COURT OF FIVES

KATE ELLIOTT

LITTLE, BROWN AND COMPANY

Copyright © 2015 by Katrina Elliott
Map illustrations copyright © 2015 by Mike Schley

Little, Brown and Company

Hachette Book Group
1290 Avenue of the Americas, New York, NY 10104
Visit us at lb-teens.com

Little, Brown and Company is a division of Hachette Book Group, Inc.
The Little, Brown name and logo are trademarks of Hachette Book Group, Inc.

The publisher is not responsible for websites (or their content) that are not owned by the publisher.

First Edition: August 2015

Library of Congress Cataloging-in-Publication Data

Elliott, Kate, 1958–
    Court of Fives / by Kate Elliott. — First edition.
        pages cm
    Summary: When a scheming lord tears Jess's family apart, she must rely on her unlikely friendship with Kal, a high-ranking Patron boy, and her skill at Fives, an intricate, multi-level athletic competition that offers a chance for glory, to protect her Commoner mother and mixed-race sisters and save her father's reputation.
    ISBN 978-0-316-36419-5 (hc : alk. paper) — ISBN 978-0-316-36424-9 (ebook)
    [1. Social classes—Fiction.   2. Sisters—Fiction.   3. Contests—Fiction.
    4. Friendship—Fiction.   5. Racially-mixed people—Fiction.   6. Fantasy.]   I. Title.
    PZ7.1.E45Cou 2015
    [Fic]—dc23

                                                                            2014016743

10 9 8 7 6 5 4 3 2 1

RRD-C

Printed in the United States of America

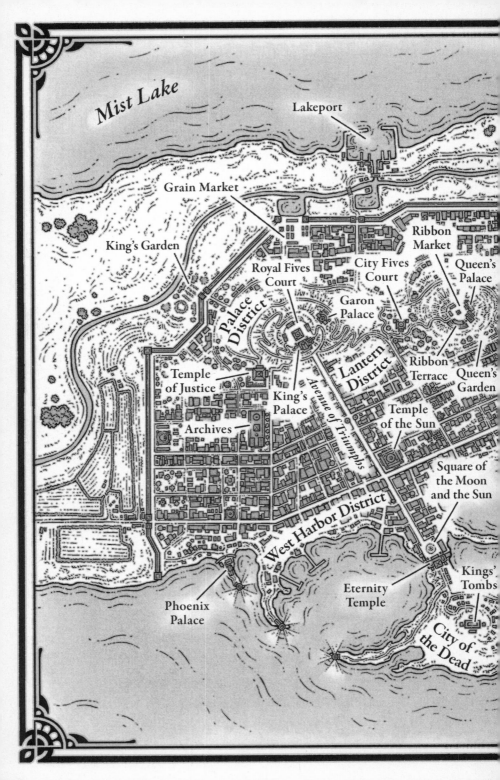

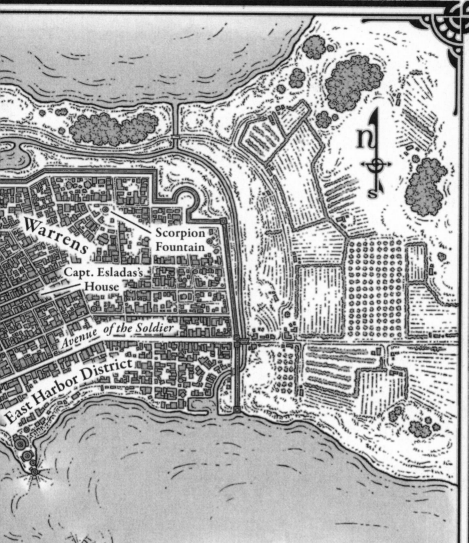

Warrens

Scorpion
Fountain

Capt. Esladas's
House

Avenue of the Soldier

East Harbor District

SARYENIA

Fire Sea

The oracle speaks:

The tale begins with a death.

Where will it end?

There could be a victory

a birth

a kiss

or another death.

There might fall fire upon the City of the

      Dead, upon the tombs of the oracles.

A smile might slay an unsuspecting

      adversary.

Poison might kill the flower that bloomed

      brightest.

A living heart might be buried.

Death might be a mercy.

1

We four sisters are sitting in the courtyard at dusk in what passes for peace in our house. Well-brought-up girls do not fidget nor fume nor ever betray the least impatience or boredom. But it is so hard to sit still when all I can think about is how I am going to sneak out of the house tomorrow to do the thing my father would never, ever give me permission to do.

I say to my elder sister, Maraya, "What are you reading, Merry?"

She hunches over an open book. Its pages are bathed in the golden light of an oil lamp set on an iron tripod. The words so absorb her that she does not even hear me.

I say to my younger sister, Amaya, "Who are you writing to, Amiable?"

She flashes a glare from her heavily kohl-lined but nevertheless lovely eyes. "I am writing poetry, which I am sure is a sophisticated and elegant skill you have no acquaintance with, Jes. Now hush, I pray you, for I just thought of the most pleasing way of describing my eyes."

She pretends to brush a few letters, but instead she retrieves a folded note from its hiding place beneath the table. I happen to know it contains execrable love poetry smuggled in from a secret admirer. As her poem-worthy eyes scan the words she blushes prettily.

I glance at my twin sister, Bettany, thinking to share a joke at Amaya's expense, but Bett sits in the shadows with her back to us. She is weaving string between her fingers, muttering words in a rough undertone. I do not wish to know what she is saying, and I hope she does not intend to share it.

Mother sits on the marriage couch, the plushly cushioned double-chair that she and Father share when he is home from the wars. A gauzy silk gown spills over the huge expanse of her pregnant belly. Her slightly unfocused stare might in another woman be described as vapid, but in her it simply means she is thinking of Father. All is harmonious and peaceful, just as she likes it.

I want to get up and race around. I want to climb the walls, which is the plan for tomorrow when Bettany has agreed to make a screaming diversion during which I will clamber up one of the sturdy trellises and escape unseen over the roof.

Instead we will sit here until the Junior House Steward comes in to announce supper. Girls like us have to be more decorous and well-mannered than the daughters of other officers because our father is a lowborn army captain fighting to make his fortune through valor and bold leadership. Which one of us would dare jeopardize his steady, hard-fought climb through the ranks by indulging in disreputable behavior?

"You are restless, Jessamy," Mother says in her sweet, pleasant voice. "Is something troubling you?"

"Nothing," I lie.

She examines me a moment longer with her soft gaze. Then she picks up her embroidery and begins to stitch with the easy patience of a woman who is accustomed to waiting for the reward she loves best.

The handsomely decorated courtyard gleams in lamplight. In his last campaign, Father won enough prize money from his victories that he had the courtyard repaved with marble. We now sit on carved ebony-wood couches with silk-covered pillows, just as highborn people do. What matters to Father is that the courtyard has become a respectably fashionable setting in which Mother can entertain without embarrassment those wives and mothers and sisters of army officers who will accept her invitations.

I turn my thoughts again to the forbidden thing I am going to do tomorrow. I have it all planned out: how to get out of the house, how to be gone from midmorning to midday without anyone except my sisters knowing, how to bribe Amaya to keep my secret while finding a way to repay Maraya and Bett for all the times they have helped me sneak out without Mother becoming suspicious. I've done it a hundred times.

Everything is set for tomorrow. It will all go exactly as planned, just as it always does.

I smile.

And that is when disaster strikes.

2

mother looks up as an eruption of voices and clattering footsteps rises from the front of the house. Out of the clamor we all hear a man's robust laugh.

Another woman might gasp or exclaim but Mother calmly sets her embroidery wheel onto the side table. The smile that paints her mouth is gentle, yet even that mellow touch of happiness makes her beauty shine more brightly than all the lamps and the moon and stars besides. I hasten over to help her rise. Amaya hides the note under the table.

Even Maraya looks up. "Has Father returned home early from the wars?" she asks, squinting in a way that makes her look bewildered.

Bettany shouts, "How I hate this false coin and the way we all lie to ourselves!"

She jumps up and rushes into the kitchen wing, pushing past a file of servants who spill out into the courtyard because they have heard the commotion. Just as Bett vanishes, Father appears. He is still wearing his armor, dust-covered from days of travel, and holds his captain's whip in his hand. It is how he always arrives home, wanting to greet Mother before he does anything else.

"Beloved," he says.

He passes the whip to the Senior House Steward who dogs his heels, then strides across the expensive marble pavement to Mother. Taking her hands, he examines her face as if to assure himself that she is well and healthy or maybe just to drink in her remarkable beauty. His gaze drops to the vast swell of her belly and he nods, acknowledging the obvious.

She says, "Welcome home, my lord."

Her tone is as unruffled as the sea on a windless day. She is the ocean, too deep to fathom.

Father releases her hands as he turns to address the Senior House Steward. "I require a bath, after which the Doma and I will dine in our private rooms."

Then, of course, he walks back to the entrance and sweeps the curtain aside to go in.

Mother says, "My lord, your daughters await your greeting and your blessing."

He blinks, as if he has just remembered that we exist.

After a moment's consideration, he walks over to us. We line up in order of age.

He kisses Maraya on the brow. "Maraya, you are well?"

"Yes, Father. I have memorized the fifth set of Precepts for the Archives exam. Do you think the Archivists will allow me to sit for it? Can it be arranged?"

He glances down at her feet. His eyes almost close as he fights off a frown.

Of all of us girls, Maraya resembles Father most in looks except for the one accursed flaw: every other Patron man would have smothered at birth an infant born with a clubfoot. When he is not home she wears only a light linen sock over the splint.

"I always wear my boots when I go out. No one will know as long as I hide the foot in public." I admire Maraya for the way she reminds him of her deformity to make him uncomfortable enough to actually listen to her. She never shows the least sign of resentment. "No suitable man can offer to marry me. A position as an Archivist at the Royal Archives would be both respectable and secure."

"True enough. You have studied diligently, Maraya. I will think about it."

With that, she wins the first round.

He moves a step on to kiss me, his lips dry against my forehead. "Jessamy, you are well?"

"Yes, Father."

He pauses, waiting for me to say something more.

Of course I am glad he is safe and alive, but I cannot believe the ill fortune that has brought him home early.

"No questions about the campaign?" he asks with the faint half-smile that is the closest a somber man like him ever comes to affectionate teasing. "I had to devise a new formation using the infantry right there on the battlefield because of the peculiar nature of the enemy tactics."

What am I going to do? I have never tried to sneak out while Father is at home. His entourage of keen-eyed, suspicious, and rigidly disciplined servants runs the household like an army camp, in a way quite unlike Mother's relaxed administration.

"Jessamy?" He raises an eyebrow in expectation of my response.

"Yes, Father."

Realizing I have no more to say, he frowns at the empty space where Bettany should be standing next to me.

"Bettany is ill," says Mother.

"Has the doctor been called?" He sounds puzzled.

"It is her usual affliction," she answers, her voice as placid as ever. "Do not concern yourself, my lord."

He glances again at me. When I say nothing, he kisses Amaya's brow and takes one of her hands in his. "Well, kitten, you are looking well."

"I have missed you so dreadfully, Father. You cannot know!"

He chuckles in that way he has when one of us has pleased him. "I have a special treat for you, something I know you have been hoping for."

She glances past him as if expecting one of the servants to walk in with a suitable bridegroom whose status will vault her into a better class of acquaintance. "Whatever could it be, Father? For you must know that your return is what I have been hoping for most!"

I glance at Maraya, thinking to share an eye-roll, but she stares steadfastly ahead into the middle distance. Probably she is running Precepts through her head and isn't listening anymore.

"Better than all that, I promise you." He releases Amaya to look toward Mother, for it is obvious that the "treat" is an offering he places at Mother's feet. "Our army has won a crucial victory at a village called Maldine. I have received a commendation and will be honored with a place in the victory procession tomorrow morning."

"Esladas!" She forgets herself enough to use his name in front of others. "At last your courage and service are recognized as they ought to be!"

Her pleasure makes him glow.

I envy them sometimes, so complete together. We girls could as well not exist, although it would be different if we were boys.

"It will take some days to set up proper victory games, so tomorrow's procession will finish with the usual weekly Fives. Lord Ottonor has requested our family's presence in his balcony box for the occasion."

Amaya shrieks. Even Maraya is surprised enough to gasp.

I shut my eyes as the full scope of the disaster blows down over me. My plans, my hard work, and the scraps of money I have saved for months: all washed away. If I had Bettany's temperament I would rage and stomp. Instead I fume, thoughts whirling. It's as if I am two people: dutiful, proper Jessamy on the edge of bitter tears, and confident, focused Jes determined to find a path through what looks like an impossible Fives maze.

"I know you all know how to behave in public from our various excursions," Father goes on. "Furthermore, an official royal victory Fives games will follow in eleven days at the Royal Fives Court. If you girls make a properly good impression, Lord Ottonor may invite you to attend him there as well."

"Oh, Father! I have so often dreamed of having the chance to attend the games at the Royal Fives Court!" breathes Amaya so ecstatically that I wonder if she will wet herself from sheer excitement.

Mother examines Father with a furrowed brow. "You are not one to boast, my lord, so this must be much more than an ordinary victory. It is unexpected indeed that we here in this house should be invited to Lord Ottonor's balcony at the City Fives Court. For us to also be allowed to attend the games at the Royal Fives Court is extraordinary."

"It was no ordinary victory, that is true." Like Maraya, he assesses himself and his situation with clear eyes. "In his own way Lord Ottonor is a fair man and means to see me rewarded for my achievements."

"Are you saying his star will rise in court because of your victory?"

"He has long hoped the king will give him the title of lord general. It would be a signal honor."

"Especially since Lord Ottonor isn't even a soldier. He sends his officers into the field to win glory for him!"

"Kiya, that is how it has always worked. Bakers' sons do not become generals. Or even captains. I have done exceptionally well for a man of my birth and situation. You know that." He glances at us girls and then at her pregnant belly.

A shadow chases through her eyes. "Is it wise to bring your family into such public view, Esladas?"

"I am not ashamed of you!"

All three of us girls startle. He never raises his voice at Mother.

"You are tired and dusty from your long journey, my lord." With a gracious smile, she takes his hand. "A bath and supper will restore you."

He leaves without a backward glance at us. Mother casts

one last look over her shoulder as she follows him through the curtain. Then they are gone.

All the breath goes out of me like I've been punched.

Amaya whoops. "Lord Ottonor's balcony box tomorrow at the City Fives Court! Oh, I will die of joy! Wait until I tell Denya that she and I shall stand at the balcony rail and watch the Fives together!"

I sink onto the couch, hitting my fists repeatedly against my forehead. "What a disaster! I'll plead illness and stay home. Then I can sneak out once you're all gone."

Amaya flings herself down beside me and grabs my arms. "You have to come, Jes! Bettany won't go, and who would want her to, anyway? Father won't let Maraya attend lest someone notice her accursed foot." She gestures toward Maraya's splint. "Father will never let me go alone with him and Mother. Highborn people never bring a daughter alone. They bring a daughter only if they also bring a son."

"Which Father cannot do, as he has no sons," remarks Maraya.

"Oh, I hope Mother does not talk him out of going!" cries Amaya, wringing her hands.

"No chance of that," says Maraya. "She will wish him to receive all the accolades he deserves. You have to go, Jes. Think of all the slights Mother has endured over the years. Think of how Father has been loyal to her despite everyone telling him he should marry a Patron woman to advance his career. He

12

wants to honor her by showing he is not ashamed of her and their children on the day of his extraordinary triumph."

I think of what he said about devising a new infantry formation and how he wanted to share the story of his victory with me. I'm so proud of him and so angry that he came home today of all days. But I can never tell him why.

So I snap at Maraya. "You just think if he gets a promotion and reward he will agree to you sitting for the Archives exam."

She shrugs, my ill temper rolling right off her. "I like the thought of sorting through all those dusty old books looking for arcane references to ancient oracles."

Amaya wilts against the couch, pressing a hand to the back of her forehead in a pose copied from the theater. "I would weep and wail every day if I had to suffer that. As I will for the next year if I can't go tomorrow," she adds threateningly. *"Every day."*

"You couldn't pass the exam anyway, Amiable," says Maraya with one of her rare thrusts. Yet her gaze fixes on me. "What else do you suggest I do, Jes? No Patron man can marry me, not even if he is the lowliest baker's son from a humble hill-country town back in Saro-Urok. Furthermore, Father cannot let any of us marry a Commoner. It would be illegal, even for us."

"I don't want to get married," I say, crossing my arms. "I don't want to live Mother's life."

"Don't be selfish, Jes. Father would marry Mother if it

weren't against the law. Think of how much easier and more secure that would have made her life. So don't sneer at her and the choices she's made. We live because of her."

I look at the ground, scraping a heel over the marble.

Maraya goes on in her relentlessly calm way. "I do not want to be trapped in this house for the rest of my life. My point is that if Father feels his position is strong enough despite his domestic arrangements, he'll let me become an Archivist. So if you won't do it for Mother and Father, then I pray you, do it for me."

"I saved for a year to get enough coin to pay the entry fee for this week's trials at the City Fives Court! I chose this week because none of us heard anything about Father coming back so soon. If I'm trapped on a balcony box the whole time, I can't run. That's a forfeit. I'll lose my coin."

Amaya throws her arms around me, burying her face on my shoulder, her voice all weepy. "We've never been invited to Lord Ottonor's balcony before, Jes. Never. The other officers already look down on Father. This is his chance to shove us in their faces. Not that you care about that."

I push her away and jump up to pace. Frustration burns right through me. "How do you think I feel, training for years without ever having a chance to actually compete in a real trial? I have run the Fives a hundred times—a thousand times!—on practice courts and in practice trials. Now my one chance to experience a real trial is ruined. My one chance!"

14

"Please, Jes. *Please.*"

The stars must hate me, having fallen out in this ill-omened way. I walk with Mother every week to the City of the Dead to make the family's offerings to the oracles. Can the oracles read my angry thoughts, as rumor says they can? Is this their punishment for my not being content with my lot? For my not being a dutiful-enough daughter?

"It just isn't fair! We have to pretend to be proper officer's daughters even though no one will ever believe we are. It's Father's reputation we are protecting, not ours!"

Yet alongside my furious ranting, my mind races, assessing options, adapting to the way the situation has just changed. None of their arguments matter anyway. With Father in residence I have no hope of sneaking out when his aides and servants are looking for the slightest break in the strict routine they impose.

I circle back to the couch. "Very well. I'll accompany you, if you'll cover for me."

Amaya grabs my wrist. "You can't mean to sneak out of Lord Ottonor's balcony to run under everyone's noses! In front of Father! What if he recognizes you?"

"No one will recognize me, because Fives competitors wear masks. It's just one run."

Maraya pries Amaya's fingers off my arm. "Jes is right. No one ever knows who adversaries are if they don't win. It's only when they get to be Challengers or Illustrious that people can tell who they are by the color of their tunic or by their tricks and flourishes. No one will guess it is Jes because they won't think she's out there."

I grab Maraya and kiss her. "Yes! Here's how we'll do it. There's bound to be small retiring rooms for the women at the back of the balcony. Mother won't use the one assigned to her because she'll think it her duty to remain out on the public balcony the entire time so everyone knows Father's not ashamed of her. I can claim to have a headache and pretend to rest in the retiring room. Amaya just has to make sure no one goes back to see me."

Amaya's eyes narrow as she works through her options.

"You can wheedle Father, Amiable," I add, "but you can't wheedle me."

She grunts out a huff of displeasure. "Very well. But you owe me, Jes."

"Agreed!"

I tap my chest twice, which is the command Father has always used when he wants his soldiers, his servants, or his daughters to obey without question. And when he lets us know we have fulfilled his orders to his exacting specifications.

She straightens into the stance of a soldier at attention and taps her own chest twice in answer. Then she ruins the martial posture by jumping up and down with her arms raised.

"Thank you, Jes. Thank you! Wait until Denya finds out we get to watch the trials together and practice flirting."

She scrawls out a note to her friend and calls for a servant. A boy hurries out from the kitchen wing. His mouth is smeared with honey from a sweet bun he has sneaked off Cook's table. He's a scamp of a boy, maybe ten years old, one of Mother's rescues off the street. My father gave him the name Monkey because Father names all our Efean servants after plants or animals. But when Father is not home Mother calls him by his Efean name, Montu-en.

"Run this over to Captain Osfiyos's house at once, Monkey," declaims Amaya in her best Patron voice, all condescension and clipped-short words. "Give it into the hands of the personal maidservant of Doma Denya, no one else."

"Yes, Doma." The boy takes the folded paper and dashes off. I envy his freedom to race through the streets of an evening and loiter on his way back.

Amaya seals away all her writing things, then pauses to look at Maraya, who has gone back to reading. "Merry, I don't think your foot is cursed and Mother doesn't either. I'm sorry. That was mean of me." She grins, mischief lighting her face to its prettiest. "Not that I mind being mean, but I like to save it for times when it will improve my social standing."

Maraya laughs, and so do I. All my pent-up frustration spills into a river of expectation, a rush carrying me into this new scheme.

The maidservant assigned to serve us girls appears at the curtain, looking curiously toward us as if wondering what we have to laugh about, the daughters of heroic Captain Esladas and the beautiful woman he can never marry.

Maraya closes her book and signals that the maidservant, whom Father named Coriander, may approach and speak.

"Doma Maraya." Coriander uses the formal term even though we can't actually claim the right to be addressed as *Doma*, for it is a term properly used only for women born into the Patron class. It is not meant for girls whose father is a Patron but whose Mother is emphatically a Commoner. Yet inside our house Father insists the servants call us by the title. "Doma Jessamy. Doma Amaya. Your supper is ready for you in your rooms. Will Doma Bettany be joining you?"

Maraya glances toward the sky. "Only the oracles know."

As we leave the courtyard with its bright lamps, I smile, eager for tomorrow.

3

When he was twenty, my father left his homeland of Saro-Urok and came to the land of Efea to make his fortune. The very day he arrived on the wharfs he saw a sixteen-year-old Commoner girl in the market and fell in love with her beauty. This is not a remarkable story. As foreigners say, there are more women in Efea than stars in the sky. The foreign men who come here to make careers in the royal service are generally young and unmarried and thus quick to fall into and out of love.

What is remarkable is that my father has stayed loyal to my mother for twenty years.

Even though he is only a baker's son, he is still considered Patron-born. Patrons are people either born in the old empire of Saro or descended from ancestors who emigrated from Saro to Efea any time in the last hundred years. The law forbids people of Saroese ancestry from marrying the native people of Efea, who are called Commoners.

As Father moved up the military ranks he could have contracted a marriage with a Patron woman to help advance his army career. It is the usual path for ambitious and successful Patron men. Commoner girls are for youthful liaisons. Patron wives are for status and sons.

That all he has to show for the relationship with our mother is four daughters, two stillborn sons, and several miscarriages makes his loyalty all the more unusual. Most Patron men would have abandoned one Commoner concubine and taken another, hoping for a son. Most Patron men would have smothered Maraya at birth and handed unlucky twin girls like Bettany and me over to the temple.

Father did none of those things.

But I'm certain he will kill me if he finds out I've been running the Fives during the months and years he is away from home at the wars.

4

Every victory procession parades along
the wide boulevard called the Avenue of Triumphs.
Mother and Amaya and I wait at the side of the avenue in the
family carriage, which has a roof for shade against the blister-
ing sun and bead curtains to conceal us from improper gazes.
I am strung too tight by the thought of running the Fives to
care about the procession, but when Amaya parts the strings to
peek through I scoot up beside her, realizing that I am excited
after all. I don't want to miss a single thing.

"Look! Here they come!" Amaya is bouncing on the
seat hard enough to make the carriage rock. "Make sure you
remember everything so we can tell Maraya all about it!"

"Bett, too!"

Amaya sniffs. "As if she cares."

Mother sits calmly but she is also holding the beads to one side so she can see.

First the horse guards sashay past. Everyone cheers and whistles as the horses prance and the proud cavalrymen show off their splendid uniforms of flowing gold silk and red leather boots trimmed with golden tassels. Next ride the royal heralds flying purple banners marked with the white sea-phoenix, the badge of the royal house. Blasts from their curved trumpets announce the approach of the royal carriage.

Cheers fade into a sullen quiet.

The royal carriage is open for all to see, and today both the king's and the queen's seats are empty. That is not unusual; the royal carriage leads the way in every victory, festival, and funeral procession whether anyone sits in it or not. Perhaps it is for the best. The crowd's harsh murmurs remind me how unpopular the king and queen have become.

Abruptly shouts of praise and triumphal whistling begin again as people see Prince Nikonos. The king and queen's younger brother sits in a smaller carriage that follows right behind the royal carriage. He wears formal robes of purple and gold. His hair is cut short in the fashion of soldiers because he is a soldier too. He stares straight ahead as people press their right hands to their hearts and offer the bow of gratitude.

Mother and Amaya and I do the same even though no one can see us. When we straighten, the royal stewards' carriage is passing. They fling coins into the crowd.

22

"Mother, please!" says Amaya. "Can I jump out and grab one? They say a royal coin brings good fortune."

"No, Amaya, it would displease your father," says Mother in a kind but firm tone. "This is not the day to draw attention in such a way."

By now even Mother is shifting restlessly as musicians march past, drumming and singing and trumpeting to announce the arrival of the soldiers being honored in the procession. The victory carriages are garlanded with flowers and ribbons. The first two hold lords, who always take primacy regardless of what they accomplished in the field, and the third holds the generals who actually commanded the army. Lesser officers will follow in the lesser carriages.

"Mother! Mother! Do you see him?" Amaya jerks forward, almost sticking her whole head through the beads until I drag her back.

My mouth drops open in utter amazement. Father is seated alone in the third carriage, dressed in his best polished leather armor and holding the brass-studded whip that marks his captain's rank. He looks so dignified and solemn that if it weren't for the whip no one would ever guess he isn't really a general.

Never in my life and dreams have I ever imagined such remarkable distinction would be shown to a humble baker's son.

Mother looks radiant as she wipes tears of joy from her cheeks, but she says nothing. All around us I hear people talking about the stunning victory at Maldine.

Am I really going to risk running the trial after I have seen this? I grip my fingers together like I can squeeze all the heart out of me and leave only dry sand. The dutiful part of me knows I should just let it go, be obedient, don't take the risk. But it could take me another year to scrape together enough coin to pay the entry fee. Anything could happen. What if I never have this chance again? Just once I want to run a real trial and pretend to be a different girl with a different life.

The lesser officers pass, followed by ranks of victorious soldiers and then wagons heaped with captured weapons. As high-ranking prisoners in chains shuffle past, the ground begins to tremble with thuds. A deathly hush spreads across the gathered crowd.

A cohort of spider scouts brings up the rear of the procession. The spiders are giant eight-legged mechanisms, each one given life by magic and directed by a soldier strapped into the carapace of the metal beast. They are mostly used in the desert, where they can move quickly and for longer distances than foot soldiers or cavalry. On the avenue they clank along with an ominous thunder that causes the packed crowds to cower.

It makes me angry to see people afraid, because my father served with distinction as a spider scout in his first years in the Efean army. I squeeze Amaya's hand. "People should remember how often spider scouts catch bandits trying to sneak into villages and towns! They should be thankful, not scared!"

"Denya says the king never calls them into the city unless he means to wield them against his most dangerous secret enemies," she whispers. "Anyway, they're creepy. Don't you wonder how the priests use magic to wake up a metal body and make it live?"

"No. I have enough to think about," I mutter, remembering that the biggest event of my life is about to happen.

The victory procession moves out of sight along the Avenue of Triumphs. As the crowd thins out, our carriage takes a side street up the Queen's Hill to the City Fives Court. Mother's eyes are still closed, as if she is seeing the parade again in her mind's eye.

After what seems like forever, our carriage arrives at the plaza in front of the court.

A Fives court is the name we give the playing field on which the game of Fives is run. It is also what everyone calls the huge, round, roofless stone building, several stories high, that rings the playing field and where spectators sit to watch, gossip, bet, eat, drink, and cheer.

From all over the city people are streaming into the court to find seats. Trials are held every Fivesday but because of the victory procession today's trial will be especially crowded.

Our carriage comes to rest in a fenced-off yard reserved solely for the Patron-born. We wait until Father arrives. He has changed out of his armor into formal attire, a waist-length fitted tunic and a draped ankle-length skirt called a keldi and worn only by men. Captain's whip in hand, he escorts our party through a private entrance that leads past the tiered seating where Commoners cram together and up to the special section where only Patrons may sit. When we attend the games as a family, Father rents a box in this section with cushioned benches and attendants to hold umbrellas to block out the sun.

Today, however, he leads us to the private tiers where Patron lords enjoy the trials, cordoned off even from ordinary Patrons. At an archway flanked by guards, Father flashes an ivory token. The guards wave him through with formal congratulations on the great victory. They carefully do not glance at Amaya, but they eye me in my linen finery. I can tell they are wondering how I fit in.

Father ushers us toward a balcony box marked by a flag depicting a three-horned bull, the badge of Lord Ottonor's clan. Lord Ottonor stands at the entrance greeting each of his guests. They are all men whose careers he has sponsored in the military, the administrative service, or mercantile ventures. He greets Father with the look of a man who cannot believe his great fortune at having discovered gold baked within a humble loaf of bread.

"Captain Esladas! You have brought glory upon Clan Tonor!"

"It is all due to your magnanimity, Lord Ottonor," says Father in his usual serious tone.

Lord Ottonor's smile acknowledges his own generosity in giving Father the chance to excel. When he sees Mother he blushes a little and clasps his hands together like a shy lad who doesn't quite know what to say. He is careful not to touch her. "Here is the lovely Kiya. 'What a soothing sight beauty is to the weary heart.'"

It is a quote from a popular play.

Mother never bows nor cringes before Patrons. She has the knack of smoothing all paths. "Your gracious welcome honors us and our daughters, Lord Ottonor."

"Your daughters!" His eyebrows arch as he sees us standing behind her.

"This is Jessamy," she says.

Obviously I am not what he expected, looking so like a Commoner as I do.

"Your gracious welcome honors us, Lord Ottonor," I say in my sweetest voice, with a glimpse toward Father to see if my tone and expression are acceptable. Father gives me an approving nod.

"Here is Amaya," says Mother as Amaya pushes herself forward.

Amaya makes a graceful bow, one perfectly appropriate to an unmarried Patron girl greeting an elderly lord. "'What honor the generous lord bestows upon we the humble among his servants.'"

A genuine smile lights his face. "A line from *The Hide of*

the Ox. Do I make the acquaintance of another devotee of the theater?"

She arranges her prettiest expression on her pretty face. "I am the most ardent of devotees of the theater, Lord Ottonor. I have seen you there in your box, if you do not mind my saying so. Of course my family attends when we can. I am also sometimes allowed to attend with Captain Osfiyos's household. His daughter Denya is my particular friend."

"Delightful! What a lovely girl, Esladas!"

Father moves us along with just enough haste that I realize how whenever we are in public he does his best to prevent us from speaking to Patron men. People are taking their places, ready for the trials to start. Every part of the floor of the court except the central victory tower is covered with canvas, concealing the layout of today's obstacles. The covers will only be pulled back when the first trial starts. I want to be out there so badly that I can taste the kick of the sawdust and the grit of chalk. I have to check in before the gate to the undercourt closes or I'll forfeit.

My mouth goes dry. I'm going to do it even though I know I shouldn't. I'll be obedient forever after this. I will.

As Father settles Mother into a chair I lag behind, patting my forehead with a scrap of cloth and pretending to grimace in pain. Amaya points me out to him and he walks back to me.

"Jessamy? It's not like you to retreat from a challenge. I hope you are not afraid of appearing in public."

28

"Of course not, Father. The noise and dust have given me a headache. If I can close my eyes for a little without being disturbed, I am sure I will feel better right away and I will come back out."

He nods. I slip into the long tent that stretches along the back of Lord Ottonor's box. Curtains divide the interior into small private rooms. Coriander is waiting at the far end of the tent. She quickly slips a servant's blank leather mask over her face. Seeing me, she relaxes and pulls the mask off. We go into the tiny retiring room where she has stowed our satchels.

"Give me your servant's token," I say.

She hands over a cord strung with a servant's ivory pass. "As you command, Doma."

"If anyone comes looking for me, fetch Amaya."

She nods and goes out. I pull my game clothes out of the satchel: a short tunic, leggings, and shoes sewn out of a leather so supple that they fit my feet like gloves fit hands. I change quickly and pull an ankle-length green tunic over everything. My mother embroidered the sleeves and collar herself. It's nothing fancy, the kind of linen sheath gown a Commoner girl would wear in the market. A gauzy shawl conceals my hair, and one of the plain leather masks worn by servants conceals my features. Then I get on my belly and peek out from under the tent's base, which isn't pegged down. A servants' aisle runs between the back of the tent and the tall stone back wall of the Court. In a moment when no servants are in sight, I wriggle out.

Every time a servant rushes past me bearing a covered tray of food for the Patrons or carrying out a covered bucket of waste to dump in the sewer, I expect them to shout and expose me. But they think I am one of them. Pretending to be a servant isn't hard at all. Amaya and Maraya could never manage it because they look too much like Father, but no one takes a second look at me. With shoulders hunched and head bowed I slip past the guards while they are admitting a large party walking in under a palace banner, people so highborn they use only lowborn Patrons as servants, not letting any Commoners at all into their household. I hurry down the outer stairs and down a ramp into the nether passages of the ground level.

It is customary for competitors to arrive at the trials and descend into the undercourt with their masks and game tunics already on. In a shadowy alcove that smells of urine I tug off my tunic and stuff it and the shawl into the satchel. Quickly I bind back my hair in a tight net. A nondescript player's mask of silk, thread-wrapped wire, and fine leather cord conceals my face. Most competitors wear fancy bright masks and color-ful tunics, meant to draw the eye. My mask and tunic are an ordinary brown, like me.

There is only one gate into the undercourt, where the Fives players, called adversaries, assemble before trials begin.

The guards let me through when I show them my adversary's token. I join the stream of players moving down the stairs to the attiring hall, where we'll be assigned our starting round and belts. Just as I reach the bottom, a bell rings and the gate slams shut above me. No one who arrives late will be admitted, in order to keep competitors from discovering ahead of time what configurations of the Fives will be unveiled when the canvas is pulled back.

I hurry past locked doors behind which lie the mechanisms and structures used to build and manipulate each new Fives course. The people who work there belong to a guild sworn to protect the sanctity of the Fives. It is said that men have been killed for revealing the secrets of the undercourt.

But all that has nothing to do with a girl like me.

Still hidden behind my mask, I walk into the attiring hall. There are benches, open spaces for warming up, and curtained alcoves and basins for washing. I gawk as I look around. I've never been in a real attiring hall. I've worked my way through practice trials at unofficial neighborhood courts where a girl like me is anonymous among crowds of Commoners and slumming Patron men seeing what competition is out there. It's only because anyone with enough coin can purchase a token to enter the Novice-level City Court official weekly trials that I can finally walk here.

A custodian collects my token and satchel with no more interest in me than she would have in a faded old tunic. She checks the numbered token against a ledger. "You're in the first trial."

My heartbeat quickens. I'm really going to do it. I have no trainer to wish me good fortune as I enter the ready cage, which is a lamplit chamber with a ladder at each corner.

I get my first look at the other three adversaries I'm running against. They are masked, of course. Since we're entered in the Novice-level division, they must either be fledglings who have yet to win a trial or Novices trying to move up. You have to win ten Novice trials to move up to the next division, called Challenger. I want to win so badly. I want to prove to myself that if I truly had the opportunity I could run the Fives and succeed.

I look over my competition, trying to seem calmer than I really am, because really I *am* about to crawl out of my skin. I dig down for the other Jes, the cool, collected Jes who knows how to measure and make fast decisions with no margin for error, like my father on the battlefield.

The others have each already been handed a wide colored belt to mark their start position. They all happen to be male, but the stocky one wearing the red belt looks too muscle-bound to be flexible and the skinny one wearing the green belt is already sweating; that will make him slip. The one tying on the blue belt wears a fancy gold mask and a gold silk tunic far too expensive for a Novice, so that probably means he is from a palace stable where they can afford such a wasteful display. What matters to me is that he looks fit and calm; he'll likely be my main competition.

The ready cage custodian hands me the last belt. It has the same brown color as my gear, so when I tie it around my waist it blends with my humble clothes. Brown means I start at the obstacle called Pillars. I smile, pleased by my good fortune. Pillars is a maze, and I'm adept at mazes.

I follow my custodian up one of the ladders. The crowd's noise rumbles through the stone, sinking into my bones. This is really going to happen. Tears of excitement sting my eyes.

We walk through a dim tunnel that ends in a small chamber beneath a closed hatch. This is the start gate for Pillars. Yet another custodian stands here. This one is watchful, assessing my height and build, wondering how I'll do. I rub chalk on my hands and on my leather shoes to absorb sweat. I open and close my hands, feeling every crease and callus.

The gate-custodian and my attendant custodian remain silent. Above us the crowd roars as the canvas is hauled back and today's configurations revealed. Spectators chant along with the formulaic ceremony that opens every trial, the recitation of a set of verses that describes the court, the obstacles, the game itself. But I have already ceased hearing and seeing anything except what is right in front of my eyes. I am ready to run. I am ready to win.

Except that I can't win.

I've always known I can't win, because winning will bring disgrace on my father.

Too late I realize I should not be here. I should not be doing this. It isn't worth the risk that someone will recognize me behind my mask.

Horns blare like knives in my ears. The crowd quiets to a surging mumble.

Deep in the undercourt the start bell rings, and the hatch opens.

All my doubts fall away. I forget everything except the promise of the ladder and the challenge that awaits me above. Heart racing, thoughts sharp as a spear, I climb.

The trial begins.

5

∽IIIII∽

Imagine you are a magician and can see through
the eyes of a crow flying above the City Fives Court. Below
you lies the huge round stadium built of stone and wood. You
see the tiers of seats and the shaded balcony boxes filled with
people cheering and shouting. The Fives court in the center
is divided into four quarters, each one of which is an obstacle.
At their simplest they are easily described: Pillars is a maze,
Rivers is water crossed via moving stepping stones, Traps is
bridges and beams to balance along, and Trees is climbing
posts. The first person to negotiate the four outer obstacles and
then get through the fifth and center obstacle, called Rings,
climbs the victory tower to claim the victor's ribbon. To win
you need to be strong, fast, smart, and flexible, and have excellent balance and agility.

Through the crow's eyes you look down on a girl crouched on a raised wooden platform about three paces by three paces square. She is panting, catching her breath. Blood dries on her left palm where she scraped herself while climbing on Trees. She is grinning, every part of her body and spirit filled with elation.

That girl is me.

I have successfully made my way through Pillars, Rivers, Trees, and Traps. This platform is one of two entrance points for Rings. From the height I look around to see where the others are. The red-belted adversary is still stuck in the maze of Pillars. If you're not smart enough to figure out the maze you shouldn't be running.

The green-belted adversary is wavering as he crosses a high beam on Traps. I suck in a breath, pulse racing as I see him overbalance. Too late he tries to center himself! He slips and falls. A shout explodes from the spectators as he hits. I can't see the floor of Traps from here but men race out with a stretcher. There is a moment of utter silence as people stare.

My heart is pounding and my throat feels raw with apprehension. What if Green Belt is dead?

Laughter and good-natured cheers erupt from the crowd: Green Belt must be injured but not dead, aware and awake enough to make light of his fall. I've gotten distracted even though only five breaths have passed since I arrived here. I should be looking for Blue Boy as I decide on a strategy.

A Rings configuration is set up as a maze, like Pillars. The spinning rings turn at different speeds, just as stones move in Rivers. You have to avoid traps; this one has smaller rings that turn separately, nested within the larger rings. Rings are stacked so you can climb, as in Trees, to a higher and more difficult but faster level, or play it safe on the ground. Rings is my specialty. I'm not the strongest nor the fastest, but I'm agile and I'm patient and I'm calm. Most of all, I know how to grasp the whole pattern and figure out the fastest path. You can beat me anywhere else on the court but no one beats me through Rings.

Since Blue Boy isn't yet here, how am I going to lose on purpose without everyone guessing? Even though Father doesn't know it's me, I want him to admire the girl in the brown belt as she falls just short of winning. Worse than losing would be overhearing him remark on how that girl had run poorly.

A foot slaps the ladder behind me. To my utter relief Blue Boy hauls himself up onto the platform and drops into a crouch beside me. It's a good tactic, confronting me directly as we enter the last challenge. He's about my height, lean and muscled. A gold silk half-mask covers his eyes and forehead but I see his smile and his even, white teeth. He looks like he's having a good time and is perfectly happy to share that good time with me.

"Salutations, Adversary. Do you let me pass, or do you contest my right to enter first?"

I can tell by his high-class accent that he's way above my place in the world. He's as pure Patron as they come but there's no glint of condescension in his voice.

"Salutations, Adversary," I answer, pitching my voice low to disguise it.

He drops the pompous formalities with another flash of the friendly grin. "I have to say, I'm impressed. I don't remember running against you before. By the way you took that twisting leap over the rope bridge in Traps, I'd have remembered you."

"How did you see that?" I ask, surprised both that he was able to observe my run and that he would have paused for long enough to watch.

He points to a cluster of poles sticking up in Trees. "I had just reached the top of the center-post. Your leap was impressive. You're not wearing a stable badge. Who trains you?"

"What makes you think I'll give up my secret?" Cheerfully I snap out the informal court challenge used only between players. I can tell he's expecting it by the way he laughs. "Kiss off, Adversary."

From the platform there are three possible rings I can reach on my first jump. I've already chosen my path. I leap for the middle ring just as it turns full on open, facing me. I brace my feet on its wooden curve and grasp each side, spread-eagle. The thrill is what I live for, the timing, the way I can hit it just right.

He whistles sharply, amazed by my audacity. After a hesitation he jumps through the right-hand ring and starts climbing down into the spinning maze. I stay holding on through three complete turns of the big wooden ring. I'm comfortable braced here. Anticipation curls smugly in my gut as I watch him dodge and climb and backtrack along the ground.

There is always more than one path through Rings. The key is finding the most direct one instead of the most obvious one.

Getting bored, the crowd begins singing a popular song about a lovelorn adversary:

I'll wear my mask and I'll wear my ribbons
And to the wharf I'll gladly go
For my love has said he will meet me there and—

A man's voice pierces above the clamor: "Wait for it, sweet pea!"

Whoever the man is, up in the stands, he knows exactly what I'm going for: on the fifth turn a straight path will open to the tower. It's a hard choice to make because all the rings are continually moving. Once you start leaping you have to keep moving as the tunnel opens in front of you and closes behind you. If you stop, you'll fall. But if you're bold you can race through a wave of opening rings like opening doors.

I'm bold.

The path opens. I run right through, the curved wood rings scraping on my feet as I propel myself to the next one and the next. Blue Boy is working the slow but sure way. He's good but I'm better.

I'm going to reach the tower first.

So the moment I have to decide to fall feels like stabbing myself. I gauge the speed of a wheel's turn so I can just miss getting a good brace on the rim. Pretending to slip, I sit down hard on the edge. It cuts into my rear as I slide and let myself fall until I am hanging by my hands. The grip bites into my fingers like a reminder of what I'll never have. With a grimace, I let go.

When I hit the ground I roll to absorb the shock but pretend to sprawl, taking up precious time to allow him to get farther along.

Sand chafes my face. But it is the burn of hating myself for having to lose and look clumsy that chases me the slow way along the ground to the tower. He swarms up the ladder ahead of me, not looking back.

With my foot braced on the lowest rung and a spike of anger slashing through my chest, I watch as he snags the victor's ribbon and pulls off his mask to the crowd's roaring approval.

In official trials the winner has to take off the mask in front of the entire assembly.

That's why I have to lose.

To my disgust he's good-looking, with cropped-short, straight black hair, dark eyes, and a pale golden complexion, the very model of a lord's son, one of the highest Patrons of all, palace-born. Most likely his household has its own Fives stable of players and a private training court.

He glances down at me. A narrow-eyed frown shades his face.

He's not as happy about his win as he ought to be.

Shaking, I crawl down the ladder into the undercourt.

As the crowd roars, I remember Amaya. What if she couldn't keep Father from coming back and checking on me? I'd better hurry.

I jog along a passage to the retiring hall, separate from the attiring hall so no one who has run the court can exchange information with someone yet to race. An attendant gives me my satchel and a cup of the sweet nectar that only adversaries and the royal family are allowed to drink. I knock it back in one gulp and almost choke on the syrupy flavor. The attendant says nothing—they aren't allowed to talk to the adversaries for fear of bribes and favors trading hands—but her brow wrinkles with curiosity. I still have my mask on.

Setting down the empty cup I hurry on.

Gate-custodians allow me out the narrow exit stairs, guarded below and above.

I emerge into the nether passages. After I change in the shadowy alcove I'm just another sweaty Commoner girl in her one nice dress, except for the clamor of my thoughts.

I did it! I ran a real, official trial. I can almost call myself a real adversary now, even if I'll never be one.

The air reverberates with the noise of spectators calling out bets and predictions as the next set of adversaries begins. Vendors shout. I didn't notice them before but now the smell of food drenches the hot breeze: bread dipped in oil, shelled roasted nuts and salted seeds, and toasted shrimp.

I return the way I came.

To my relief the curtained retiring room is empty. As I strip off my long tunic, I try not to cry. It was everything I'd hoped: the exciting course, the crowd's cheers, the smell of sawdust and chalk.

I rub a few tears off my face, then ladle water from a ceramic pot into the washbasin and wash the drying blood off my hand. I cherish the pain because the scrape proves I did it.

A haughty voice rises outside. "Open the curtain!"

The drapery lifts, handled by an unknown servant wearing a mask. Amaya sweeps in. While I've been gone she has powdered her skin so it is as golden-pale as Maraya's.

"You almost won! I could tell you wanted to! If you had taken off your mask in front of everyone it would have humiliated Father on the very day of his great triumph."

"Which is why I didn't win." The cool water soothes my exercise-flushed skin but my mind keeps seeing how I could have run right through the rings to the tower.

She shoves me onto a stool in front of a dressing mirror. With a lighter hand than her temper suggests she teases out the worst tangles in my hair with her fingers, then uses a little oil to comb the rest.

"How could you do that to me, Jes! When the green adversary slipped I thought he'd broken his neck and then I thought you would break your neck when you fell—and I screamed!"

"You screamed? You never scream."

"I was so frightened. If you were injured everyone would have seen your face! And then when I screamed everyone looked at me, so Father wanted to bring me back to join you and I thought we would get caught for sure. I told him a bug ran over my foot."

I snort. My pounding pulse is finally slowing. "As if bugs ever scare you. You're the one who flattens them with your sandal. Bett's the screamer."

"Father doesn't know that, does he?" She yanks my hair back into an unfashionable puff-tail, a quick way to make my coily hair look neat. "It was a close call. If he found out, my life would be over! I'm done covering for you, Jes! This is the last time!"

"The oracle speaks," I mutter.

"Don't say that! It's bad fortune to mock the oracles!"

She stamps a foot, which makes me giggle, which makes her pull my hair even harder. In all fairness she makes it look good, and afterward pauses to stare at her own tresses all tied up in pretty ribbons. She drinks in every bit of Patron beauty she has inherited from our father: the perfect bow of her eyes, her straight black hair, the lips whose color she emphasizes with carmine stick. Yet even Amaya can't quite pass as a Patron. In the way her lips part slightly I see how it hurts her, knowing she will always be second best in the circles we live in.

"You look lovely," I say.

"Amaya? Are you in here?" Her friend Denya waits behind the closed entry drape for permission to enter. "Lord Ottonor is about to receive visitors! You better hurry!"

I grab my linen finery as a servant lifts the drape. Denya steps into our little refuge and stops, trying not to stare at me pulling the long sheath of a gown down over my dark body.

Amaya places herself between Denya and the couch to hide the Fives clothes draped in full view. "Glad tidings! Who is coming, Denya?" she asks in what Maraya calls her bird-twitter voice. "I simply can't wait to see!"

"A party from Garon Palace. It's a great honor for Lord Ottonor to host a palace lord at his balcony!" Denya is a soldier's daughter, like us, but both her parents are Patron-born. She has the courtesy to be embarrassed at being caught staring, for which I like her. Her gaze catches on the tunic and leggings, and her forehead wrinkles as she puzzles. "Is your headache better, Jessamy Tonor?"

"Salutations, Denya Tonor," I reply, for every person who lives under a lord's sponsorship takes the clan name as their surname to mark their allegiance. "While languishing here

with a headache I have been reciting poetry to improve my
character:

> *At dawn face the east to sing in the new day.*
> *What the oracle speaks, your heart yearns to obey.*"

"You are so dutiful, Jessamy Tonor," Denya says politely
as she grabs Amaya's hand and hauls her to the entry drape.
For all that Denya is pure Patron and pretty enough, she
knows Amaya is the lamp that draws the moths. "If we hurry
we won't miss Lord Gargaron's party as they arrive. I've seen
them on their balcony. His nephew is really good-looking. If
we pick the right place to stand, he might speak to us!"

"Truly?" Amaya's interest shifts away from the damning
clothes to the far more interesting prospect of flirting.

They slip outside just as a roar of disappointment bellows
from the spectators. An adversary has failed to complete one
of the obstacles. I slowly tuck the clothes away in my satchel.
It was far easier to climb up the ladder onto the Fives court
than it is to go stand among people who will stare, wondering
why Father allows a daughter who looks like me out in public.
But I don't want him to think I'm a coward. And hiding will
dishonor Mother. So I walk out along the cloth-walled passageway to the balcony where Lord Ottonor and his entourage
watch the trials under the shaded comfort of an awning.

Lord Ottonor sits on a cushioned chair with an excellent view of the playing court below. My father's sponsor is an
avid spectator of the Fives. He ran them himself when he was

young. I find it hard to look at this old man with his sagging jowls, patchy breathing, and complexion gray from ill health, and imagine him as a Fives adversary good enough to compete at the Royal Court, much less as an Illustrious.

"This set has no adversary as adept as that last pair," he wheezes as everyone listens attentively. They don't even notice me enter. "Look at the fellow wearing the green belt. He'll never get past the rope bridge if he can't figure out it is rigged to collapse. I put no odds on the red-belt girl. She's slow like day-old porridge, ha ha!"

The men standing beside his chair all laugh politely. A table laden with fruit, roasted shrimp, spicy beans, and sweet finger-cakes dusted with sugar sits close enough that he can gesture to whatever he wants. Right now my father is offering him a platter of shrimp from which Lord Ottonor is picking off the fattest and juiciest with a pair of lacquered tongs.

None of Lord Ottonor's blood relatives are here today, only people he has elevated through sponsorship. Besides my father there are three other military officers, an administrator wearing the long sleeves of a bureaucrat, and one dour merchant. The men have been allowed to bring their marriageable children.

Amaya and Denya have taken a place at the railing at the edge of the awning, where they can get the first look at any visitors coming through from the back. Another Patron girl joins them; I don't know her name and have never seen her before. Three boys about our age watch the game.

My mother is the only Commoner seated beneath the awning. All the other Commoners here are masked servants, none of whom would ever sit down in the company of Patrons, because they would be whipped.

I don't want to talk to Amaya and her friends so I find a place to stand at the far end of the balcony. The only thing I really care about is what is going on down on the court. The green-belted adversary is stuck at the rope bridge in Traps. My father sees me. With a stern nod he indicates the platter in his hand, so I hurry over and return it to the table.

My movement catches Lord Ottonor's eye. "A shame about her, Esladas, no? The other girl is so pretty."

I busy myself with arranging the platter among the others, keeping my face averted.

My father says, "Jessamy is an obedient girl, my lord. Obedience must always be valued above beauty in a woman."

"I suppose so," said Lord Ottonor. "Although when obedience goes hand in hand with beauty, the world smiles more brightly, does it not?" He nods at my mother, whom he allows to sit beside him because he enjoys admiring her.

She is embroidering a length of cloth. Her hugely pregnant belly should make the work a little clumsy, except my mother can do nothing clumsily. No ribbons confine her hair, which she wears in its natural cloud. She makes no effort to lighten her complexion, nor does she need to. Men have written poems to the lambent glamour of her eyes. She looks up with a kind smile.

"I think all my daughters are beautiful, Lord Ottonor, both the two who look like Esladas and the two who look like me." Her silk-soft voice is as exquisite as her face and rather than scolding him seems to be agreeing with him.

I don't know how she does it. I don't think she knows. I think she just is that way, like a butterfly whose bright wings capture the eye simply because it is a radiant creature.

"Four daughters, Esladas!" Lord Ottonor drones on. "I'm surprised you kept them all, since they will just be a burden to you when you have to pay to marry them off. If you can marry them off." He pops a shrimp in his mouth as he considers the vast swell of my mother's belly. "Perhaps this one will be a son."

My father says, "If the oracles favor us, it will be a son."

My mother's eyebrows tighten. Although she takes an offering tray to the City of the Dead once a week in the manner of a proper Patron woman, she herself never consults the oracles, not as Father and all Patrons do.

At the railing Amaya tugs on Denya's sleeve. A party of men enters the balcony box. My mother rises from her chair and retreats to the back benches where sit the Patron women who are the wives of the soldiers. Out of respect for my father's new fame as hero of Maldine they allow her to rest among them. Anyway, they like her.

Once I am sure she is settled I sidle to the far corner railing out of the way as the newcomers are announced. Lord Gargaron is a slender man of about my father's age, a thin-faced fellow with thin eyes and a thin nose and a thin smile. Lord Ottonor laboriously rises to greet him.

I am as invisible as any servant. Which is a good thing, because I sustain a shock that jolts right through my body as my hands clutch the railing.

One of the people with Lord Gargaron is Blue Boy.

6

Blue Boy is called Lord Kalliarkos. He is the nephew of Lord Gargaron.

Tidied up and dressed in lord's clothing, he is the same youth I allowed to reach the tower first. He patiently acknowledges the men being introduced to him by Lord Ottonor, but by the way his gaze keeps flicking to the court below I can tell he wants to be watching the game.

"Ah, you just ran that trial, did you not?" says Lord Ottonor. "Shame about your last adversary falling from the Rings. I thought it a funny slip for her to make."

"So did I," says Lord Kalliarkos.

A mighty shout rises from the spectators. Everyone looks to see what has happened.

The green-belted youth has figured out the trick with the

rings but his rhythm is off as he leaps from one to the next. The turning rings are about to cut him off. If he is smart he will stop and swing down to the ground, but he sees the girl in the red belt running along the ground and he doesn't want to lose.

I suck in a breath. A terrible thing is about to happen.

"Stop. Stop, you fool," I whisper. I know what it is like to have your pulse pounding in your ears and your breath surging in gasps and your entire being so fixed on the handhold you are reaching for that you don't see the gaping chasm opening at your feet.

I grip the railing so hard it bruises my fingers.

Just as Green Boy leaps into the next ring, its nested smaller ring cuts inside the larger ring, which he is holding. The crowd shrieks as the ring crushes him. He falls, screaming. The roar of the spectators drowns the thump of his body onto the ground. From the angle of his neck and the sprawl of his limbs, anyone with eyes can tell he is dead.

Sucking in an oath, I push back and look around.

Even Amaya, who has not the slightest interest in the Fives, is clasping hands with Denya and staring avidly at the dead youth. It's not that the spectators want adversaries to die. It's just that it adds spice to the game, not to mention spatters of bright-red blood on the sandy ground like the spots on a tomb spider's brown back.

As the crowd cheers, the red-belt-wearing girl climbs the ladder to take her triumph.

Kalliarkos is staring at me with the same narrow-eyed frown I saw when he pulled off his mask on the victory tower. He glances around Lord Ottonor's retinue, spots my mother, and looks back at me. He walks to the railing next to me and glances at my feet in the five-toed foot-hugging leather game shoes I did not have the wit to change.

In a low voice he says, "Doma, I swear by the oracles that you remind me of someone who was wearing scuffed leather shoes exactly like those, down to the three lines of chalk smeared across the right foot."

My gasp causes Kalliarkos to smile.

"I won't tell if you don't want me to. Where do you train?"

"I can't say. They don't know I run." My cheeks burn.

"Any of them?" he demands, almost laughing.

"Shh! My sisters know. Not my father and mother."

He studies the Patron men surrounding Lord Ottonor. "Which one is your father?"

My father happens to look our way at that moment, mouth tight and expression hard.

"Ah," says Kalliarkos. "The hero of Maldine. I should have guessed."

I want to know why he "should have guessed," but it seems rude to ask a lord what he is thinking. No lord has ever spoken to me before today. Father will not like the attention he is showing me. I should want him to walk away but I don't.

"You lost on purpose," he says.

I stare down at the playing court, trying to ignore him so he'll leave. Men roll the dead adversary onto a stretcher.

"It made me feel my victory was a cheat," he adds.

"My apologies, my lord. It was not my intention to make you feel like a cheat." It is hard not to snap, because I still feel the moment when I had to fall. I manage a calm tone. "But I can't win."

"That's not true! You're really very good. . . ." He trails off, tracing the polished wood of the railing with a finger. "Oh."

"If I'd won, I'd have had to take off the mask. Then they would have seen."

A smile teases his eyes, one that doesn't quite touch his lips. "That must be frustrating, having to lose when you know you could have won."

"It is—!" I break off. "Not that it wasn't close, I mean."

"That's kind of you to say, but the truth is I didn't see how the rings would turn into a tunnel. You would have beaten me."

I bite my lower lip to stop myself from agreeing with him. Instead I gesture to the court. Men carry the stretcher off while the ground is sprinkled with sand and wood shavings and raked for the next run. "You have to get the timing of the rotation exactly right. If you don't, the smaller rings turning inside the bigger ones will break your grip or crush your fingers. Like what happened with that adversary, may the gods judge him kindly."

He doesn't even look toward the court. Instead he leans toward me. "Rings is my weakness. I need to be good enough to make it out of Novice and into Challenger. That's never going to happen if I can't succeed at Rings. You saw it all, where it was and where it was going and how it would get there. How do you do that? Where do you train?"

"Kalliarkos," calls Lord Gargaron, making no effort to keep his voice down. "Kalliarkos, pray pay attention when I speak to you. Lord Ottonor ran the Royal Court when he was your age, did you know? He could give you a piece of advice or two, well worth listening to if you ever want to be good enough to get past Novice and not just dabble at the Fives as it seems you do."

I wince.

Kalliarkos's handsome face turns to a blank mask, utterly still, so you can't tell what he's thinking. But by the bleak splinter of doubt in his eyes I see that his uncle has poked him with this knife before, calling his skill into question in front of others.

"Maybe Rings isn't your strong point," I mutter in a low voice, "but you can learn some tricks to help you see how the timing falls into place."

"Kalliarkos, do not speak to the servants. Ottonor, why is that girl standing idly by? If you must employ Commoners to serve in your household, please be sure they wear a mask."

Lord Ottonor's flushed face betrays his embarrassment as

he glances toward my mother. The moment he looks toward her, the women seated around her move away.

"She is the daughter of Captain Esladas." Lord Ottonor's tone is stretched so tight that it grates.

Lord Gargaron's thin face sneers in condescension. "I have heard of your excellent tactical breakthrough at the battle of Maldine, Captain Esladas. I would think a man of your talents would have arranged a beneficial marriage with a woman of proper Saroese ancestry years ago. With adequate sponsorship and a suitable wife, you might go farther than a second-rate captaincy."

The group under Lord Ottonor's awning goes deadly quiet. The flush on Ottonor's face drains to a pallor. He looks a little sick. He presses a handkerchief to his brow but makes no reply. What emotion smolders in the press of my father's gaze I dare not guess, but Father does not move nor speak.

Gargaron eyes my mother with a pinch of hostility, then looks straight at me. "Regardless, I am surprised you parade the girl before her betters in this unseemly way. Surely you are not hanging her out in the hope of attracting a buyer."

"Forgive me, Lord Gargaron," says Father in a soft voice. "I brought my daughters with me today in the hope of giving them some polish. That they are allowed to mingle in company with their betters cannot but improve their characters."

Kalliarkos stands with the fingers of one hand pressed to his forehead, gaze fixed on his sandaled feet. Most of the other men have the courtesy to look away but Denya's father is smiling as if my father's public humiliation is a long-hoped-for prize. To my surprise, Denya does not step away from Amaya but remains stubbornly at her side, holding her hand, even when her father gestures for her to come over to him.

Amaya looks at me. Tears sparkle unshed at the corners of her eyes. By the fixed intensity of her gaze I can tell she is furious. I stare at her, wordlessly promising that we will endure this. Words cannot humiliate us unless we let them. We have seen our mother accept much worse and smile graciously.

"Daughters?" Lord Gargaron professes innocence as he glances at Amaya. "Have you more than one? An expense that surprises me, given your humble origins. I believe you are a baker's son, are you not? Come to Efea to make your fortune?"

"I have four daughters," Father replies. "Amaya is my youngest, Jessamy a year older."

"Where are the other two?" asks Lord Gargaron.

Father glances toward the tent as if he fears by some malicious mischief we have hidden Maraya inside with her shameful crippled foot. "They are not here, my lord."

"Have you eight sons to match your four daughters, as the oracles tell us, 'Let your sons be double in number so your wars will flourish'?"

"I have hope of sons, my lord," says Father.

Every person under the awning, even the masked servants, looks at my mother's pregnant belly.

"Merely a hope of sons! Meanwhile you suffer four living daughters to be ensconced in your household! You have gone native indeed, Captain Esladas. Everyone knows the Commoners spend themselves into penury for the vanity of their daughters. No wonder you are stuck at a captain's rank despite your famous exploits. You will rise no farther if your feet are stuck in the mud."

Kalliarkos actually gasps. He glances at me although surely he understands I cannot react.

Father takes in a long and slow breath, and he lets it out in a long and slow exhalation. Mother calmly chain-stitches white petals to fill out an embroidered rose. She does not look up nor does her hand falter. One might be forgiven for thinking her simpleminded, or deaf.

"Friend Gargaron, shall we not watch the trial?" says Ottonor feebly. "They are about to begin a new trial."

"So they are," says Lord Gargaron, settling back to observe. "Let the girl bring me something to eat." Father beckons to me at the same time as Lord Gargaron adds, "The other girl, the pretty one."

I stop short, panting a little, because I'm both angry and scared. Amaya looks confused and apprehensive, not sure if she should be flattered by the lord's attention or worried about it. She hesitates, looking toward Father for direction.

"I'll get what you need, Uncle." Kalliarkos shakes his shoulders as if releasing himself from a rope that has pulled him up short. He walks to the buffet table. "These shrimp look particularly succulent. Let me add one of these stuffed mushrooms, your favorite, Uncle. And here is coriander bread shaped as fish!"

Trumpets blow to announce that the next four adversaries are taking their places at the ladders in the undercourt. Father grabs hold of my arm, his grip like iron, and drags me inexorably away from the railing. I can't see the start as the bells chime down the familiar melody.

The crowd sings along:
Shadows fall where pillars stand.
Traps spill sparks like grains of sand.
Seen atop the trees, you're known.
Rivers flow to seas and home.
Rings around them, rings inside,
The tower at the heart abides.

A mighty shout signals the start of the run, but of course I can't see anything from back here.

Mother glances our way but Father lifts his chin, his way of saying, *Stay out of this.*

A masked servant lifts the entry drape, and Father hauls me into the stuffy interior. The cloth-screened passage seems dimmer than it did before. We are alone.

He slaps me hard across the face.

"You made a spectacle of yourself, Jessamy. I do not care what pleasures his smile offers, or how well-intentioned he seems. If I bring my daughters into public, I expect them to be dutiful and modest. Amaya is the only one of you girls who has any chance for a respectable alliance. Do not ruin it for her by hoping to become a rich lord's whore!"

My mouth drops open. The unfairness and crudity of his scolding scalds like boiling water.

"That *you* would cast your ribbons at a most unsuitable young man shocks me. I expect *you* to know better." The way he examines my face and person makes me feel I am a worm crushed under the sole of his boot. "Not only is Lord Kalliarkos nephew to Lord Gargaron, his grandmother is a princess of the royal line, a wealthy woman who owns an entire shipyard. You will never speak to him again, do you hear me?"

7

I **stare at** the three chalk marks on my leather slippers. My cheek stings. "Yes, Father."

"He can have no interest in a girl like you except for what can never be allowed. What exactly did he say to you?"

My breath is coming in gulps as tears trickle alongside my nose. A headache jolts up the back of my neck and my sight swims.

"He just talked about the Fives. I felt it polite to reply. I didn't know what else to do."

He frowns more in sorrow than in anger. "I suppose you could not have refused to answer when he spoke directly to you. Very well. Wait for me in the retiring room."

He goes out.

A masked servant enters, perhaps the same one who held

the drape. All I can see of her face is her eyes. She tracks me as I retreat to the retiring room. A breeze stirs the cloth walls as I enter. Sinking onto the couch I fold forward and rest my throbbing head on my arms. The golden day has turned sour and horrible.

The curtain swings aside and Father steers Amaya in.

"You two are leaving immediately."

Amaya chirps in her sweetest voice, "Father, with our mother so close to her time, perhaps you will permit me to remain here in the retiring room. Denya can sit with me so I won't be alone. That way I can look after Mother should she become over-tired before you are released from your duties by Lord Ottonor."

He takes a step toward her. "Your mother is safe with me!"

Amaya does not cringe. "Father, I only seek the best for our mother. We girls worry for her when she is so close to her time." She launches her next attack. "Since Maraya couldn't come, she particularly asked Jes and me to make sure Mother is comfortable."

His skin darkens with a flush, for any reminder of Maraya's deformity shames him. "You will accompany Jessamy back to the house."

Amaya resorts to her wheedling voice. "I'm so disappointed we have to leave early. Denya mentioned one of the military men is looking for a wife, and I prayed to the oracles that maybe he would notice me. But I suppose there is no hope for that now. I know Jes was foolish and selfish but I have to say that Lord Gargaron was rude to us." She flicks a convenient tear from her eye as her voice catches on half of a sob.

"A lord of his rank is accustomed to speaking as he wishes," says Father, "but I will not hear my daughters spoken of in such insulting terms. I can make no objection to such a man so I am sending you home to get you out of his way."

She sniffs. "Can we at least still go by the Ribbon Market on our way? Mother said we could, to buy ribbons to celebrate your great victory and a banner to decorate the house. Our chaperone will be with us, and Steward Polodos and our maid-servant and a groom and a driver. It will be perfectly proper. You promised me a new mask for the Shadow Festival the last time you were home. I thought I would be a cat this year."

"No. You are going straight home. Wait here until I return with Steward Polodos."

He departs.

"I never get what *I* want and it's all your fault!" Amaya looks ready to spit with anger. "Aren't you suddenly turned into the flirt! I've never seen you go after a boy like that! You should know better than to speak to a lord's son. It makes Father look bad."

"He spoke to me first! It would have been rude if I hadn't answered."

"You should have moved away from him. But you didn't. You thought he was handsome. Admit it!"

"Handsome?" I pause, remembering the way he looked atop the victory tower when he pulled off his mask, the perfect representation of a triumphant adversary. "Yes, he is. But that's not what happened." I lift my right foot to display the three white smears. "Lord Kalliarkos recognized the chalk marks. He's the adversary who won my round. He wanted to know why I let him win."

"What a disaster! What did you tell him?"

When I think back I can't help but smile even though my cheek still hurts. It is very flattering that he knew I should have won. "I told him I can't unmask. Then he asked me about Rings. He was remarkably courteous and treated me like an adversary, not a Commoner. He thinks I'm good, Amaya!"

"Oooh! Jes's heart has been slain by a man complimenting her on her skill in running the Fives!"

"What a relief he wasn't speaking to me because he found me pretty!"

She grins with the charm that makes her irresistible when she chooses. "That's not what I meant. But you have to admit it is just like you to care more that he praised your skill than your beautiful eyes. Jes…" She curls a ribbon around a forefinger, suddenly somber. "If he knows your secret, then he can tell Lord Gargaron. Or Father!"

"Hush," I say, for I hear footsteps.

A servant lifts the entry drape. The painted mask she wears gives her the look of an ancient statue brought to life to serve the highborn. It also hides her expression so I cannot tell what reaction she has as she steps aside to allow Lord Gargaron to walk into the retiring room.

With a look, he measures me from my scuffed leather slippers to my coily hair. His lips sneer as if he is imagining some dire calamity like a great tide of seawater destroying the city or my modest charms seducing his nephew. The frown fades as he examines Amaya with a more luxuriously measuring stare. I grasp Amaya's hand; she squeezes mine, taking a step away from him.

"Where are the other two?" he asks. "Four daughters and no sons. A man ought to be ashamed."

"Our sister Bettany is frequently unwell, my lord," I say, for I do not want him to think he can command Amaya's attention whenever he wants. "Our eldest sister, Maraya, is studying with the hope of being allowed to take the examinations to be admitted as an Archivist in the Archives."

Father returns with Junior House Steward Polodos in tow. His surprise on finding Lord Gargaron alone with two innocent girls cannot be disguised.

"My lord," Father says as he places himself between us.

Lord Gargaron studies us as if we are furnishings. "The Archivists who investigate the workings of the world believe that a woman who has an excess of heat and vigor may give birth preferentially to daughters. As it is the nature of Commoner women to be overburdened with the heated constitutions more appropriate to men, it would explain the unusual numbers of daughters among Commoners. Not like the women of our people, Captain, who are properly cool and reserved."

Father sucks in a breath so sharp that the lord deigns to notice.

"Had you a comment?" he asks with a raised eyebrow.

Father's anger snaps in his eyes like a storm but his tone remains flat. "It was nothing, my lord."

"No, no, indeed, I insist you speak."

Gripping my hand even more tightly, Amaya shuts her eyes. Usually nothing scares Amaya but she is trembling now.

I won't let such a poisonous man humiliate Father. We have heard this slur before, and I need only repeat words Maraya has said more than once. I know how to speak exactly like a full-blood Patron, each word crisp and clipped short. "In truth, my lord, the unusual numbers of daughters found among Commoners might more easily be explained by them keeping all their girls instead of giving younger-born daughters to the temple in the City of the Dead as Patrons do."

"Argued like an Archivist," says Lord Gargaron. "Are you sure you are not the one who should take the examinations, rather than your unseen sister?" Amusement creases his brow, and yet I wonder at the twitch by his left eye: Is he angered by my forthrightness? "These intellectual questions are not mine to decide. I have estates to run and a war to fight. The king recently named me lord governor general of the Eastern Reach. Do you know the intricacies of the eastern command, Captain Esladas?" He nails his gaze onto our father.

Father's lips crease with a curl of anger, quickly suppressed. "By reputation only, my lord. I have not fought there."

"No, indeed not. Your talents have for the most part been wasted on the tedious mire of skirmishes in the northeast desert. A shame Lord Ottonor has given you little scope in which to shine so as to burnish your shield of rank." He sweeps a hand in the half-circle gesture by which Patrons honor the god of Fortune, since what balances atop fortune's wheel may as quickly fall beneath. "Let me remove myself from this private room, where a man who is no kin of yours cannot be welcome. I was looking for a different sort of chamber."

Too late, we display our palms and bow our heads in deference to his lordly rank. The lapse makes him smile as he leaves.

"You cannot get out of here quickly enough." Father takes Amaya's arm. I grab our satchels. The Junior House Steward stands at attention in the manner of a lowly foot soldier. "Polodos, keep your eyes open to make sure no servant of Lord Gargaron follows you."

Polodos taps his chest twice. Like soldiers on a fast march we hasten to the shaded area where Lord Ottonor's servants prepare food and wait to run errands. Coriander is ready to go.

Our chaperone is an elderly Patron woman named Taberta

who holds the beads of an ill-wisher. Every well-to-do Patron family with children keeps an ill-wisher to guard its progeny, for such a woman can cast the evil eye onto any person who tries to harm her charges.

Father leaves us with Taberta and hastens back to the balcony and Mother.

Taberta greets us with a nod. Her tongue was cut off on the day the oracles named her as an ill-wisher. She notes Amaya's tears and lightly taps my arm with her ebony baton. The click-click-click of her ill-wishing beads accompanies us as we emerge into the wide carriage yard. Drivers doze in the shadows of carriages. Our senior groom comes stumbling out of the shade and kicks the driver to wake him up. Both men smell of barley beer.

Taberta clambers up beside the driver, where everyone can see that this carriage must not be molested by beggars, thieves, or hucksters. As I get inside I hear Amaya talking to Polodos before she gets in after me. Once again the bead curtains conceal us. The carriage rolls, the servants walking on foot outside.

Amaya studies me. "You do look a little bit like Mother. It isn't entirely impossible that a Patron man who wants that kind of thing might look at you."

"Goodness, Amiable, you truly do hate to admit that any one of us except you might be attractive. No wonder you and Bettany don't get along."

"Bettany is Father's problem, not mine, thank the oracles!"

"Don't be mean about Bett!"

Amaya has a startling glare when she narrows her eyes to slits. "Bettany makes life hard for herself! Don't blame me for pointing it out. The person you ought to feel sorry for is Mother but you never do!"

"Father loves her! That's always been enough for her!"

Amaya shakes her head. "You're so blind, Jes. When Father's gone all you think about is the Fives. When he's home you follow him around like a loyal dog waiting for scraps."

"I do not!"

She snorts. "You're the closest thing to a son he has. Don't you understand why Father doesn't want a lord talking to you? If your handsome palace-born Lord Kalliarkos informed Father that he wanted you, Father *could not refuse*. He would have to hand you over! He worries about what will become of the three of you, even Bett! That's why you ought to do everything you can to help me make an advantageous marriage."

"Because you are the only one who can hope for a respectable life, as you forever keep reminding us?"

Amaya's eyes get a droopy look that makes me think I have choked the fragile hope she has nurtured. "I don't want to live in Father's house all my life! If I marry well, you can come live with me and sneak out to run the Fives as often as you want."

"I thought you wanted me to give up the Fives!" I hiss.

"As long as we live in Father's house, it would be safer if you did." Her voice rises.

The thought of never again running the Fives smashes down like a vast rock. My eyelids flutter as I crush back tears. "It doesn't matter. What point is there in training if I can never compete?"

Her expression darkens, like the breath of an oracle pushing an ominous cloud over the bright eye of the sun. "You should have lied to the young lord. Why should he keep your secret?"

"How could I lie when he saw my shoes? Anyway, he promised not to tell."

"There will be trouble," she mutters, and lapses into silence.

The horses labor, pulling uphill, and I wonder where we are going because our house lies downhill from the City Fives Court. When the carriage glides to a halt I peek outside. To my astonishment we have stopped at the Ribbon Market.

"Amaya! Father told us to go straight home!"

She leans in to whisper, "You ran your Fives! Now I'm going to go buy my cat mask."

Before I can react she hops out of the carriage and, with Coriander and Taberta in tow, strides away into the Ribbon Market.

8

I **jump out.** Junior House Steward Polodos waits in
the shade of the carriage with his arms crossed. He came
from Saro-Urok only two years ago, from the same town as
Father. For months after arriving he wore his straight black
hair long and tied back in a club as Patron men do in the
homeland, but recently he cut it off into the short style all men
wear here where it is hot year-round and soldiers go clean-
shaven. It's as if he is trying to impress someone.

The groom and driver are standing at the horses' heads,
talking together, looking agitated.

"Steward Polodos! What is going on?" I demand.

He regards me with a pleasant and entirely unruffled
expression. "There's been some trouble with the horses' harness, Doma. We just have to stop here a moment to fix it."

No one is fixing anything.

He turns his face back toward the sea, a faint smile on his usually serious face as he gazes at the view. The promenade is built on a crater rim and offers a splendid view across Saryenia, the royal city of Efea. Saryenia is famous for two conical hills, the King's Hill and the Queen's Hill. The King's Hill is crowned with the massive king's palace, the Royal Fives Court, and the many administration buildings and military offices. On the Queen's Hill, the queen's stately palace oversees banking and merchant offices and the markets. The Archivists say these hills were once tiny volcanoes like the Fire Islands that seed the western sea.

I can imagine exactly how fiery Father's reaction will be if he learns we have disobeyed his direct order.

"Amaya wheedled you into doing this, didn't she? I mean no offense, Steward Polodos, because Mother speaks highly of your skills. But if you harbor some sort of romantic feeling for Amaya, you must know she has her sights set on a dashing military man. Not a mere household steward like you who besides that is as lowborn a Patron as our father."

If my words offend him he does not show it.

"Almost any man would find Doma Amaya hard to resist," he says with another smile. "I respect Captain Esladas more than I can say, Doma Jessamy. But it will not harm your sister to find a little happiness by buying a mask. The Ribbon Market is always perfectly safe. Lest you wonder, the groom and the driver both had a drink of celebratory beer while on duty. Should your father hear of it they will be whipped and lose their employment. So they will say nothing. Will you tell your father that we came here?"

The thought of Father finding out about this reckless escapade and thus causing Amaya to tattle about the Fives makes me want to scratch my fingernails down my cheeks and scream.

"I'm going to find her and bring her back."

"Doma, your sister took the servant and ill-wisher with her for propriety's sake. You must stay here with the carriage."

"Will you tell my father that I walked alone into the market when you weren't meant to bring us here at all?" I stalk off before he can answer.

Nestled inside the Queen's Hill crater, the Ribbon Market is a maze of stairs and narrow aisles shaded by canvas awnings. I know exactly where Amaya's favorite mask vendor has her stall, but when I make my way to the place down several flights of twisting stairs, Amaya isn't there.

I want to strangle her. Where has she gone?

I head deeper into Mask Lane. There are wooden masks and thin hammered metal masks and fragile glass masks and inexpensive canvas masks and woven reed masks. Masks ornamented by beads sit beside masks sewn entirely of feathers.

Numerous side alleys make Mask Lane a maze for shopping but fortunately I spot Amaya on the central aisle. She is standing at a stall holding a pair of cat masks so she and Taberta can look them over. The ill-wisher loves shopping with Amaya because my sister includes her in decision-making and slips her extra coin to buy trinkets for herself.

As angry as I am, I cannot help but be amused by the sight of several young Efean men loitering nearby, waiting to see if Amaya will look their way. They're not direct like Patron men. They wait for you to speak first. But Amaya is uninterested in good-looking boys who cannot offer her an advantageous marriage, especially if they are not Patron-born.

"You have an audience," I murmur as I come up beside her. "We have to go."

She doesn't even look at me. "Shhh. I'm about to start bargaining. You owe me for helping you today. This will make us even."

"Amaya! We can't take the risk!"

"You should talk!"

Turning her back on me, she begins haggling with the vendor over the pair of gold-sequined cat masks with silver-wire whiskers and tufted, feathery ears. The sky would have to rain fire before Amaya would cease bargaining once she has started, so I decide it will be faster to let her get what she wants and then go.

What if someone we know spots us? I look around, studying the ground as I would a Fives course to identify paths of escape.

On the Fives court, the pace is focused and tight. That's what I'm comfortable with. Here in the market people relax; they smile; they pause to take a drink of juice or tea. They set down their work and chat for a while with a friend who has come to talk. On mats under awnings, artisans carve and weave. Most of the vendors and artisans are Commoners, as are many of the shoppers. Patron rule has brought prosperity for Patrons and Commoners alike.

In the next stall over, my eye catches on a woman who is embroidering spots on a cloth-and-wire butterfly mask. She considers two spools of thread for her next set of stitches, one a delicate rosebud pink and the other a starker bloodred. Glancing up, she looks me right in the eye. With a lift of her chin she spits on the ground, never taking her gaze off me.

Heat flushes my cheeks as I glance toward Taberta, but the ill-wisher is caught up with Amaya. My sister and the cat-mask vendor have settled into a drawn-out haggle that is beginning to attract attention for its masterful display of competitive bargaining. To show respect to the vendor Amaya bargains in Efean rather than Saroese. Like all of us girls, Amaya speaks the Commoner speech as easily as the Patron language, although never in front of Father.

"The work is exquisite, and far too dear for the likes of me, Honored Lady. I am only a soldier's daughter. I cannot hope for any such fine vanities as these perfect masks. Yet I cannot help but admire them. They are worth far more than a mere two silver bars. I am ashamed even to mention such a price, for I mean no insult by it."

"Doma, were I able to give them to you for nothing I would, for they will surely ornament your beauty. Or, I should say, your beauty would ornament their humble craftsmanship. But what can I do? I must pay rent to the Patron lady who owns this stall. I must feed my children and my husband. For all this I am obliged to sell such work for no less than eight silver bars."

While they haggle I risk a glance back at the embroiderer. She has chosen the thread the color of blood to decorate the butterfly's sapphire-blue wings. Now I wonder if I imagined her contempt. Am I just being jumpy?

Amaya drops five silver bars into the vendor's payment bowl and receives both masks wrapped up in cotton batting. She turns to me. "Victory is mine! Are you ready to go yet? I've been waiting forever for you, Jes!"

"Where is Coriander?" I ask, ignoring her stupid joke.

Her gaze skips past me to light upon the embroidering woman.

"Honored Lady, that emerald butterfly is so lovely!" she exclaims, stepping around me. "Its beauty reminds me of my mother, delicate yet strong, and in harmony in all ways. The gods have honored you with a gift."

The woman's surly frown thaws beneath Amaya's soothing charm. "My thanks, Doma," she says in a husky voice as she hands over the one with emerald wings.

"Amaya, we have to go," I mutter as the woman glances between us, trying to sort out our relationship: Amaya with her straight black hair, eyes with a slight fold as Patrons have, and light golden-brown skin, and me with my coily hair and dark brown skin. It's my Saroese eyes that give away our sisterhood.

"Won't Father love to see this on Mother?" She turns back to the woman. "This is so like my mother's beauty and grace that I could not possibly bargain. Please do not be insulted if I tell you I have only three silver bars left in my purse."

So the haggling begins.

"Taberta, we have to go," I say, begging help, but the ill-wisher is looking around for Coriander.

Has the servant girl run away? Has someone abducted her, as we've heard sometimes happens to servants? Then I see her farther down the lane. She steps out of the shadow of a stall where racks of plain white linen-over-wire masks stare blankly, empty faces awaiting decoration. She is speaking to a person out of my sight, and she grins with a brilliant smile I have never seen on her face in our house, not in the entire year she has served us.

The constant hammering emotions of the day have crushed my patience to dust. I stride down toward her. She sees me coming and hurriedly trots to meet me, gourd bouncing on her hip, eyes cast down. There's an old scar on the top of her shorn head that I have never before noticed, the score of a whip.

"Please give me your pardon for wandering off, Doma."

A scowling young man with pliers in hand steps into view from out of the stall. He's tall, broad-shouldered, utterly Commoner, like her. His anger and suspicion strike like a bolt of lightning quivering through me. My hands curl into fists. Who is this nameless youth to judge people he doesn't even know?

"Keep going," he says to her in Efean. "There's no cause for you to beg a pardon from the likes of her."

She scurries on but I cannot allow such disrespect to go unchallenged. His eyes flare as I approach, but he's an Efean male and so he waits for the woman to speak first. A jagged scar on his face gives him a menacing look but it is the sneering curl of his lip that really annoys me.

With a false smile pasted on my face I address him in the Patron language. "I am looking for a sturdy, well-constructed mask at a fair price. Might I find that here?" My smile crashes as I unleash my anger. "Or would you just try to cheat the likes of me?"

He replies in the Patron language, his words tinged with the same Commoner accent Mother has. "You're one of that spoiled litter of half-sour kittens my sister serves."

It's like slamming into a wall of scorn.

He adds, "You must be one of the twins. Which are you? The sullen schemer, or the screamer?"

How dare he call us names!

Above, Amaya, Taberta, and Coriander hurry away up

the lane, Amaya beckoning imperiously for me to follow. But I already had to lose once today. I want to beat him before I go.

"What a rude and selfish boy you are!"

"Selfish?" He gestures toward the stall he came out of. On his right forearm five parallel scars stand out against his brown skin, like he was clawed. "I labor dawn to dusk to help keep my family's household fed and sheltered. I'd labor into the night but we haven't the money to buy oil for lamps. Can you say the same?"

"I mean you are selfish to feel the need to insult me even though you must know that a single word, and I could have your sister whipped and put onto the streets. My father would never tolerate a servant who says such things about his daughters. Not that he will know! Because I don't think it's right that your sister be harmed just because you need to prove you can insult me to my face as if that makes you a man."

He stiffens. "It wasn't my idea to sell her labor into service. She's had whippings before from your kind—"

"Not from my father!"

"No, not from him or his household," he admits grudgingly. "But our uncle has plenty of work she can help him with here. It wouldn't involve hauling out Patron piss buckets to the sewer—"

A throbbing bell tone rings through the air, followed immediately by a clacking of wood sticks like a signal. Abruptly people start lowering their awnings to show their booths are closed. A burly man emerges from the curtained back room of the stall. He grabs the young man's arm to pull him off the lane but halts when he sees me.

"Doma! You do not belong here." The burly man has the accent of someone who has learned the Patrons' language just well enough for the marketplace. "Go. Please. Go!"

He spits Efean words at the youth, calling him *pigheaded* and *wretched fool* and a phrase that refers to the withering of his reproductive organs. For one breath I enjoy the scolding, because the old man is really ripping into the youth. But the discipline I learned from my father kicks in. The last thing I need today is to get caught in whatever commotion is unfolding in the market. Nearby a child starts to cry with screams of helpless fear.

Amaya is already out of sight. As I back away, a rumble of tramping trembles through the ground. Gears and joints tick over. Sunlight flashes on tiny mirrors. A curved metal body looms into view above the market stalls. A slender metal spider, twice my height, pivots into the lane. The child's hysterical bawling cuts off as the huge spider slams to a stop in the lane.

The luster of brass makes the creature shine. Five of its eight legs are braced against the ground. One uses an auxiliary pincer to lift up the corner of a striped awning to examine what lies beneath. One has unfolded into a pair of blades, ready to strike anyone who comes too close. I can't see the last leg, because it is cut off from my sight by the spider's carapace head and sleek abdomen.

Puffs of sorcerous mist rise from the metal belly. The tilted carapace shelters a soldier, his back protected by the shell and his front by boiled leather armor. By the way the body is swiveling from one side to the other, the spider scout is searching for a dangerous criminal or a traitorous spy. People scurry out of the way like vermin trying to escape the sweeping broom of a vigilant housekeeper.

I take another slow step back, hoping the scout will not notice me.

A screaming woman shakes off a pair of men trying to hold her back and runs under the spider. Two of its legs move, shifting its carapace to a new angle. I can now see the eighth leg. Horribly its splayed foot has crushed the hips and legs of a child. The tiny head lolls peacefully, a chubby hand tucked under the chin as if the child were merely asleep instead of dead.

Several people race out and drag the woman away as she fights to stay.

Suddenly the pincer leg rips free of the striped awning and points right at the stall where I'm standing. With a curse, the burly man shoves the youth into the back room.

When the spider moves it eats up the ground. I barely have time to suck in a shocked breath when a leg slams down so close that air shudders in front of my face. With a shout of fear

I skip back. Its pincers tear apart the canvas and pinion the youth like a fish caught by a sea eagle. As easily as I would pick up one of Amaya's old dolls, it lifts him. He kicks once, then gives up. Tears stain the burly man's face, but he makes no protest.

My gut is clenched, and my face feels numb, but I have to get out of here. I don't owe them anything and I can't afford to get caught. Falling in among other people I hurry up the lane in the direction in which Amaya went. I pray to all the gods that she has already reached the promenade. But before I get to the stairs, soldiers in boiled leather armor march out to block our way.

I am trapped between the spider scout and the infantry-men on foot.

The soldiers push forward from both ends of the lane.

They are rounding up all of us who look like Commoners.

9

Always scout your ground. That is one of the first lessons the woman who trains me teaches her fledglings. It's also what my father says about impending battle.

When I was waiting for Amaya at the mask stall I noted that there were two alleys on the right and one on the immediate left. The one on the left runs alongside a two-story building with a narrow balcony. I shove through the milling people and bolt into this alley. Jumping, I catch the rim of the balcony. But when I try to swing a leg up to hook over the railing, the sheath skirt of my linen gown won't let me kick, much less climb. I drop back down and frantically tug up the cloth just as two Patron soldiers run into the alley. A burst of fear and determination gives me a rush of energy. I leap, catch, and swing myself over.

One soldier levels his crossbow at me as I pry at the closed shutters but they won't open. The other kicks down the door and stomps inside as the inhabitants cry out in fear. A crossbow bolt thunks into a shutter a handbreadth from my shoulder.

"The next one will be in your head," calls the soldier.

A shutter slams open, and I grab it because it will give me enough leverage to clamber up onto the roof and get away. Then I see the other soldier inside. He holds a spear in one hand and a baby in the other.

"Please, Domon, don't hurt my child," gasps an Efean man who is trembling in the shadows.

In the distance the woman is still wailing over her dead child. I let the soldier take me into custody. He seems to take pleasure in repeatedly jabbing me in the ribs with the spear as the two men escort me back to the lane. Desperately trying to come up with any kind of a plan I stumble into the clot of huddled prisoners. The woman who makes the butterfly masks steadies me reflexively, then recognizes me and pushes away with a curse as if I am the evil shadow whose whispers bring misfortune. People examine me with so much hostility that I tense.

A second spider scout stamps up, crested with a captain's horns. Soldiers shove Coriander's brother forward. His arms are already trussed up behind his back, and his face is dirty, like they deliberately and maliciously rubbed it in the dirt. His nose is bleeding, and for an instant I feel sorry for him.

"That's him." The captain surveys the shattered stalls and frightened craftspeople. "These people must have known who he is! Arrest them all for harboring a fugitive!"

The thought of Father showing up at the Queen's Prison to bargain for my release makes me choke.

"Jessamy!"

I almost leap out of my skin.

Lord Kalliarkos rushes up, wearing the same rich clothing he wore on the balcony. The gold scarf flapping at his neck marks his grandmother's royal lineage, so naturally the soldiers give way at once. He hauls me over to the spider captain.

"My lord," says the captain wearily, as if he already knows what is going to happen.

Kalliarkos is so highborn he does not even identify himself. "You may release this young person into my custody."

Soldiers avert their faces, knowing better than to smirk. I wish a trap would open and swallow me. Coriander's brother's look of disgust is like hot ash blown in my face.

The captain's words fall with rigid politeness. "Then if you will be so kind, my lord, and move out of the way of our operation, I would be all gratitude."

Oblivious to the man's contempt, Kalliarkos tugs me past

the spider scouts. The dead child is gone, having left behind a puddle of blood and a forgotten little sandal with one broken strap.

"Why are you here?" I demand as I trot along beside him. I'm too breathless and too horrified by what I've just seen to be in awe of a rich young lord sweeping out of nowhere to rescue me.

"You never told me where you train."

"You followed me to find out where I train? You must be desperate, my lord."

His smile has an edge. "You should be very glad right now that I am that desperate."

My father's words dog me: *You will never speak to him again.* But I need answers. "How did you know I was here?"

"After your father took you off the balcony I made my way around to the servants' area. I just meant to find out where you live but when I saw you leaving I followed. Good fortune for me that you got yourself into trouble. Now we can talk."

"Good fortune? There's a dead child, and people getting arrested!"

His bitter smile curls into frowning displeasure. Without a word he leads us to a long straight stair set off with tall railings and guarded by silent soldiers. They bow to Kalliarkos and let us pass. We climb forty steps in silence. No one else uses these stairs; they must be reserved for highborn Patrons. At a landing he pauses, setting a foot on a bench.

"My lord, I beg your pardon for my disrespect." The placating words stick in my throat because I am still angry, but no lord will let the likes of me scold him. He can destroy my father's career. "I have no right to speak to you that way."

"No, you are right to speak. It is easy for me to make light of a situation that does not threaten me. Honesty isn't disrespect."

He gazes thoughtfully over the roofs and awnings of the Ribbon Market. The many lanes and stalls take up almost all of the crater. A thread of smoke marks the place where I was captured. Spider scouts moving through the narrow alleys flash as the sun hits their polished carapaces at just the right angle. It reminds me of how a good adversary can use the sun's light to gauge where traps are concealed. There are a lot of clues and cues an astute player picks up on. Kalliarkos's tense posture tells me something. I just have no idea what.

I can't help but notice the things Amaya would. His profile has the classic beauty of the Patrons in the slope of his cheekbones, the curve of his eyebrows, the cut of his eyes. His black hair is so short it stands straight up, and with a restless gesture he combs a hand through its stiff strands.

"I didn't mean to force the secret of you running the Fives from you like that," he goes on. "I won't tell anyone."

He looks so serious that I nod like I'm tendering a payment

even though I feel all at sea, unable to gain my footing. "My thanks, my lord."

He looks relieved that I am not angry at him, as if a lord would ever care about my feelings. "You can thank me by telling me where you train. If I don't master Rings I can't win ten Novice trials and become a Challenger. If I don't get good enough to run as a Challenger, my family will send me into the army. That's the last thing I want."

"Every Patron man wants to distinguish himself in the army."

"I don't."

"How can you not want to serve in the army? The army is the glory of Efea. Soldiers are the truest servants of King Kliatemnos and Queen Serenissima. It is the army that keeps Efea's people safe!"

"You're a captain's daughter. That's all you've ever heard. It's not why we fight."

My irritation spikes again. How dare he dismiss my father's valor! "Efea's enemies are always attacking us. We have to fight lest we be overrun by people who want to steal the grain out of our fields and the gold and iron from our mines."

With a heavy sigh he starts climbing, and I match his steps even as I feel the ache of a bruise coming in where the spear-butt jabbed me.

"I mean no disrespect to your father, the hero of Maldine.

But it isn't that simple, Doma. The noble ancestors of our king and queen fled the empire of Saro over a hundred years ago."

"Yes, I know. That was when the last emperor was murdered and the empire fell apart."

"Most of the people we fight are really just our distant cousins, the ones who stayed behind and built the kingdoms of Saro-Urok, West Saro, and East Saro out of the old empire. It's like one huge, nasty, bloody, generations-long family quarrel." He waves a hand airily. "The point is, I'll never be allowed to learn what I need at my family's Fives stable."

"Why not?"

"Because my uncle doesn't want me to run the Fives. Unlike your father with you, he can't stop me running, not as long as my grandmother allows it. But the trainers at Garon Stable know it will displease him. They can't go against his wishes."

"You feel trapped too!" I say eagerly as I forget I am talking to a lord.

"Yes!" As our gazes meet, a spark of understanding flashes between us. "Please tell me where you train. I'll do anything."

We reach the top of the stairs, which give onto the promenade. Soldiers guard every avenue that leads off the terrace into the city. Patron carriages are lined up, waiting to be given permission to exit. Everyone looks nervous.

Amaya stands by the carriage next to Polodos. He

surreptitiously slips a folded scrap of paper to her. Can stolid, boring Polodos possibly be Amaya's secret suitor, the one who writes execrable paeans to her beauty on scented rice paper?

The brush of Kalliarkos's fingers on my elbow jolts me.

"Please," he says. "I know you understand."

"I do understand." I am sure the sky will open and the gods' judgment pierce me with a mighty arrow for talking to him when Father told me not to. "But you see how it is with me."

"Plenty of girls and women run the Fives."

"Yes, Commoner women do, and if I were a Commoner my family would be proud. But Patron women do not."

"Your father is the hero of Maldine. Surely that counts for something."

"His daughters must be the most proper Patron girls of all, even if we will never truly be Patrons."

He frowns, thinking over a situation a highborn youth like him has never faced. "Of course you're not a Patron girl. You're a mule."

I flush at the word.

"Forgive me, I meant no insult." That he blushes in his turn shocks me. Why does he care? "Of course I see your father feels he must be doubly strict given the peculiar nature of your circumstances. Considering how good you are, that must be frustrating for you."

His unforced sympathy opens my heart. "It is frustrating.

I train at a little stable run by a woman named Anise. It's near Scorpion Fountain."

His eyes widen. "That's a bad part of town."

"No it isn't. Maybe you've heard it is because only Commoners live there. Anise takes any comers, even Patrons. She won't treat you differently from the others just because you're a lord's son."

"I don't want to be treated differently because of who I am." His expression is so serious I believe he believes it. Were a lowborn Patron like my father to attempt to rescue a Commoner girl from a mass arrest it could kill his career, but such magnanimity in a lord's son is charming eccentricity.

"Anise doesn't run adversaries in trials like the competitive Fives stables do," I add. "She's not interested in reputation and making money like everyone else is. She's not like the palace stables, competing for royal favor and a seat closer to the king's throne if their adversaries win. All she does is train those who want to learn. That's why she's got no fame. That's why I can train there."

He clasps my hand warmly. "Thank you! I'll meet you there, won't I?"

The pressure of his skin on mine makes my chest tighten in a strange way that Amaya would tease me for were she to see me now. Which she will, if she happens to look this way. I am suddenly aware of how many people swarm the promenade, any one of whom might recognize him and then me. And tell Father, or use gossip to harm Father's reputation.

I pull my hand out of his grasp. "I have to go."

"Scorpion Fountain. Anise." He hurries away through the mob of waiting carriages.

10

"Jes! There you are!" Amaya waves. "Hurry!"

I trot over, hating how the fashionable sheath gown makes it so hard to climb or run. But if I'd escaped the soldiers, Kalliarkos wouldn't have rescued me. Thinking of the way he casually treated me as just another adversary makes me smile as I reach the carriage.

"Thank the oracles!" Amaya grabs my hands so tightly I think she might actually have been worried. "How did you get separated from us? We have to get home."

"It was stupid to stop here!" I say as we clamber in.

"It's stupid of you to run the Fives in defiance of Father. Do you want to have this argument again, Jes?"

No one is more annoying than Amaya gnawing on an argument so I tweak aside the curtains and stare outside to ignore her. The view seaward is stunning from this height. The city has two harbors that are almost perfect circles, their rocky rims washed by water. Many ships sail in and out bringing in goods from foreign countries and taking away the grain, gold, spices, and cloth that our enemies covet. Between the harbors rises the peninsula that houses the City of the Dead and the tombs of the oracles. The deep blue sea stretches to the horizon to the south and west, its waters glittering under the sun.

Far away to the south, much too far to see from here, lies the land of Saro, where my father was born, the same land out of which the ancestors of the current king and queen fled during a terrible civil war a hundred years ago, as Lord Kalliarkos has just reminded me. With their army and their priests the newcomers established a royal dynasty here. But even so, it wasn't far enough away, because the deadly hostilities they left behind plague us still.

My gaze drifts back to where Coriander waits like a person drugged by shadow-smoke. I wonder what terrible crime her brother committed. Probably he murdered someone in a fit of rage.

"What are you looking at?" Amaya shoulders me aside. She glances toward Coriander but then turns to look forward for so long that I wonder what she is looking at. Finally she sits back. "How I wish I could trade places with Coriander! Then I could walk anywhere I wish in the city instead of being trapped by Father's honor!"

"As if Coriander ever gets a day free." The memory of her brother's accusations grinds at my thoughts.

Amaya unwraps one of the cat masks and turns it from side to side. "Have you ever been in love?" she asks too casually. "I know you've done things at the training stable you're not supposed to. I won't tell."

"Kissing people who are attractive to see what it feels like is not the same as being in love!" I smile the bold smile I usually only wear at Anise's stable, the one that shows I'm not really a dutiful daughter at all. "It is fun, though."

Amaya rolls her eyes and then lifts the cat mask to her face. For an instant, as I see her dark eyes shining through the slits, the mask seems to melt into her. For an instant, her skin takes on a sheen of silky fur and her teeth sharpen and gleam and her painted fingernails elongate into viciously pointed claws.

Startled, I blink, then rub my eyes.

She lowers the mask with an overwrought sigh, just an ordinary pretty girl.

"Why did you buy two cat masks?" I ask.

"So Denya and I can match." She wraps the mask back up. "Are we ever going to leave?"

She sticks out her head, looking forward. I see the way she catches in an excited breath, the way her head tilts flirtatiously like she's smiling at someone she wants to notice her. Abruptly our carriage jerks forward and she sits back heavily in the seat, fanning flushed cheeks with a hand. She closes her eyes and smiles triumphantly.

I peek out again. A young Patron woman is peering out of the heavy beaded curtains of the carriage ahead of us. Her hair is a dramatic sculpture of ribbons, elaborately layered tails, and braided plaits. Thickly drawn kohl outlines her eyes as if with wings. Seeing me, she frowns in surprise and withdraws inside.

A moment later I see Kalliarkos—of all people!—stride up to that very carriage and swing inside. He's grinning like he just won a trial. Guards wave their carriage through the gate.

When our turn comes, Polodos walks confidently up to the guards and we are waved through without incident.

"Polodos doesn't seem like the kind of ambitious, dashing man you would be interested in," I say, still peering out through the beads.

"You need to pay attention to something other than the Fives, Jes. Polodos is very ambitious."

I sit back in astonishment. "Is he really the one who writes that leaden-footed poetry devoted to the mysterious pools of your star-ridden eyes?"

"It's not leaden-footed. They're the most beautiful words ever written!" She hasn't opened her eyes. "Could you just let me have some peace?"

The grind of the wheels on the street, the clip-clap of

the horses' hooves; and the pad of the servants' feet as they walk alongside out in the sun blends into a soothing rhythm. In a pleasant baritone Polodos sings a lover's song about a sailor stealing off his ship at dawn to meet his beloved so she can "wash his clothes." I shut my eyes and pretend I am climbing the victory tower, that I reach the top and pull off my mask.

It's just a dream. It will never happen.

Amaya elbows me. "Jes! Wake up. We're home. Thank all the gods! Father's not here yet."

We live in a district where lowborn Patron men who have gained a certain level of prestige and wealth have set up households behind high walls. The green gates of our house are marked with Ottonor's three-horned bull. We get out in the carriage yard and hurry indoors past Father's parlor and study, past the reception room and garden where he hosts what social gatherings he can afford, and into the family quarters.

"We did it!" Amaya takes hold of my hand. "Father will never know because everything went perfectly!"

The tension and the emotion of the day finally begin to drain and I start to relax.

Just as we enter the family's gracious parlor we hear Bettany screech.

"I can't anymore! I won't! And you can't stop me!"

That tone is trouble and this is not a day on which we want any further notice from Father. Amaya and I run down the passage and into the suite we four girls share. I bar the door behind us.

Bettany faces Maraya. The contrast between them could not be more stark. Maraya has the same short, stocky build as Father. Bettany towers over her. Her hair spreads like an aura around her head. Hers is the beauty that crushes rather than soothes.

"What is going on? Why are you bullying Maraya?" I demand. Bett and I aren't much alike, but we did share a womb so there isn't really anything I won't say to her.

"I'm not bullying her. She's the one who got in my way." Bettany picks up a laden basket and slings it over her back. "I am leaving this house forever. And I'm not coming back."

"If you ruin the family's reputation by running away, I'll never make a good marriage," cries Amaya.

Bettany measures Amaya in the hard way that makes Amaya blush. She hates that Bettany is far more beautiful than she is and hates even more that Bettany cares nothing for her beauty. "I weep for you, Amiable. You can tell Father I died."

"You might spare a thought for what will happen to the rest of us," says Maraya calmly. "We will be punished for what you did."

"Don't you care about Mother?" Amaya demands.

"That fat cow! Grazing inside the fence she allowed to be built around her while she waits for the bull to come home and cover her."

"There's no reason for you to be deliberately coarse!" I'm astonished at how much her comment annoys me. "If not for her, you and I would have been handed over to the temple."

Her anger makes the room hum. "Yes, we all like to praise her for that. But what if Father had insisted on giving us to the temple? Would she have stood up to him then?"

Maraya raises a hand. "Your argument is a sieve that doesn't hold water. Maybe he didn't insist. But maybe he did and Mother refused. All we know is that I am alive and you two are not servants in the temple."

"Or worse," murmurs Amaya. "You might have been dedicated to become attendants to a living oracle. Think of how awful that would be! Shut up in a tomb until you die."

We all turn on her, even Bettany. "Shh!" "Hush!" "Amaya! How can you speak such an impiety!" Our words roll together into one.

But it is too late.

Maybe our bad fortune has nothing to do with Bettany's rebellion and Amaya's blasphemous words. Maybe it started when I so arrogantly presumed that my day would go exactly as planned. When both Amaya and I defied our father's wishes. Maybe it has nothing to do with us girls at all. To lords

98

who live in palaces, we are nothing more than sticks in the current to be rolled along in waters far more powerful than our fragile lives.

A commotion rises from the house. Shrieks and shouts split the air.

A staff hammers on our closed door. The voice of the Senior House Steward startles us, for in the normal course of our lives he is far too important to be bothered with mere girls. When he speaks he sounds frantic, like a man about to fall into a vat of poison.

"Open up! Doma Maraya, you and your sisters are demanded at once in the master's study."

11

A **horrible sick** fear worms its way into my heart. I can't breathe. Father has found out!

Amaya mutters a crude curse under her breath. Even Bettany stares, stunned speechless by the distress in the steward's tone.

Maraya recovers first. "We shall come at once, Steward Haredas."

His footsteps lumber unsteadily toward the front of the house, like he is injured and limping.

"What if something happened to Mother and the baby?" A tear trickles down Amaya's face.

"Hide the basket, Bett!" I snap.

When that is done Maraya leads us down the passage

with her rolling walk. We hasten through the family parlor and along the shaded walkway that skirts the formal garden. Taberta kneels at the public altar, a stone basin set on a big block of granite. She clicks through her ill-wishing beads, mouth moving in prayers she can no longer utter aloud. Tears streak her face.

Something has gone terribly wrong.

We walk into the reception room with its floor tiled with a scene from one of the stories told in old Saro: that of the fledgling firebird that fled its nest and found a home in a new land.

The family's servants huddle here, whispering and weeping.

Fear tastes like bile in my throat.

Polodos stands guard at the closed door to Father's study. He lets us pass.

Mother sits in Father's chair, her brow furrowed but her face clear and healthy. Father stands behind her with a hand on her shoulder. As we enter he steps away from her. His clothes are streaked with blood.

He is a strong and good-looking man, hardened by war and yet unmarked except for a few minor scars. That is why the smears of drying blood on his brow shock us girls into mute statues.

The door opens. Polodos enters with Cook, who carries a tray of drink and food.

"I could not eat a thing after seeing that," says Mother in a trembling voice.

"You will eat," says Father.

We wait while Cook pours a cup of broth and ladles out fruit and almonds. Father stands like an arrow held to the string, poised at the edge of release. Only when Mother has eaten does he speak.

"Lord Ottonor went into convulsions on the balcony. Although a doctor was in attendance there was nothing she could do. He is dead."

Cook hands him a cup of his favorite tea, and he drains it in one gulp like a thirsty man who has just crawled out of the Desert of Rocks.

"Is that his blood on your clothes, Father?" I ask. Trying to make sense of it all is the only way to stay calm. "Why was he bleeding?"

"He fell and cut his scalp open. He also coughed up blood."

Mother says, "He was poisoned."

Father shakes his head. "No. He was old and ill. He has had convulsions before. It is why he had a doctor in attendance at all times."

Bettany stiffens. I hiss at her under my breath but she cannot keep her mouth shut no matter what damage it does.

"Now you have no lord sponsor, Father. What is to become of us? You and your pregnant concubine and your four inconvenient daughters and your shameful lack of sons and your household that has clung to the hope that you will gain a higher office even though you never do? What lord will wish to sponsor a man of your birth and age who has no wife and no heir, a mere field captain in the Royal Army with no prospects for advancement whatever his victories?"

"Bettany," says Mother in a calm voice, "I cannot approve this disrespectful tone toward the man who gave you life."

"Cannot approve my tone? Yet you want those questions answered too, don't you?"

"Do not try me, Bettany," says Father. "You and I have clashed before and we will again, but this is not the time. Whatever you think of me you need to consider right now what this means for all of us."

I think Father is a little afraid of Bett, not in a cowardly way but as if he fears the havoc he has unleashed on the world. He slapped me! Yet he *speaks* to her.

"Father," says Amaya in a small voice, "if you can find no lord to sponsor you, then there is no chance I will ever find a husband, is there?"

"Enough, Amaya," he says in a tone that starts her sniveling. "A tomb will be opened in the City of the Dead. Lord Ottonor's corpse is being prepared for his journey to the afterlife. The rituals are being sung, and the priests are braiding his self and his shadow and his name into the husk of his flesh so he will be able to walk to the gods' country."

He stares at his palms. An old white scar cuts across his left hand, memory of a desperate struggle. For as long as I remember he has had that scar. I don't know how he got it.

He looks up. "Polodos, you will buy reeds. The women of the house will weave them into mourning mats. We will sleep and sit on these mats only. All other furniture is to be covered and not used until after the funeral. The women's ribbons and masks and fripperies must be burned. The household will wear mourning shrouds."

"Burned!" Amaya fights not to break down.

I'm already planning where I can hide my gear.

He goes on. "Once the mourning prayers are begun we will imbibe only water and bread until Lord Ottonor enters his new abode in the City of the Dead. The food we would have eaten will be given to the oracles. Is that understood?"

Cook is of Patron parentage but she was born and raised in Efea. She looks aghast as she protectively pushes the platters closer to Mother.

"My lord father, is that necessary?" asks Maraya in her calm way. "It is not commonly the custom here in Efea to follow the harsher laws of the old empire. I can show you the Archival records of funeral feasts observed even in the greater and lesser palaces...."

"We must observe mourning with complete propriety, exactly as it was observed in the days of the empire." Father is a blade of steel, sharp and unmerciful. "This house especially cannot be seen to take a single step wrong, as Bettany has seen fit to remind us. We are not a palace to bend custom to our convenience."

Mother curves a hand over her belly. "My lord, of course the household will obey the holy customs of the old empire. Is there no exemption for small children and the aged and infirm, who may suffer if they cannot take a bit of broth or goat's milk to strengthen their blood?"

My mouth drops open. Never in my life have I heard Mother question one of Father's decrees, not in front of us girls.

"No." His tone whips us. "The gods protect those who are fully obedient to their decrees. The oracles see all. Everything must be done with the most scrupulous observance."

We stand as silent as if we have had our tongues cut out. It is hard to swallow.

Dried blood flakes off his hand. "I must wash off this blood. Make a pyre for all our clothing. The ashes of our vanity will be placed in Lord Ottonor's tomb when he is interred after the funeral procession."

His gaze holds each of us in turn. Even Bettany says nothing, for once cowed just like the rest of us. When he looks at me I shiver, for I am not sure I know this man with his angry brow. His right eye twitches as if a flash of light has made him want to blink.

A terrible idea rises up in my heart. This turn of events is not anything he thought would happen, not yet, not now. He fears what Lord Ottonor's death will bring. But I am not so sure he fears on behalf of his daughters. I am afraid he is not thinking of us at all.

12

At dusk we begin burning clothes in a brick hearth hastily built at the open front gate. We drape ourselves in mourning shrouds, wrinkled linen sacks with holes cut for arms and head. We stand all evening at the gate so everyone can see our piety. Ribbons blacken and curl. Ash seeps everywhere.

Saroese priests sing the proper ritual songs, which drone on and on. An elderly Efean servant called Saffron faints and is taken inside. Half of the household is coughing from the smoke. My eyes stream but not from grief. I am sorry Lord Ottonor is dead but I am not bereft. Father stares straight ahead. Shadows haunt my mother's gentle eyes. Bettany is silent. Maraya looks as if her carefully tended dreams have been demolished. Poor Amaya sobs as she places the three beautiful masks she just bought onto the flames.

I hid my Fives gear in a rice basket. Will the oracles punish all of us for my disobedience? Yet I do not go and fetch it out. If I lose the Fives, I will turn into ashes too.

Long after everyone has stumbled off to catch what sleep they can on mats on the floor, I sit alone in the family's private courtyard. My heart is gray, burned to cinders. My thoughts chase like adversaries through a maze.

It is true that Lord Ottonor rode Father's military victories to a higher place in court. But all lords gain benefit from the achievements of their sponsored men. He did not compel Father to marry a Patron woman of Ottonor's choosing. He allowed Mother to come to private social gatherings and treated her with tolerant respect. He could have forced Father to get rid of us daughters but he did not. In his own way he accepted us. He allowed us to stay together.

I bury my face in my hands, trembling. I thought such mean and petty things about him and now I wish I could take them all back.

A rustle of movement whispers from the kitchen courtyard where the hearths and oven stand. I tiptoe inside. Mother kneels all ungainly beside a mat where the old servant Saffron now rests. She is shading into a delirium, her self and her name coming unmoored from her body. Saffron isn't her real name anyway; it is just the one Father assigned her when she came into the household.

Mother glances at me, then slips a tiny leather bottle from

the crook of her left elbow and slides the bottle's tip between the old one's withered lips. Saffron suckles as might a lamb. Bettany stands in darkness against the wall. As far as I know everyone else is asleep.

But suddenly lamplight winks, then sprays the kitchen courtyard's walls with shadows. Father appears. "Is this how I am repaid?" he says with clenched jaw.

Instead of begging his pardon Mother steadies the bottle at the old woman's lips. He backhands her so hard that drops of oil splash onto her perfect skin, pale flecks against brown.

I jolt back a step, heart thudding, a hand clapped over my mouth in shock. Before this night I have never seen him raise a hand to her.

Her expression tightens as she looks up at him. "How can your Saroese gods demand an old woman suffer for the sake of a man who never knew she existed?"

"I have allowed you to keep your useless strays at some cost to my career. But now is the crux. If I cannot attract a new lord sponsor in the wake of Ottonor's death, then what do you suppose will become of her? Or of you?"

"You fear for your own honor, my lord. Your own ambition. That is what drives this unreasoning mood. It is not like the man I know."

"When they see you they laugh at me for my weakness." He lifts a hand.

I flinch, thinking he means to hit her again. Bettany leaps forward, yanks the lamp out of Father's grasp, and throws it onto the hearth. The ceramic bowl shatters, and oil blazes up. Mother kneels with a hand pressed to her cheek.

"You're the one who got her pregnant all those times!" Bettany shouts. "You could have let her go but you never did!"

"Bettany, calm yourself," says Mother. "The death of Lord Ottonor has upset us all. We will weather this unpleasantness and find peace again."

Ashamed at my hesitation, I hasten forward to help her rise with my arm around her back.

Father grabs an unlit lamp from the table. He lights it before the glow of the spilled oil fades. When he looks at us with that dark frown, I tremble.

"Am I?" he says. "Am I the one who got you pregnant?"

Never before in my entire life have I seen anger pinch Mother's mouth.

"Dare you speak so to me, Esladas? Out of your own fear? Had I desired another man I would have left you. Had any of your daughters not been born of your seed I would have honored them by telling them the name of their father. I would not have lied and worn a mask of deceit. Never believe I will accept such insulting words. For it is not just me you insult. It is yourself, and your girls."

Fierce Bettany begins to cry but I am numb. My lips are numb. My heart is numb.

I watch Father for any hint of how the hidden wheels of the undercourt will turn and whether a trap will open beneath our feet. Mother is a rock in my arms. She is not even shaking, but where her taut belly presses against my side I feel a pressure, a push, and then a little kick. *Their baby.*

The only sounds are the hiss of the wick and the husky breathing of the old servant. Lamplight bathes Father's face in a mask of light while we stand in shadow. I imagine he must examine his troops with just this implacable stare before he sends them into a battle from which he knows few will emerge alive.

Without one more word he walks out of the courtyard, leaving us in darkness.

Mother takes hold of Bett's arm. "I hope you have not cut yourself when the lamp shattered."

Bettany commences sobbing in gulps. She rarely cries, but when she does, it is floodwaters. "That he should speak to you in that tone!"

"We enter a perilous time. He knows things may go ill for our household and his military camp, all the people under his command. Beyond all else he does not want to fail us. So he listens to his fears instead of to his wisdom."

"You always make excuses for him!" She stomps away into the house. Each thudding footfall makes me wince.

Mother says, "Help me down, if you will, Jessamy."

As I ease her to the ground and kneel beside her, I hear the creak of Saffron's frail voice.

"Blessings on you, Honored Lady. May your mercy be rewarded by the five."

"Hush, Safarenwe. The old Efean beliefs cannot be spoken of in this house. You must finish the milk."

"Mistress, you saved me already from what was worse than death. The passage from this world into the next is no hard journey. Do not harm yourself by helping me."

"You are too weak to drink only water and eat only a crust of dry bread. I insist."

I remain crouched beside them until Mother sees the bottle emptied. The creamy smell of the milk makes my stomach growl. When Saffron is settled peacefully, I help Mother up.

"I will sleep with you girls tonight," she says. "A blessing on you for staying with me, Jessamy."

I am ashamed I did not help her sooner, that I stood by while Father hit her.

As if she can see into my heart, Mother says, "It is the only time he has ever laid an angry hand on me. I would never stay with a man who abused me. Do not think this is how he is."

When I speak my voice sounds like a little child's. "He was never so rigid about the old country Saroese ways before."

"This will pass, I promise you. Be patient."

He does not seek her out that night. We girls stack our mats so Mother can have a softer resting place and ourselves lie right on the hard floor.

For the next three days Father is gone all day to stand

attendance at Ottonor's household as the lords of the city pay their respects to the dead man. Our household sits shrouded in the ashes of our finery. Each morning at dawn Cook places a round of fresh bread on the altar while saying a prayer:

"You who command the wind and the rain and the sun and our destiny, accept this offering of the first food of the day. If this meal be pleasing to you, let the household find favor in your eyes and prosperity in the days to come. Let the Doma be well. Let her merciful heart and her affectionate temper be blessed and sheltered by the mantle of your protection, holy ones."

I moisten dry bread in a cup of well water whose metallic taste coats my tongue, but the scraps do not dull the restless uneasiness that dogs me. Bettany and I cling to Mother, wipe down her sweaty face and arms with a cool cloth even though mourning people are not allowed to bathe. Amaya sits listlessly in the shade, grieving for her burned treasures. Maraya reads as if words are food. Old Saffron's spark fades in the quiet of night and she dies before dawn. Her body is carried out of the house while Mother whispers a prayer in Efean that I have never heard before. But when I ask what it is, she shakes her head and refuses to answer.

Late at night on the third day Father returns home at last and shuts himself in his study. We four girls walk with Mother to the closed door. He does not answer her query but I hear him pacing. The scuff of his feet on tile is broken by the creak of a chair as he sits down and then stands up again. Haredas speaks to him but he does not reply.

Polodos guards the door. It is he who, after glancing at us, murmurs to Mother: "Lord Ottonor left massive debts, Doma. His heirs are ruined and his household in disorder."

Amaya begins to cry. "How will we eat? Where will we live?"

"Imagine having to endure Amaya's bawling over being forced to eat stale bread!" Bettany mutters.

Maraya pokes her. "Or your gloating over her bawling."

Bettany snorts, amused by Maraya's wit, and Polodos looks our way, shaking his head. They quiet at once. No one wants Father to come out and scold us.

"Dry your tears, little Amaya," says Mother, brushing her fingers along Amaya's cheek. "No doubt your father has some scheme in mind. It will be better in the morning, you'll see. Let's go to bed now."

When I wake at dawn, all the others are still asleep.

Mother looks peaceful, her breathing as soothing as the becalmed sea. I love her so much.

Maraya sleeps with a smile on her face. She's probably dreaming of dusty old Archives.

Amaya is curled up as tightly as a bug, her head tucked against her knees. She looks so young, like a girl instead of a budding young woman.

Bettany sprawls with arms flung out like wings. In sleep

all the anger has melted out of her face. I feel I am glimpsing another Bettany, one I've not yet been introduced to in the waking world. Among Patrons Bettany would be criticized as too tall, too broad-shouldered, too kinky-haired, too dark. But no one would ever dare call her anything except beautiful, for she is like finest silk tossed in among serviceable linen.

Every body has five animating souls:

The vital spark, the breath, which separates the living from the dead.

The shadow, which hugs us during the day and wanders out on its own at night.

The self, which is the distinct personality each creature has, that makes one person different from any other.

The name, which consists of a person's lineage and the reputation that person builds through deeds and speech.

The heart, which is the seat of wisdom, the flesh in which we live. The heart binds the five souls into one.

When Bettany sleeps, her shadow walks elsewhere, and I think it is her shadow that crawls with the anger that makes her lash out. In our shadows sleep our passions and our crookedness and our sly wit and our determination to survive and to eat and to live. I wonder what I look like to the others when I sleep. Where does my shadow wander? Does it ever run the Fives, and win?

A scrape alerts me. I roll over to see Father standing in the door, studying us. The gray light paints his face with a silver sheen, as if it is his shadow that has crept to the door to stare at us, leaving his body behind. He wears his soldier's sandals and a loose linen shroud that drapes from his broad shoulders to his knees, leaving his powerful calves bare. For a moment I wonder if it really is his shadow and not him at all. For a moment I see a stranger who has invaded our house and does not like what he has found within.

What does he see when he looks at us?

At length he vanishes.

Instinct stirs in my bones. Something bad is about to happen.

I rise and creep after him.

13

He has paused in the garden to stand in front of the altar with his head bowed. Movement just out of my sight catches my attention, and I freeze behind a pillar.

Polodos steps into the garden from the reception room.

"He is here, my lord," he says.

Nothing lies in the altar bowl except crumbs of bread pecked apart by birds during the night. A brightly plumaged bird called a dawn-throat sings its spilling melody, one long fall of plangent notes.

"Forgive me for what I am about to do," Father says to the gods. "It is better this way."

There is a trap here. I taste it in Father's bitter tone; I see it in the way he clenches his left hand; I smell a sweet aroma like temptation.

When he leaves the garden, I sneak after him through the empty reception room and to the door of his study. Father stands with his back to the door in the posture of a soldier awaiting sanction from a superior. Lord Gargaron stands at Father's desk as if *he* were head of the household. He wears spotless court clothes, a linen vest over a wrapped ankle-length skirt whose pleats are as sharp as knives. He is looking through Father's correspondence, examining the pages and then setting them aside.

"You have a superb record, Captain Esladas. Your victory at Maldine is being compared to the triumph our forces had at Marsh Shore in Oyia ten years ago when they defeated and killed King Elkorios of Saro-Urok. Your quick thinking at Maldine's harbor salvaged five of Princess Berenise's ships that would otherwise have fallen into enemy hands along with a number of Efean merchant vessels that were carrying valuable cargo. The princess knows your name, Captain. All of Garon Palace knows your name."

"My lord," says Father in a wooden tone.

"Your exploits have been spoken into the ear of King Kliatemnos himself. Queen Serenissima has also heard your name mentioned in her royal salon. Their brother Prince Nikonos has been heard to speak of your distinguished service in the army. This is a high honor for a man who began life in the hill town of Heyeng in the remote province of Everlasting

Janon. A sixth son so superfluous he could not even expect to inherit a share of his father's humble bakery."

"My lord," says Father.

Lord Gargaron looks up, straight at me. He blinks but in no other way betrays my presence. Father cannot see me because I am behind him. Gargaron smiles just a little, like he takes pleasure in the fact that I have to stand here and listen.

He sits in Father's chair and turns over another page. "Your finances are in arrears, Captain. Yet you are no spendthrift. It looks as if you have gone into debt because of Ottonor's demands on your purse. Not that I wish to speak ill of the dead, but the man was a fool, a weakling, a wastrel, and a bad manager besides, which in my opinion is the worst of it. A man of your capabilities should have years ago been given a larger command, not stuck in the desert. You should have been sent to the Eastern Reach where the real war is going on."

"Lord Ottonor's purview was along the Reed Shore and in the northern desert, my lord. That is why I served there."

"Yes, but he is dead now, and his son and heirs are sunk in such a ditch of debt that I daresay as soon as the lord is entombed the family will be packing up to rusticate in the country for a generation. They cannot possibly afford to maintain a suitable household in the city, nor will the king and queen allow them to retain a presence at court. The royal family can forgive any transgression except financial stupidity and of course blasphemy against the gods. Yet when Ottonor's household breaks up, what is to become of a competent military man like you, Captain?"

Father does not reply. From the way Lord Gargaron smooths a hand over the last dispatch on the desk, rather in the way I imagine a man strokes a reluctant lover's skin, I realize that Father has not been invited to speak. He is obliged to listen, just as I am.

"It is a great expense to elevate a man of ordinary birth from a captain's rank to that of general."

Father sucks in a breath as hard as if he has been punched in the gut. Impulsively I take a step forward with the ridiculous thought that I can somehow protect him from the very reward he must have dreamed of achieving all his life.

Lord Gargaron's gaze flashes up. The look he gives me stops me like a door slammed in my face.

"First, your financial affairs must be disentangled from those of Ottonor's heirs before the creditors descend. This must be accomplished at the same time your household scrupulously observes all the proper mourning rituals so your low birth is never a reason for suspicion."

He has arranged the papers into three stacks. One is the household financial records. One he has already pushed aside as of no interest to him. He keeps a hand open and flat atop the third stack. From this distance I cannot read the words but by the shape of them I can guess it is the careful record

Father keeps of his day-to-day service, everything he has seen and done while at war.

"Second, a general must have a proper wife. Not this infamous concubine. She is tempting in the way Efean women can be. How much more so she must have been twenty years ago, fresh and ripe and young. But you are no longer a young man. A young man's toys and pets must be put aside if a man has ambition. Do you have ambition, Captain?"

"To put aside my...my..." Father will not insult her by calling her his concubine, and he cannot call her his wife. "She is a woman, not a pet or a toy."

The thin smile I so dislike creeps onto Gargaron's thin lips. I want to scrub its foul kiss off my skin.

"Good Goat, man! How you struggle! Let me be plain. I can offer you a generalship in the Eastern Reach if you agree to marry my niece and enter my sponsorship with no encumbrances."

"Your niece?" Father sounds dumbstruck.

I am sure I have misheard. But Lord Gargaron goes on quite matter-of-factly.

"She is a lovely girl, unusually intelligent and showing an astute grasp of financial matters, like her grandmother."

"I beg your pardon, my lord, but I must ask why a highborn woman with royal lineage would be willing to marry a man like myself?"

"Ah." Lord Gargaron pushes the third stack of paper

out of the way and pulls to him a bright blue butterfly mask. It is the only ornament Father keeps in his study, set on his desk to remind him of my mother. He didn't burn it, even though he was supposed to. "My niece was married two years ago. There was an unpleasant parting of the ways and some unkindly gossip within the court. Not to put too fine a point on it, Captain, but among the matchmakers of the court she is now tainted goods. No lord will marry her, and as you know by law only a married woman can conduct business. By this means I crush two birds with one stone. She will gain the legal standing she needs to continue in the family business, and you will gain the respectability and connection you need to make your way as a general."

"To gain this exceptional reward I must put aside the woman I have lived with for the last twenty years. What if she gives birth to a boy?"

"What if she does? Such a boy cannot legally inherit from you regardless. You can sire another son but this is the only chance you will ever receive to burnish your fame and reputation by being henceforth known and obeyed as General Esladas."

I wait for Father to shout Lord Gargaron down, to proclaim his undying loyalty to Mother and his daughters. I wait for him to claim us as the only legacy he cares about.

Father says nothing.

Gargaron is the one who speaks. "There would be one other stipulation. I want your daughter."

Father cracks. He takes an aggressive step forward, then stops himself. "How can I expect to maintain an honorable standing at court if it becomes commonly known that one of my daughters is being used as another man's concubine? You cannot demand this of my honor."

"Concubine? Ah, you mean the pretty one. She is an attractive morsel, to be sure. But I mean the one who runs the Fives."

The simple words choke me.

Did Kalliarkos confess the whole after telling me he would keep my secret?

But it is too late now to hide the truth I have kept from Father for so long.

Unaccountably, Father laughs. "None of my daughters runs the Fives, my lord. A man of my rank and position could never permit that."

Gargaron lifts an eyebrow. I think he is going to laugh out loud. Instead he turns the butterfly mask in his hands and raises it so he looks out at my father through slits cut for prettier eyes than his. "You have not permitted your daughter to run the Fives?"

"Of course not! Why would you even insult me with such an accusation?"

Gargaron lowers the mask. His gaze flickers to mark me as he covers his mouth with a hand as he smiles. What sort of awful man would enjoy my consternation and my father's ignorance?

"I fear I must then accuse you of a graver misapprehension, Captain Esladas. You seem not to know what is going on in your household at all. I would hate to think the entire scheming cabal of females has been concealing the truth from you all this time. For it is sure that one of your daughters has been running the Fives. But perhaps you would like to ask her yourself."

14

F ather did not become a highly decorated captain by being slow to observe the obvious. He turns. Surprise flashes through his face but he absorbs my presence swiftly, for he is a man who never hesitates, even when the tide of battle turns against him.

"Jessamy! Tell Lord Gargaron that none of your sisters runs the Fives."

"None of my sisters runs the Fives," I echo obediently.

"There, my lord! Your accusation is unfounded."

"I have made no accusation," says Lord Gargaron. "There is nothing illegal or criminal in a girl wishing to run the Fives. Although I perfectly understand why you would not wish it known among your peers, Captain Esladas. The half-blood daughter of an ambitious man like yourself must behave in keeping with the old customs of the Saroese home-land, where daughters are few and kept indoors until they are safely married to a respectable husband. I would not like to see the lords and officials at court laughing at a man I had sponsored because his concubine's daughter was running Rings around him."

The moment Father realizes what my echoed answer means, his expression darkens with a look of such betrayal that all I can think about is the recrimination in his eyes.

"Come inside, Jessamy," says Lord Gargaron in a voice that cannot be disobeyed.

I enter the study. It would have been better to be crushed in turning Rings and my body dropped all bloody to the sand.

All at once Father acts decisively. He strides forward without the lord's permission, and rings the handbell on his desk to summon a steward. As we wait in silence, Father stares at the rug. The knotted wool is framed by a border of immortal firebirds as rosy as dawn. For years Mother saved coin from the household budget and engaged in a bit of marketing on the side to earn enough to buy him this carpet as a gift.

Footsteps approach, and Polodos halts at the open door, eyes wide as he takes in the scene.

Father speaks in a cold tone that scares me. "Polodos, go fetch..." He is about to say "the Doma" or "the mistress of the house" but these are titles he cannot give to my mother in front of Lord Gargaron. "I wish Jessamy's mother to attend me at once. Then make sure we are not disturbed."

"As you command, Captain."

Polodos closes the door as he goes out.

Lord Gargaron smiles his thin smile, and I shudder. The three tiny gold rings in his right ear mark him as a man who commands a palace household, although he is not himself born of royal lineage. "Tell me something, Jessamy," he says.

I wish desperately he would stop using my name in such a familiar way but I cannot object.

"You ran impressively against my nephew. Why did you allow a lesser adversary to win?"

Instead of answering I look at the rug. I have failed Father in the worst way: I have caused him to lose face. He knows it, and so do I.

"Answer Lord Gargaron, Jessamy."

"I did not dare win, my lord," I say in a low voice.

"Why is that, Jessamy?" Gargaron asks.

"Because the winner must unmask, my lord."

"You did not want your father to know you run the Fives, is that it?"

"Yes, my lord." I finally look up.

Father is actually too stunned to speak as the extent of my insubordination hits him.

Lord Gargaron oozes on, his unctuous tone like slime in the air. "Garon Stable is shorthanded in promising young

Novice adversaries. Your daughter appears to have real skill. More than that, she possesses an aptitude for the finer points of the Fives. My nephew Kalliarkos is a good boy, a pleasant lad, but he doesn't have the edge that determines loser and winner just through sheer guts. You know what I mean, Captain. You see it among the men you have fought beside, those who, like you, have the necessary grit to see the battle through. Your daughter takes after you in that way. Do you not think so?"

"You, Jessamy? *You* were the one I trusted most."

I will not give Lord Gargaron the satisfaction of seeing me break down. But it is so hard to stand here with my father staring at me as if I am a scorpion crawled out of the night to sting him with its venom.

A tap rattles the closed door.

"Enter," says Lord Gargaron.

Mother comes into the room, and Polodos closes the door behind her to seal us in.

Even in her shapeless mourning shroud and with the bulk of her pregnancy before her, she glides like the most beautiful of ships, resplendent, moving gracefully under sail.

"My lord," she says, and I am not sure which man she addresses.

For an instant I think neither Father nor Lord Gargaron is sure either.

Part of what makes her beautiful is that she has the discipline to regret nothing. Even under Gargaron's censorious eye she does not wilt or fade.

"What is your wish, my lord?" she asks, addressing Father directly.

"Has Jessamy been running the Fives without my permission?"

"She didn't know!" I cry, for above all things I do not wish Mother to take the blame.

She sighs with such gentle reproof that she could as well have slapped me. "Of course I knew, Jessamy. Do you think I don't know everything that goes on in this household?"

"You knew, Kiya?" Father raises a hand as if to strike in sheer, frustrated rage, glances at Lord Gargaron, and lowers the hand. "You let it go on despite knowing I could never allow it?"

"What harm? Amaya is youngest of the four and she is now the age I was when you and I met. When I was her age, I worked in the market. I came and went as I pleased. It seems to me it was in part my freedom to come and go that attracted you because it was so different from how women behaved in the land of your birth. Our daughters are no longer girls. They are becoming young women. Do you mean them to live shut up in this house all their lives?"

"As you have done? Is that what you mean? Was this

house not good enough for you?" He is shouting. He has forgotten that Lord Gargaron watches all, a vulture waiting for the beast to die so he can consume the carrion.

Mother never shouts but there is a stony weight to her voice that is worse than any chastisement. "I have no complaints nor have I ever made any. I chose this life with you. I knew what it would be. But our daughters have had no choice."

"So you let them sneak around. Good Goat, woman! What else have you allowed them to do?"

"They are good girls, Esladas! There is nothing wrong with Jessamy running the Fives. Many girls run the Fives."

"Not my daughters! Not the daughters of men like me!"

Always Mother has championed us and encouraged us. Defended us. "She is good at it. In all the months and years you have been gone to the wars, what harm? I have been careful and so has she. She does it for the love, not for glory, not to shame you. So I ask again, what harm?"

"The harm is what falls on my honor and my reputation! But how can I expect you to understand a man's honor? How can I expect you to understand the shame it brings on a man when his household of unruly women disobeys his few rules because he has wielded too generous a hand?"

Mother is as tall as Gargaron and a little taller than Father. She does not shrink or slump as they stare at her. If anything, she grows more magnificent. "I acted as I thought best to make this household a peaceful refuge for you, my lord. No whisper of shame or disobedience has ever met my ears. Have such whispers reached you, Lord Gargaron?"

"Indeed, none have," he says with amusement and a flicker of respect. "The household of heroic Captain Esladas is never spoken of at all except as a curiosity. Yet it was not so difficult for me to discover the truth about this girl Jessamy." Despite the brief courtesy he shows Mother, he bends the severity of his gaze on Father. "You have been imprudent in your supervision of your women. They have made a fool of you because you have been too compliant, more like an Efean man, henpecked and hog-tied by the women in his sad eunuch's life. Yet I am willing to overlook the situation if you will agree to the offer I have set before you."

He speaks to Father, looks at Father. But like currents striking stepping stones in the obstacle called Rivers, the words flow toward a different shore.

Mother blinks as their impact hits her. As she understands what this truly means for us. The radiance of her face dims. She staggers, and I grab her arm to support her.

In all my life I have only seen my mother cry three times, twice when we carried stillborn boys to the City of the Dead and its Weeping Garden where infant sons of Patron fathers are buried. The third time was when my father left for the campaign in Oyia across the sea, because she knew he would be gone for years and might never return.

Now she sucks in gasping, ragged breaths as she struggles

not to break down right here in front of him and Lord Gargaron. Twenty years have been cut loose with casual words flung in her face.

Father will not even look at her. He has already made up his mind.

"How could you? You selfish pig!" I scream.

"Jessamy!" Mother's voice shatters into coarse slivers. "Do not humiliate us."

Lord Gargaron sighs. "I cannot spend all day enduring a woman's tears. Steward!" He rings the handbell.

The door opens and Polodos enters, bowing. "My lord?"

"Take the concubine away," says Gargaron.

Father says nothing.

Turning so I don't have to see the man I have looked up to all my life, I help Mother toward the door.

"The girl stays," adds Gargaron. "She will come with me."

I stop dead.

Mother's shuddering and silent tears cease on the instant. Her gaze rises to Father's shame-ridden expression.

"Esladas, you cannot mean to hand Jessamy over to this man?"

"Lord Gargaron is my lord now and thus my household is his to order as he wishes," says Father in a tone so rough I suddenly realize he is on the edge of weeping.

She steps between us. "I will not allow it! She stays with me!"

"Ah," murmurs Lord Gargaron. "Now at last we see the scorpion. Defiant and disloyal when her true face is revealed!"

"Mother, it's all right." I am so afraid that Gargaron will demand Father punish her that my thoughts tangle up in a dead-end maze of terror. But I can sluggishly think through what Gargaron has already said. "He just wants me to go train for the Fives in the Garon Palace stable. That's all."

"Of course that is all." Gargaron laughs. "Please do not believe I would ever touch a woman of your blood and breeding, much less any of your litter. If I need a concubine, I can engage a woman of my own people. Ottonor has died in such destitution I can pick and choose from among the prettiest of his young kinswomen. Now, if you will, remove the concubine to her quarters."

"I won't let you go, Jessamy," Mother cries, clinging to me.

"You must let her go," says Father in a brutal voice. "She is mine, Kiya. I allowed her to live, so I hold the power of life and death over her. Let it be that if the girl was willing to defy me by running the Fives without my permission then she can live with the choice she made."

I see Lord Gargaron fingering his whip. He'll whip her, I know he will. I tug on her arm frantically. "Mother, I'll be all right. You have to go."

Polodos peels her away from me. The young steward's expression is closed and disapproving. He obeys without a questioning word and leads her out of the room. I hear her sob with wrenching despair before the door closes.

I stumble, overcome by fear and grief, and barely catch myself against the door that has locked me away from my mother and sisters. The whole world has broken apart around me.

"Very good, Captain," says Gargaron in the pleasant tone of a man who approves of the bread and wine set before him. "You will not regret this. Together we will do very well."

"Yes, my lord." So easily he acquiesces! The thought of Mother's grief-stricken face keeps me silent. I will not cause more trouble for her. "But if I may, my lord. It would be dishonorable of me to leave before Lord Ottonor's mourning procession and his journey to the City of the Dead. As one of his sponsored men, I am required to attend with my household."

Lord Gargaron waves a hand as if brushing away a fly. "But you are no longer Lord Ottonor's man. You are mine now, so you are not required to observe this obligation. Besides, I stand among Ottonor's creditors. Clan Tonor owes my clan a great deal of money. By taking on your sponsorship I do his memory and his household a service by erasing part of his debt."

"My lord, I obey. But..." His hesitation lasts only a moment before he forges on. "Legally I have no further obligation. But Lord Ottonor supported me in my early years when I came to Efea with nothing but the clothes on my back and a hope to make my fortune here. Honor declares that I must show my gratitude properly. Had Lord Ottonor not given me the chance to take up a military career I could never have gained the honors I did and thus come to your attention."

"Your honor does you credit, Captain. I will make sure that members of your household are granted the honor of sitting the overnight vigil with Ottonor on his first night in the City of the Dead. However, I need you to depart right away. I received word yesterday that there has been an attack on the outpost of Seperens, beyond the Green River. I need a reliable and intelligent commander there as soon as practicable, so today you will be escorted by an honor guard of Garon soldiers to my villa at Falcon Hill. My niece will meet you there. You will sign the marriage contract. After Ottonor's funeral we will celebrate the wedding feast and you will sail east to the war."

Father's eyes have darkened with a surging storm-sea of emotion but he collects himself. He is like a man who has been commanded to throw overboard his most cherished treasure and yet will steel himself to do so in order to keep the ship afloat in wave-tossed seas.

"Yes, my lord."

"You must make a start on getting a son before you depart for the frontier. Let me assure you there is nothing wrong with the girl, no unsightly blemish or defect of character. You will find her appearance pleasing, her manners polished at the queen's court, and her acumen for matters of business quite up to the mark."

"Yes, my lord." Father curls his hands into fists, opens them, and at last fixes them together behind his back in a soldier's waiting stance. "My lord, the woman...my daughters... it would be dishonorable to just abandon them."

"It's not as if you have tossed them into the Fire Sea without a raft! You are a more tenderhearted man than your valor and hard-mindedness on the battlefield have led me to believe. Still, every man has his little flaws and quirks. I will have my stewards make provision for the women so you can travel to the frontier with peace of heart and a calm spirit ready to do battle."

Father glances at me.

"I will never forgive you for this," I mouth, and though my words are silent, he understands them and looks away. I pray he is ashamed of the work he has done this cruel morning!

Gargaron smiles. "Gather your arms and armor, Captain, and your military aides and senior staff." He glances down at the butterfly mask with its bright blue wings and cheerful strong color like a glimpse of the embracing sky. "I have taken a fancy to this mask, Esladas. I will just take it when I go."

Father swallows, choking down the final shard of refusal. "Of course, my lord. If I may ask..." His gaze darts to me in my shroud. "What of Jessamy?"

"She will come with me now. All the gear and clothing she will need will be supplied at Garon Stable."

A sob catches in my chest like a knot of whirling winds. "Can I not even say good-bye to them?" I whisper.

"No time for that." Lord Gargaron claps his hands three times.

I take a step toward the door, thinking to dash to the back of the house just to kiss them for the last time.

Father taps his hand twice against his chest, and I freeze and tap mine in reply, as I have been taught. Obedience traps me. The door opens and three resplendently garbed Garon Palace stewards appear like the dread guardians who defend the gates at the entrance to the afterlife.

My path is blocked.

I take the only road open to me, the one that leads me out of the household where I grew up and into the household of the lord who has just ripped apart my family.

15

I **feel dead** in my shroud as I walk out of the house. In ancient days in the empire of Saro, a dead emperor was accompanied to his tomb by living servants who were buried with him.

As I step out onto the street my vision blurs and a wave of dizziness causes me to trip over my own feet. I steady myself with the breathing I was taught at Anise's stable to prolong my stamina. Because I do not know where else to stand, I halt behind the back wheels of Lord Gargaron's carriage in the same place Coriander would walk behind ours.

Servants hauling carts and leading donkeys trudge along the sun side of the street on errands for other households while the carriage waits on the shade side. A lord has the right to the shade, and now I have stolen a tiny bit of it for myself, as the old saying goes: "The lord's shade also shelters the lord's servant."

Creditors have gathered beside the gate, clutching silver-banded ledgers. They crowd forward when Lord Gargaron emerges with Father beside him.

"Have the shrouds taken down," he says to Father. "Now that you belong to Garon Palace you are no longer in mourning."

One of his stewards dismisses the creditors as Lord Gargaron mounts into the open carriage. It needs no concealing curtains like the ones Patron women hide behind when they go out.

Harness bells ring to announce his departure. The carriage rolls forward. My feet scrape on the ground as I follow. At the gate Father stands at attention. Of my mother and sisters I naturally see no sign.

Father glances toward me as I pass. Is that a tear glinting on his face? Hope batters at my chest. He will shout that it was all a mistake. He will run after me and bring me home.

But he lets me go without a word of farewell.

We leave the house behind. It's like I'm trudging to my tomb.

The worst thing of all is that I understand why he did it. When you run the Fives you make choices in order to win. He will soon have achieved the highest honor a man of his birth could ever dream of. And he has thrown us away to get it.

Our procession heads uphill. We live on the rumpled skirts of the Queen's Hill, too high to be Common and too low to have any pretension toward highborn status. After we cross the saddle between the two hills, we climb higher on the King's Hill than I have ever been in my life. Modest compounds like ours give way to lush gardens and spacious courtyards. How beautiful the sea looks from up here and how lovely the harbor with its masts and colorfully painted ships. Out on the water, sails flash like wings atop the waves. Their easy grace makes me think of my mother and sisters. Tears seep down my cheeks.

Where will they go? What will they do?

The brass-striped gates of Garon Palace loom in front of me as the carriage halts. My lips are dusty and my eyes sting. Lord Gargaron steps down and to my horror he walks right up to me. The scent of cardamom and myrrh wafts off him, the perfume of rich men who wear fragrant oils to cover the smell of sweat and dust. I hold my ground like a soldier.

"Let me be clear, Jessamy. Do not for an instant believe you are here as a hostage for your father's good behavior. A man like him cannot help but reach for the victory tower. He fights to win regardless of your fate. You are worth nothing to me except as an adversary. I have taken on considerable debts in order to bring your father into my household. If you do not pass muster at the stable, I will have you sold into servitude to make up some of what I have paid out. A tall, strong girl like you would be welcome in the gold mines. Do you understand me?"

"Yes, my lord." My voice is little more than a scrape.

He beckons over a stout woman dressed in the leggings and tunic worn by adversaries. She cannot possibly run competitively because she is missing one hand. The stump is shiny. She is the only Commoner I have seen among the Garon Palace servants. "Tana, if she does not pass muster, return her to my stewards and they will dispose of her."

"Yes, my lord."

He climbs back into the carriage. The grand front gate opens and the carriage, servants, and guards proceed in to the palace. Beyond the open gate I see pavilions, gardens, and courtyards stairstepped up the hillside, as beautiful as a painting.

"Girl! Stop daydreaming and come with me!"

The woman leads me down the lane to a smaller gate, also painted with the horned and winged fire dog mascot of Garon Palace. The gate stands open, flanked by a pair of guards who give me a bored look like they've seen a hundred fledglings walk in hopeful and walk out rejected.

Inside, a Fives court takes up most of a huge central courtyard. An elderly Patron man is running youths and men through the traditional form known as "menageries," a formal pattern dance meant to imbue adversaries with the mental discipline necessary to succeed on the court. Four women are warming up on a set of posts set to different heights, a standard beginner's configuration of Trees. To my surprise, one is a young Patron woman with her hair clubbed up in the style of the old country. I have never seen a Patron woman running the Fives.

Tana leads me past a kitchen with an open dining shelter where the midday meal is cooking. My mouth waters. She ushers me into the dim confines of a bathhouse built into the wall that separates the stable from the palace. The front space has benches for changing.

She gestures at my shroud. "I didn't know people still wore those. While you wash I'll get you clothes for today. If you pass muster, you'll be measured for an off-duty tunic and sandals, two sets of Fives gear, and palace livery for formal occasions. You aren't in your bleeding, are you?"

"No."

"They'll explain about that, if you stay," she says as I tug off the shroud. "Don't go in the hot room or pool; just use the washroom. Take a towel from the shelf." She gives my naked body a stare from top to toe. "You look strong. Where did Lord Gargaron get you?"

"He picked me out of some rubbish that was thrown away."

Mother always says that bitterness is poison but I am swimming in it.

She gives me a long look, measuring the secrets behind

my eyes, then shrugs and leaves. The entry curtain slaps down behind her.

The floor of the changing room has not a speck of dirt except from my grimy feet. I venture into the washroom, which is magnificently set up with a trough in which to stand, sieved basins hung from the ceiling, and pitchers, cups, and sponges lined up on shelves. Pipes bring water, with levers to start and stop the flow. Because there is no one around I creep into the hot room just to see what it looks like. Steam hisses over stones. In the room beyond lies a tiled rectangular pool. Voices echo through the chamber, people on the other side of the wall using a palace bathhouse that shares the same plumbing system. I scramble back to the washroom.

As I begin to wash myself I think about Gargaron's threat to sell me to the mines. Father once told us that prisoners and indentured servants sent to the mines are forced to work the most grueling and dangerous jobs.

But I don't want to think about Father or anything he ever told me, so as I scrub myself down I pretend I am scouring all traces of him out of my flesh and my heart. After I've washed I rinse down my hair and blot out as much water as I can. The towel is a square of linen the length of my arm. It isn't big enough to wrap around me so I sit and drape it across my lap.

Then I wait.

My thoughts scurry home. Has Lord Gargaron evicted

Mother and my sisters? With their clothes burned, what will they wear? Can I run away and find them?

So abruptly I am not prepared for it, the curtain sweeps aside and three men enter. Two are Commoners and one is a Patron. Their skin is sheeny with sweat and gritty with sand and scrapes. They don't see me in the corner as they begin stripping out of their Fives gear. The Patron is talking all the while.

"And then he said, 'I'll wager ten bars that the brown girl beats him,' and Nar said, 'Ten bars? I wouldn't take that bet if it was for a sip of beer because it's obvious she's going to beat him....'"

I cough.

Startled, they peer into the shadowed corner where I huddle.

The Patron waves as at a fly. "Girl! You can't be in here. It's men's bath time now. Get out."

"I have no clothes."

As the words slide out of my mouth, I realize nothing but this scrap of cloth conceals my genitals. I grab a second towel and hold it over my breasts.

"Good Goat," says the elder Commoner, a man with a shaved head who appears a bit older than my father. "You must be a fledgling."

The Patron has an oddly familiar face but I don't know him. He laughs. "How like Tana to forget about her. Is the old mare sucking shadow-smoke again?"

They yank their clothes back on and tromp out.

Sooner than I expect Tana reappears, muttering about goat-footed smoke-heads and their disrespect. She tosses a bundle of clothes at me, underthings, leggings, a Fives tunic, and a belt; she has a good eye for size. Last, she offers me several pairs of five-toed leather slippers, and I find the best fit.

"We eat at midday at the bell. I'll show you where to get water."

Beside the kitchen a pipe empties in a trickle into a brass basin surrounded by a decorative brass tree from which brass cups dangle.

I reach for a cup but she slaps my hand away. "You'll get your own cup if you pass muster."

She deserts me again. Each cup is etched with a different mark: a flower, a spiral, a hand. I'm so thirsty. I glance around to make sure no one is in sight, then cup my hands and drink in gulps until my thirst eases.

Looking around I spot a spectators' terrace, a raised set of stepped benches under an awning. Tana climbs to the highest benches and joins the three men now sitting there. They are the ones who interrupted me in the baths. I sit below them at the edge of the shade so it doesn't seem like I'm encroaching. Yet they pay no attention to me. Evidently I will remain invisible unless I pass muster. It's better that way.

Everything seems distant and unreal, like my shadow has come half unmoored from my body. I can't even recall when I was last happy until I remember how I felt while I was waiting to climb the ladder for my one chance at running a trial. The memory of the crowd singing drifts through my head as I look over the practice court. I'm so dazed that patterns seem to unfold across the course to the rhythm of the well-known song.

Canvas walls block out a maze in Pillars, throwing shadows along the ground as if they are pinned there waiting to leap out and swallow unsuspecting adversaries, as it says in the song: *Shadows fall where pillars stand*.

Traps is a series of balance and maneuvering exercises, beams and ropes and a bridge with basic traps, but when I blink, motes of light spin in my vision, sparks like grains of sand swirling along the dark lines of rope and beam the way blood rushes in veins through the body. Posts of various heights and with a mix of handholds and angles crowd Trees; standing at the pinnacle is like displaying your reputation of honor and glory to all people, your name so bright that everyone knows you.

I rub my eyes, trying to focus, and when I open them the world looks ordinary again.

Rivers is a shallow pool measuring twenty by twenty strides; painted wooden roundels just big enough to stand on are being drawn back and forth by ropes as a pair of lads no older than me try to jump from one to the next without getting their feet wet. The boys are fledglings. Once I might have scoffed at their clumsiness, but Anise taught us that scoffing at people who aren't as skilled or as established is a sign of weakness. As the shorter boy splashes into ankle-deep water, the spectators laugh. I cautiously look more closely at Tana and the men.

By the evidence of his clubbed hair the Patron man comes from the old country, yet his lack of beard means he now considers Efea his home. "Where did those two boys come from? Why are they even here?" Like my father he has the choppy accent of a man who learned to speak Saroese in the old country. The Saroese spoken here sounds different, influenced by the lilt of Efean speech. "They are just as bad as Kalliarkos when he started."

"Hard to believe anyone could be that bad," says Tana with a relaxed chuckle. "They are here as a favor for one of Princess Berenise's merchant partners. But I believe it is Lord Kalliarkos who convinced his grandmother to insist the boys be given a chance to train."

"Does that mean we're saddled with them for a year or more? No offense to you, Tana, but for all this new push to build Garon Stable so it can truly compete with the other palace stables, this place will never amount to anything until the princess stops doing favors for her grandson."

"Kalliarkos has improved a great deal."

"Yes, he has, but if the quality of adversaries here does not improve a great deal more than he has, my honor will demand I leave."

"Garon Stable will fall apart without you, Lord Thynos," she says in alarm.

"That I had to sit through that embarrassing performance by Kalliarkos at the City Fives Court four days ago was bad enough. I have never seen Gar as angry as when that brown girl slipped on purpose to let Kalliarkos win!" But he laughs as if Lord Gargaron's anger amuses him.

"I would not like to be her if he ever finds out who she is." Tana does not laugh. "When he gets to cursing like that, you know he wants revenge."

"Do you think Kal paid off that adversary so he could get another win?" asks Thynos.

Tana scowls. "He is no cheater. You know that as well as I do."

"I suppose not. It would never occur to him to cheat."

I finally realize where I've seen Thynos: he is an Illustrious who runs under the Fives name of Southwind. I've seen him run at trials. Players who have reached the highest level get their faces painted on murals throughout the city.

The conversation veers to how Garon Stable may fare at the victory games to be held at the Royal Fives Court in six days: my father's victory games. Thinking of how Mother wept with joy at seeing him honored makes me want to tear out my heart just so I won't hurt so much. Grief sinks into me with the heat.

The sun reaches its zenith. A whistle marks the end of

practice, followed by the ringing of a bell in the kitchen shelter. Everyone ambles over to the dining area. Heat and hunger make me woozy as I clatter down the steps. No one pays me any mind as I take the last place in line. No one speaks to me. It's like I don't exist, like I'm already handed over to the stewards and asphyxiating in the mines.

As they get their food the adversaries scatter along the tables in groups. A kitchen girl yawns as she hands me a lacquered meal box. I decide it is most prudent to find a seat alone and just fill my stomach. There is warm bread and salted vegetables and a huge portion of savory chicken stew heaped over rice. I murmur the polite offering under my breath: "With both humility and gratitude my body accepts this gift of food, holy ones. Creatures who were once living gave of their spark and substance to nourish mine. I honor them."

The words rise with a sour taste. Father would speak them while we awaited his permission to eat. I don't want to think about him. My hunger twists into despair. But I have to eat to keep up my strength. If I get sent to the mines I can't help my mother and sisters. And the chicken stew does look good.

"Jessamy?"

The spoon halfway to my lips with my first bite, I freeze. Kalliarkos stands with a meal box in his hand, wearing a tunic and leggings just like any other adversary. The way he said my name draws the attention of every person in the shelter. They stare as he sits opposite me.

I set down my spoon because my hand is trembling. Un-expectedly, anger cascades out of me in a harsh whisper. "You said you wouldn't tell anyone that I run the Fives. But you told your uncle!"

"I did not speak of you to him at all!" He looks taken aback.

"How else could he have found out? He humiliated my mother in front of my father just for the pleasure of seeing her cry."

Abruptly he gets up and walks away. At first I think I have offended him but he returns with two mugs of barley beer, the usual midday drink in Efea, a thick brown brew as rich and nutritious as bread. He sits and offers one to me as he speaks in a low voice.

"Perhaps seeing my uncle in action helps you better understand why I do not wish to follow his orders, since they so often lead to unpleasant things."

A fist in my chest unclenches. "You didn't betray me."

"No, I didn't. If my uncle was interested in your father, he would have investigated everything about him thoroughly." He sips contemplatively, then sets down the mug. "What I don't understand is why you are here. Your household is in mourning for Lord Ottonor."

Everyone is still looking at us. I liked it better when they ignored me.

I shift closer, whispering even more softly, "Lord Gargaron took my father into his household and made him a general."

Kalliarkos whistles. "That can't be possible."

A spike of irritation burns through my flesh. It's as if he's two people: a young man who really understands me, and an oblivious fool. "Of course it's possible. Your uncle wants the hero of Maldine to command the Eastern Reach. What's so strange about that?"

He looks at the sky as at the gods and their inexplicable actions. "I had no idea. I thought it was a lord from the old country, someone with military experience overseas...."

"What are you talking about?" My hand tightens around the mug. I need something to hold on to when I get the bad news I am sure is about to come.

He runs a hand through his short black hair.

"My older sister left this morning for our villa at Falcon Hill. She's to marry a military man newly come to the service of Garon Palace."

16

My father is marrying Kalliarkos's older sister. I stare as the scraps and hints of information I've overheard all fall into place.

"Have I done anything to make you think I make rash promises without meaning to keep them?" he asks in a low voice.

A woman I did not know could remain a mirage, but every time Father looks on his bride he will see the face of a highborn woman whose brother he told me I must never speak to again. Because I'm not good enough for such a man.

"When I said I would keep your secret, I meant it," he adds.

It's odd how annoyed he sounds, like I'm doubting his honor. I'm grateful to him for keeping his promise but the news is a knife in my throat. I can't speak.

We eat the rest of our meal in silence. At last Kalliarkos makes an awkward retreat.

Tana shepherds me to the women's barracks for the usual lie-down people take in the worst heat of the day. Canvas curtains hang from the roof to create eight cubicles with two cots each. She directs me to a cot placed by the door where normally a servant would sleep.

"Rest here. We'll run you at the afternoon practice, see how you do." She leaves.

In the gloom I strip down to my underthings and lie on top of the blanket. Having sisters and servants, and training at Anise's stable, has killed any shyness I might ever have felt about undressing around women.

The curtain flaps as the Patron girl strides past without a word and goes into the cubicle at the far end. Three other women jostle up to look me over.

The tallest is a strapping Commoner woman with big hands. "Please don't tell us you're Lord Kalliarkos's latest pity rescue."

"Pity rescue?"

The short one breaks in. "The useless fledgling adversaries he brings in are a waste of everyone's effort. This stable will never be able to compete at the highest level if his uncle doesn't put a stop to it."

"Lord Gargaron?" I ask, thinking about the mines.

All three make the sign against the evil eye.

"Don't ever mention his name," says the tall one. "We're talking about Lord Thynos."

"Lord Thynos is Lord Kalliarkos's uncle?"

"He's the younger brother of Kalliarkos's mother. When she was shipped here to marry his father, he was sent along with her. He was just a boy then."

The one who hasn't spoken yet looks at me. "Maybe she can actually run."

"Maybe I can!" I say with a flash of confidence that punches through my misery. "I'm no pity rescue!"

"How else can Lord Kalliarkos know you?"

I know better than to tell the truth so I just shrug. They walk off. Tallest and shortest share a space. The quiet one's cubicle is hung with so many pretty masks and ribbons that it reminds me of Amaya. Melancholy swells in my heart. I would drown in grief except that the heavy meal, the mug of beer, and the drowsy heat combine to make me sleepy as my thoughts eddy.

I can't die in the mines. I have to help Mother. I can't abandon her as Father did.

Every night when we went to bed she sang an Efean charm over us to keep night-walking shadows and their fingers of illness off our vulnerable little bodies. She would never sing it in front of anyone else, not even the servants and especially not Father. It was her secret mother's gift to us, she always said. The charm would lose its power if any ears but hers and ours heard it. As I drift off to sleep the memory of her voice whispers in my mind:

Sea and stone and wind and seed
Sky above them, pay me heed.
Let no wandering shadow's kiss
Harm my girls or steal their strength.
Let their shadows safely roam
On night's dark path, then bring them home.

I dream in snatches: a bird-haunted ship on the water rolling amid stormy seas; a lamp's blazing wick being doused by the pinch of a finger; a baby born with no spark of life in its flesh...

I bolt upright, my heart pounding, my face soaked in sweat. What am I still doing here? I am invisible to these people. I can run away and find Mother. Father made his choice; let him live with it. I don't have to obey him anymore.

I tug on my clothes. The other women are moving as they start to wake up. Outside, afternoon shadows stretch across the training court. I stroll past, then veer toward the open gate. The same guards stand there, still bored and now sweating profusely. The moment they see me they cross their spears in my path.

"We have orders not to allow you out until we get word that you've passed muster."

"Just seeing if there's a view." I force an ingratiating smile. "I've never been up this high on the King's Hill before."

The street is angled to create a spectacular view. On a clear day like today the closest of the smoking islands of the Fire Sea can be seen on the western horizon, but the most prominent sight is the peninsula between the harbors, the City of the Dead. From this height it looks rather like a squat tree, with its narrow trunk connected to the land and its spread branches marked by paths winding past white stone tombs. The paths flow up toward the crown of the hill at the peninsula's center. The temple is a long, narrow building stretched like a wall across the "trunk" to control all access into and out of the tombs.

"Very impressive!" I say brightly before I turn to go back. My jaw hurts from smiling.

Tana and the elderly trainer sip tea in the dining shelter. I drink at the basin and splash water on my face to cool down my flushed cheeks. Slowly my bleary thoughts focus on the only thing that matters now: I have to pass muster. Everything depends on that.

The other adversaries are on the forecourt warming up with a round of menageries. I find a space at the back and step into the rhythm. The dance unfolds through a changing pattern whose movements are named after animals: cat, ibis, elephant, snake, dog, falcon, bull, wasp, jackal, butterfly, gazelle, crocodile, horse, gull, monkey, scorpion, horned lion, crane, sea dragon, firebird, tomb spider.

My arms and legs are stiff as I begin, but as I arch like

a cat, sway like an elephant's trunk, stretch my arms wide as a falcon's wings, I loosen up. My feet tread the coarse stone pavement as the bull paces his field. The linen headband I've tied around my head grows damp as I become the lazy but explosive crocodile. Sweat trickles down my scorpion's curved back. My arms flex and extend as I stalk the proud path of the horned lion.

Within the discipline of the menageries my despair drains away and my resolve creeps back into my heart.

Anise taught us that every training ground, like every person, has a unique soul. I seek the soul of this place through my dusty, callused feet, the taste of the air on my tongue, and the pitch of my beating heart. This training ground feels fresh and unformed, still discovering itself, not like Anise's whose stones felt old and patient. I think I could belong here. I think this ground likes me.

As we finish up, still in unison, Tana and the old man, called Darios, arrive.

Tana whistles to me. "Girl, you start on Trees. Lord Kalliarkos, if you will, on Rivers." She points to the two fledgling boys. "Pillars. Traps. Take your places."

"Is there chalk?" I ask.

She raises an eyebrow, as if she had not expected me to ask that question or perhaps any question. "Chalk at each gate."

Everyone else retreats to the viewing terrace, not bothering to hide their anticipatory smiles. Kalliarkos catches my eye and smiles to reassure me, and when I hear laughter from the spectators' benches I am sorry I looked at him.

I shake off their amusement as I trot around the outside of the court to find the crooked crossed hatch-mark that is the symbol for Trees. A bowl of chalk sits on the ground by the curtained gate. I tighten my slippers and my fingerless gloves before dusting my palms and the soles of my slippers with chalk.

The warning bell rings.

As I face the entry gate a sliver of hope lightens the dreary misery in my heart. A whisper trembles up from the ground like the heart of the Fives court speaking to me. It reminds me that I don't have to lose. I don't have to cheat myself here, and if I pass muster, they will want me to win.

The start bell rings.

Energy pulses through me, driving me forward. The heavy canvas curtain gives way as I shove it aside. Some adversaries swarm right up the posts of Trees and pick a path as they go, but that is not what Anise taught us: *Sailors chart shoals and currents, so must you chart your path before you set sail. Seek the most efficient route, not the shortest one.*

The configuration is a basic course set for speed and strength. Because I am not usually as strong as the men I have learned to use speed and agility to create momentum that will carry me up handholds on high posts and across gaps between clusters of posts.

I am going to win because the Fives is where I belong.

The world narrows to the grain of wood beneath my fingers, the press of my foot against a post as I shove into a leap, the impact that jars through me as I catch the next post and steady myself. When I land on the resting platform, I'm more winded than I ought to be but that is likely because I was eating only bread for three days.

A murmur of voices rises from the spectators' terrace.

Half the challenge of the Fives is the choices you have to make on the fly. Because the court has four starting gates, one for each obstacle, and only one center obstacle, each adversary has a choice when she successfully completes her first test: which direction to go next. The choice here can make the difference between winning and losing.

The gate to Trees is always sited facing the southeast, Rivers to the northeast, Pillars to the northwest, and Traps to the southwest. I must choose either Rivers or Traps next. I don't want to chance that I might pass Kalliarkos where he started on Rivers because it would embarrass us both. So I climb down and race along a canvas tunnel that leads to Traps.

No sooner do I ring the gate bell and dart through the canvas than I see one of the fledglings fighting to maintain his balance on a slack rope. In the time it takes me to confirm that this configuration of Traps holds no maze or height complications, only a straight shot through every basic sort of balance and trap, the lad falls. He catches himself with a good two-footed release, then runs back to the beginning because if your foot touches the ground you have to start over from the gate. I'm already up the opening incline.

My heart is centered; this is my joy and my brilliance. I race across the narrow beam, rock along the taut rope weave, and relax into the slack rope. The bridges and traps are so simple that I am a little irked when I cross the resting platform and charge for Pillars.

In a training maze, hanging canvas walls can be easily moved into new configurations. When I was sitting up on the terrace in the morning I charted this Pillars course and memorized its turns. Did the trainers change it while we napped?

Given the number of footprints smearing and smudging the sprinkling of sand I decide that if they haven't even raked it then they likely have not changed its course or added any complications. Still, I don't want them to guess that I memorized the pattern in case they decide that's cheating.

Counting branching corridors keeps me so occupied that I slam into the back of the other beginner where he has paused trying to decide whether to go left or right. Without a word I dodge past him. He's a bright boy; he follows on my heels, right behind me as I climb to the resting platform.

He says, "How did you come all that way already?"

A few years younger than I am, he has the wheat-colored hair commonly seen among Soldians, sailors whose homeland lies far to the east.

I offer him the best piece of respect I can, by treating him as an equal.

"Kiss off, Adversary," I say.

His startled smile flashes in answer as I jump down to Rivers.

This configuration is dead easy, hopping from each slowly moving tiny roundel of wood to the next. It's just balance and timing. The fledgling actually just stands on the shore to watch me. As I climb up to the last resting platform I see him start across, mimicking my choices, my pace, and my way of jumping. Pleasure flames my cheeks at the imitation.

A foot scrapes the ladder below. Kalliarkos climbs up. He crouches with a hand touching the floor as he catches his breath. He glances at me, then ahead at Rings.

It is a fledgling's version used for basic training. Rather than the usual upper and lower paths, its twelve large wooden rings are arranged to make a circular path around the victory tower. A hidden mechanism turns each at a different speed. All you have to do is jump onto the first and gauge the right timing and angle to leap to the next.

But he hesitates because the first ring has already swung wide on to face us and so he has missed the best point to anticipate the jump. His lack of confidence is a knife pinning his foot to the floor.

I spring past him and onto the first ring. Hooking fingers along the curve I shove off with my foot and launch myself to the next ring before Kalliarkos has even left the platform. I'm no longer breathing hard; I'm flying. He is not halfway along as I scramble up the ladder and grab the victor's ribbon at the top of the tower. The feel of the cloth in my hand never gets old, even on the practice court.

This is how it should be.

This is what I live for.

17

⌘

Grinning seems like a child's cheap boast but I can't help it. By the way the spectators are staring I can tell I have surprised them.

Kalliarkos reaches the ladder and with a hand on the lowest rung calls up, "You didn't even hesitate! How do you do that?"

His face is so open and welcoming. I like his eyes, the way they flare, how dark they are, the thick curl of his eyelashes. There is a smudge on his cheek I would wipe clean in a comradely way if he were an ordinary adversary, but I never could touch a lord like him.

Once my heart has stopped pounding, I climb down. "You have to take enough time to study the rhythm and the pattern, not just plunge in. Once you decide, you can't hesitate."

"That's exactly what I'm talking about." He laughs as if he doesn't care that I've beaten him. "You have it all in your head already. Now you just have to teach me."

A bird has been trapped inside my heart, wings beating. "I guess now that I'm here there's nothing to stop us from working together every day if you want."

Then I hate myself, remembering my mother and sisters.

"Are you all right?" His brows draw down in concern.

I look around but we're still alone. "It was a shock to leave my family."

He leans against the ladder like we have all day to gossip. "Do you really have three sisters and no brothers? What's to become of them?"

"I don't know," I mutter as my jubilation shatters into dread. Yet it astounds me that he even thought to ask about them.

"Being here is a great opportunity for you. I can give you news about your father's campaign. Any prize money you earn you can give to your family."

I must blink ten times as his words sink in. If I pass muster, Garon Stable is the best place I could be.

He smiles as if my startled expression is the best reward he's ever been given. "Didn't you already think of that?"

"I didn't ask to come, my lord."

"I deserved that! You would say it was easy for me to forget how you got here, wouldn't you?"

His casual stance and confiding words confuse me. "You don't act like—" I bite the words back, recollecting prudence and propriety.

"Like what? Go on."

"The way lords are supposed to act."

"The way my uncle Gargaron takes what he wants when he wants it? The way my grandmother is the sweetest woman you could ever meet, until her will is crossed? The way my sister..." He shifts so his broad shoulders press along a rung, and he crosses his arms. "I decided years ago not to be like them."

Daringly I say, "What did you decide to be like?"

He examines me intently. "Why do you want to know?"

A shrill whistle interrupts us.

"We better go," I say.

He walks ahead as he must because he is a lord. When we emerge together onto the forecourt, Tana is waiting. I can't interpret the straight line of her mouth.

"Lord Kalliarkos, if you will, get a cup of broth from Cook. You too, girl. We're changing up the obstacles and you will run against Gira and Dusty."

My grin returns. I am so ready to run again.

Tana notes my anticipation with a flick of a finger that whisks a piece of sawdust off my elbow. "You're not what I expected."

"Come on, Jessamy. They won't give us much time to

recover." Kalliarkos taps my arm and flashes another of his grins.

The casual touch of his hand makes my smile vanish. It's foolish to be flattered by his attention, so I put on my game face. We walk to the dining shelter to drink a cup of broth swimming with bits of meat and herbs like heal-all and brave-man's-iron. The rich liquid slides down my dry throat.

Kalliarkos sips. "I always hesitate on Rings. It's like I have to wait until it's exactly right and I'm exactly sure before I can go in."

"You have to make your own openings, Lord Kalliarkos."

"Just call me Kal. We're all adversaries here in the stable."

No matter how well we get along we will never be just fellow adversaries, but I nod because when a Patron gives you an order, you obey it. "All right. My sisters call me Jes."

The thought of my sisters chokes me all over again. What will Merry do now she's lost any chance of being an Archivist? Poor Amaya and her broken dreams. Will Bett desert them and Mother? Where will they sleep? How will they live? I hope the broth's steam swirling around my face disguises the tears that prick in my eyes.

This time he is so wrapped up in his own troubles that he doesn't notice. "I went to the stable by Scorpion Fountain. That woman Anise turned me away. She said I would just bring trouble down on her and her people."

He's so indignant. He doesn't want to be like other lords,

yet it has never once occurred to him that the rest of the world won't just give way when he gives them that cheerful smile.

"She probably guessed that you are connected to a palace."

"I didn't tell her my name!" He leans closer, watching me. "Whatever you're thinking, you can say it to me."

It's uncanny how well he understands me. I know I shouldn't feel this comfortable with him but I do, so I risk truth. "Your clothes and your highborn looks and the way you carry yourself tell a woman like Anise everything she needs to know about who you are and why you have come to her begging for training."

"What do you mean?"

I sigh. "If you got angry at her or demanded special treatment, you could make trouble for her. If you were hurt, she could lose everything, even her life. She's a Commoner, and you are a palace lord. Surely you see she might not want to risk having you there."

He frowns.

I turn my mug around to do something with my hands. "You said they won't train you here, but they *are* training you here. I don't understand why you think you need Anise."

"Real adversaries train every day except Sevensday. It's their life. It's all they do. But I have duties in the palace. I have a tutor. I have to learn the Precepts. I have a sword-master and a driving instructor. I'm required to attend court functions even though I have no interest in gaining influence at court.

I want to train every day but my uncle forbids it by requiring me to do all these other things. If I show up here on days when he's not given me permission to train, Tana and Darios must turn me away. Not that I fault them for their obedience," he adds hastily. "It's a trap my uncle has set for me."

"Can't Lord Thynos train you? Doesn't your mother have some say in this? She's Princess Berenise's daughter, isn't she?"

With a finger he draws a circle on the steam-dampened table like drawing a circle around words he knows he's not supposed to say. "No, she isn't. My father is Princess Berenise's son, but he died years ago. Because my mother was brought from old Saro to marry my father, she has no support among the lords and royal court here in Efea. That means her brother, Thynos, has no power either. He is completely dependent on my mother's treasury. He runs the Fives because he needs the prize money to keep up a separate establishment so he doesn't have to live in Garon Palace. Even my sister is afraid of Uncle Gar. The only person I've ever seen stand up to him is my grandmother when she told him to give me a chance to prove myself at the Fives."

His confession emboldens me to ask a question I would never have dared ask a lord before this moment sitting over cups of broth. "I know you said you don't want to go into the army, but would it be so bad? Of course a soldier might die in battle but an adversary can die on the Fives court from a bad fall. You gain honor and reputation either way."

A bleak expression darkens his face. "There's more to my situation than that."

Voices interrupt us. His hand tightens on the cup. Adversaries stroll in under the shelter, ostensibly to take a draught of passionflower juice or a cup of broth but obviously because they are curious about Kalliarkos and me. He bends toward me exactly as a conspirator would. With everyone looking I should not respond, but I lean closer too. His breath heats my cheek.

"Maybe we could go to Anise's together. You could introduce me, tell her I won't ask for special treatment. That I'll behave just like all her other Novices."

"Let me think about it," I temporize.

Darios beckons.

"We should go limber up," I say with relief.

Kalliarkos rises. "This run won't be as easy. Dusty has already run seven Novice-level trials, and won one in the provinces. Gira—Giraffe is her Fives name—is a ranked Novice, with five victories, like me. She's good."

"So am I," I retort.

He grins.

Tana assigns me to Trees again and Kalliarkos to Rivers. Gira, the tall woman, gets Pillars, and Dusty starts on Traps.

I chalk up at Trees. The conversation whirls in my head: His confiding manner. His dark eyes. He's so easy to talk to. He listens. All these thoughts slow me down and make me stumble. I have to wall them off and focus.

The start bell sounds.

Anise taught us that when a court is changed quickly, it means the big things remain the same but subtle tricks have been introduced, easy-to-overlook details meant to catch you up. So it proves: on Trees they have shifted one set of posts closer together and removed the handholds to create what is called a "blind shaft." I have to brace my back on one post and my feet on the other to work my way up. They've added an extra rope and beam to complicate Traps, but balance is easy for me. Pillars has a few shifted canvas walls. Rivers is exactly the same only they have greased all the roundels, which I am fortunate enough to notice when the sunlight glints off them. I take the crossing at a speed that is almost but never quite uncontrolled so my feet don't press for long enough to slip.

I hit the resting platform for Rings at the same time as both Kalliarkos and Gira. I dodge between them and leap at the last possible moment, just before the first ring turns edge on. As I twist to squeeze through sideways my nose scrapes the wood. I jump again. At the sixth leap I throw in a spin and by the last I have enough momentum to launch myself into a tight somersault and still land perfectly.

When I swarm up the ladder to the victory tower Gira lets out a whoop from the base as Kalliarkos trots up behind her. From a post in Trees, Dusty shades his eyes as he spots me at the top.

I climb down.

"That was splendid!" cries Kalliarkos.

Gira slaps me so hard on the shoulder that I stagger. "Hammer's Curse, girl. You spun those Rings like a spider on a filament."

I can't stop grinning. "Nothing is better than this!"

Kalliarkos bumps me, shoulder to shoulder. "This is where you're meant to be, Jes. Many successful adversaries support their families off their winnings."

Gira glances between us but says nothing. I'm still floating on my victory but my smile fades as we reach the forecourt where Tana and Darios are waiting. Lord Thynos ambles up, looking at me in a way that makes me shiver. I've drawn too much notice on myself when I should have won in a less showy manner. For all that he pretends to treat Tana and Darios as equals, they give a dip with their chins and step back.

"Now I'm intrigued," he says. "Tana, set up a new course. Run her against me, Inarsis, and Talon."

Inarsis is the Commoner man somewhat older than my father whom I saw in the bathhouse. He comes up beside Thynos, chuckling. "The way she flew across those Rings gave me a turn. My old bones can't match that."

Only a man who knows he can beat me would make such a joke. He catches my eye and nods, and my courage falters.

Talon is the name of the silent Patron girl. The look she gives me is as friendly as an asp.

"You must want another cup of broth before you run

again," Kalliarkos says as he again nudges my shoulder so companionably that I reflexively thump his shoulder back.

"Go away, Kal." Lord Thynos waves a hand in dismissal.

Kalliarkos's chin comes up. Suddenly he looks a lot like a prince surprised that a man whose grandmother is not Princess Berenise feels free to order him around.

"Nephew, you may go."

Age trumps royal blood. Kalliarkos retreats to the dining shelter, glancing several times over his shoulder. Thynos doesn't need to give the order to anyone else. They clear off.

He is a good-looking man ten or twelve years older than I am. This year, as an Illustrious, he will run for the champion's wreath at the King's Trials at the Royal Fives Court.

He takes a step closer to me. "I've finally figured it out. You're the brown girl, the one who lost on purpose to Kal. You can't hide your flair. It's striking and attractive."

He doesn't mean attractive as a hopeful lover would use the word. He means it as an adversary considering the skills of a competitor. Victory matters, but flair seduces the crowd.

He takes hold of my chin and turns my head to one side and then the other, gripping so hard that my jaw aches. "What in the hells does Gar want with you?"

"He wants me to run the Fives, my lord," I say in a squeezed voice.

"There is more to this than that. Does Kal know you're the girl?" He releases me and his gaze narrows. "Of course

172

he knows. Who exactly are you? That you're a mule I can see. What else? Don't lie."

If he kills me right here he will never be called to account for my death.

Yet because I run the Fives I cannot help but sort through the implications, just as I analyze Rings before I go in. Will telling him about my father give me an advantage, or will it hurt my tenuous status? Can I lie convincingly? Will Lord Gargaron tell him the truth, if Thynos asks because he is dissatisfied with my answer? Are he and Gargaron allies or enemies in whatever internal politics trouble the peace of Garon Palace?

I have to make a decision, so I leap.

"My father is Captain Esladas, the hero of Maldine."

"By the gods!" He rocks back as his chin comes up. "Does your father acknowledge you? Was your mother his youthful concubine? A whore, perhaps?"

As if Bettany's shadow slips inside me, all the helpless rage I have had to hold in claws out. My arm comes up, hand in a fist.

"He kept faith with her, and she with him!"

I have betrayed too much. With every particle of my being I breathe calm back into my shadow. The blaze of fury cools as I lower my arm and uncurl my fingers.

He catches both the move and my restraint, and his brows draw down more in curiosity than in affront. He is too powerful to fear me.

"The hero of Maldine. My niece's new husband. A man about forty years of age who, so the story goes, was wedded to the army and never to a woman, for he served the king and queen with his whole heart. But the story that was sung at my niece's betrothal feast missed a few verses, did it not?"

"Her betrothal feast was last night?" I blink as the words sink in. Lord Gargaron hadn't even asked Father before he announced and celebrated his niece's forthcoming marriage. He was that sure Father would agree.

Lord Thynos lifts a hand to command my wandering attention.

"I ask again. What does Lord Gargaron want with you?"

"I could not say what is in the lord's mind. But surely my presence at this stable will improve its reputation." I hold his gaze for just as long as I dare before dropping mine.

"No wonder Kal likes you. You have the confidence and the spine he lacks."

I want to defend Kalliarkos but I know better. I keep my mouth shut.

"Now we shall see if you can pass muster," he adds with a heartless smile. "Your first two runs were just a warm-up. This is your test."

18

Once, and only once, Father told us about the battle in which he won his captaincy.

At that time, twelve years ago, he had already risen to become a sergeant in command of a cohort of thirty-six spider scouts. Sergeant is the highest rank to which a man of his birth could aspire. The desert garrison was part of a string of small forts put in place to guard against the incursions of barbarians, desert bandits, and the merchant-mercenaries called Shipwrights who raid villages for slaves and supplies. One day, outside an isolated village on the edge of the Sand Desert below the Bone Escarpment, the vanguard of an unknown force brushed the web of scouts.

A hundred years ago, when the last emperor was murdered, the empire of Saro splintered into the three kingdoms of Saro-Urok, West Saro, and East Saro. Many rival princely clans fought among themselves across the imperial homeland, each hoping to claim a kingdom.

After surviving an assassination attempt, Prince Kliatemnos heeded the advice of his wise elder sister, Serenissima, and set sail across the Fire Sea. With their three younger sisters and many ships full of soldiers and refugees, they made landfall in the dusky and mysterious land of Efea with its beautiful women and magical masks. Kliatemnos married the last living daughter of the old Saroese imperial house, but it was his elder sister he named as queen to rule beside him. Together they overthrew the luxury-loving Efean monarchs who did nothing but drink beer and write poetry all day, and they buried the temples of the fraudulent Efean diviners and their vile superstitions beneath mounds of dirt and crushed rock.

Five generations later, Father identified the advancing army as the Silver Spears, elite forces under the command of the king of West Saro. Like the king of East Saro and the king of Saro-Urok, he was a descendant of one of the rival clans, all of them cousins of the royal family of Efea and still squabbling over the corpse of the old empire like jackals over bones.

Father's captain dismissed the report as impossible, for before that day, armies from old Saro who invaded the new kingdom of prosperous Efea always came from the Eastern Reach through its rich agricultural lands. They never attacked out of the north through the bone-dry desert. He ordered

Father to strike aggressively at the enemy because he was sure they were bandits who would be easily driven off.

The desert garrison had not the numbers to turn back a massive invasion. All they could do, Father said, was hold their ground defensively and take their losses for long enough to give messengers time to reach the king and call the main army into play.

He commanded the defense with such skill—for the main army had time to be alerted and march to the rescue—that he was rewarded with a captaincy. We never heard one word more about the highborn Patron captain, although we suspected our father had killed the man to stop him from dooming his troops to a complete slaughter. Of the 512 men garrisoned at the five desert outposts, 128 survived. Father remembered the exact numbers, and the day he told us the story he recited their names in the form of a praise poem.

Even when you face defeat, he told us, *you must not falter.*

19

All adversaries know that the architects of Fives courses can rig them to favor an adversary based on political favor or a crowd's preference. Tana and Darios have changed the practice course to emphasize upper body strength over agility. I have no hope of defeating Lord Thynos and Inarsis on a court rigged for pure strength.

But I am a soldier's daughter. I won't falter.

Naturally Tana starts me on Trees, my weakest obstacle. This new configuration emphasizes straight climbing up and down poles and includes a rope climb that I manage by leveraging my leg strength. My arms start aching sooner than they should. My left elbow develops a persistent "pop" every time I bend it. The obstacle finishes with a ladder that has no rungs.

Hanging from a wooden bar I have to jump it up four pairs of posts.

I've trained on the "jumping bar" but rarely managed a complete set. The first try I miss getting the bar into the hooks and fall, butt to sawdust. The second I get up two posts but miss my timing and crash, rolling to avoid a clumsy stumble. The wooden bar hits my face. My nose hurts but is not broken. What if I can't do this?

In the mines, you're whipped if you don't work. People get whipped to death.

I get back up.

The third time I focus on how the swing of my legs gives me lift. Sheer grit propels me. When I reach the fourth set of posts and lurch onto the resting platform, I collapse, panting. My arms feel like they're going to break apart, my nose throbs, and my hands won't open because they are cramping.

In the mines, overwork, rockfalls, or bad air will kill you no matter how obedient and hardworking you are. No person sold to the mines comes out alive.

I breathe through the first few moves of the menagerie called cat, all slow stretches.

Finally I stop shaking, uncurl my hands, and go on. I enter Rivers rather than Traps next because I'm betting they'll have rigged Traps for strength too. The spectators watch in silence, brushed by flows of murmuring as one of the others manages a neat trick, nothing I can see.

I get through Rivers well enough but I know I am far behind when I hear an adversary enter the maze of Pillars behind me. I am pretty sure it is Lord Thynos. I scramble hard, refusing to let him pass me, and in fact I catch a glimpse of him in the maze as I climb the resting platform and then dash for Traps.

When I brush past the gate, I see Talon on the ground rubbing her ankle. Daggers would have a friendlier impact than the piercing stab of her gaze. I stare back at her in a way I ought not.

No one on the court will ever intimidate me. Never. This is the only place I am truly myself.

A trainer's whistle shrills. A crease of fierce anger lights Talon's face so startlingly that the whole world seems to shift under my feet like I'm seeing a vengeful spirit instead of a person. Darios has pulled her from the run and she's furious.

I've allowed myself to become distracted. Focus. Focus. Focus.

The first task in this Traps is another jumping ladder, this one higher than the last. It's the only way to reach the beams and ropes. My courage plummets.

Think first, Anise taught us.

Don't see what everyone else sees, Father would often say. *See what they are missing.*

The rules of the Fives give each obstacle a specific restriction: In Trees you have to complete all the climbing tasks,

180

although you are offered a choice between a short path with harder tasks and a longer path with easier ones. In Traps you have to get through the entire course without touching the ground; otherwise you have to go back and start over.

So I race up the ramp, leap, and just catch the bar. I don't jump the bar because it's not required in Traps; that was Talon's mistake. I hook a knee over and pull myself up so I can just climb the side post. It's got no flair but it's easy. The rest of the balances and bridges are simple except for the intimidating height, but the trap is sprung when I discover that the last trap needs the wooden jumping bar to fill it in. It's easier to go back to the beginning and do it over again, this time bringing the wooden bar with me.

I have just scrambled up the resting platform when Lord Thynos reaches the top of the victory tower and grabs one of the practice ribbons tied there. Inarsis is halfway up the ladder below him, calling up congenial curses whose crude nature makes me blush.

Lord Thynos scans the obstacles to find me. The rush of adrenaline after a challenging run always makes me a little cocky, something else I never reveal at home. I wave mockingly, but in truth I have done better than I expected.

He does not wave back.

I have nothing to be ashamed of, yet when Tana releases me to go to the dining shelter while sending the other adversaries onto the course to train, I drag my feet. Just as I feared,

Lord Thynos and Inarsis join me. They pepper me with questions.

"Who trained you?"

"Why did you go to Rivers instead of Traps after you finished Trees?"

"Do you have a strategy for solving the maze?"

"Which was the hardest task in this trial? Which was easiest? Where did you falter?"

"My concentration," I say. "I got distracted several times."

Tana appears. Lord Thynos and Inarsis rise.

"She needs specifically to work on strength in addition to her regular training," Lord Thynos says to Tana.

The men then walk away and Tana returns to the training ground, leaving me alone.

It takes that long for me to realize I have passed muster.

I am an adversary training in a stable.

I sit there with my mouth gaping like a fish for so long that my shoulders start to stiffen up. My whole life has been turned upside down, all the bad and the good churned together. Thoughts muddle around in my mind: Mother's tears; the feel of the victor's ribbon clutched in my hand; Amaya's lovely cat mask that she threw in the flames; the way Father nods when he approves of something I have said or done.

Talon limps in and sits down. She props her ankle up on a bench; it is wrapped in seaweed. In the kitchen, Cook and her assistants clatter around, preparing the evening meal.

The sun sinks toward the west. The piping strains of a flute ensemble serenade us from over the palace wall, elegant and haunting.

I collect my scattered souls, sucking in a big inhalation to calm myself. It is time to make an ally. "I'm called Jes."

Talon nods to acknowledge that I have spoken.

"It's a lovely practice ground. It feels new but it's welcoming," I add.

She makes no reply. Her complexion is flawless except for a smear of dirt on her chin. The mask of her expression tells me nothing.

I try one more time. "How long have you been training here?"

She looks away.

We sit in awkward silence while the sounds of training drift on the air. Finally she unties her clubbed hair and combs it out through her fingers. It falls all the way to her buttocks, so thick and silky that I can't help but admire its beauty. I would love to comb it like I do my sisters' hair while we talk and argue and laugh about anything and everything, but it seems impossible to ask her after she has rebuked me. She keeps her gaze fixed on the roof of the bathhouse as she braids her hair into three tails and then braids those three tails. Only the mercenaries known as Shipwrights wear their hair this way. It looks strange on a Patron woman.

The silence hangs so uncomfortably that I'm glad when

the other adversaries crowd in to wash and line up for supper. I look around for Kalliarkos but he does not appear. Perhaps he has a court function to attend. No person can truly succeed as an adversary if they don't devote their life to the Fives. He's caught in the same way I was, between his dream and the pressure of those who command his life.

Tana brings over a brass cup and hands it to me as the others stamp their feet and whistle. It's hard not to strut.

"You need a Fives name," says Tana.

"Oh. Uh...people usually call me Jes, short for Jessamy. The flower."

"No, no, you don't get to choose your name," she says with a laugh.

By now everyone has begun shouting out suggestions. I am grateful so few are lewd.

Just as they seem likely to vote on a stupid, sentimental name like Sailwing or Spinflower, Lord Thynos reappears with Inarsis. They are scrubbed clean and dressed in such silken lordly garb that they must be going straight to the palace. I can't figure how a Commoner like Inarsis can accompany Lord Thynos as an equal.

Lord Thynos says, "I have already named her."

Everyone shuts up. I'm so nervous I clasp my hands behind my back as Father's soldiers do when at parade rest, but really my fingers are clutched in a death grip.

"She'll be called Spider, for the way she spins herself through the air."

The sun just then drops below the wall. Light turns to shadow all across the courtyard like evil tidings. A shiver of cold runs up my arms.

Spider is an ill-omened name because it is a powerful name. The spider scouts protect our kingdom, and the magic that gives the metal beasts life is a secret known only to the magicians who serve the king. More dreadful yet, wickedly poisonous tomb spiders protect the City of the Dead from grave robbers and impious people who think to corrupt the oracles who guide us.

Spiders may guard tomb and desert but they are not our friends.

The other adversaries look down at the ground or up at the darkening sky, anywhere except at me. They are troubled and embarrassed too.

I am suddenly certain that Thynos and Gargaron are engaged in a game I know nothing about, one that involves lords and palaces as far beyond my common reach as the stars in the sky.

I incline my head to accept what I cannot change.

Lord Thynos departs, Inarsis walking beside him. Once they're gone the conversation jolts back to life as everyone mingles, relaxed and easy.

"Jes! You want to sit with us?" Gira waves me over to her table. "This is Shorty, and Mis," she adds, introducing the other two women.

They smile. Nothing feels more natural than to sit down together with the three of them as all my life I have sat alongside my sisters. Missing Merry, Bett, and Amiable gnaws like a pain in my belly, and I desperately wish they were here, but the cheerful way Gira, Shorty, and Mis include me makes my grief easier to bear.

Talon stays off by herself. The praise the adversaries throw my way is sparse, like a passing shower of rain, but I can tell they are glad to have me. People sing as they drink cups of passionflower juice and graze through bowls of nuts. I could learn to love this.

After bathing I pick my own cubicle, one near the door. I'm issued Fives gear, a long, sleeveless linen sheath gown for everyday wear, undergarments, sandals, and a worn but serviceable set of formal clothes pressed and folded. An oil lamp. A bed with a linen sheet and a pillow. All the necessities for grooming, monthly bleeding, and washing. Exhausted, I stretch out on the bed.

How swiftly fortune changes!

Everything I took for granted has dissolved into mist and shadow. That which I never dared hope for has come true. Is there an oracle at the heart of the world who whispers a fortune into unhearing ears and we never know until it is too late? Or does fortune fall at random like ripe fruit dropping when a passing wind shakes it free?

Tonight Father will lie down with his new bride and his new rank. He has made a fresh bed for his ambition that doesn't include us.

What will happen to Mother and my sisters must concern me above all else. Just as Kalliarkos said: dedicate myself to the Fives, and give my prize money to help my family build a new life. I can make this work. I'm sure of it.

20

I **wake up** the next morning as an adversary. No matter how many times I say the word to myself I have trouble believing it. The curtained cubicle with not a scrap of decoration and only a small chest of folded garments and necessaries is all the luxury I have ever desired, because I am now training at an official stable. Light as air, I float out to join my comrades.

Gira and Shorty and Mis wave me over to sit with them for breakfast. Mugs of broth with flakes of green heal-all and bits of meat go down smoothly, a light breakfast before training.

"Do you like the theater, Jes?" Gira asks. "We're trying to decide which performance to see this week."

Shorty says, "I want to see *The Hide of the Ox*."

Mis groans. "Not that again. You've seen it ten times."

"A hundred times will be too few. All those battles and duels, and then everyone dies at the end."

"Everyone dies?" I exclaim with a look of shock.

Mis screws up her face apologetically. "Oh, no, now you've ruined it for her!"

Shorty is a nice woman who will never be a top-ranked adversary. I am pretty sure Tana is training her to be a trainer. Shorty smirks, lifting her chin. "Look at her eyebrows. She's already seen it. She's messing with us to get a squawk like she just did from you, Mis."

Everyone chortles.

I set down my spoon. "Do you go often to the theater? It seems like staying out so late would interfere with training."

"With an attitude like that they're going to love you," says Gira with a laugh. "All work and no fun. We don't train on Sevensday so most people go out on the town on Sixth-day night. We three usually go to the Lantern District and see a play. You can join us if you want. What would you like to see?"

Talon has taken a seat at the other end of our table. It is obvious she is listening by the flicker of her eyes when Gira invites me along.

My mouth opens and closes. Except for Amaya's excursions with Denya's respectable family, my sisters and I are only allowed to go to the theater when Father is home to accompany us. The idea of going on my own with fellow adversaries hammers home how totally my life has changed. "I don't know. My sister Amaya's favorite is *The General's Valiant Daughter* because of the doomed love story between the daughter's brave maidservant and a handsome soldier who is a prince in disguise. She often goes with a friend but I've never seen it."

"I wanted to see that new play, *The Poet's Curse*," says Mis. "But it never opened."

Tana halts beside our table, shaking her head. "A good thing it did not open. The king's own seal bearer closed the theater's doors for good and all the actors were sent to the provinces. The man who wrote the play got arrested and thrown into the king's prison for murder."

Mis says, "The playwright killed someone?"

"He was charged with killing the reputation of the royal family by humiliating them in public. I heard a rumor that the play concerned a reprehensible story about the honorable and deified Serenissima the First, mistress of favorable winds and daughter of the great goddess Hayiyin who causes the water to rise and the grain to sprout." Her glower cows us. "An appropriate theatrical entertainment would be one of the comedies playing on Trifle Street. Or that other old favorite, *The General's Valiant Daughter*, as Jes mentioned. That should have enough swordplay, backstabbing, old enmities, and wicked bandits even for your low taste, Shorty."

The training bell rings, and we hurry to line up for menageries. Kalliarkos doesn't show up so it must be one of the days he has other duties. Lord Thynos and Inarsis separate me from the rest and push me through a grueling session on Trees. They make me climb, and climb, and climb. They show me a better method to work the blind shaft. They make me hang until my shoulders feel like they're going to rip off. They make me pull my chin up to the bar and lower myself back down until my arms become more porridge than iron. Then they count while I stand on my hands with my feet resting on a pole.

After this brutal initiation, Inarsis races me and Dusty through Rivers five times to see how much my eye for pattern and speed gets thrown off by fatigue. By the fifth pass I'm not much better than Dusty, but I still beat him.

Then they race us on parallel ladders set horizontally across poles. We swing from hand to hand, side by side. Dusty with his lean strength beats me, which makes him crow out loud and flap his arms in mock triumph, and that makes me laugh helplessly as I drop to the ground in a heap. Thynos walks off as Inarsis calls over a pair of stable attendants to adjust the posts.

Dusty sits beside me, wiping chalk off his hands. "I'm utter glad to have another one like me here," he says cheerfully. "Gets lonely being the only mule."

"There's not so few children born to Patron men and Commoner women," I object. "Nor should it be shameful. That's why I don't like that word."

"Heh. I don't like it either. Is your mother here in Saryenia?"

"Yes. She raised us." I glance at my hands but unlike Kalliarkos he doesn't notice anything odd in my expression.

"Good fortune for you! In my village not only was I the only one, but my mother and grandmother are both dead. I'd no mother's shield to protect me. I had only my uncle and he's addicted to shadow-smoke. It was a glad day I was sent off to the city to work."

"How did you come to run the Fives?"

His grin widens, like he is pleased by my attention. "Always ran it. The only place the boys who didn't like me couldn't beat me up. The dames would never allow fighting on the court. Said it disgraced the game."

"Dames?"

"The grandmothers who oversee the village. Don't you know anything? They run the warrens here too."

"Dusty, you're going again," Inarsis interrupts as Thynos appears with Kalliarkos in tow. The spotless neatness of Kal's Fives gear makes me shake my head.

"What?" Kalliarkos demands, smiling.

"I suppose servants clean and press your gear every night," I say. He glances at his clothes with a look of such utter surprise that I laugh. "You've never even thought about it, have you?"

"Spider!" Thynos cuts in. "You sit out. You two lads, up the blind shaft."

I settle on a pole rolled off to one side, glad for the rest.

Watching Kalliarkos and Dusty, I try to find rivalry or friendship, but all I see is polite nods that could mean anything. Kalliarkos is really good on the blind shaft. It's a pleasure to watch his blend of tension and strength as he nimbly climbs up various widths. He easily beats Dusty.

The interaction between Lord Thynos and Inarsis interests me too. As they talk, discussing Kal's technique or Dusty's inefficient breathing, they touch each other on the arm or back without thought, in a way I have seen at Anise's training stable where I observed that kind of casual contact between longtime friends or lovers. Once I saw my father talk to another man in a similar fashion, with an intimacy that had to do not with flesh but with trust; he told me later that he and the other captain had served in the Oyia campaign, where together they had faced death. Will I ever be able to truly trust Kalliarkos?

After he finishes a climb and waits for Dusty, Kalliarkos catches my eye and tilts his head, as if he can tell I am thinking of him. He is sweaty from training, his hair slicked against his neck, his face glistening, and his damp leggings sticking to muscled thighs. I try not to grin but then I do, and he winks at me. I cover my mouth to stifle a giggle.

Thynos thumps him hard on the back, gaze flicking between the two of us. "That's enough, Kal. I think we can break for our meal now. You go back to the palace. Isn't your poetry tutor waiting for you?"

"My tutor didn't come today. They're all busy preparing for the wedding feast on Sixthday night."

Remembering how Father abandoned us hits like a kick in the belly. I clutch my arms across my body.

Kalliarkos's brow wrinkles with concern as he takes a step toward me. "Jes, are you all right?"

"Kal, I told you to return to the palace." Thynos stands with arms crossed. "Are you arguing with me?"

Kalliarkos holds his uncle's stare for just long enough to save face, but both Thynos and I can tell the moment before the prince gives way. Without looking at me, he stalks off with Inarsis dogging his heels like a guard.

Thynos waits until they are out of sight before brushing his hands free of chalk and grit. "Dusty, take a break. Spider, at attention."

I stand as Dusty hurries off. Thynos paces around me, forcing me to turn to keep facing the ominous thunder of his frown. When he stops moving he rests two fingers just above my breastbone and increases the pressure until I take a step back.

"With training and discipline you could go far, Spider. Don't throw it away for something you can never have."

"I'm not doing anything illegal!"

"I didn't ask for your opinion. Go join your fellow adversaries."

I fumingly retreat to the dining shelter, where the others have already started eating.

"How'd it go?" Gira asks, searching my face. "Dusty says you were run flat by Lord Thynos."

"I suppose I was," I say, thinking of his words. Abruptly I'm cheered by his warning because it means he wants me to concentrate on the Fives.

Tana pounds her cup on a table to get our attention. "Adversaries, tomorrow there will be no training. As members of Garon Palace we are required to attend the funeral procession for Lord Ottonor. Darios and I will be busy this afternoon to prepare, so you have the rest of the day off. Don't get used to it."

"Whoo!" cries Mis, pumping her arms skyward as Gira, Shorty, and I laugh. "Let's go to the Lantern Market. I need to buy a charm for my sister's new baby."

I have never in my life been allowed to go to the Lantern Market but I'm too embarrassed to tell them that.

"Can we just walk out into the city when we're not training?" I ask, and from the way the others look at me, I can see I've puzzled them. "I mean, we don't have to ask permission? Or have an escort?"

"We're not Patron girls to be shepherded around by an

ill-wisher," says Gira with a glance toward Talon, who sits at the far end of the table picking the pine nuts out of her stew and ignoring us. "We're adversaries. As long as you keep your Garon badge on, no one will bother you. Anyway, Shorty and I are going to stay in for a change. You two have fun."

Walking out the open gate with Mis is like being blown by the wind of freedom. No one stops us. No one questions us. Our honor is our own to guard. All my life I have been either a dutiful daughter bowing to propriety or a disobedient girl flouting my father's strict rules. Mis and I can stroll down the street with not a care in the world. She's not like my sisters at all: she is easygoing and relaxed. As an adversary she's not yet as good as Gira or Dusty but she's coming along.

"How did you get started running the Fives?" I ask.

"My grandaunt ran them back when she was my age. The whole family goes all the time to trials. So they decided I might as well have a go at it. They paid my way in."

"How many siblings do you have, that you can train while they work?"

"I'm youngest of eight, five girls and three boys."

How like Efeans! Five girls and only three boys! But I don't say that aloud.

"I have three years to prove myself. If I don't make Challenger in that time, I'll just go back to the family business."

"What business is that?"

"Perfume. It's how I got my Fives name. I reeked of the distilling factory when I got here."

I laugh. "Because your Fives name is Resin. I wondered."

"What about you, Jes? There's a rumor going around that your father's an officer in the army." She hesitates, then goes on hastily as if she has already said the cruel thing out loud and now must apologize for it. "You know what they say: Patron eyes and Commoner skin."

We walk for a while in silence. I don't know how much I can say, how much I want to say, how much is prudent to reveal.

She finally says, "It's just you have such a Patron way of talking and acting, like you're kin in a lord's household. But you can't be."

I am a Patron, I want to say, and yet I know I am not. I cannot defend the people we girls all pretended we were.

"I'm sorry," she says. "I meant no insult by it."

"It's all right, Mis. Yes, my father is in the army. And my mother is Efean. It's hard to talk about."

"You have nothing to be ashamed of!" she says stoutly. "And if anyone says you do, you can just run their ass flat on the court."

We're laughing as we reach the West Gate of the Lantern District. Two huge brass wheels are suspended from the underside of the gate, each hung with a thousand ribbons fluttering in the breeze. According to the decree of the king and queen, all public entertainment must take place in the Lantern District. At night people congregate on the tiered stone seating of its many small amphitheaters. Whether Commoner or Patron, the people of Efea take their poetry and theater very seriously. The old epic plays can last until dawn if the audience keeps demanding new scenes be added or if they argue with the actors over their interpretation of a famous dialogue. I once saw a death scene repeated five times before the jeering audience was satisfied. The best-beloved playwrights and poets are as celebrated as any Illustrious.

As Mis and I walk down the main street she points at the different banners advertising the many plays. "See that gap there? That's where the banner for *The Poet's Curse* was hanging, but they've taken it down."

The empty space in the row of banners looks suspicious. "What reprehensible story did *The Poet's Curse* tell?" I ask.

"Shhh! If the playwright was arrested, then we don't want anyone to hear us talking about it! Come on, the market is this way."

It's so strange not to have to bow to Father's strictures. If I win prize money I can come here as often as I want with my sisters, when I find them. The day seems so glorious. Possibility opens everywhere around me, as if my five souls swell with well-being. What felt like bad fortune looks like good fortune if I turn it over and examine it from the other side.

Because the theaters open only at night, during the day the Lantern District is called the Lantern Market because you can buy other pleasures there. At the street stalls a person can buy protective amulets; perfume; every sort of cosmetic; jewelry, cheap and expensive; and little gifts suitable for lovers. It is emphatically the kind of place a proper Patron girl would never, ever walk, even with an ill-wisher in attendance, and certainly never alone with a friend. I can't stop staring. What goes on behind these closed gates is the sort of thing Father wished to protect his daughters from, because girls like us who aren't really Patron or Commoner sometimes end up selling sexual favors. Such acts are the lowest thing a Patron woman can do. That it isn't seen as shameful among the Efeans makes Patrons scorn Commoners even more.

Mis browses along a lane with amulets meant for newborns: shell anklets to ward off sickness, polished stones to weight their souls to their flesh until they fully attach, and carved amulets as a shield against shadow-walking.

Having no coin to spend, I am content to watch people. Because of Saryenia's harbors, people come to this city from all over the many lands strung along the shores of the Three Seas: handsome Amarans so famed for their administrative skills that every kingdom seems to have a few serving in its official-dom; straw-haired Soldians who work as sailors all along the Three Seas; a pair of seafaring Tandi guildwomen taller than most men; bowlegged cavalrymen from the grasslands of Dey;

veiled desert men; and more besides. Like ribbons they come in every variety, wide and narrow, bright and muted, precious and ordinary. Three different times a passing Efean man catches my eye and smiles, nothing more, leaving it up to me whether to call after him.

"Jes? Sorry to take so long. I hope you weren't bored."

"Loitering in the market is a splendid luxury better than any sumptuous feast or treasure chest of rich jewelry!"

She laughs, thinking I am joking, although I'm sure Kalliarkos would understand. "I'm going on to see my family. Do you want to come with me? We'll eat at dusk and then go back to the stable afterward."

Among Commoners, to be asked into the house is a way of saying you are trusted. Her merry expression offers me friendship. I grasp her hand. "My thanks, Mis. I do want to meet your family but today I need to go see about my mother."

"Of course you do! Next time." She slaps me on the shoulder in a comradely way, and we part. The moment she can no longer see me I tuck my Garon badge under my clothes. I don't want any random passerby to wonder why a servant of Garon Palace is walking where I'm about to go.

By now it's brutally hot so I keep to the shade side of streets as I make my way from the Lantern District, which lies at the base of the King's Hill, over to the skirts of the Queen's Hill. I'm sweating and thirsty by the time I reach the compound where my family once lived in amity and trust. What

I hoped for I don't know but the gates are shut and barred with thick locks. Around the back I climb up my usual escape route, creep past the cistern on the roof, and look down into the private courtyard and under the archways into the rooms beyond.

All the furniture is gone. Even the marble pavement acquired at such expense by my father has been dug up to be sold off elsewhere. Nothing stirs except dust under the feet of a little flock of starlings probing for insects. They are the only family that lives here now.

The sun beats on my head like the hammer of grief. If I just knew where they were I could be easy, I could truly flourish in my new place. Not knowing is a festering worm gnawing at my heart. Surely Mother will have left a message for me somewhere she knows I might go.

Anise's stable.

The starlings take wing in a rush, circling the roof once and flying away toward the warrens. Maybe it is coincidence, but maybe it is a sign.

I leave behind the house I grew up in and walk down off the wide avenues and sprawling compounds of the Patron-born into the close-packed, crowded lanes of the Commoners. I have walked this route many times on my way to Scorpion Fountain and Anise's stable. There's one little boy I see every time sitting on the steps of a shop that stinks of smoked fish. He has a clubfoot, but he's well cared for, clean and neat and with a polished walking stick that he waves at me in greeting. I wave back. He's not hidden like Maraya.

I've walked right through the heat of the day and am glad for a drink at Scorpion Fountain with its curved spouts. By the time I reach Anise's stable, a flock of fledglings and experienced adversaries is pacing through a warm-up of menageries on the stone forecourt. This Fives court is said to be the oldest in the city, its walls and ramps worn to a shine by generations of feet and hands working across it. The furnishings around the courtyard look strikingly poor to me now compared to the fancy new architecture of Garon Stable. No baths, no barracks, no dining shelter, no warehouses for extra equipment to change up the obstacles. Instead of a viewing terrace covered by an awning there is just a dingy set of steps up to the ancient compound wall from whose height Anise can walk all the way around the court.

I know a lot of the people. I've exchanged casual remarks and friendly banter with many of them for years without becoming close enough to have to tell them who I really am. Now I pin the Garon badge where everyone can see it and, with a jaunty wave, saunter in. Anise cuts across the courtyard to meet me. She is taller than Mother, fat and powerful in the way of respected Efean women. Silver hair crowns her age. How old she is I do not know, and it is impossible to tell from her face because she has so few wrinkles.

"Honored Lady," I greet her. "I wanted to know if my mother perchance left a message for me here?"

"No message. I've heard nothing from your honored mother." She steers me into the shade by the gate, away from the others. "I heard your father now serves Garon Palace."

I am almost bouncing on my toes because I am so excited to let her know my news. "He's been made a general. I'm training at their stable. I'm finally going to be a true adversary."

Her gaze drops to the Garon badge and then moves back up to my face. The silence draws out so long that I stop bouncing and wipe my forehead instead.

"Did you send that boy to me?" Her tone flicks me like a whip's tip snapped in my face.

I flinch. "He wanted to know where I trained, that's all."

"Mm-hm." She taps a foot on the ground like she's impatient with my stupidity. "Do you know his grandmother set up Garon Stable just for him?"

I blink, startled by her cutting tone.

"Do you know his maternal uncle is the Illustrious Southwind?"

"Yes."

"He made his reputation at Asander Stable and yet by one means or another was convinced to transfer to a fledgling stable without a single victory to its name. For Garon Palace to set sail on such a daunting venture means they think they can make some kind of brilliant profit from all this. What profit they make does not include folk like you and me. You are swimming in dangerous waters, Jessamy. Maybe you have been thrown into the Fire Sea without a raft, for which I am sorry, but do not involve me or mine."

I shrink back, head ducking. For four years she has trained and encouraged me, and now I just wish I could vanish into a hole in the ground. "I'm sorry, Honored Lady. I meant no harm."

"A polite and handsome lad, I'll give him that. If he smiled at you I suppose it would have been hard to refuse."

I take in several sharp breaths rather than admit she is right. "I had to let him win at the trial. Giving him your name was my way of apologizing because he knew I lost on purpose. Anyway, he's desperate. They won't truly let him train like other adversaries. They want him to go into the army." I'm babbling because I cannot bear the way Anise stares at me as if I've failed her.

She lifts a scolding hand. "Don't tell me secrets that aren't yours to share."

Behind us the adversaries flow through the transition from the ambitious flight of the firebird to the creeping death of the tomb spider, the last of the forms.

Taking hold of my hands, she turns them over to examine my calluses and scars. Then she looks up into my face. "I promised your mother I would do my best by you."

"My mother talked to you?"

"Of course she talked to me. She would never have taken the risk that you might be harmed when you went out of the house on your own. You are the best I've trained, Jessamy. You have the intelligence, the stamina, the strength, and the flair, and most importantly you have the discipline and the fire. But as long as you train at Garon Palace, you must never come back here again."

21

Despite having died in disgrace and in debt, Lord Ottonor must be allowed a final procession to the City of the Dead because that is the prerogative of a lord who was head of a clan and thus must be honored by burial in an oracle's tomb.

We assemble for the funeral at dawn. The royal carriage, the seven noble palaces, and all the lordly clans with their retinues are required to accompany the procession. Tana pushes me into line with Gira, Shorty, Mis, and the cook's girl, filling in a row of five.

I lean toward Gira. "Why did Talon stay behind in the stable?"

She steps on my foot. "Stop talking."

We march in time to the mournful pulse of funeral drums.

I have never before worn formal household livery because my sisters and I never officially belonged to Lord Ottonor's household. The adversaries of Garon Stable wear a version of the parade uniform worn by Garon soldiers. As we walk I adjust my knee-length sleeveless vest. Its back is stitched with the horned and winged fire dog that represents Garon Palace. Three buttons close the bright yellow silk across my chest, allowing it to flow open to either side. Beneath the sleeveless vest I wear a knee-length tunic cinched at my waist with a lacework of three belts. Loose trousers are tucked into boots. The color of the processional scarf marks the occasion: we all wear long, narrow white funeral scarves.

Anise's harsh words haunt me. Whatever it is Garon Palace wants, it will not hesitate to trample anyone who stands in its way.

By the time we get to the bottom of the King's Hill I am sweating all over. Father told us stories of his childhood and how it got cold in a season he called "winter," but I don't understand why Patrons wear all these layers of clothing in warm Efea. Even my eyelids are sweating.

As all the households reach the Avenue of Triumphs, they line up according to status. Clans whose animal talismans bear no wings naturally give way to palaces, whose talismans do. Among the palaces there is a further hierarchy, depending on who stands highest and who lowest in the royal favor. Although every lord's clan we meet halts to let us pass, we are required to give way to all six of the other palace clans. How Lord Gargaron must hate having to let another palace go ahead of him! Finally we take our place.

A staggered formation of Garon soldiers stands in the first rank to protect the household. Behind them, with the best view, the lords and ladies of the palace assemble. In the third rank gather the lesser relatives, officials, and officers. The highest-ranking servants and Challenger-level adversaries stand in the fourth rank, and we Novice and fledgling adversaries and the lower servants are crammed at the back with the worst view.

Kalliarkos stands between Lord Gargaron and an elderly woman carried in a chair. He is wearing an elaborately tasseled hat. I catch glimpses of his bare neck as the beaded strings sway each time he shifts.

"Stop staring at him." Gira nudges me with her heel.

Flushing, I try to think of how Amaya would salvage the situation. "Why do Patrons wear those ridiculous hats?"

Gira snorts.

A servant in the fourth rank hisses displeasure, so we shut up.

Pipes, bells, and a chorus of singers announce the arrival of the king and queen at the head of the funeral procession. The royal banners glide into view, carried by officials wearing robes embroidered with blood-thorn roses, white death-flower, and skeletal falls of bone-vine. A hooded sea-phoenix perches quiescent in a cage, its folded wings glittering. When the royal carriage rolls past without king or queen in it, I hear a murmur of spiteful satisfaction. Not even Prince Nikonos has come to honor the dead man. People will discuss this dreadful insult for months.

The funeral wagon passes, devoid of the embroidered banners and garlands of painted masks that would usually drape the flatbed with its open coffin. A lord's burial casket should be gilded with gold flakes and studded with jewels. Ottonor's coffin is humble wood painted with cursory daubs of lozenges, straight lines, and handprints to depict the three gods and their attributes of fecundity, martial prowess, and justice.

Lord Ottonor does not lie in the coffin yet, of course. Dressed in formal parade wear embroidered with the three-horned bull of Clan Tonor, his corpse lurches forward one awkward step at a time. The priests have bound his self, his shadow, and his name into his body, where his heart still resides. With the mystical power held by the priests, they have motived his flesh with a fresh spark of life taken out of another creature and fixed into him.

Kings and princes and lords walk to their tombs this way.

His expression is a peaceful mask, face waxy with the paraffin that has been rubbed over his skin to preserve it. Only the jerking motion of his limbs betrays disquiet within the four remaining parts of his soul, as if he fears to approach the judge who rules the afterlife.

Four priests attend him, one at each of the cardinal

directions. Each holds a ribbon attached to the silver chain at his waist.

His male relatives follow. Heads bowed, they pace in shame. Steadily rising whispers spread like fire among the onlookers.

Father's decision to join Lord Gargaron's household no longer seems quite so heartless and ambitious. Now it seems more like prudence and desperation. What would have happened to us had Father's fortunes tumbled into the pit with Ottonor's clan?

The crowd's whispering conversations quiet.

The oracle comes.

In the empire of old Saro, a dead emperor was accompanied into his tomb by servants. They would be smothered to death and arranged in the chamber so as to serve him in the afterlife. Last of all, an oracle would be brought into the tomb and given poison. In her death throes the priests could read a prognostication of the next emperor's reign. But when King Kliatemnos the First died, his devoted wife, known as the Silent Orchid, refused to condemn another woman to that cruel tradition. She and her four daughters walked with the king into the tomb, the only time Patrons have ever had anything good to say about a man having four daughters. Out of respect for her dignity the priests allowed her and her daughters and the oracle who accompanied them to live. If you can call that living: walled up in a tomb until you die.

Girls chosen to be oracles grow up in separate cells in the temple, never seeing another person and speaking only to the priestesses who pass them food and water and the priests who instruct them in the lore of the gods. This procession is the only occasion an oracle will ever have to glimpse the sky and the sea and the city and the faces of people.

The curtained wagon passes in silence. No one wants theirs to be the last voice heard by an oracle on her way to her tomb. She might carry some fragment of your five souls—a taste of your heart or a thread of your shadow or a sliver of your self or, worst yet, the memory of your name—to dwell among the tombs forever.

The silence makes my skin prickle like ants crawling all over me. I shift my feet nervously but even that faint scuffing reverberates like a clap of thunder. The curtains sway. I hold my breath for fear the oracle will catch the spark of my breathing and steal it.

Only when the wagon passes out of my sight do I exhale.

The oracle's vehicle is followed by twenty tomb attendants walking in ranks of five. These women from Lord Ottonor's clan have been granted the honor of sitting vigil overnight as the borrowed spark drains from the body of the deceased. Mourning shrouds cover their bodies from neck to ankle and they have all done up their hair in a tower of braids wrapped around a conical funeral hat. I see Amaya's friend Denya among them, looking pale and sad.

Behind them walk the five servants who will be walled into the tomb at dawn to serve the living oracle. They are faceless and nameless. Shrouds cover their heads and drag on the ground so even their feet cannot be glimpsed.

The shrouded attendant who walks at the center staggers like a wounded creature with a swollen belly. I blink.

Suddenly I am absolutely sure it is my mother.

My heart pounds so hard I think it is going to leap out of my throat. A headache spikes between my eyes, my vision growing blurred. Another of the attendants is tall like Bettany, and one has a slight lurch to her walk as Maraya would. One is short and delicate like Amaya, and the fourth could be me if I wasn't standing here, torn away from them.

"Mother," I gasp.

Gira grasps my wrist. "Shhh."

The bricklayers' wagon trundles past, followed by a file of royal cavalry and a squadron of six spider scouts. The clanking of their metal feet on stone shakes me back to earth.

It cannot be them. Tomb attendants are raised in the temple just as oracles are. My thoughts are just a wandering madness because I don't know where my mother and sisters are.

The princely and lordly retinues follow the funeral procession through the city and past the harbors to the temple and Eternity Gate. I walk as if dazed by shadow-smoke, my hands clammy and my face hot.

Just past the temple wall rise the mudbrick tombs where

ordinary Patrons inter their dead, one hundred to a small chamber, packed in like bricks. Richer Patrons can afford family tombs where, for generation after generation, their dead are wrapped in shrouds and stacked onto granite shelves. The tombs of the lords and the palaces stand on the hill, with the royal tombs at the crown. Only highborn Patrons are served by oracles, as it is said, "Let the king and his sons heed the word of the gods even in the shadow of the afterlife."

All the households wait in the heat as the dead man is led into his tomb. The sun hurts my eyes but every time I close them I see a nightmare vision of my mother wrapped in a shroud.

The palace households ahead of us start filing in to pay their last respects. We creep up the hill. At length a porch and low door appear before us. Bricklayers wait under an awning, bricks and mortar and tools ready for tomorrow's dawn.

My hands clench as I climb the five steps onto the porch. A simplified version of a three-horned bull is carved into the lintel, a few lines incised to identify this as the tomb of Clan Tonor. The opening into the tomb is so narrow we have to turn sideways to go in. I shuffle behind Gira through an outer chamber with an offering trough to the right and a latrine trough to the left. People have already urinated into it, and the smell makes me wince. The tomb also stinks of the sweat of so many hot, anxious people trudging through. How horrible to be trapped inside here for the rest of your life.

We pass under an arch into the central chamber with its stone bier. Offering cups and bowls filled with flowers, beads, coins, and magical amulets surround it.

Dead but breathing, Lord Ottonor lies on top of the coffin. The spark that gives him breath will fade over the course of the day and night. Just before dawn the priests will place him inside his coffin and seal the lid. His corpse and coffin will rest on the bier until his oracle dies.

How do the priests fix that spark into him? Did it come from an animal or a person? All I know is that it must come from a similar place as the magic the king's magicians use to animate the spider scouts, whose metal bodies are given life by sparks taken, so Father once told us, from desert spiders.

The twenty vigil-sitters face the walls, their backs to the mourners who file past. The five shrouded attendants kneel in the archway that opens into the third chamber, where the oracle resides. From behind they look like sacks.

The quiet in the tomb presses like weight. The world outside, the sough of the ocean, the cry of gulls, the speech of people: these have vanished. All I hear is the scuff of feet and the occasional sucked-in breath as people enter the tomb behind us and get a lungful of the fetid air.

We pace up the length of the middle chamber. The moment I reach the head of the bier, the line halts. I look down on Lord Ottonor's waxy forehead. His eyes are horribly open, staring sightlessly at the ceiling, which is painted black with white specks for stars. His chest rises and falls. I am caught between the bier and the veiled attendants who block the doorway into the third room.

This end of the tomb smells fresher because in the oracle's chamber there is both an air shaft and a hole for speaking to people outside. Five lamps burn, illuminating a table set with a basin and pitcher, a stack of books atop a wooden chest, and a curtained bed where the oracle must be seated, hidden from the mourners.

One of the bed curtains stirs. I stiffen, holding my breath so I don't shriek out loud.

Pale fingers brush through a slit in the curtains, probing from the inside.

She sees me. I know it. A wave of dizzy fear makes me sway.

The oracle speaks in a whisper like the scratch of a poisoned thorn.

"The tale begins with a death. Where will it end? There could be a victory, a birth, a kiss, or another death. There might fall fire upon the City of the Dead, upon the tombs of the oracles. A smile might slay an unsuspecting adversary. Poison might kill the flower that bloomed brightest. A living heart might be buried. Death might be a mercy."

Shorty nudges me from behind. The file is moving. I stumble in Gira's wake, accidentally brushing the clammy skin of Lord Ottonor's dead hand with my own. Sweat breaks down my back. A pulse pounds in my ears and I am not sure if it is my own or that of the spark that animates the corpse's chest. Maybe the oracle's heart beats in time with mine.

I do not know where I am going.

I cannot think.

At the archway that leads out from the chamber I glance desperately back toward the five attendants, realizing I have lost my only chance to try to communicate with them, just to make sure they are no one I know. With a hiss through teeth like a snake giving warning before it strikes, Gira drags me after her. I stagger through the outer chamber and onto the porch where with a gulp of fresh air I see the blue sky unfolding above. A sob knots in my throat, but I keep it down in my heart where it must stay.

I feel like a walking corpse as we return through the city to Garon Palace.

The training stable gate with its horned and winged fire dog greets us like a refuge.

It is already late afternoon as we wash up with the ritual prayers. Many servants remained behind to spend the day preparing a huge repast to celebrate the dead man's safe passage to his next house of existence. The leavings we receive in the stable are the most magnificent feast I have ever laid eyes on. None of Father's victory feasts nor any of the social engagements we girls were allowed to attend boasted platters of gingered-orange quail, date-stuffed chicken, wine-soaked beef, white fish garnished with almonds and saffron, salted eel, barley cooked with herbs and onions, honey cakes, and enough beer to drown a city.

I force myself to place a moist honey cake on my tray.

"Did you hear anything in the tomb?" My voice quavers. I am afraid they will say yes, but I am even more afraid they will say no.

"No, but it sure smelled," says Gira, wrinkling up her nose. "Why do you ask?"

"No, thank the gods." Shorty cuts her off. "And I'll thank you not to repeat the question."

"It would be ill fortune," adds Mis. "The oracle never speaks until the tomb is sealed."

The honey cake sits uneaten.

I imagined the words. That's all.

The party looks likely to spill late into the night, so I make excuses and creep off to my bed. Wide awake although exhausted, I listen to the adversaries singing lewd songs as they get drunk. From over the palace wall, a melody of tuned bells mingles with the breath of flutes. At intervals a male voice rises to sing sonorous stories of the splintering of the old empire and of how the first Kliatemnos and Serenissima bravely defeated the corrupt magic of the old Efeans and erected a new and pure kingdom on Efean soil.

As I drift, a horrible certainty swims to the surface of my mind. Through her oracle's magic she was speaking to me alone. For Gargaron's poisonous scheme to work, he must remove Mother from Father's reach forever in case Father is tempted to seek out the beautiful woman he has loved for half his life. How better than to bury her where no one can look for her and where religious law prevents her rescue?

I wake with a jolt, like I have been stabbed.

I will have my stewards make provision for the women, Lord Gargaron told Father.

And so he has.

22

My guts twist in knots as I struggle not to throw up. I lie shaking so hard I cannot stand.

When the fit passes I dress, finding everything by feel. It is the middle of the night but I have to go there now. I have to save them. I pin my Garon badge inside my tunic in case I need it, but for now I must not advertise where I come from.

Outside, a single lamp burns by the drinking basin. The tables are clean, benches set atop them for the night. It is so quiet and still that as I pad past the Fives court I don't at first notice a person standing on one of the beams. She is balancing on her left leg while holding her right leg straight out in front of her with her hands grasping the flexed right foot. Not a wobble disturbs her. She might as well have been turned to stone. By the shadow of her clubbed hair I know it must be

Talon. I freeze, waiting for her to shout, to betray me. But I am met with silence.

By easing back a step I fade into the shadows along the wall. I have to keep going.

The stable gate is closed and barred. Pressing my ear against it, I listen for the guards but hear nothing.

I crack open the pedestrian door set into the large gates. The guards lean against the porch pillars, dozing, a crock of spicy plum wine open at their feet. They too have partaken of the funeral toasts to a dead lord no one liked or respected.

I creep past them, scarcely breathing until I am out of sight of Garon Palace.

Father told us a hundred times that girls like us must never go out alone at night. When he was gone to the wars I often sneaked home at dusk from Anise's stable, but I have never in my life been out alone at night. The dregs of funeral feasts spill here and there into the streets. Men reel along in clots of singing and laughter. Three Commoners, wearing the white ribbons of people willing to take coin in exchange for sex, chat about a poetry contest that they plan to attend on the next full moon. A woman pushes past with a cart for selling toasted shrimp. Her bucket is empty, a good night for her, and she is singing an old Commoner song about the young woman who slept with the incarnated moon. She looks unthreatening so I pace along behind her.

My thoughts careen all over everywhere. For once in my

life I can only stumble forward into darkness, blinded by a mask that no longer fits. The laws of the gods are good and true. That's what I was taught. But this is wrong.

The shrimp-seller stops so suddenly that I bump into the cart and leap back with an apology.

She is my mother's age and as mean-looking as a dog about to do battle with a razorbird. "You mean to steal my coin, you'll do better to make your move before we get into the warrens."

My mouth drops open at her ugly tone. "I meant no harm. I'm just out walking."

"Where do you dwell?" she demands.

"I'm an adversary in training."

She cuts me off with a rude gesture. "You think if you wear the mask of their speech and their customs they will accept you as one of them, but they never will. Move off my shadow, mule. I don't want your kind thinking you can shade me."

I stagger past her and, driven frantic by fear, break into a run even though I know this will draw attention.

The Avenue of Triumphs is scattered with smears of fruit, sprays of vomit and urine, and sweet-smelling wreaths of flowers hanging from the stone statues of the heroes and gods who line the avenue. A night-soil wagon creaks as it trundles down a side street. The eerie lament of a night-chat warbling in a nearby garden heralds the coming dawn. I hurry across the grand Square of the Moon and the Sun. Seen from this side, the temple looks like a fortress, its long windowless wall guarding the City of the Dead.

Eternity Gate stands open to accommodate the last of Ottonor's mourners.

As fortune has it, a file of soldiers comes walking behind a captain wearing the two-horned mare badge of the Kusom lordly house. Head bowed, I slide into the end of the line of attendants. The gate-wardens grasp ebony-wood staffs that gleam with priestly magic. They let me pass because they think I am with the soldiers, the girl who does their washing.

Lit lamps mark the open tomb on the dark hill. All of Lord Ottonor's kinsmen and household have spent the night prostrate on the ground outside, watched over by a cohort of wardens, the men who patrol and supervise the City of the Dead. The bricklayers are starting to set out their tools and mortar by lamplight.

As I approach the porch I have no idea what I'm going to do once I get inside.

But it doesn't matter. Before I reach the steps a tomb-warden lowers a staff to cut me off.

"You are not wearing the badge of Clan Kusom. Who is your master?"

I hesitate, trying to think of an excuse he will believe without having to show my badge.

"Hoping to steal from the offering cups, no doubt! You can tell your lies to the chief warden. Come with me."

I skip sideways to avoid him, and he whacks me so hard on my left leg with his warden's staff that I grunt and drop to one knee.

A man grabs me from behind. I brace to rip myself from his grip, but when he speaks his familiar voice makes me pause.

"Jessamy! I told you to wait beside the path." Junior House Steward Polodos uses the harsh tone of an angry master, although I've never heard him speak harshly to our servants. "My pardon, Warden. I wondered where my servant had gone."

The tomb-warden, seeing a Patron man like himself, returns to his guard duty.

Polodos tugs me away out of the lamplight. My leg throbs.

"Doma Jessamy, what are you doing here?"

"We have to get them out. Hurry! It's almost dawn." I yank on his arm but he doesn't budge.

"What are you talking about?"

The captain of Clan Kusom emerges onto the lamplit porch, looking shaken by what he has seen inside. The first seeps of gray lighten the sky.

"My mother and sisters are being entombed as the oracle's servants."

His eyelids flicker as my words hit him, but he shakes his head. "A pregnant woman can never be entombed, because she might be bearing a son. Did you actually see or speak to them?"

"No, but I know it's them." My voice cracks.

"It can't be, Doma Jessamy. It would be blasphemy. The priests would never allow it."

My certainty wavers. Of course it isn't them. Bettany would have fought and kicked the entire time. Amaya would have pleaded and cried, and Maraya would have argued. These attendants walked all that way on their own legs.

"You must go back to Garon Stable, Doma Jessamy. I expect you are out without permission, just as always."

The words sting. I snap back, "What do my father's rules matter now? He threw us away."

The placid young man he used to be has vanished to become someone with an edge. "You are quite mistaken. General Esladas wishes to make sure the Doma has money enough to set up in whatever business she desires. He has arranged for her and your sisters to take lodging at the Least-Hill Inn in the West Harbor District until they can sort out their circumstances."

My heart clenches, half in anguish and half in triumph. "Father did that?"

He goes on like he is explaining to a child. "The general sold his captain's armor and gave the money to me to bring to Doma Kiya."

"Even though Lord Gargaron promised to make provision for them?"

"A man of honor makes sure of his family without going through an intermediary."

In excitement I grab for his hand, then remember I am pretending to be a servant. "Is my family at the inn?"

Behind us the priests begin the hymn of sealing. Five of them progress into the tomb, each carrying a large silver cup for the final toast.

"No. I am to take them there but I haven't been able to find them. When I went to our compound I found it swept clean, the Doma and all her servants gone. A neighbor told me that Garon stewards sold the debt of the Commoner servants into bonded labor to pay for the expenses of closing down the house. So I came here to speak to Lord Ottonor's stewards. They tell me they had nothing to do with General Esladas's household once Garon Palace took it over. I don't dare apply to Lord Gargaron's stewards to find out what happened to the women, lest they suspect the general's intent."

The bricklayers move in to lay the first course within the doorway.

"We have to make sure they're not in the tomb!"

He takes a firm hold on my wrist. "Doma Jessamy, be calm. Of course you are worried on their behalf. I am too. I will start looking for them tomorrow in the city and I promise you I will find them. Now I'll escort you back to Garon Stable. You shouldn't be out on your own."

The bricklayers stand aside as five women step over the brickwork and hurry down the steps to Lord Ottonor's household, which awaits the final blessing. The bricklayers begin the second course of the big mudbricks. They work with the speed of long practice.

Polodos walks away and I follow, because of course he will look for them tomorrow, and I will have some freedom to help him. While he strides swiftly on, I glance over my shoulder. Five more attendants duck through the doorway and descend the steps. Denya walks among them. The bricklayers begin the third course.

"No." All my terror resurfaces. I halt.

"Doma?" He pauses about twenty strides ahead of me, turning to look back.

He won't believe me.

"You've got to go ahead, Polodos. We can't be seen together or word might get back to Lord Gargaron. Imagine what would happen to Father if we were discovered! Hurry! Lord Ottonor's people might have seen us already."

Flustered by the possibility that he may have put us in danger, he does not argue. "Are you sure you'll be safe?"

"I have a Garon badge. I'll get word to you at the inn."

He hurries off into the gloom.

I take slow steps backward up the path. When the file of Kusom soldiers jostles past, cutting me off from Polodos's sight, I hasten toward the tomb. The third group of attendants is already out, the women drenched in tears as they walk free of the stones and the stink.

The bricklayers place the fourth course. Dawn lightens the air.

Lord Gargaron strolls into view from the other side of the tomb, accompanied by Garon soldiers. His glance takes me in with the merest flicker of surprise, and he changes course to cut me off.

"Here you are, Jessamy. I suppose I should have expected it."

"Why should you have expected to see me, my lord? Garon Palace has already paid its respects and given its offerings to the dead man."

He glances toward the tomb with a thin smile. "Yes, so we have."

In that smile lies the truth: their fate was determined from the moment Lord Gargaron decided he wanted a new general.

He nods as he examines my expression and draws his own conclusions about my thoughts. "You have something of your father's instinct for strategy. I saw it when I watched you run against my useless nephew. You calculated each obstacle. You found a way to lose without making it obvious you had thrown the game. That makes you an adversary to reckon with."

All my caution flies out the window. "You came here to make sure they were bricked into the tomb, did you not?"

He considers me with a look I cannot fathom. "A man cannot serve if his heart lies in two pieces. General Esladas must not be distracted."

"She's pregnant!"

"We are at war," he says as if that answers everything.

"I'll tell the priests! It's blasphemy!"

"Do you think you will ever be allowed to get close enough to the priests to speak to them? Do you imagine anyone will listen to the mad rantings of a mule?"

The last group of women crawls out over what is now more a window than a door. The song of the priests drifts out from inside, the final blessing during which they cut away the dead man's shadow and seal his flesh into the coffin. Over time his self will dissolve and his heart decay, but as long as the tomb stands Lord Ottonor's name will remain alive in the world.

The oracle was telling me what I could not yet understand. Death might be a mercy.

"Put me in there with them, I beg you. That would be propitious, would it not? Like the Silent Orchid and her four obedient daughters. Let me go with them into the tomb. Please!"

"I think not. You will bring glory to Garon Palace, just as your father will. I will accept nothing less from you than the heights of the Illustrious."

The priests crawl out of the tomb, the last to emerge. With hands raised on the porch, they sing the hymn of triumphant justice while the bricklayers stand atop benches to finish the final courses and seal the tomb.

A scream of despair rips out of my throat and breaks

through my body as I dissolve into grief-racked sobs. But all of Lord Ottonor's household is wailing too, in the customary manner. The women scratch at their chests and the men throw dirt onto their heads. My voice is so lost among theirs that it stops me cold.

I am not the screamer.

Why is Bettany not screaming and shouting? What of Amaya's piercing whine? Have they smothered them as was the custom in the old country?

Are they dead?

The prayer of the priests reaches its crescendo in praise of the heavenly triumvirate of gods who have given the people prosperity, justice, and victory. In what was once a doorway the bricklayers leave only a thin gap for air like a mouth barely parted as it gives up its last breath.

My knees dissolve, all strength gone. The soldiers do not even glance at me. I am nothing to them.

I am nothing to myself. I am no longer Captain Esladas's daughter. My mother is no longer a woman named Kiya but a faceless and voiceless ghost. My sisters are gone.

I collapse over my thighs, fists on the dirt.

Lord Gargaron's feet shift in front of my face. I lift my head and see him motion to a captain, who escorts Denya to a carriage. Tears and exhaustion stain Denya's face, yet even so I see how pretty she is.

I remember what my mother said when she came home

from the City Fives Court on the day Father's clothes were washed in Lord Ottonor's blood: *He was poisoned.*

Lord Gargaron has taken everything he desired from the ruins of Lord Ottonor's household.

"Bring her," he says.

I walk before the soldiers can drag me. My legs stump like weights that belong to another person. Ahead wait two carriages. Lord Gargaron climbs into one. Denya is escorted to the other. I make ready to trudge behind the carriage but to my surprise the steward orders me in with her.

Its blue awning floats like the heavens, painted with cranes and sunbirds. I climb inside.

Denya looks up sharply, scrubbing tears from her cheeks. "Jessamy Tonor!" She laughs a little too wildly. "No, it is Jessamy Garon now, is it not? Just as I am Denya Garon."

With a snap of reins from their drivers, the carriages roll.

As a courtesy I pretend not to see her cry. "So you are bound for the palace too, Denya Garon," I say, the words as starched as waxed linen.

"Why are you so elevated? The lord would not take one like you to be a concubine." She breaks off, realizing how the words sound.

"Why would I want to have to endure that man's attentions in the bedchamber? I am at the Fives stable."

She sniffs, drawing up her chin. "Yes, of course. Amaya

said you were always sneaking out to run the Fives. My father would have whipped me."

"Was Amaya tattling to all her friends?"

"No. Just me."

There falls a silence. Denya was a loyal friend to Amaya. She deserves better than me hitting out at her in fear just because she's the only one I can touch.

I try again, attempting a kinder voice. "What will happen to your father, Captain Osfiyos?"

Her mouth twists as she makes several messy snorts of grief. It is an embarrassing sound but I cannot laugh at her. Probably this is the only time she will be allowed to cry. At Garon Palace, as a woman brought in to please her master, she will need to show a smiling face.

"He was broken down into the ranks. My brothers must start over as apprentices. Our family was ruined because of Lord Ottonor's debts. There was talk of me marrying a captain from Lord Nefelyan's household but that is all gone."

Just when I think she is going to collapse entirely she stiffens her spine and ruthlessly wipes her cheeks because she is a soldier's daughter too.

"I shall have elegant clothing that my father could never have afforded. I just wish Amaya could see it. If she and I could go shopping together we should have such pleasure. At least my older sister is safely married out of the household. We had a younger sister but she was dedicated to the temple as an infant." She stretches out her arms to study her hands as if imagining the rings she will wear, but the twist of her mouth betrays the rank taste in her throat. "I would rather endure Lord Gargaron's attentions than be buried alive."

He has buried them alive! An abyss has opened in my heart and I am tumbling endlessly, for there is no succor and no mercy.

Denya reaches across the gap, the pressure of her fingers like fire, her eyes lifted to mine all wide and trusting. How many times have I seen her and Amaya whispering together, hands clasped?

"You look sad, Jessamy Garon. Have you news of Amaya? Where did she go?"

I blink.

She doesn't know. No one knows. He has hidden it because he knows it is wrong.

She leans closer, her shoulder touching mine. Her lips touch my ear as she whispers, although how anyone could overhear us as the wheels roll and the horses clop along I cannot imagine. "I'm so worried about her. If you get news can you please find a way to slip a note to me? You helped her smuggle the notes in before."

"Was that awful poetry from *you*?" The mention of those dreadfully mundane and ridiculous love paeans breaks through my agony. She ducks her head as though to avoid a blow. "Unfolding petals and tongues of flame?"

Blushing, she struggles to meet my gaze. "We were just practicing. A married woman has to know how to...write love poetry and do other things. After she has given her husband sons, then people will look the other way if she wants to do things that unmarried women aren't allowed to do...." Like an actress playing the part of a modest lover, she presses a hand to a cheek.

Memory pulls me deeper despite the pain that recollection causes: the family courtyard with its lamps and the marriage couch where Mother loved to sit, content to know her man would return to her. Amaya would read plays aloud in her expressive voice, and we would laugh, or pretend to cry, or gasp in fear, or murmur in shocked surprise, according to her pleasure and the passage she was declaiming. Amaya was always brilliant at acting a part.

"We didn't mean anything by it." Her tone has an anxious lilt.

Perhaps for the first time in our years of acquaintance I really look at Denya. Her beautiful eyes are so brown they are almost black, with brows a perfect bow. The shroud drapes her body, hinting at a shapely form beneath. Her hair is clubbed up, but if let down it would be as straight and thick as that of the actresses on stage who are renowned throughout the land for their beauty. Dressed in finery, adorned with cosmetics and jewelry, she will be lovely. But it is the grief and fear and hope in her face that tell the truth of her heart.

"Were you and Amaya lovers?" I blurt out.

She draws back with an intake of breath but the truth is written all over her face, as good as a confession.

"I don't care what you did with Amaya," I say in a voice too accusing, for it isn't Denya I rage at. How have I been so blind? "I just hope you will be well treated by Lord Gargaron."

"I don't want your pity. Go run your Fives, Jessamy Garon." Her anger scalds over me. "You never saw anything but what you wanted. You only helped Amaya so she would help you."

She turns her face away and closes her eyes to make it clear the conversation is over. A tear slides down her cheek but she makes no sound.

Nor do I make a sound. I am bricked up and my heart is buried, but that does not mean I cannot fashion hate into a weapon. Yet I cannot confide anything to Denya; I cannot be her friend. Someday soon she will be in bed with him whether she wants to be or not. She might give up the secret of my hate without meaning to. She might give it up in exchange for a reward.

Beyond the curtains the city slowly wakes up to the dawn. Folk trundle past with carts and wagons. Files of donkeys clump along but I do not peek out to see what goods they are hauling as I usually would. A woman laughs, and another woman laughs in answer, happiness shared. Probably I will never laugh again.

Out of my fog of wretchedness and desolation one clear thought surfaces:

The only person who will believe me is Father.

23

I **am dropped** off at the stable and Denya is taken
away to the palace. Smoke streams from the kitchen as
adversaries eat porridge and fish for breakfast. I walk over to
where Gira, Shorty, and Mis sit. At the far end of the table
Talon sips a mug of broth. She looks up as I approach but says
nothing.

Gira gives me a big-eyed goggle. "Where did you go so
early?"

"Out for a walk."

Father would have stood me in his office and demanded
answers with question after question until I satisfied him that
I had by no means besmirched the family honor, but they just
go back to their food.

Tana bangs a brass cup on the table to get everyone's attention. "Come up here, Spider."

She hands me the cup. Its shine glints in my eye. A spider is carved into the brass. Its long legs wrap the cup like fate, and its mouth bears a set of pincers. Horribly, its long abdomen bears the jagged lozenge markings of the dreaded tomb spider.

Is Lord Gargaron mocking me?

"Lord Thynos brought this by at dawn, Jes. He himself had it engraved." Tana lowers her voice. "I can see you are troubled by it, maybe think it a bad omen. But I could not refuse it, nor can you. So make the best of it. Make it work for you."

Does Lord Thynos know? Is he in partnership with Lord Gargaron?

Fortunately it is a serious occasion so my grim look goes unnoticed as I walk to the water basin, dip my cup, and drain the water in one gulp. It has a metallic taste, spiced with the flavor of a metalworker's furnace. When I hang the cup from one of the hooking branches of the brass tree and sit beside Gira, no one says a word. We just eat.

Eventually Gira and Mis begin arguing over whether to see *The Hide of the Ox* or *The General's Valiant Daughter*. Their words wind like a maze through my dark thoughts. Today is Sixthday, and most of the adversaries will go out on the town.

"You better go change," adds Gira. She and the others are already in their Fives gear.

I run into our barracks, change, and make it back in time for the lineup. The slow pace of the opening menagerie with its stretch and reach for warm-up soothes the tightness of my limbs and allows my mind to pace through Lord Gargaron's game. He fears Mother because he respects her. Talking to her made him understand why Father remained loyal to her all these years.

A baton slaps my buttocks.

"Pay attention," says Darios. "When you are on the training ground I want your mind and heart on the court as well as your body. Do you understand, Spider?"

The other adversaries reach through the movements so I pretend I am their shadow instead of me, the girl whose living heart has been buried. When we sweep a turn, I see Kalliarkos in line where two animals before he was not. He has the privilege of showing up late, at whim, on the court that was built for him. When your grandmother is a princess of the royal line, it must be difficult for anyone not of royal blood to tell you what you can and can't do.

Darios whacks my rear again, harder this time. I nod, but as we complete the menageries, my mind is already running Rings and devising a plan. When we assemble at Rings I make my move.

Meant to be paired with Dusty for a race through Rings, I let Gira go ahead so I can move back beside Kalliarkos.

He taps me on the elbow. "Are you all right, Jes? You look tense and tired."

"I thought you wanted some tips for Rings."

His expression lightens. "Of course!"

I start tapping my foot against the earth in a steady rhythm. "Because there are mechanisms in the undercourt to turn the rings, the rate of turn remains constant. It's different for each individual game. It might be a quick one-two-three one-two-three one day, and another day it might be a slower one-two-three-four. Find a way to identify that rhythm in your head. That's how I judge the pace of the turns. That's how I time the leap from ring to ring." With a hand I indicate Dusty and Gira as I tap my foot loudly to emphasize the pattern.

They're a little off, trying to judge by eye rather than beats.

"But the rings aren't all turning at the same time," he protests.

"Each ring starts up at a different moment. That's how you get that unfolding movement. But they all turn at the same speed once they've started. The first ring starts turning and then a beat later the second one starts, and a beat later the third starts.... Does that make sense?"

He tugs at his hair, mouthing numbers as he counts, "One-two-three-four...but that one—no wait, I see what you're saying. This is a six-count turn." Because he's staring with such concentration and I'm watching him, I don't notice Darios come up behind us until the baton slaps my butt. I'm so startled I jump and stumble and have to catch myself on Kalliarkos's arm.

"I told you to run with Dusty, Spider!"

"Her shoelace came undone," Kalliarkos says while I'm still biting my lip because Darios really whacked me and my rump stings. He doesn't let go of me and I lean into his strength like it's the only thing stopping me from falling into the abyss of terror for my family.

"Yes, sorry. My shoe. I told Gira to go ahead of me."

"Don't take it upon yourself to change my training!" The old man looks genuinely irritated as he glares directly at where Kalliarkos's warm fingers are curled reassuringly around my elbow. Kal releases me and steps back like a chastened child. "You two are up. Move!"

The beat of these rings already runs through my bones from the foot-tapping I used to show Kalliarkos. But he hesitates, blinking, and as he starts counting all over again like he didn't already do it before, I fling myself into the first turning hoop. I beat him easily, and Darios sends me off with Dusty to train on Rivers while holding Kalliarkos back to run Rings again.

When the break comes I walk to the dining shelter with Dusty and Mis. She is teasing him about the way he planted his face in the water on Rivers. His nose is bleeding but not cracked. I pretend to laugh. In another life, the one in which my mother and sisters haven't just been buried alive, I would be laughing with my heart and not just my mouth.

Darios calls Dusty away for tending. Mis and I grab a mug of broth and sit.

"You seem tired," she says. "You were a little slow. You all right?"

I want to break everything on the table, smash it to pieces. My hands clench.

Mis glances toward the counter where Kalliarkos is bantering with the serving girl as she hands him a bowl of broth. "He flirts with everyone, Jes. He doesn't mean anything by it. He likes people to like him."

He scans the dining shelter, spots me, and with a smile starts our way.

Mis coughs. "I mean this in a friendly way, Jes. Don't play with that fire. Nothing good will come of it."

She stands up and makes way for him to sit down. He nods at her in the same friendly manner he uses with everyone, but he doesn't think of asking her to stay seated with us, nor does it seem to occur to him to ask why she is leaving.

"I worked on counting. I was just starting to get the pattern of it and then Darios told me to stop talking to myself. Like he doesn't want me to figure out a way to improve. So I counted in my head. Is this something Anise taught you?"

"I just always did it, from the first time I tried Rings." I see the opening and take it. "You said we can help each other. I need your help."

The rim of the bowl has just touched his lips but he lowers it without drinking. Steam curls into the air like hope stirring. "With what?" he asks.

"Help me get to my father. I need to see him."

The rough movement he makes with his hand, like pushing my words away, tips the bowl, but I grab it before it spills.

His eyes go wide. "You can't see him. Uncle Gar told me General Esladas is never to see any of his old household again, on pain of death. He was only allowed to retain his military people."

Around us, adversaries are getting up to return to training.

As I stand, I angle so close to him that I could kiss his cheek if I wanted. My lips brush his ear, and I feel the way his body shivers.

"This is why you're stuck at Novice," I say in a low voice, and I mean every word. "You won't take risks."

I walk away. Although I know he is staring after me, I do not look back.

"Hey, wait up," I call to Mis.

Shaking her head, she slows down. "Don't say I didn't warn you. But maybe I should warn him. You'll eat him alive."

Eating means a feast. Suddenly I see a possible route to my father.

"Maybe I will." I try to smile boldly but all I can manage is a grimace.

"He is good-looking. But his grandmother will find out and put a stop to it. You'll be lucky to keep your place in the stable. I don't see how you dare risk it."

The family of General Esladas can be thrown away as easily as the shards of a broken cup. My life means nothing if I do nothing. I would rather die in the mines. But I can't say that to her. I have to distract everyone so they think I'm involved in something that has nothing to do with my father.

I say, "Kal and I knew each other before I came here."

She whistles. "You call Lord Kalliarkos *Kal*? Don't tell me you've already—"

The practice bell interrupts her and we hurry to take our places in line. It takes every measure of will I have to pace through a short set of menageries: cat, jackal, and crane. I slog through the training with the other fledglings. If wool stuffed my head I would think more clearly. Everything ebbs and swells in a fog around me. I can't keep my balance on Traps, and I miss my timing on Rivers. Tana blames my lapses on a lack of fitness so she assigns me to run laps around the court while the others train. Running I can manage: all I have to do is set one foot in front of the other in time to the pulsing agony in my heart.

When the meal bell rings I veer into Trees because that's where the Novices are climbing under the supervision of Lord

Thynos and Inarsis. Everyone else is taking off except Kalliar-kos and Dusty, who are coming down the center pole. Dusty hits the ground first. The moment Kalliarkos drops he turns to stare at me in a way that causes Dusty, Inarsis, and his uncle to measure me as if expecting me to sprout monstrous pincers and four more limbs.

Thynos raises a hand. "Your grandmother is waiting, Kal."

Kalliarkos doesn't even look at him. He only looks at me. "I'll be there when I get there, Uncle Thynos. Don't wait."

"Kal!" Thynos takes a step toward him.

But Inarsis snags Thynos's arm and drags him away. Dusty coughs as if he's got something stuck in his throat and follows them. The chatter of adversaries leaving the court and heading to wash up stirs over us like a gust of wind.

When we are fully alone Kalliarkos's lips press to a thin line and his eyes cut with annoyance. For an uncomfortable moment he looks a little like Gargaron. "I'm sure it is under-standable that you wish to see your father. But. You. Can't."

"I can if you'll take me. You said the wedding feast would be at the villa on Sixthday night. That's this evening. Surely you are going. Take me with you."

"It's forbidden. It's dangerous. I can't."

"*I can't* is what you tell yourself every time you face Rings."

His eyes have a bright intensity, a window into his burning need. "It's not the same thing."

"It's exactly the same thing. It's why you won't ever become a Challenger, because the first thing you see is what you can't do instead of what you can do." His face flushes, thick with hot blood as I goad him. "Maybe the army can make a man of you, Lord Kalliarkos. But I doubt it."

There it is: the slack rope pulled taut, the gleam of defiance that wasn't there before.

"How do you propose we manage it?" he demands, but even as he speaks I see his gaze shift past me toward an idea that has just occurred to him. He mutters, "No...yes...I could...it might work...."

When he looks up, I know I have won.

"All right, then. But you have to meet me where I say, and do as I ask." He sticks out a hand, palm up and open in the gesture of merchants everywhere.

I lay my palm flat atop his. My skin is cool, and his is hot.

Thus the deal is made.

After the meal everyone lies down in the heat of the day but I am too restless to sleep. If I close my eyes all I see is bricks sealing my family away.

Because it is Sixthday there is no afternoon training. I wash with the others but plead a headache and retreat to my cubicle instead of soaking in the hot pool because I cannot bear their chatter. I dress in my underthings and my leggings, tie my Fives slippers just below my knees like I used to do when I sneaked out of the house, and wrap my Fives court tunic around one thigh. Kalliarkos wants me to be ready in case I have to climb the villa wall. The everyday loose linen sheath gown they issued me covers me from shoulders to ankles, hiding the other clothes. The ordinary garb of Commoner women makes me inconspicuous.

When I hear Gira, Shorty, and Mis leaving at dusk I hurry after so everyone else sees me leave with them. "I'm feeling better! Which play did you choose? Can I come?"

"*The General's Valiant Daughter*," says Mis with a laugh. "Come on, then."

It does not take us long to reach the West Gate of the Lantern District.

Beneath the flowing ribbons I halt. "Listen. Will you meet me here later?"

Mis presses a hand over her eyes as if to hide whatever folly I'm planning from her sight.

"Lord Gargaron is a hard man, Jes." Gira waggles a finger in front of my face. "Don't cross him by trying to romance his nephew, no matter what his nephew says."

"How could I be meeting him? The palace has some kind of wedding feast tonight, doesn't it?"

Gira frowns. "That's right. They do. Where are you going, then?"

Amaya has a look we sisters call her sad kitten eyes. I try it out now. "I can't say. Please."

They look at one another. After a moment Shorty shakes her head, foreseeing no good end to the night's business, but points to the big brass water clock with its ticking gears, elaborate catchments, and column of trumpets that stands to the west of the gate. "We will be here when the fourth night-trumpet blows. If you're not here, then you're on your own."

"Thank you! If you have to go back without me, say I vanished into the crowd and you lost track of me. It is Sevensday tomorrow anyway. It is our free day, isn't it?"

"It is our free day, and you don't have to be in until dawn on Firstday," says Gira curtly, but I can see she is revising her opinion of me, wondering what kind of troublemaker I will turn out to be. "I don't like to be the kind of person who gives advice, Jes, but whatever it is, I think you shouldn't do it."

"Who ever listened to good advice? I never did!" Mis's laugh is drowned out by a blast of singing that washes over us from a determined group of revelers who swarm past, already drunk.

Gira seems ready to scold me again but Shorty pulls her away. I wait as they walk under the ribbon wheels. When I am sure they are out of sight I stride down through the lively streets, past the night market just opening for the evening with its tempting foods, and along the Avenue of Triumphs where my father was cheered. That day seems like it happened years ago.

Halfway down the Avenue of Triumphs stand monumental twin pillars carved with the victorious deeds of the much-loved and justice-seeking King Kliatemnos the Fourth and his wise and benevolent mother, Serenissima the Third, who acted as regent for him when he was a child. The side streets of this district are awash with taverns that cater to Patron military men and foreign mercenaries. Tonight the place is swarming with soldiers. I did not realize there were so many in the city. In a nearby tavern a man is singing a dreary account of the battle of Reef Cliffs, where as an adult Kliatemnos the Fourth died with a knife in his back just as his army achieved a decisive victory over the king of East Saro.

Kalliarkos wanted to meet here instead of outside the Lantern District because we're less likely to be recognized and because it will not look strange for a young woman like me to get into a carriage belonging to a young man like him. In fact, while I'm waiting, four different foreign men crudely proposition me, and an unknown man in the crowd pats my buttocks in passing. A drunk Soldian actually tries to touch my breasts before I elbow him hard enough to wind him.

"Try that again and I'll brew a magic to make your testicles wither," I snap in my most highborn Patron manner. "Am I wearing white ribbons, that you feel you can accost me?"

His comrades drag him away, muttering about arrogant mules.

I move away up the street, scanning the traffic, and admire a small carriage that is being deftly woven through the wagons, carts, foot traffic, and fine carriages. Rigged for speed, it is just large enough to seat a driver and two passengers, although the passenger bench is empty. The driver wears a sand scarf wrapped around his mouth and nose, the sort of gear worn by a traveler in the desert. He pulls down the scarf, looking for me. In his court clothes, whip in hand, he looks so striking that I stare and stare as he almost drives past. Then I remember to push out of the crowd.

Seeing me, he deftly reins the carriage to a halt.

He grins down from the high seat. "As I promised, Doma," he says with a laugh that makes his whole face light up.

From the height of the carriage, he offers me a hand. His grip enfolds my fingers and I'm breathless as he pulls me up. He overweights his tug and I accidentally thump into his body, forcing him to grasp me around the waist so I don't fall. His chest presses against mine. Our faces almost touch, his lips so close to mine I need only exhale to kiss him.

Why shouldn't I take the risk? Father's rules no longer define my life.

My lips brush his mouth.

"Jessamy," he murmurs as his arm tightens around me.

The carriage jolts under us as the horses back up a step. I slip as he lets go to better grip the reins. What am I to him, really? Something with which to defy his uncle?

The bricks of the tomb rise between us.

"We must hurry," I say, scrambling for the passenger bench.

Kalliarkos's muttered curse makes me jump. Have I offended him? Is he like his uncle, angry if he's challenged?

Then I see that we are no longer alone.

Lord Thynos stands at the horses' heads, holding the harness, while Inarsis leaps up into the carriage beside me and pulls down the canvas curtains to conceal the passenger bench. The carriage rocks again as Thynos climbs up onto the driver's bench beside Kalliarkos.

"Keep moving, Kal," says Thynos.

After a moment the carriage rolls. I peek out between the curtains to see Kalliarkos's rigid back.

"Did you follow me, Uncle?"

"My dear nephew, long ago I promised your mother that I would never, ever let you walk about the city unattended. She fears you may be kidnapped and held for ransom. Or murdered, which would be less expensive but far messier. You've made my task easy so far. Am I correct in thinking that this is the first time you have sneaked out on your own?"

Inarsis chuckles. "Not the first. On the other occasion he followed our young tomb spider to the Ribbon Market."

"What do you want?" snaps Kalliarkos, sounding embarrassed and thwarted.

Thynos sighs with a dramatic emphasis worthy of Amaya. "Either you don't intend to feast with your sister and her new husband tonight and instead plan to ruin the prospects of an extremely promising adversary, or you are expressly defying Gar's injunction that all ties between our heroic General Esladas and his irregular family must be severed. Which is it?"

"None of your business."

Lord Thynos's eyebrows fly right up his forehead. "Do not tell me what is and is not my business, puppy. Answer me!"

"Enough, Thynos," says Inarsis in a genial tone. "Be glad our young man is finally showing some spine. It was a good ruse, Lord Kalliarkos, to have this carriage made ready in the back alley and meanwhile tell your mother you were riding with your grandmother, and your grandmother the opposite."

"Not good enough," mutters Kalliarkos.

"I am an experienced campaigner, my lord. Not much gets past me."

Thynos laughs. Kalliarkos does not. Neither do I. They will ruin everything. I twist my hands together, wound tight with anguished frustration, but I see no way to be rid of them. They have all the power and I have nothing but my wits and determination.

We turn a wide corner and pick up speed. Peeking out between the curtains I see we are headed toward the eastern gate along the Avenue of the Soldier, so called because so many armies have marched out of the city along this wide boulevard. I'm a little surprised Thynos has not taken the reins, but in fact Kalliarkos drives with an impressively brisk confidence even though his expression is stiff with anger. I can't stop looking at the way his hands masterfully handle the reins and how his gaze flits along the traffic to find narrow spaces to slide our carriage through so we don't need to slow down.

Lord Thynos glances back at me, his smile turning to a flat stare. "Spider, that was an imprudent place for you to agree to meet a man. A crowd of drunk soldiers is not safe for a woman, especially one like you."

I do not need to be scolded about such matters by a man who isn't my father! "Because I am young or because I am a mule?"

"Because you are both. Patron women are protected by their clans. And every foreign man who reaches these shores soon learns that Commoner women are protected by the magic of their father's mother. A dame's evil eye can kill a man's potency. But one like you has no clan and no Commoner grandmother on her father's side. Your father was no fool to raise his daughters as if they were Patron girls. I feel sure he knew exactly how far his shield of protection extended."

There is no answer to that, but no trace of humiliation or offense will show on my face. I keep my head high and my eyes forward, as Mother taught us girls to do.

We approach the huge gate with its sentries, lamps burning as the purpling twilight sinks into the full darkness of night.

"Kal, take that cursed scarf off your face. The guards need to see an uncle and his nephew on their way to a joyous wedding feast, not a prince skulking about playing at banditry."

Kalliarkos tugs down the scarf so it wraps only his neck and leaves his face visible. As we come to a stop, he hands the guards a piece of fired ceramic with a cipher stamped on it, giving us permission to leave the city. Inarsis pulls the curtain out of my hand and shrouds us behind it before the guards can get a close look. So have my mother and sisters been cut off from everything around them. I clasp my hands in my lap and, trembling, wait out the crossing, but quickly enough we are allowed to pass under the triple gates and over a wide plank causeway that spans the canal that rings the city.

Beneath the wheels the grind of wood turns to the rumble of stone as we roll onto a paved road and head out of the city into the countryside. Inarsis ties the curtains up out of the way.

The Royal Road follows the coastline of Efea from Saryenia all the way to the easternmost fortress at Pellucidar Lake in the mountainous Eastern Reach, a journey that takes weeks. At night the road is lit with sturdy glass lanterns fastened to pillars. Iron cages posted at intervals contain the remains of dead enemies scavenged off the battlefield and left to rot. The bones of those the king has defeated are ground to dust and, so it is said, mixed into the goat's milk drunk by King Kliatemnos the Fifth every morning to strengthen his blood.

"What do you mean to do now, Uncle?" asks Kalliarkos. His raised chin and brusque tone give him a lordly arrogance that makes him seem a stranger, not the amiable young man who first spoke to me on Lord Ottonor's balcony.

"Must I do anything? Can I not enjoy this lovely ride

through the countryside on our way to your sister's wedding feast?"

The view here just outside the city is not that lovely. Regimental camps sprawl alongside the Royal Road, each surrounded by a wall. Every gate has a company badge painted on it: a looped cross, a triangle finned with two bars, a hatched circle. By these marks soldiers can know their own company and form up again in the disarray of battle, so Father taught me. He praised me for memorizing the name of every regiment in the king's army. I see some of them now: the Striking Fours, the Bronze Blades, the Old Spears.

Beyond the last camp of the king's army lie the temporary camps of mercenaries eager to take the king's coin. Their flags fly but I do not know their names or origins or even what languages they speak. All I know is that such people fight for money instead of honor and loyalty.

Inarsis stirs beside me. "As the man hired by your grandmother to protect you, Lord Kalliarkos, it would be prudent of you to inform me what your intentions are this evening so I may plan for every contingency."

I tense, waiting for my secret to be exposed, but Kalliarkos does not hesitate. "Is it so surprising that for once I wanted to choose my own company for the journey there and back? It took years to convince my mother that it was humiliating for me to have an ill-wisher at my side at all times, like I was still a little child. Now I have you two nursemaids following me

254

everywhere. I have decided to act as a man instead of a boy. Does that content you, General Inarsis?"

The name jolts me. "General Inarsis? The victor of the battle of Marsh Shore during the Oyia campaign?"

"The same, Spider. As for you, Lord Kalliarkos, your explanation does not content me."

"How did I not know who you are?" I mutter, partly because I am stunned and partly to distract him while I think.

"Inarsis is a common name among Efean men," he says with an amused smile.

"I know it is!" I should have guessed that a man of Commoner ancestry who walks like an equal beside a Patron lord must have an exceptionally distinguished reputation. "You are the only Commoner to ever command the king's army."

"We call ourselves Efean," he says in a mild tone that rebukes me.

"Yes, but—" His quiet confidence flusters me. "But all the high officials and lords in Efea are Patron-born. For instance, no matter how well a Commoner—I mean an Efean—learns Saroese, they cannot become an Archivist, only an Archivist's assistant. I thought it was the same in the army."

"I assure you that I began the day as a junior officer in the only Efean regiment, which itself was commanded by senior officers, all of whom were Patron men. The battle was a bloody, violent conflict with massive casualties on both sides. I had to step forward after all the senior officers were dead or incapacitated."

"Did you actually kill King Elkorios of Saro-Urok? With your own hand?"

"I did. For my service I was generously recompensed in money and given the fine and mighty title of general so they wouldn't have to say that a noble king was killed by a lowly foot soldier. Immediately afterward I was relieved of command and replaced by officers of Saroese ancestry. Some of them as young and inexperienced as Kalliarkos here."

"But you were fortunate to be in the army at all. My father served in the Oyia campaign. He said yours was the first company of Efean soldiers assembled and commissioned in the king's army."

"That is correct. Before the reign of Kliatemnos the Fourth, Efeans were not allowed to serve in the military."

It seems shameful to remind such a courageous man of what he already knows so I change the subject. "Father often spoke of your company's bravery and skill. My mother liked to hear of your exploits."

"Did she?" His features are obscured by night, but I sense he is suddenly fascinated. "We all knew of her. Not because Captain Esladas spoke of her—he never did—but because we all knew he was living with an Efean woman as if she were his wife. We knew he had four daughters and no sons. It is a measure of his skill as a commander that he continued to rise past higher-born Patron men. The Patron officers saw his loyalty as a sign of weakness but we Efean soldiers knew it for a sign of strength that he kept faith with a woman he cared for."

"Until ambition poisoned him," I mutter.

Inarsis replies in a low voice, "Sometimes in battle a man must choose between two bad outcomes. Please do not think your father had a choice once Garon Palace became involved. I am sure it pained him deeply to set her aside."

I do not want his sympathy. But I will use it to get what I need. The quaver in my voice gives my words the ring of truth. "I asked Lord Kalliarkos to sneak me in to see my father so that I can tell him I have passed muster and will train as an adversary in the Garon Stable."

"I am sure General Esladas knows that already," remarks Thynos.

"Not from my lips," I say. "Please, Lord Thynos. General Inarsis. Just this one favor."

By now we've left the encampments behind. The road cuts through land divided into fields with a network of canals. Burning lanterns recede before and behind us like gems strung on a wire necklace. The beauty of the lit road catches in my heart: the pathway of these glimmering lights could lead to triumph or disaster. Yet I can't truly appreciate the scene as I sit poised to bolt and run if the hammer falls.

For the longest time no one speaks.

Suddenly Thynos taps Kalliarkos on the shoulder. "The

twin sycamores mark the servants' lane. We'll drop her off in the palm grove and come around by the back."

All my breath gusts out of me as I sag in relief. "Thank you," I murmur.

Kalliarkos easily maneuvers the carriage off the main road and onto a hard-packed earth track. In the distance a firefly string of lights marks the main entry road through square fields of barley and wheat. A cluster of lights reveals the villa near the seashore.

We cross four canals before we enter a village surrounded by sycamore, fig, olive, and date trees. The locals stare from their verandas. Every house is connected to the others by raised walkways. The children run naked but their faces are clean, and the women wear long linen sheaths like mine while the men wear the short keldi that covers only from hip to knee.

Is this the kind of village my mother came from?

We continue along a path between vineyards, smoke coiling out of pots to keep insects away. Ahead rises an orchard, trees like persimmon, pear, and cherry brought from old Saro. We come to rest off the lane, hidden among the thick pillars of date palms. The gentle slope of the ground toward the sea gives us a view of the villa. Night makes it hard to see but by the way lamps are placed I can tell there is an outer and an inner compound, and that the inner compound has two wings, two squat towers, a garden, and a courtyard at the center of the sprawling house.

"Now, Kal," begins Thynos, "here's what we'll do."

Inarsis coughs. "Perhaps you should let Lord Kalliarkos devise the plan."

"Here's what we'll do," I interrupt. "You three will attend the feast as expected. I can easily get inside."

"Gar doesn't allow Efean servants in Garon Palace," says Thynos.

"I know that! I thought I would climb inside, if Lord Kalliarkos will explain the layout to me."

"You don't need to," Kalliarkos interrupts. "Out here in the country, we do use Efean servants, especially when we need to hire in extra help from the village for a feast like this one."

"So if I wear a servant's mask, no one will look twice at me."

He nods with a triumphant glance at Thynos. "That's right."

"Excellent. That's settled, then. You three go about your business as usual. I will return here after I see my father and wait for you. Where am I likely to find my father before the feast? Is there a private chamber of some kind where he may be preparing for the evening?"

"There you go, Nar, the daughter you always wished for but never had," says Thynos with a laugh. "Gives orders like her father, doesn't she?"

How can he know how my father gives orders?

"The eastern tower is set aside for the husband." By

Kalliarkos's pleased expression, he is enjoying the way we are running Rings around the men assigned as his minders. "It was my father's before he died. You will find General Esladas there before he comes down to greet the guests."

"Is there anything else you can recommend, Lord Kalliarkos?" I ask.

Inarsis smiles, obviously amused by our interplay, but Thynos frowns.

Kalliarkos glances up at the starry sky. "We will meet here when the Four Sleeping Sisters rise in the east, about midnight. I have no desire to linger at the feast while my sister ornaments herself in the flattery and congratulations of the courtiers and guests. We can return to Garon Palace long before dawn."

He looks at me, his gaze smoky and intense. A spark leaps between us, as if he is promising another adventure before sunrise. I am so taken aback by the challenge that at first I don't move.

"Go on," he says, daring me. "I will be waiting."

24

It's easy to be a Commoner. I just have to keep my head down, never look any Patron in the eye, and always step out of their way. When I reach the servants' gate with its trio of bored soldiers standing guard, I ignore the way they ogle me. The hardest part is trying to copy the way most Commoners pronounce the Saroese language.

"Domon, I am hired for the laundry. I was riding in a wagon but it broke down so I had to walk." As I speak I pat the Garon badge pinned to the shoulder of my dress. One of the men is smirking, one looks as if he is wondering if he can get away with squeezing my breast, and the third frowns suspiciously.

Smirker gives a wheezy laugh.

"Guess your mother didn't want to whore you out like she

did herself, eh, mule?" says Squeezer as his hand drifts toward my torso.

"Leave it." Suspicion slaps the other man. "Look at her arms. She's wrung plenty of laundry and maybe a few men's necks. Go on, mule. Just as a favor this once, if you are ever caring to return it." He winks, expecting me to be grateful.

I fix my gaze on the ground lest I betray myself by looking him right in the face with the pride and dignity I deserve. When I curve my shoulders down to make myself seem smaller, they let me go.

The villa boils with activity. In the outer courtyard a quartermaster and his company are readying high-slung military coaches and cargo wagons. In the inner stable yard people load twenty wagons with chests and furniture while others prepare carriages fitted with gold-threaded curtains and cushions. I walk briskly through the commotion. Once inside the servants' wing I snag a featureless leather mask and fasten it over my face.

A trip through the bustling kitchen nets me a precious lacquered tray complete with a covered cup. A crisp word to a harried girl fetches a pot of hot water and a little basket of pungent herbs. I have helped my mother prepare this mix of dried petals and needles a thousand times. It is one of the niceties she loves to comfort him with after a long day. I used to think her devotion to us all made her a little dull. My hands tighten on the tray: she will never again serve him a cup.

The modest, boring household life I once complained of and wished to escape seems the most golden and treasured memory now.

I approach the main building from the back through the rear garden. The central building rises two stories high, flanked by square towers. Lights burn in both. From the western tower floats the laughter of women; shapes move within the upper chamber. In the eastern tower a person stands at the window looking over the garden. Being lit from behind obscures his face, but I would recognize my father's posture and the cut of his shoulders anywhere.

In this villa owned by a princely family, servants swarm like rats. The lacquered tray fends off unwanted questions. No one calls you over to give you a task when you are already about an urgent matter. The guards stationed at the bottom of the tower stairs wave me through. Evidently Father's nightly tea is already an established fact in his new household, although it is now a servant who brings it, not a loving partner.

My pulse surges in my ears far beyond the effort of climbing the steps. The air seems to swim past my vision as lamplight flickers. I have to pause to catch my breath on the landing of the second story. An open door looks onto a chamber bare except for a large bed where an orderly is laying out two nightrobes. I flinch away from the sight and scurry up two more flights of stairs.

On the top floor soldiers wearing the Garon badge guard

the open door. They wave me to a halt and I am oddly thankful they are so cautious of my father's safety.

"Have the rest of the wedding furniture boxed up," my father is saying to a man whose gray-streaked hair and fleshy back I recognize as belonging to Steward Haredas. "I am sure Lady Menoë has a warehouse in Garon Palace for all the finery."

He glances up, alert to the movement at the door. I stand framed by lamplight, the tray in my hand and my face masked. For a moment he does nothing but look.

Then his nostrils flare as he takes in a sharp breath. His lips silently form my name: *Jessamy*.

He has recognized me even in my mask.

"General, is all well?" Haredas asks. "You look as if you have seen a rat."

The steward notices me. He flaps a hand as his brow wrinkles with lines of anger, for unlike my father he sees only what he expects to see. "The general drinks his tea before he goes to his bed, not now. Be away! Must I speak to your supervisor and have you whipped?"

"No, Haredas, I asked for tea to settle my stomach." Father wears a mask too: a mask of indifference. But he clenches his left hand. "I will take a few moments to drink it in peace before I descend to greet the guests and my wife."

Does his tone bite on the words *my wife*? Is he embarrassed, or ashamed, or angry that his unwanted daughter has shown up where her presence can harm him?

Haredas gives a disapproving grunt. "This must be one of the local girls hired in for the feast. Lady Menoë does not allow Efean women among her servants."

"Go see that the wagons are being loaded properly," says Father.

I step aside to let Haredas leave. He does not give me a second glance.

"Bring the tea," says Father in his command voice. As I step into the room, he adds to the soldiers, "Close the doors. I need a few moments without interruption to collect my thoughts before the evening's ordeal."

The guards tap hands to chests. "Yes, General."

The doors close.

I stand in the tower chamber with the father who threw us away. He wears clothes of remarkable richness, a long red silk keldi that falls to his ankles and a red silk jacket trimmed with gold braid and embroidered with shimmering gold thread on the shoulders.

"Set down the tray and pour," he says in the firm but not harsh tone of a man used to having raw recruits feel intimidated by his stare. In all the years of my childhood I did not see him lose his temper. No one would call him a gentle man, but he is never rash nor cruel. He is a soldier who has suffered wounds and dealt death, but once after I had accompanied him to his regiment's encampment and he and I were returning home, he told me that the most painful wound of being an officer was sending men to die.

I fear what I must tell him. I fear what his answer may be. When I set down the tray and pour, my hand trembles and the stream of tea splashes messily.

"So, Jessamy, here you are, come where you are forbidden to be."

"How did you know it was me?"

"Do you think I do not know my own daughters? Except when they are running on a Fives court, so it seems. I suppose I should not be surprised after discovering you had all this time plotted out a secret campaign and waged it behind my back in direct insubordination of my orders."

I set down the pot and rake the mask back from my face. "Do you know what provision Lord Gargaron made for Mother and your other daughters after you abandoned us? Do you?"

"I did not abandon you! Do you have any idea what would have become of the household if we had fallen with Lord Ottonor? All the years of careful stewardship to maintain our finances in good order were wiped away to nothing by his undisciplined luxuries and endless bad decisions. In one way he was a good man. He gave a humbly born man like me a true chance to flourish by my own efforts. But in the end he did not take care of the people he was responsible for."

"Do you think Lord Gargaron has taken care of us?"

He picks up the cup, takes a long swallow, and sets it down, looking grim. "Why are you here, Jessamy? Have you been mistreated?"

"Lord Gargaron has had Mother and your other daughters bricked up in Lord Ottonor's tomb. That's how he made provision for them!"

He blinks.

At first I think he is about to deny it, to protest, to slap down the ugly accusation.

But I recognize the flashes of expression: the tic of an eye, the quiver of his upper lip, the way his brows draw down and afterward lift; he is running the Rings in his head, assessing the information at hand. My face must look similar when I crouch on the last platform and let the height and spin and speed of the obstacle settle into my brain until the pattern emerges.

He staggers, barely catching himself on the table.

"Kiya," he whispers so softly I cannot truly hear him, but I have seen her name on his lips for all my life, and it looks like nothing else he says because it always shakes him to the heart.

The agony that twists his face gives me a stab of joy because I want him to suffer the way they must be suffering, knowing he condemned them to a living death.

He sinks onto a chair, hands braced on his knees. His lips move in a prayer, but he has not the breath to voice it out loud.

The spicy fragrance of the steeping tea hits my nose, drawing me hard into the memory of the quiet evenings when we would sit in our courtyard as night embraced our content little family.

I hate him.

He gave up Mother's devotion and our laughter for this sour victory.

After a while he looks up, and he says, "Jessamy."

He sounds so wounded that I cannot help but creep over to him. I kneel as I used to do when I was younger and lean my forehead against the chair with its armrests carved in the manner of firebirds in repose. Mother bought him this chair.

He rests a hand on my hair and strokes a thumb over its coils.

"Jessamy," he says again, as if the shock has torn all other words out of his mouth.

His raw grief is little enough recompense for the pain but I can't revel in it. I can't bear it.

"You have to get them out," I whisper. "If anyone can, you can, Father."

His voice is hoarse with choked-back tears. Its vulnerability makes me press a hand to my chest lest my heart pound right out of my skin. "It was the very day I got off the ship. I was only twenty years old, wandering around dazed because Efea was a dazzling vision like nothing I had ever imagined. I remember the very moment I saw her in the market. At home we had no garden but for a strip of dirt that my father's brother cultivated for dill and peppers to flavor the bread. Only at a festival could we afford to trade bread for a few precious, shriveled persimmons, the last of the crop. Then in Efea there was an old woman selling persimmons so bold and orange that they caught my eye. That's when I saw her. She was laughing."

Mother has told the tale of their meeting before but made a jest of it. She tripped and a young foreigner caught her before she fell facedown into a vat of urine. Confusion resulted because neither spoke the language of the other.

The yearning in his face burns out my hatred. My anger turns to ashes.

"Did you fall in love with her at first sight?"

"No one can fall in love at first sight. Love is built over years, not snapped into existence like a flame that can be as easily extinguished. But I was so struck with her beauty and the pure joy of her laugh that something deep within me changed. Where I grew up I never saw beautiful young women laughing boldly in the market, like they belonged there. The poets sing that a man come to foreign soil leaves his heart behind in the familiar and beloved earth of the village where he grew up. But in that one instant my heart leaped all the mountain vastness and the wild and windy sea to come to rest here on Efean earth. I would never go back to the old country. Maybe I was Saroese once. But I am an Efean man now, and I will fight for Efea."

"Fight for Lord Gargaron, and his palace, and his ugly schemes."

He cuts a hand through the air to silence me. "I suppose it seems to you I did not fight to keep you. That I let ambition sway me. In what gauzy theatrical tale do you think I could have said no to Lord Gargaron? The instant he stepped into the house, our fates were sealed."

Tears choke my throat. "We can't leave them there."

His stern voice comforts me. "We won't leave them there. For her to have a life away from me I can live with. But if I walk away now, knowing what I know, I cannot call myself a man. And if I am not a man, then I might as well be dead. Besides that, it is the worst kind of blasphemy to entomb a pregnant woman. It is spitting into the faces of the gods."

"Can you tell the priests?"

"Don't be naïve, Jessamy. To get them entombed means at least some priests already know about it. Lord Gargaron has offered them something they want in exchange. Or they fear him. A man like that has many ropes with which to bind people to his will. Now let me think. The City of the Dead is guarded day and night. The tombs are sealed with bricks, impossible to enter or leave unless you break them open...." He trails off, wiping a hand wearily over his brow.

"I can get into the tomb through the air shaft," I say, my voice tentative because I am unsure if he'll approve of the plan. "If I have rope, a climbing harness, and an ally outside, then the people trapped inside can be lifted out. A diversion, like a fire, will keep the priests' attention elsewhere. Mother and the girls can't wear mourning shrouds on the street, so I'll bring each a change of clothes. Also, it would have to be done at night."

His gaze fixes on a point beyond my head as he works through the possibilities. This must be the face he wears in battle: unflappable and deadly serious. "It's risky, but it could work. You'll need a Patron ally, someone who can move in and out of the City of the Dead without suspicion. Polodos can help you."

"I saw him at Lord Ottonor's tomb. I tried to tell him, but he wouldn't believe me. Do you think he has enough courage to aid me?"

"Do not underestimate Polodos." He grasps my hands. "Even if he does not, he will obey you because you have the mind and the heart and the courage of a soldier, Jessamy. You should have been my son."

My lips curl as I yank my hands out of his. "I don't want to be your son! I want to be your daughter who matters to you as much as a son would."

Another man would protest that I do matter to him, or would push me aside in disgust. He catches my chin in a hand and tips back my head. In his eyes I see myself: not as a reflection but in their brown color, their shape, the thick lashes, the intensity. In the face of his scrutiny I begin to cry silent tears because I want him to care, and I have never truly been sure that he does.

His mouth tightens. "Never think my daughters do not matter to me. Never believe it. I am proud of all four of you even if I have not known how to show it." He releases my chin. A smile peeps out as he shakes his head. "Down the air shaft. I suppose that is an idea you picked up from the Fives. I expect you are good, are you not?"

I have to bite my lower lip to stop from bawling. All I can do is nod.

"Of course you would be."

I put a hand on his knee like a supplicant. "Father, come with me."

He sets me back, stands, and takes an agitated turn around the room. "Garon stewards watch me. Garon guards stand at every gate. My movements are under constant scrutiny. My usual military stewards and orderlies have already been sent east to prepare for my travel. Except for Haredas, I am alone among people loyal to Lord Gargaron. After tonight's feast they mean to parade me at the victory games and then send me east to the war."

"That's when we can do it! The day of the victory games!"

"They would find me out in a moment. I cannot walk out that door without a guard on either side. Besides that, my involvement would endanger your mother even more. A man who would commit blasphemy to separate her from me will murder her if he knows she is free."

He halts at the window to gaze down over the courtyard

in its blaze of lamps. The tense set of his shoulders eases as he wills himself into calm.

"I must go to war, just as I always do. I will fight to keep Efea free from invasion because soldiering is my duty. The king needs me to command his army." He turns, and I rise, standing at attention as I have been taught. "Freeing your mother and sisters is your task, Jessamy. You must devise an attack and carry it out. I can never see her again, do you understand?"

I wipe away tears because he has allowed me a glimpse into his five souls, his deepest heart: it isn't just Gargaron's ruthlessness he fears, it is his own love for her. If she dies, he will blame himself. He already blames himself. "Yes, I understand."

He taps his chest twice, and I respond with the same signal.

I have been given my orders.

A bell rings in the courtyard. Servants rush to the feast like the sweep of wind. Women's laughter spills on the night air, unmarred by grief or care.

"You can find Polodos at the Least-Hill Inn by the West Harbor," he adds. He cocks his head as we both hear a noise at the closed doors.

"Open up at once. General Esladas must see me immediately."

I would know Lord Gargaron's voice anywhere.

25

꒰꒰꒱꒱

I pull my mask down over my face. The tray is in my hands before the door opens. Father remains at the window.

With bowed head I step out of the way as Lord Gargaron strides in. He cannot be bothered to glance at a masked servant. All his attention is reserved for the man he has elevated. His disapproval clouds the room.

"General Esladas, I thought you would be downstairs already. The procession is gathering."

Father flips his sleeves, then smooths them. "My apologies, my lord. I am not yet accustomed to the formal manners of a palace and the stately customs by which every nightly meal is embarked upon." No agitation mars his tone or manner.

Lord Gargaron's frown lifts as he joins Father at the window. "It is just as well you've lingered here because there is a small matter I wish to speak of while we still have privacy."

"My lord." Father inclines his head obediently.

Lord Gargaron leans out to examine the courtyard, then steps back as if fearing arrows will pierce him from out of the night. "On the road, it is likely you will be joined by your wife's brother."

"Likely? Is there some doubt of it?"

"His grandmother insists he be given one final chance to prove he can make something of himself running the Fives, even though I am altogether opposed. Still, I have given my word to allow him a last trial. If he can win at your victory games, he may devote himself to the Fives. If he loses I will finally be allowed to send him into the army as has been my intention all along."

He rubs a cheek with a finger, as if rubbing a gloating smile off his lips.

"My lord." The acknowledgment offers nothing and betrays nothing.

"I expect you to keep him close. Let him see how a campaign is run. Give him a chance to prove himself in protected circumstances, with you making the important decisions. Above all else, keep him safe."

"What manner of temperament may I expect to be dealing

with, my lord?" Father asks with the patience of a man who has overseen any number of hapless lordly whelps sent out to endure their first and possibly only campaigns.

"He's a smart boy but naïve. He needs seasoning and experience. The one thing you must cure him of is that he wants people to like him. He is inappropriately friendly toward those who are not of his station. He believes he can rescue forlorn wretches. He has a bad habit of doing favors for people to win their approval."

Father is far too disciplined to glance my way but the twitch of his shoulders and the cant of his body betrays that he is abruptly wondering how I got here and who might have helped me.

"Cleanse him of that desire for camaraderie, if you can. But above all, I need him back sound in mind and whole in body. A few brave injuries would not go amiss to mark him as a good soldier. Your fortune will rise with his, I promise you."

I rock back a step to catch myself.

"My gracious lady wife speaks little of her brother," Father remarks. "I am not sure she has mentioned him even once within my hearing."

"Though close in age, they are not much alike." Lord Gargaron looks around to see me standing like a statue by the door. He flutters a hand. "Out! These creatures! Too stupid to take initiative."

Father's gaze flicks toward me, then back to his lord.

"Good soldiers undertake their duty and accomplish all that they have been ordered to do," he says as I depart.

The words are meant for me.

My head is buzzing. The stone steps slip away, like they are falling farther and farther from my feet, and by the time I reach the bottom I am halfway to flying. Only my trained reflexes keep me from slamming into one of the guards.

"Slow down!" he barks.

Panting, I duck my head and slide away at a more measured pace although my heart stumbles.

The corridor is awash in a locust cloud of voices. Because I do not know the layout of the villa, I miss the route taken by the servants and find myself in a large atrium in which a company of finely dressed Patron men and women are gathering. Across the room I see Lord Kalliarkos, Lord Thynos, and General Inarsis chatting amid a circle of brightly dressed courtiers, and although Kalliarkos glances around the room, my mask protects me as I creep along the wall like a shadow.

Lords and ladies mingle, chattering and laughing. The women wear linen sheaths, the fabric covered with embroidery and tiny beads to create flowers and vines and butterflies. Bright ribbons tiered in clusters and waterfalls in their hair swirl and swing as their heads move.

At the still center stands Prince Nikonos. No adornment gilds his gold keldi and sleeveless jacket; unrelieved gold silk is all he need wear to mark his status as the younger brother of the king. No one stands close to him, leaving him alone in a sea of laughter. He looks up at a woman with her back to me. Their gazes cross like sparks spitting and, making the gesture a deliberate snub, she greets a woman with an effusive smile and a cheek touched one to the other's.

I have seen that face before, so striking with decorative kohl artistry turning her eyelashes into the spine of wings drawn onto her cheek. The architecture of ribbons in her hair spreads like a fan to frame her round face. She is the young woman who was peering out of the carriage at the Ribbon Market the day Coriander's brother was arrested and Kalliarkos saved me from the same fate. Kalliarkos got into the carriage because she is his sister, and now my father's wife.

Her gaze catches on me as on a hook. She gestures to one of the less glowingly dressed women and pulls her close, a hand curled possessively around the other woman's arm as she speaks to her.

Why have I been so stupid as to stare? Praying the wall will hide me, I head for the far entrance, but before I reach it I am intercepted by the steward whose dour face kills all hope in my heart.

"You stupid country girls." She pinches the underside of my arm so hard I choke down a yelp. "You were expressly told not to walk through the atrium. In these kitchen clothes as well, the worst sort of alley dress. Lady Menoë is displeased you have spoiled the efforts we made to have all the decorations exactly as she wishes. Believe me, you will regret you came to her attention. You have lost your pay for the week. Be in my office at dawn. What is your name?"

"Coriander," I squeak in a voice not my own.

Mercifully she releases me to scurry on my way.

I make it out to the courtyard just as the atrium swells with the excitement and noise of more arrivals. When I glance back, I catch a glimpse of Lord Gargaron accompanied by my father. Unseen musicians sing the famous prayer for victory from the play *The Firebird's Revenge*, which ends with the beleaguered general defeating all his evil foes, although, in typical fashion, he dies just before the messenger, who is his lost son, arrives to announce that the enemy has been utterly vanquished.

I flee past the courtyard and hurry through the bustling servants' wing, where I find a random surface to place the tray. It is a relief to tug the smothering mask off my face, although I leave it pushed atop my hair just in case. A woman waves me down.

"Here, girl, take this to the kitchen."

She hands me a bucket brimming with glistening oysters still in their shells and stinking of brine. I wander dazedly to the kitchens, gripped by the scents of baking bread and roasting fowl, the platters of fruit carved into the shapes of winged dragons and horned lions, and the sculptures of dates and honey built into miniature facsimiles of famous buildings like Saryenia's lighthouse or the Gem Gardens of ancient Saro, where the last emperor was murdered beneath a flowering peach tree.

Steam wafts over me like the breath of the firebird. Smoke from grilling meat stings my eyes. I have no idea what to do with the oysters. Just as I have identified a table where I can stow them and flee, another woman accosts me, takes the bucket, and directs me to a table where girls are chopping onions, leeks, radishes, and cucumbers. I am set to peeling grapes, which a woman arranges in pleasing patterns on lacquered trays. My head is thick and my limbs move as if encased in lead. An anchor weighs down my heart. Seeing my father has set me as into a stormy sea, tugged this way and that but ever caught on the cable that ties me to him.

Can I really save them? Is it possible to unbury the dead?

How long I stand with the smell of food making me ravenous I do not know. But when a procession of young men in formal skirts and jackets appear to carry away the trays of grapes, figs, and cut melons, I wake as from sleep. Fruit marks the last course of the feast. Soon Kalliarkos, Thynos, and Inarsis will make an excuse to leave. If I'm not in the palm grove, Kalliarkos may decide to prove himself by sneaking in to find me, and that would be a disaster.

Fortune favors me. I am marshaled into a group given baked fish wrapped in lettuce to feed the wagoners making ready to return to Saryenia. Outside, some wagons are already leaving in a rumble of dust and noise. I hop onto the back of one as if I am part of the cavalcade and gulp down the delicious fish in its moist wrapping. With such a vast procession departing, the guards take not the least notice of me as I lick the last lingering taste off my fingers.

The wagons roll along the beaten earth lane, their way lit by young men pacing alongside with lanterns. I scan the heavens. The Four Sleeping Sisters have already risen. The moment the shadowy ranks of date palms come into view I jump off. Not until the procession has faded into the night do I run into the palms. To my relief, Kalliarkos and Thynos await me.

Kalliarkos hurries to greet me, grasping my hands and staring so intently at me that I can't take my gaze off his dark eyes. "I thought you were captured! I was about to go in and rescue you!"

A spark of brilliant joy surges up from my weary, grief-stricken heart. I squeeze his fingers a little more tightly, enough to make him really notice how strong my grip is. "That's why I had to hurry. I was afraid you would run in to rescue me and get caught and then I would have to rescue you from your rescue of me."

He laughs, glances at Thynos, and defiantly plants a quick kiss on my mouth. "You never stop competing, do you?"

Thynos coughs.

Kalliarkos releases me but I just stand there. I touch my lips, sure I can feel the pressure of his mouth still lingering.

He grins cockily. "That's the first time I've made you blush."

I cross my arms and lean just a little closer, chin coming up. "You won't manage it again."

"Won't I?" His fingers close on my elbow.

"Come along, children, enough playacting," says Lord Thynos sharply. He leads the horses down the path between the trees, calling over his shoulder. "I can hear Menoë's cavalcade rattling along the road. She never travels anywhere without twenty wagons of furnishings and five carriages of personal servants, and her drivers have specific orders never to let any vehicle pass her household's wagons unless it belongs to the king, the queen, or Prince Nikonos. We need to get ahead of them or we won't reach the city gates until dawn."

Thynos keeps walking, expecting us to follow, but neither Kalliarkos nor I move. His hand braces my arm. Our bodies touch like they are eager to learn more about each other. He examines me in a way that makes me feel he is searching for my every least secret simply because I fascinate and concern him so much.

"Did you see your father? Did you get what you desired or needed from him?"

I don't hesitate. I leap.

"I need your help to do something so dangerous and

entirely forbidden that bringing me here to see my father is trivial in comparison. If we are caught, we will both be executed."

His warm hand slides caressingly down my arm to capture my hand. "What could possibly be that dangerous and forbidden?"

I am both terrified and exhilarated because I have seen something in him tonight that no one else has ever believed in. That I didn't really believe in until right this moment.

"Your uncle entombed my mother and sisters with Lord Ottonor to keep them away from my father forever. I'm going to rescue them. I can only do it with your help."

He lets go of my hand as if I've burned him. Crouching, he buries his head in his hands. A whisper escapes him, words I can't quite hear. He rocks back and forth in some kind of pain.

Out of the darkness, General Inarsis trots into view. "Lord Kalliarkos? Are you injured?"

Kalliarkos jumps up so fast that Inarsis draws a long knife and spins a full circle to fend off attackers, but there is only me.

From the other direction Lord Thynos runs up, sword drawn. "Who has assaulted you?"

"'I am assaulted by impiety, injured by blasphemy,'" cries Kalliarkos. It is a famous line from a tragic play, and he speaks the words with a vehemence that chills me.

Taking a step back, I make ready to run. My rash confession has jeopardized everything.

He grabs Thynos's elbow so aggressively that Thynos looks startled and Inarsis almost leaps between the two men. "Did everyone know except me?"

Thynos looks at the fingers gripping his arm and smiles perilously. "What am I meant to know?"

"Uncle Gar has committed a terrible crime."

If the ground had dropped out from under my feet and I had plunged into the furnace where the unjust are blasted and blinded by flames for eternity, I would have been less surprised. "You believe me?"

Kalliarkos's chest shakes in a false, fierce laugh. "Of course I believe you. It's exactly what he would do."

"What are you two talking about?" demands Lord Thynos.

"Uncle Gar entombed Jes's pregnant mother and her sisters as the oracle's attendants in Lord Ottonor's tomb."

"Ah!" sighs Inarsis. He sheathes his long knife.

Kalliarkos begins to pace, but his gaze sticks to me. "The priest-wardens will not just let us break open the brick door. What do you propose?"

"We'll go in and out the air shaft," I say. "It has to be at night, but I will not be allowed into the City of the Dead on my own."

Kalliarkos considers the plan as if it is a maze. "I can walk in and out at any time without being questioned. Everyone will expect me to have attendants with me."

The world waits to bow at his feet, and he is finally starting to see the power of his rank.

"You're serious." Thynos crosses his arms.

"They both are." Inarsis lowers a suspicious gaze on the other man. "Did you know?"

"Sun of Justice!" Thynos swears. "With the gods as my witness, I knew nothing! Nor would I ever be party to such an act. Bad enough they bury living women in the tombs of every lord and prince and king here in Efea. To entomb a pregnant woman on top of that! It's sickening. It wasn't like this in the old country."

"Then you'll help us, Uncle," says Kalliarkos, his words more command than request.

"You can't free them." Thynos stares Kalliarkos down. "No one can."

This time Kalliarkos does not give way. "Yes, I can. Jes and I can. And we are going to. So your choice is either to aid us or get out of our way."

26

At the speed to which Kalliarkos whips the horses we quickly return to the city. Inarsis directs us to a barracks compound for Efean soldiers, where he obtains the things we need. The gate-wardens at Eternity Gate allow Kalliarkos and Thynos to enter the City of the Dead without a single question, even though it is the middle of the night. Inarsis walks ahead, carrying lamps, and I walk behind, carrying a jug of broth slung over my shoulder and a covered tray that the priests believe is an offering, but which really contains clothing.

The lower paths that lead through the community mausoleums and the Weeping Garden are quiet. A few mourners wait with tomb wreaths and offering trays to set before the bones of their ancestors. Path-wardens bow as we walk past. Partway up the hill Lord Thynos veers off, leaving us.

Out of the darkness Lord Ottonor's tomb rises before us. A single oil lamp burns on the porch, as it is said, "The everlasting flame of memory burns on the strength of a man's fame." Years from now, when his living oracle ceases to speak, offerings will no longer be laid at his door, because his clan has been exiled. Its seal of bricks will be broken, his bones interred in a vase, and the tomb cleaned and anointed for a new inhabitant, one whose fortune may burn brighter and flame burn longer than Ottonor's fortune and fame, marred as they have been by his disgraceful ending.

We proceed around to the oracle's alcove at the back of the tomb. The alcove is a narrow cleft built into the wall where supplicants can kneel and hear the oracle's voice through a tiny opening no bigger than my hand laid flat. I kneel and peer through, but no light burns within. What if Lord Gargaron had them smothered the way tomb servants were back in the old empire?

My pulse roars in my ears. I dare not whisper to see if anyone is alive inside because the oracle is not our ally and might call for the priests.

After making sure no path-wardens are in sight I pull off my linen sheath, fasten on my Fives jacket, and wriggle into a climbing harness used to train fledglings as they learn more advanced skills. Kalliarkos hands me a packet of tapers and flint for light. I climb up on Inarsis's shoulders. My feet balanced on his hands, he hoists me so I can scramble up onto the roof.

From this height I look around. The City of the Dead is a low hill with the four kings' tombs on the central height, each marked by three lamps. Below the kings' tombs lie the palace tombs, each lit with two lamps. Lord Ottonor's tomb lies among the lesser lords' tombs lower down.

The air shaft has a short brick chimney with gaps in it to catch the crosswinds. Its mouth is covered by an iron grate. A smell wafts up, thick with death and tainted with blood.

What if they truly are dead?

Suddenly sparks spin aloft from the far side of the hill. Distant shouts stir the slumberous night. Thynos's diversion is in progress.

The grate shifts easily. A whisper of sound alerts me to movement inside the tomb.

Faintly I hear a woman say, "That's right, Doma. Breathe. You have given birth before."

Mother is alive.

Heart racing, I swing my legs over the shaft and feel out the courses of brick. The opening is exceedingly small, no doubt to discourage tomb robbers. While Kalliarkos stands watch, Inarsis grounds himself as my anchor and lowers me into the tomb. I fend off the walls with elbows and knees, scraping my way down. It's a very tight fit. When my feet touch the floor I slip out of the harness and give a pair of tugs to show I am in.

Invisible in the darkness, fabric flutters across my left hand like the brush of wings. A cardamom-scented breath hisses along my cheek.

"What unwanted demon's shadow troubles our holy rest?"

Its raspy voice makes me jump with a flare of such panic that for an instant I can't think. Then, fumbling, I unwrap one of the oiled linen twists, strike a spark on flint, and light the taper. A woman at my elbow winces back, shielding her eyes. She is not young, as newly entombed oracles are meant to be. She is so old that her hair is as white as bone. But she is highborn Patron through and through. Her painted hands bear no calluses. This woman has never done a day's labor in her very long life.

"Get out, foul shadow! Be banished! Return to your flesh and disturb us not."

Her burning stare unsettles my fixed determination. Oracles are sacred. We honor their connection to the gods. But she looks more than a little crazy, trembling with fear and indignation. She's in my way and I won't let anyone stop me, not even the gods' voice.

I dodge around her and stride to the arch that opens into the central chamber. The taper burns hotly in my hand, its light revealing all.

Maraya sits on the floor, bracing up our mother.

Mother is ashy and drained of vigor, her body slumped.

Coriander kneels in the gloom beyond Maraya. How has *she* come to rest in a Patron tomb? Her face is streaked with smears of drying blood. She holds strips of torn linen, which she is plaiting to make pads to soak up blood.

Cook crouches between Mother's spread legs. Her hands are blotched with stains. The taper's flame is not bright enough to illuminate color but I can smell the overpowering scent. My mother lies in a seeping puddle of blood.

A dark globe crowns between her legs.

Cook says, "Hold your breath, Doma! You must hold your breath and push."

"It is all for nothing," murmurs my mother in a ragged tone that shatters my heart. "The baby is dead."

Maraya can barely speak through tears. "There's another baby coming, Mama. You must push."

"It is better to die than chance the child will live in this tomb. You cannot wish such a death upon her. You cannot!" Despair ravages Mother's voice.

From behind, the oracle brushes past me, a dagger in her hand. "Pregnancy defiles the tomb! You have brought death upon us!"

She lunges for my mother.

Slamming my shoulder into her, I shove her sideways, then punch her in the chest. The dagger is knocked loose. I scoop up the knife as the oracle stumbles over a naked newborn on the floor. My breath floods in bursts as I gape at the tiny, empty body. The poor little thing, given no chance to breathe, no spark to brighten its souls into life.

290

The oracle paws at the lifeless infant, cradles it lovingly in her skinny arms. "They tore him away from my breast and killed him. Why torment me with this memory of the past?"

Our scuffle has drawn attention. Maraya, Cook, and Coriander all stare at me, mouths open and eyes wide, too stunned by my appearance to speak.

A new contraction shudders through Mother but she does not even try to ride it. Her self-soul has fled her body, leaving her weak and apathetic. The thought of my mother dying from despair banishes every point of confusion in my mind.

"Mother, you have to push!" I say in the sharpest voice I have. "You have to give birth to the baby and the afterbirth. Do you hear me, Mother?" I am shouting because if I do not shout I will dissolve into wretched misery.

Her eyes roll back in her head as if she is passing out, but then they steady, and they track, and they find me. "Jessamy?"

"Jes!" cries Maraya. She can't release Mother so she shakes her head over and over, blinking as if she expects me to vanish. "Is it really you?"

Cook squints into the light. "Doma Jessamy? How can you be here?"

Mother's hand tightens on Maraya's arm. "Did they trap you too, my darling Jessamy? Or is this your shadow who comes to bid good-bye?"

I kneel beside her, holding the light by my face. "I am not

a shadow. I am here to get you out of the tomb. Coriander, help Merry hold her up so it will be easier for the baby to drop."

"That's right, listen to Doma Jessamy," says Cook briskly. Maraya and Coriander lift Mother until she is in a crouch, supported by them. "Merciful Hayiyin, Mistress of the Sea, let this prayer unknot a birth that has grown tangled." She slips her hands between Mother's legs.

"Mother! Push!"

My words hit like spears. Awareness sharpens her gaze. A contraction rolls through. She holds her breath and pushes as Cook massages her below.

The baby's head emerges, its cap of black hair smeary with slime and blood. With the gods as my witness I smell life amid this blood, not death.

"You can manage one more push, Doma!"

Mother sucks in a breath, tenses, pushes. The baby's shoulders and little body slip free. Cook catches the newborn and gently places it on Mother's chest.

"Here is your daughter, Doma."

The baby lies so still that I am not sure it is breathing, but the umbilical cord pulses. Mother's eyes are closed and for a moment of sheer blind terror I am not sure she is breathing either. Then her lips part and a broken whisper emerges.

"It was the lotus flower potion the priests drugged us with to make sure we could not fight or run. Infants haven't the strength to survive it, for inside me they must have sipped as at the cup I was forced to drink. I wish I had died with them. Then I would not have to know." Some wicked creature's shadow has slipped inside her and means to swell and swell until the last of Mother is pinched into oblivion. "I made secret offerings to the Mother of All...."

"Doma! That's an Efean superstition!"

Mother seems not to hear Cook's remonstration. "She has turned Her back on us because we turned our backs on Her. My poor children. All dead."

I look past her and see a limp figure sprawled at the foot of the bier. How anyone can sleep through such a crisis I cannot understand. Then I realize it is Amaya, tangled in a shroud. My whole body clenches as I struggle not to cry out. Oh, terrible, terrible!

I cannot see for tears stinging my eyes. Why did I mock her when she was fated to suffer this horrible end?

Stricken, I stand there for the longest time. I don't know what to say, or how to say it.

"Here it comes," says Cook. With another contraction, the red veiny mass of the placenta drops into her waiting hands. The baby makes a sound, echoed a moment later by Maraya choking down a sob of relief.

Just as the flame from the lit taper is about to singe my fingers I see an unlit lamp in an alcove. "Coriander, bring that lamp over here."

The last spark from the taper is enough to light its wick.

Lamplight flares so powerfully after the sour yellow glow of the taper that my eyes water. I pass the knife through the flame several times and hand it to Cook, who cuts and ties the cord.

"Give me the baby," I say, for everyone is as silent as if we are already dead and only waiting for the dust to cover us. "Coriander, hold the light."

The oracle is moaning, rocking my dead brother in her thin arms. Cook starts wiping up the blood. Mother's eyes close; she is still breathing but I fear she has passed out from blood loss and exhaustion. I cut off a length of Mother's rumpled shroud and dry off the baby, then swaddle her in the last bit of clean cloth.

She has a flat cap of black hair and it is likely her eyes will resemble Father's more than Mother's. Beyond that it is impossible to say anything about her except that my heart expands until all my souls glow with love for this frail little spark. Her lips are perfect. Her cheeks are puffy. Her eyes are open and they fix on me. When we look at each other, we see something that can never be taken from us: our sisterhood.

Maraya presses a hand against my side to make sure I am solid. Her voice is so shaky it terrifies me. "It's really you, Jes! I thought I was dreaming when I first saw you but it's really you."

I crush her hand in mine. "Yes, it's me. What happened?"

Tears cloud Merry's face. "We were told we were being given the honor of sitting the overnight vigil at Lord Ottonor's

294

tomb. But when we were taken to the temple they fed us lotus flower syrup to dull our minds and afterward the priests netted our flesh with shadows that compelled us to walk to the tomb."

Thinking of the way they lurched along makes me shudder. "Where's Bettany?"

"Mother didn't trust the Garon stewards. She thought it best for one of us girls to stay behind to oversee what became of the servants. Since the man in charge couldn't tell the difference between Coriander and Bettany, they switched places. Mother was so broken when Father repudiated her. Yet she worries about what will happen to the people who depend on her."

"Of course she does. What happened to Amaya?"

"When we woke up from the lotus syrup, the tomb was bricked in. I was so frightened, Jes!" She pants a little as she remembers. "But there was a fine tray of food. Naturally Amiable grabbed at it first. She couldn't resist the candied almonds even though they are supposed to be given to the oracle. I wish we had fed them to the old witch, because someone poisoned the food offering."

A dreadful gaping hollow opens in the pit of my chest. "She's dead, isn't she? Oh, stupid Amiable! Stupid, stupid Amaya."

"How could she have known? How could any of us have guessed this would happen?"

"To entomb unwilling servants, and a pregnant woman among them! And then poison the offering to make sure they die! He wanted to make sure you were all truly gone."

"Who do you think did this, Jes?"

I glance around but he has no spies to overhear. "Lord Gargaron."

She shuts her eyes, then opens them, nodding. "Yes, I see. He wanted Father without encumbrances. Can you really get us out?"

"Of course I can. I'm lifting you all out the air shaft." I smile grimly. In my mind's eye I see the Rings opening to the victory tower. Lord Gargaron can't ever admit to what he did, so he can't demand they be pushed back into the tomb. It will be easy to hide them from him because he thinks they are all dead from the poisoned food. The baby stirs in my arm and makes a crooning sound. Over by the bier, as in answer, Amaya mewls like a kitten.

I tuck the baby in Maraya's arm and hurry over. Vomit stains the front of Amaya's shroud and she has peed and voided her bowels. Her hair is slimy, like she thrashed in her own spew. The stink of her makes me gag. But she is breathing. When I lift her head and shoulders, she whimpers.

"Oh, my stomach hurts so badly. I need a bath and a massage. Why is this bed so hard? I don't like this. Make it better." Her eyes stay closed because she simply assumes someone will make her comfortable. I set her down less gently than I had picked her up and wipe my grimy hands on the driest corner of the shroud she wears.

"Just stay here, Amaya. Don't move."

Her eyes pop open. "Jessamy! What are you doing here?"

"Rescuing you, of course!"

She wraps her arms over her stomach and rocks in obvious discomfort. "Can you please hurry? I don't want to be here anymore."

I don't even mock her whining tone. We can't get out of here quickly enough. I light a new taper from the burning lamp and hurry past the others. In the oracle's room it takes me a moment to register what is missing.

Both rope and harness are gone. They have pulled up our means of escape and trapped me here.

27

"**L**ord Kalliarkos," I call as loudly as I dare. Silence is my only reply.

"Kal!"

Fortune save me! What if I've been an utter fool? No Patron prince could ever care for a mule like me. If Thynos and Inarsis were in on the plot all along, they would agree to help and then trap me here, like a kick in the face to let me know I got above myself. They are probably laughing right now as they walk out Eternity Gate and leave me buried.

Quite out of nowhere a sharp edge pricks me just under the ribs. Coriander has come up beside me, holding the lit lamp in one hand and the knife in the other.

"I'm going out first." She holds the knife like she knows how to use it. Flame glints on the blade's polished surface. The metal is incised with the mark of the winged phoenix, the badge of the royal house. "You're not leaving me in here."

My throat is tight and my heart is pounding, yet I slowly raise both hands as in supplication, but really so I can defend myself if she tries to stab me. "That's right," I say evenly, "you'll go first. I just need your help to lift me up to the shaft so I can climb out and get the rope."

Under my breath I murmur a prayer that I have not been duped. He doesn't want to be like the other nobles. He told me so.

Coriander moves closer. "Did you scheme with your twin so you two wouldn't get trapped here?"

"I didn't scheme with anyone!"

"Then how did you know we were inside? We were drugged and shrouded! No one knew."

I'm so angry at the accusation that I poke her right in the chest. "I recognized my mother through the shroud. That's how I knew. Don't you dare accuse me! Do you believe I would ever have anything to do with burying my mother and sisters in a tomb?"

A sneer twists her mouth. In this place she need not hide her feelings behind a mask: she is just as insolent as her brother. "Everyone knew you were your father's favorite. The one he took to the army camp with him. The one he treated like the son he never had. You and he came out of this the best, didn't you? He becomes a general and you get to run the Fives."

"He didn't know either!"

"Of course you would defend him."

"He never whipped you! He isn't a cruel man."

"Even the kindest Patron is cruel, Doma. They all walk on the bones of dead Efeans and never give it a thought."

"He didn't know this was going to happen! He's the one who sent me to get you out. He loves her, Coriander. You know he would never condemn her to this!"

To my relief her expression softens and she lowers the knife. "It's true I can't imagine him doing this to Doma Kiya."

Can I grab the knife from her? As if she guesses what I'm thinking she takes a step back.

"Why did you agree to trade places with Bettany?" I study her stance. Her hand is steady but if I rush in I might take her by surprise.

"Doma Kiya promised if I would sit the vigil and let Bettany supervise the house until we got back that she would speak to people she knew and see if she could get my brother freed from prison."

"My mother said that?" This is not the first time I've been knocked off my feet by an example of my mother's knowing and doing things I am unaware of. Her string of connections seems far more extensive than I ever guessed. Perhaps I too can find other allies, more trustworthy people than Thynos and Inarsis. That Kalliarkos might be in on their plot is a thought I can't stomach. They must have fooled him too.

"Sitting a nasty vigil seemed a small enough thing to do to save him," Coriander says. Her brow wrinkles with pain and agitation. "He's going to be executed."

"Is he really in prison for murder?"

"Yes." She isn't even ashamed.

"You want to free a murderer?"

Her contempt glints more brightly than the blade. "What the king calls murder is what others call truth. Anyway, what do you care? Lord Gargaron is a murderer eight times over if we can't get out. He's far from the only one. How many Efeans have died in the last hundred years as Patrons enrich themselves on our lands? How many Patron women have been entombed in this ugly City of the Dead because Patron lords wish to rid themselves of inconvenient girls?"

"Oracles and their servants go to the tombs willingly."

She snorts. "You're such a fool. Girls raised from infancy to believe this is their destiny? I don't call that willing." She takes an aggressive step toward me. "How are you getting us out?"

I gesture toward the ceiling. "Through the air shaft."

"Do you expect me to believe that? We can't reach the shaft and we can't climb it without assistance. You're lying."

"I have accomplices outside with a rope. They lowered me in."

"Who would dare help a person like you break into a tomb?"

I'm not sure it's true anymore, and yet I cannot fathom that he would abandon me here. "Lord Kalliarkos."

She cocks her head to one side, almost laughing. "Is he your lover? After your father told you never to speak to him again?"

"Yes," I lie, hoping it isn't a lie, that Kal is still out there.

She nods. This is a story that makes sense to her. "I'd have defied them too, just to show them! All right. I'll help. But your mother and Cook won't fit up the shaft."

Hearing the words forces me to acknowledge the ugly truth. Mother and Cook both are too big. No, I won't give up! There must be a way out of this maze. First I have to see if Kalliarkos has truly abandoned me, but the thought of discovering that he has makes me almost afraid to try to get out.

She nudges me hard enough that I have to take a step. "If my brother was free, he knows people from the masons' guild who can break into a tomb and get your mother out. If he was free."

"No one can break into a tomb without the priests seeing."

Her sneer reasserts itself as a mask of derision. "You think you know so much because you speak and act like a Patron. You know the lies they tell you but you don't know the truth."

Hands on hips, I lean assertively toward her. "Insult me all you want, but I know how to climb that air shaft!"

With a grunt of laughter she sets down both lamp and knife. "That's true enough."

I show her how to brace her hands on her knees. We practice her taking my weight on her shoulders until I am sure she can keep her balance. The gods are merciful because she is strong, and we are both determined. When she tremblingly straightens to her full height I can just snag the bottom of the shaft. I feel along the old brickwork for any sort of handhold. Fortunately it gives me a finger's width of purchase.

She cups my feet in her palms and, shaking hard, lifts me as I finger-climb my way up the shaft. The coarse grain chafes my skin. My nose scrapes the wall, drawing tears, but I keep going until I can't go farther. I push off her hands to give me momentum to arm-climb up enough to get my knees wedged in.

Someone has torn my arms out of their sockets and crammed them back in again but I can't stop now. Back and knees pressed against opposite sides of the shaft brace me; my arms have a moment to rest. Sweat breaks down my back. Grit tickles in my nostrils. I dare not sneeze.

Bracing and pushing, I creep my way upward one grunting exhalation at a time. This is not different from climbing a blind shaft, just tighter and more fearsome, and I'll die and my mother and sisters will die if I fall. Tears flood from the dust sifting into my eyes. My upward movement is so agonizingly slow but I can't fall.

I will save them. There must be a way if I can remain patient and stubborn.

At last my head breaches the top of the shaft and I hook myself over. I sprawl forward with my face pressed onto the tile and my lungs on fire.

Men's voices rise from nearby, loud as clarions in the night's hush. "Did you try to ignite the tombs to burn a way in?"

"No, my lords," says the hero of Marsh Shore in the tone of a man pretending to be a humble servant. "I am here as escort to my lord master, who visits the tomb."

"Where is he, then? You people always have some excuse when you are about your thievery."

Cautiously I shift my head but do not otherwise move. Partway down the path two priest-wardens confront General Inarsis. One carries a lamp and the other holds an edged staff. Inarsis stands with arms at his sides and palms forward in a posture I often see Commoner men using to display that they are harmless.

"My apologies, Your Holinesses. He is taking a piss."

A hand brushes my arm so unexpectedly I flinch. Kalliar-kos rolls up alongside me.

He's here! He didn't abandon me.

Such a wave of relief hits me that I press my face into his shoulder for comfort. His fingers tangle in mine, our hands warm against each other.

He whispers, "I heard you shouting. I was afraid something was wrong so we pulled up the rope so I could come in after you. Then the wardens came. I have to interrupt them before they arrest Inarsis."

I shudder, and his hand tightens reassuringly on mine.

"They are alive but we have to get them out fast. The food and drink is poisoned."

An exhalation of shock gusts from him. "Blasphemy upon blasphemy!"

"My mother won't fit through the shaft," I add. "We have to find another way to get her and Cook out. That day you followed me to the Ribbon Market there was a young man arrested. He was taken to the king's prison. His sister, Coriander, is one of our servants. She is trapped inside too. She claims her brother knows people who can break into the tomb. You have to get him out of prison and see if it's true."

"How can I get a man out of the king's prison?" he hisses. He sounds angry. "I can't just walk in and demand they free him."

"Of course you can. You're a prince. Act like one."

"You think it's so easy just because of my birth? Everything I do is watched and measured."

"What are you really afraid of?" I retort, made bold by the intimacy of him lying against me exactly as if we were lovers. The night, the danger, and our desperation make our closeness sharp and vivid.

"Of becoming like them," he whispers, his tone so dark it makes me shiver.

"You aren't like them because we are already fighting back."

My fingers brush the bare skin of his neck and the lobe of his ear. A spark of pure sensation flashes through my body like a wave off the sea breaking over me.

He sucks in a breath. "Jes!"

"Go!" I say. "The Rings are opening. The time is now. If you need more help seek a man named Polodos at the Least-Hill Inn."

Below, the lamp-warden booms a command. "You are under arrest for trespassing in the City of the Dead with the intention of desecrating a holy tomb. If you come quietly you'll be given the mercy of a quick execution rather than torture."

"I will return, I promise you on my honor as a man," murmurs Kalliarkos against my cheek. "The rope and harness are up here on the roof. The clothing and jug are below. Wait for me."

When he releases my hand my fingers feel so empty. He drops off the edge and hits with a loud-enough thump that the wardens exclaim. A moment later he appears on the other side of the tomb, walking with the knowledge that the world must give way before him. Both wardens make a deep obeisance.

"What trouble are you giving my servant?" Kalliarkos demands.

"My lord, criminals and troublemakers set a fire on the far side of the tombs. We are commanded to sweep everyone out while we search for the culprits. Our apologies, my lord."

"Good Goat! Are you saying I am not safe here among the

holy dead? Have you wardens shirked your duties?" His tone so closely matches that of the Angry Prince in *The Hide of the Ox* that I wonder if he is acting a part or if he has finally found his resolve.

For all Kalliarkos is a palace-born lord, the priests have their own authority separate from the court. "We must escort you to the gate, my lord, by order of our superiors."

"I am outraged by this interruption of my peaceful communion with the memory of a Fives adversary I have long admired and studied, for I must suppose you did not know Lord Ottonor was an Illustrious in his youth." His curt disdain makes me smile.

He allows them to escort him and Inarsis away. Lamplight bobs out across the necropolis as the wardens trawl the grounds for interlopers. I stretch to ease the throbbing pain in my muscles. So much for my brilliant plan. I have to believe he will do as he promised. Yet the truth is that I trust him because of the way he snared my fingers in his. That is the worst reason of all to trust, but my bitter heart will not stop singing its recklessly giddy song.

I lean over the shaft. Gilded by lamplight, Coriander stares up into a darkness in which she cannot see me. "I'm coming down in a moment. Stand away."

I secure the climbing rope around the air shaft and slip on the harness, then rappel down the tomb wall to the outside alcove to gather up the bundled clothing and the jug.

I lower it all down to Coriander. Although it is a risk to have the rope tied around the air shaft, where someone might see it from outside, I need to be able to show Coriander she has a way out in order to ensure her cooperation. As I descend hand over hand down the narrow shaft, my shoulders bumping the bricks, a muffled cry drifts eerily out of the tomb like the lament of the dead. Its timbre agitates me until I realize it is a newborn's startled wail. The baby's cry ceases just as I reach the floor.

Cook speaks in a voice of such calm cheerfulness that I marvel at her generous courage. "That's right, Doma. See how strongly she suckles!"

"What happened up there?" Coriander's gaze sears me. I never understood that her blank servant's expression hid so much dislike.

"We have to keep quiet until Lord Kalliarkos returns. He's going to free your brother."

"I should just climb the rope and leave," she says, chin jutting forward as if to dare me to forbid it.

"You still can. But I hope you will wait and help me get the others out."

She frowns at her hands, then glances into the central chamber. "For Doma Kiya's sake I will."

Maraya continues to support Mother against the stone bier. She has rallied enough to become absorbed in the baby suckling at her breast.

Cook now has the knife and is cutting the afterbirth into small pieces. "Mistress, you must eat a bit of placenta to strengthen yourself."

"I'm too tired to eat," says Mother in a murmur that dies away as her eyes flutter closed.

Maybe I gasp at this sign of her intense weakness. Coriander touches me on the arm with a flash of unexpected compassion, then pulls back her hand and rubs it over her scalp. I wonder who gave her the scars on her head.

"How did my mother rescue you?" I ask.

"That is not your story to know since you never bothered to ask before now." She sets the lamp beside the oracle's chest and like a tomb robber opens it and begins rifling through its contents.

Chastened, I go into the central chamber.

The oracle huddles in a corner, still rocking the dead infant in her arms. I cannot forget the words she whispered to me any more than I could forget scars on my body. Even now she mumbles phrases that make no sense and yet flow with a poem's music.

"The stars fall from the sky as blooms of fire...the infant bloomed with blood under the knife...the bird-haunted ship carries his sleeve of roses away from me...hope withers in a dying flower...poison has killed the flower that bloomed brightest...."

Maraya grabs hold of me as soon as I am close enough.

Her shaky voice worries me. "I thought I was dreaming when I saw you before, Jes, because then you vanished again."

"I am really here, Merry."

My voice jolts Mother's attention.

"Jessamy?" She looks so worn and broken that I want to pour all my determination into her.

Kneeling, I press my face against her sweaty cheek. "You must drink some of this broth and eat, just as Cook tells you. We're escaping tomorrow. We have to hide here tonight."

"Hiding" sounds better than "trapped."

"Is Esladas coming?" The way her voice quavers cuts my heart to pieces.

To lie to the ill or dying when they know you are lying is the worst kind of dishonesty. "No."

"First Lord Gargaron poisoned Lord Ottonor to take Esladas away from me. Then your father threw us away." She begins weeping bitterly.

"Mother, he has to fight in the war. Efea depends on the courage of its soldiers."

Her eyes are all shadow. Blood is smeared along her upper lip, and a scratch reddens her left cheek near her ear. Yet for the first time, as her sobs fade, she speaks almost normally. "How like your father you sound, Jessamy. You always did."

"He couldn't defy Lord Gargaron," I add.

"Oh, Jessamy." Her gentle gaze makes me love her so much. I would do anything to protect her, she who has always protected me. "That is sweet of you to say even if we know it is not true."

"Of course it's true!" Maraya wrinkles her nose as at a bad smell but I forge on because I must give Mother the heart to live. "When he found out you'd been trapped here he sent me to rescue you. Everything is going as planned. Now you must eat."

She allows Cook to feed her moist pieces of raw afterbirth. The baby loses hold of her breast and smacks her tiny lips. Tenderly Mother helps her find the nipple again. I pray that this frail newborn spark will fasten Mother's self and shadow and heart to the earth.

I crouch beside Amaya. "Amiable, I have salty broth to settle your stomach."

She claws for the jug. I trickle a little down her throat. At first she coughs; then she swallows the liquid greedily just as she probably gulped down the candied almonds.

"That's enough for now," I say sternly. I offer the jug to Maraya. Amaya doesn't protest, just sinks back onto the floor.

"Are we really getting out of the tomb?" Maraya asks after she has drunk.

"Yes!" I don't tell her that I can save her and Amaya and Coriander but I have to leave Mother and Cook behind. I don't say that Mother might die anyway from blood loss and despair, that she desperately needs a healer, food, rest, and comfort. Maraya knows it too.

Pitchers in the entry chamber contain wash water, for the priests do not wish the oracle and her servants to live in filth. Coriander refuses to wash Amaya so I am left to pull her nasty stinking shroud off, wipe her clean, and then dress her in the humble clothing I've brought.

She complains the whole time in her whiniest voice. "Why do I have to wear this coarse linen sheath, Jes? It's too long. Why is it so dark? I want another lamp."

I am pretty sure she is still too delirious to realize where she is. Her breath smells of bile made more sickening by being mingled with the ghastly scent of the sweet lotus potion. I pant in shallow bursts to avoid the stench. When I'm done, Coriander and I carry her to the oracle's bed. The stench permeates here too, but sachets of spices and herbs hung around the bed to keep it free of bugs leaven the air somewhat. Amaya curls up, hands pressed to her belly.

Washing and getting dressed in ordinary clothing cheers up everyone more than I expected. Maraya and I settle Mother on the bed beside Amaya. Then I go back to examine Lord Ottonor's bier. The wooden lid of his coffin is sealed with wax sigils molded and melted to prevent the spark-animated corpse from clawing its way out before the spark fades. By lamplight we study the lacquered offering tray with its poisoned morsels arranged pleasingly in decorative bowls and tiny ceramic platters. It looks so tempting that I almost pick up one of the artful little seed-cakes.

"Merry, aren't oracles buried young to keep a lord's name alive longer?"

"Do you know what else is odd, Jes?" I almost weep to hear the crisp tone so characteristic of Maraya before all of this happened, the one that means she's sorting through her archive of knowledge. "After Amaya grabbed the candied almonds we took the tray away from her, greedy pig! Cook offered the food to the oracle because she is supposed to eat first. But she refused to touch anything. She just watched Amaya like a vulture. After a little while Amiable got sick and vomited."

"As if the oracle feared poison."

"It's why the rest of us didn't eat right away. Cook made us wait for the oracle. Although she didn't mean to, the oracle saved us." Maraya glances toward the oracle's chamber, where Mother and Amaya sleep while Cook cradles the baby. Coriander is going through the treasures she has picked out of the oracle's chest: a tidy pile of expensive silk clothing, pewter utensils and cups, and a trove of wristlets, anklets, and necklaces strung of beads, pearls, and polished stones. "I wonder what Father's new wife is like."

"Very rich. Young. Palace-born. Her grandmother is Princess Berenise."

"Truly? Princess Berenise is the younger sister of Kliatemnos the Fourth and his queen, Serenissima the Fourth."

"What do you know about her?" I try to keep my

passionate curiosity from my voice. Knowing more about Kalliarkos's grandmother will teach me more about him.

"In her youth Princess Berenise was married to King Sokorios of Saro-Urok. I can tell you his exact degree of relationship to our own royal family if you want."

"No, no, that's not necessary."

Her voice lightens because now she is trawling through the dusty old Archives that often seem more real to her than the sisters chattering around her. "King Sokorios either died in battle or was murdered by his chief rival. It depends on which account you read and what faction the chronicle supports. They all tell a different story to make their side look good and the others look bad. After his death she married Menos Garon of Clan Garon. That is how Clan Garon became elevated to Garon Palace, through her status. She gave birth to one son. He served in the army, married a noblewoman from old Saro, sired Lady Menoë and Lord Kalliarkos, and died in battle. Gargaron is her husband's brother's son."

Voices float from outside as a party of loud men argue in the distance.

"Hush! Coriander, blow out your lamp. We can't let them see light in here!"

I rip several strips of cloth and hurry over to the oracle. She shrinks back as I loom over her. I must be ruthless even though she is just an old woman. If she screams, they'll know we're alive and Lord Gargaron will find out that his poisoned food did not work. She easily gives in as I tie her hands behind her back and gag her. This must be what they teach the girls raised in closed rooms to prepare them for a life in the tomb: to accept what others tell you to do without questioning.

Merry wraps the dead infant in cloth and sets him in the oracle's lap. "Maybe our poor brother's body will comfort her. How strange that she holds him as if he is her own. I wonder if she had a baby once? But how could she if she was raised in the temple to be an oracle?"

I blow out my lamp and we feel our way into the oracle's chamber to sit huddled together by the bed. Amaya snores noisily, burps in her sleep, then farts with a long gassy whistle.

Maraya shudders against me, and I can't tell if she is silently giggling or shaking with grief. I'm so grateful Amaya is alive that I can't laugh.

When Maraya speaks I am surprised by how much anger heats her whispered words.

"Father could have sneaked us all onto a ship. It's a lie to say he had no choice, that he wasn't swayed by ambition. If he really wanted to, he could get work as a soldier in a mercenary company like the Shipwrights. Mother could have taken in washing or sold goods in a market. We could have sailed away together to another land."

"Yes, that's a lovely story, Merry, but it's not that simple."

"It seems simple to me!" She shivers as with a fever. "The worst thing was waking up. It took me a while to understand

that we were trapped inside...and then I heard scratching...
and I was afraid the corpse was trying to claw out of the coffin." She chokes on the memory.

"Hush," I whisper. "The coffin is sealed. Even if the borrowed spark hasn't died, the flesh can't get out past the seals."

A long silence follows. Merry's breathing deepens and slows. I need to sleep but I am wide awake listening to the baby's fretting.

"Cook," I whisper. "Why are you here? Why didn't you leave with the other servants?"

"I could not leave your mother, Doma Jessamy, not when she was so distraught. Years ago she saved me from a bad place. I owe her my life, so obligation binds me to her. If the gods have led me to this place, then I am content with it."

"But you're a Patron, and she's a Commoner."

"I am a woman, and so is she. Now rest, Doma Jessamy. We need your strength."

My eyes close as I allow myself to relax. The infant whimpers. Mother wakes and nurses the baby while Cook coaxes her to take more placenta and broth. Afterward Mother weeps wearily, the grief seeping out of her like blood from an oozing wound. Maraya crawls onto the bed to comfort her. They all sleep while I stretch out on the floor.

Again all grows quiet, a perfect stillness. In the half-aware state between sleep and waking I sense the stone's contours beneath my legs, I breathe along its shadows, I feel through my skin the quivering of each vibration that stirs the earth beneath the tomb. Stone has a shadow and a secret name too, and maybe even a self.

A scratching like fingernails dragged listlessly along wood shudders me into full heart-pounding alertness. It sounds exactly as if it is coming from inside the coffin.

Is the body of Lord Ottonor trying to claw out?

My breathing squeezes tight as I pray it is only a rat. Yet rats might swarm at us out of the dark and gnaw out our eyes before we can wake up.

Scratch scratch scratch.

I wish I had the knife. What if Coriander murders us in our sleep? No, she loves Mother too. We are all here because Mother saved us.

Finally the scratching stops. A low moan jolts me until I realize it is the wind in the shaft. I lie still for the longest time. At last with the hum of the wind as my lullaby I let go of my anxious thoughts and sink, praying that nothing attacks me while I sleep.

28

The horns of dawn wake me from a sound sleep. Morning light gleams through the tiny gap in the wall through which the oracle speaks. A man is coming up the path singing a familiar song about a sailor going to meet the lover who will wash his clothes just the way he likes.

Maraya leaps up. "That is Polodos!"

She hastens with her rolling gait past the sleeping oracle in the central chamber and into the entry chamber. I catch up as she kneels by the slit where offering trays can be slid into the tomb. Footsteps crunch up to the porch. She whistles the melody as in answer.

His intake of breath is sharp. "Doma Maraya?"

"Steward Polodos." Her tremulous smile seems the brightest object in the tomb, the source of all light and hope.

"It is true," he whispers in a raspy voice worthy of the tragic theater. "Buried in the tomb. Blasphemy against the gods! You must think I abandoned you, Maraya."

She presses an open hand against the wall. "I knew you never would, not if you knew. How could you possibly have guessed?"

"I am here now, my dearest Maraya. If I must walk to this tomb every day for the rest of my life I will do so. I will not hesitate again, as I did in speaking to your father about us. You deserve better than my timid promises."

The adoration in his voice stuns me. My single-mindedness has blinded me to everything going on in the house.

Embarrassment makes me snap. "Did you see Lord Kalliarkos?"

"Doma Jessamy!" His tone flattens as he realizes he and Maraya are not alone. "I apologize for not believing you when we met here that night. I must say that to have a lord walk into the Least-Hill Inn took me aback for it is not the sort of place—"

"None of that matters," I interrupt. "What is the plan?"

"When Lord Kalliarkos told me about the poisoned food, I agreed to bring an offering tray so you would have something to eat and drink. As for the rest, I do not know. He was arguing with his advisers over a matter they considered too dangerous to undertake."

"Do you think they will betray us to Lord Gargaron?"

"The minds of palace men are closed to me. Whatever happens here, we will be beholden to them and they will demand an accounting. Beware, for they are not generous men."

"Are you a generous man, Steward Polodos?" How I wish I could see his expression to judge the worth of his promises.

Maraya leans a cheek against the bricks as if against his chest. "He is a patient, humble, and courageous man."

"Doma Maraya, I do not deserve such praise, and especially not from you, for I have done nothing to aid you when you were most in need."

Maraya tilts her head as she does when she is blushing. "You are here now. That is all that matters."

The march of the priests on their morning rounds nags at my ears so I break into their cooing. "Sing the offering prayers so the priests won't be suspicious. After that you can come around to the oracle's alcove and talk to Merry."

I hear him tap his chest twice, just as if my father had given the order. He intones the ritual prayer. "'Oh merciful dawn, light of justice, rise over the pure waters of the afterlife. Slake the thirst of the just as they pass through the curtain between this life and the other world.'"

The rope pulley scrapes, and a lacquered box appears from under the wall in the offering trough. I open it to find a feast of delicacies pleasingly arranged in decorated bowls and cups: ripe figs, chopped dates, almonds, walnuts rolled in honey and seeds, bread and barley beer, a wholesome lentil stew, and poached fish garnished with ginger. Polodos prays loudly for the judge in the court of the dead to bring a judgment of peace for all who are good-hearted and diligent.

We take the tray to the oracle's chamber. Amaya is still curled on the bed but sits up eagerly. The baby is nursing. Cook has wrapped Mother's hair in a band of linen to keep it out of the way.

"Figs are your favorite, Doma." Cook presses a fig into Mother's hand, but Mother lets it drop and sags listlessly.

"The lentil stew smells delicious," Cook says more desperately.

"Let me." Cook makes way so I can sit down. "Mother, you must eat so your milk will come in."

"Jessamy? Is that you?" She regards me as if she cannot quite recall who I am. Raising a hand she touches my face but after a moment slumps back.

I hold her hand, shocked by how weak she is.

Cook murmurs, "Ever since Captain Esladas left she has fallen farther into this cloud of confusion. There is a black dog on her shoulders eating into her head."

"We have to get her out of here," I say, but when I look at the air shaft my courage wilts.

Having finished his prayers, Polodos comes around to kneel in the oracle's alcove, where he can without suspicion pretend to be asking for a sliver of wisdom or a glimpse into his future. Maraya boldly sits on the oracle's stool. The gap in the wall is just wide enough to slide a hand through. She reaches in. I pretend not to hear their whispered declarations.

Amaya snivels about her aching belly as she gorges on figs and dates and bread.

"If your belly hurts maybe you shouldn't eat so much," I say.

"But I'm hungry!"

I turn away to see Coriander eyeing the food.

"Eat what you want, and afterward feed the oracle."

"Why should we feed her?" she objects.

"It isn't fair she be punished for what others did to us. Gag her after so she can't call out to the priests."

Getting food into Mother takes half the morning. Never in my life has Mother not nursed others, coaxed smiles out of tears, and settled every sour dispute in the household. She made Father laugh and encouraged him to sing in his melodious voice. She convinced him to give us rides on his back when we were little. When we were older she flattered him into tutoring us in reading and writing. By such means he, a man without sisters whose mother died when he was young, got to know his daughters.

Now her bloody smell permeates the chamber. It stinks like the life draining out of her. When she closes her eyes I press a hand to her chest to make sure she is sleeping, not dead. I am so afraid she will die and be buried in this Saroese tomb forever. She doesn't belong here. We girls have never belonged in the

Patrons' world, although we pretended we did. The harsh truth surfaces like a sea serpent rising out of the ocean to devour proud ships sailing the wide water.

As Polodos makes his farewells I interrupt. "How soon is Lord Kalliarkos coming?"

"Doma, I do not know. One day? Two days? More? I will bring an offering tray every day until you are free."

Mother could be dead in two days!

Coriander stands under the air shaft, a hand on the rope. "You are so sure your Patron lord will help you, yet here we still are," she says with an ugly laugh.

"I would like to see you do better!"

Cook looks between us and briskly says, "Come hold your sister, Doma Jessamy. What a sweet mouth she has."

I cradle the baby in my arms. She closes her eyes with a sigh that brings a little bubble to her precious lips. Her tiny face squishes up, and her belly makes a sound as she expels a load of soft waste into her linen wrapping. Cook chuckles and takes her away. We will have to ask Polodos to smuggle in fresh cloth. But what will we do with the soiled cloth? Word will get out to Lord Gargaron that people are alive in Ottonor's tomb. A priest will hear the baby cry. The priests have to be Gargaron's accomplices. As long as we are trapped in here we are at their mercy.

My agitated thoughts propel me as I pace the limits of our world: three chambers, the offering and waste troughs, a few slits for air, and the stone bier with the coffin on top. A sweetening scent of putrefaction has begun to germinate within the coffin, blending with the musky odor of the many amulets and magic-sewn sachets hung around the sealed wooden lid.

"Jes, you must eat and rest too," says Maraya. "You're no good to us if you get weak."

I crouch beside her, forcing myself to eat. "What will you do when we get out?"

"Take care of Mother," she says. "We will leave the city and start anew elsewhere."

"What about the Archives exam?"

"Without Lord Ottonor to sponsor me I can't sit the exam." She grabs hold of my forearm. "Can you truly get us out, Jes? Polodos says so but he wants it so much that I think he is just trying to make the misery endurable."

I whisper into her ear. "I can get you and Coriander and Amaya out. But Cook and Mother won't fit in the shaft, not unless they lose a great deal of flesh."

Merry begins crying. "I can't leave her, Jes. I couldn't bear it."

My face must look like Father's did as he stared into the truth of Lord Gargaron's offer. "We won't abandon either of them. But Mother's lost so much blood. We have to consider the worst. Can you raise the baby, if need be?"

She leans against me, weeping silently.

Arm around her, I hold her close until she falls asleep. I

shut my eyes. The wind moans down the shaft like a harbinger of death. Slowly its wail quiets as the breeze drops outside. The tomb's presence enfolds me. My awareness walks along its walls, tapping for the best place to anchor my thread. Another presence nags at me, a niggle of sound. Fingers are scratching again.

Probably it is just rats, although that is bad enough. I shift away from dozing Merry and tiptoe to the arch. The dim light hazes the chamber. The bier shudders as in a slight earthquake but I feel no rumble through my feet. Rubbing my eyes, I decide I am imagining things.

With a soft thump the coffin jolts a fingerbreadth sideways, and I jump back, slamming into the wall. My heart beats like a riot as my shoulders throb from the impact. Lord Ottonor's flesh is going to shove its way out of the coffin and stumble around the tomb groping and grabbing.

"Merry, light the oil lamp now," I say. "Cook, give me the knife."

What if the spark the priests stole for Ottonor's funeral procession was that of a criminal, and the criminal's shadow has wandered the night until it has reunited with its familiar spark? What if it means to claw its way out of the coffin to find living flesh in which to make a new home?

Coriander steps up beside me, lamp in one hand and knife in the other. "What is it, Doma?"

The coffin jerks so hard that it slides partway off the bier.

Coriander yelps.

Whom will I sacrifice to slow its blind rage?

I grab my dead brother off the oracle's lap. His dead flesh must be my shield against a walking corpse whose shadow might want to leap into my body, as it is said shadows can do. Let it jump into his flesh instead! He can't be harmed.

"Maraya, light the other lamp! Coriander, move to my right."

A wick hisses as a second lamp takes flame behind me. Maraya steps into the archway with a burning lamp. "What is it? What did I hear?"

With a grind and a snap the entire top of the stone bier bursts up.

A breath of cold hard air swirls out and then the stone lid slams down, too heavy to stay up.

We all scream.

The coffin slides, topples, and crashes to the floor. The seals crack, and the lid jumps open. Lord Ottonor's waxy corpse sprawls over the mess of bloody shrouds.

"Jes!" Maraya's voice is a breath short of a shriek. "Get back from there. A shadow is trying to crawl out of him."

Coriander mutters curses or prayers; I can't tell the difference, only that her voice is frantic.

My breathing comes in staggered pants as I edge forward holding my brother in front of me. The lamplight throws shadows across the chamber, distorted by our figures. A long, grasping shadow oozes out of Ottonor's flesh but that is surely only the angle of the light.

The corpse's fingers twitch as the body splays farther forward. A dead hand grabs for my leg.

"Jes!" Maraya screams.

I sprawl onto my buttocks, shoving with my feet to get away. The coffin heels over sideways and the corpse rolls toward me. Fingers drag down my ankle. His skin is cold, and yet a warm pulse throbs against my leg. I screech, drop the dead infant on top of the corpse, and scramble backward. My breath is coming in such ragged bursts that my sight blurs.

With a crack the top of the bier heaves open to reveal a maw of darkness.

"Get everyone back!" I cry as I look wildly around for a weapon, but Coriander and the knife are out of reach. Maraya holds out the lamp. Fire is better than fear. I grab it as I jump to my feet.

A muscled arm hooks over the rim of the stone bier, and tries to heave itself out of its stone cage. The arm sports five parallel white scars below the elbow, like a savage's. An unspeakable creature is alive in here, and we are trapped with it.

It speaks in a man's voice, in the language of Efea's Commoners.

"Curse it, Kori! Can you spare an arm to help me out of this cursed shaft before I fall and break my neck?"

"Ro!" Coriander shoves past me and grabs the arm.

Shaking with shock, I grab her from behind around the hips and use my weight to help lever him up. His head emerges, his chest, and he heaves himself over the rim. I let go of her.

She throws her arms around him, sobbing. "I was afraid I would die in here!"

He kisses her cheek but looks over her shoulder at me. It takes me a moment to recognize the young man from the marketplace because all his hair has been shaved off, but his broad shoulders and intense eyes are the same, as is his insulting tone.

"If it isn't the sullen schemer, just as promised," he says in Saroese. "However did you get a lordly princeling to do your bidding, mule?"

"Who is this, Jes?" Maraya asks.

"Coriander's brother. I guess his name is Ro."

"His name is Ro-emnu." Coriander glares at me as she scrubs the tears off her cheeks. "You aren't his kinswoman, to call him Ro."

"I thought you were exaggerating when you said they call you Coriander," he says to her, switching back to Efean. "As if you are a plant."

I arch an eyebrow sarcastically, replying in the same language. "I believe Ro-emnu has forgotten he is here to help us escape. Instead he means to while away the time with contemptuous argument."

His mouth quivers as if he can't decide whether to laugh or sneer.

I stare back, unwilling to give way.

"Ro!" whines Coriander. "Please, I want to get out of here before something worse happens."

From under hooded lids he glances at Maraya's twisted foot, face so impassive I almost want to thank him. "Bring the light in here, if you will, Doma."

Maraya hangs the lamp from a hook over the bier.

"Where can we anchor the rope?" He shrugs off a pack that looks to be stuffed with a rope and harness.

"We'll have to lower everyone down by hand," I say. "How did you get up here from inside the earth?"

"There is an entire complex of old Efean buildings buried underneath your Saroese City of the Dead."

"I never read of that in the Archives!" Maraya retorts.

"Why would the Saroese Archivists write of what they wanted no one to know, Doma?"

She nods slowly, a gesture that angers me, for it seems she is actually considering his explanation. "It is a worthwhile argument that the Archives can only record what the chronicler writes down. But then how do you know of this buried complex? You are not an Archivist."

"Who do you think was forced to bury the old complex five generations ago with rubble and dirt, Doma? Who built the tombs afterward? Patrons? No, they called the work unclean and corrupting, which really means it is too backbreaking and difficult. Efeans build all that your father's people will not touch. Our masons' guild knows of the existence of ancient buildings beneath the tombs, but they fear the underground spaces."

"We can't go down there!" Amaya appears in the archway looking very like an ethereal sky spirit only half-tethered to earth and likely to float up into the heavens at any instant. Her hair is tangled all loose over her shoulders. The linen sheath gown hugs her shapely curves like it was tailored to her. She looks so beautiful and frightening that Ro-emnu actually takes a step back as his eyes widen. "Denya's nurse says there are monsters and shadows hiding beneath the tombs that want to eat us! We mustn't go!"

My relief at seeing Amaya able to walk sweeps me with a wave of inexplicable anger. "You are welcome to stay here in the tomb because I don't have the energy to coax you out!"

"Don't leave me, Jes!" Amaya begins to weep, not with the theatrical sobs she would often use to get her way but with exhausted hopeless tears.

"I didn't mean it!" I hurry over and embrace her. She sags into my arms. "We won't leave you, Amiable. Anyway we have to get you out of here because you desperately need a bath."

She wipes mucus from her running nose and shakes with laughs that are also sobs. "I'll never eat candied almonds again!"

"I doubt that," mutters Maraya, but she smiles just a little to hear Amaya's complaints.

"Lord Kalliarkos told me the offering was poisoned," says Ro-emnu, watching us. "Is that true?"

Amaya draws herself up with a pose stolen from the theater, popularly called 'the Glare of Disdain.' Even grimy and sick, she is quite magnificent. "For what other possible reason might you think to discover me in such dishevelment?"

"Don't say it, Ro," says Coriander so suddenly that her defense of Amaya surprises all of us into silence, including her brother.

In the distance we hear horns trumpeting to announce the temple gates' opening.

"We have to hurry!" says Maraya. "The High Priest will make his customary third-day visit to the new tomb. That's us! He'll demand a prophecy from the oracle."

Ro-emnu shakes out a harness and beckons to Coriander. "Little sister, you go first."

"No!" I object. "Let the others go first, and her after."

"Don't you trust me, Doma?" The lazy way he pronounces the title makes me want to punch him.

"Sullen schemers never trust anyone, not if we want to succeed."

Unexpectedly he laughs. "I would demand the same were our positions reversed. Very well."

I uncurl my fists. "We need her strength to lower people down. Merry first, with the baby."

He glances at his sister, then at the door as Cook moves into view holding my baby sister.

At the sight of the baby his sneer vanishes and he actually drops the harness from sheer shocked surprise. "Blessed Lady! Bad enough that your monstrous priests bury women alive but to condemn a newborn child to this hateful prison! My apologies for doubting you, Doma," he finishes with so much gentleness that I blink. But he is speaking to Merry, not to me. Or maybe he is under Amaya's spell, because she leans against the wall, studying him from under half-closed eyes.

Despite his generous words, Cook measures him with obvious suspicion.

I lean over the open bier. Its smooth-sided shaft is not too different from the air shaft that ventilates this tomb, except it will fit Mother and Cook. Light gleams below.

"Lord Kalliarkos?"

His voice echoes oddly along the shaft. "Jes? You can't believe what's down here! It's like a vast tomb of old chambers, ones marked with mysterious writing."

His breathless tone annoys me as I struggle to comprehend that all this time I never suspected the truth. Why didn't I ask my father what happened to the remains of the old Efean kingdom after the Saroese took over a hundred years ago? A cool earthy breath exhales out of the depths, touched with a flavor like dusty cinnamon that spices my tongue. For a wild instant I wonder if this is the scent of the stories my mother's people told.

With the baby bound around her, Merry bravely steps into the harness. Coriander, Ro-emnu, and I lower her down.

"Shouldn't you be frightened, Doma?" says Ro-emnu, looking at me as he hauls up the empty harness. "We are about to descend into a place haunted by the restless dead slaughtered by your father's people long ago."

"The only thing that scares me is the thought of having to listen to you try to impress me with your sarcasm." I grab the harness out of his hands. "Amaya, you're next."

Her chin quivers as she steadies herself. She may be a sniveling spoiled brat of a younger sister, but she is a soldier's daughter too. "I'm ready to go."

She staggers a little, and I will be cursed for a shadow if Ro-emnu doesn't hasten forward to catch her just as if he has been lovestruck by her delicate features and proud courage. I roll my eyes and happen to catch Coriander's look at the same moment. She has covered what I am sure is a snicker of laughter by clapping a hand over her mouth. Probably Amaya stumbled on purpose so she can lean on the arm of a large, strong, attractive man, even a Commoner, just because she has to make sure she can charm every man who crosses her path. Then I remember Denya's tear-streaked face as she begged me to get word to Amaya, and I realize I don't know what to think, that everyone and everything is wearing masks. Just like me.

Faint but clear, three triple fanfares announce that the High Priest and his procession are entering the City of the Dead.

We lower Amaya down. As I'm untangling the harness, Ro-emnu straightens with a hiss.

Mother appears in the archway supported by Cook. She wears a loose linen sheath. Her skin looks blotchy and she can barely stand upright.

"Jessamy?" she whispers. "Where are your sisters? Who is this young man?"

"He has come to help us escape, Mother."

He coughs. "So this is the woman who paid the coin of her life to sleep with the enemy."

I shove him so hard that he staggers back. Before he can catch his balance I push him again so he slams against the wall. "What gives you the righteous purity to speak of her in that way? My mother is a woman, and she deserves respect!"

He gets his hands up between us but he does not touch me. Instead his gaze flicks past me to where Mother leans.

She says in a frail voice, "Jessamy, let it go. If he helps us escape then it does not matter what he thinks of me."

This is how she has lived all these years. This is how she has kept her dignity. Tears well up in my eyes and I step back because I do not want him to see me cry.

Yet to my utter astonishment he walks past me, touches both hands to his forehead, and makes an odd dip with his knees. He speaks in Efean. "My apologies for my harsh words, Honored Lady. The dames of my clan would whip me if they were to hear of my rude disrespect. I beg you to spare me the indignity of being scolded in public by them in front of all the assembled households."

His words bring a smile to her lips, as if she has remembered the woman she once was. "Your secret is safe with me. What is your name, young nephew?"

"My mother gave me the name Ro-emnu but my aunties call me Ro. I personally pledge my five souls to the task of bringing you and your people to safety, Honored Lady."

Tension fills her jaw. "I must find the strength. My daughters need me. Where is the baby?"

"Already down, with Merry," I answer.

As Cook and Coriander adjust the harness to fit her, my mother looks at me. "There was another baby, Jessamy. The son your father wanted. We cannot leave him here in this hateful place."

Ottonor's corpse conceals my poor dead brother beneath a fleshy arm and outflung sleeve. I don't tell her how I used him because I am afraid she will hate me for it. "I will bring him, Mother. I promise."

Mother is my height, tall and well built, no lightweight even before the pregnancy. It takes all our bracing and grunted effort to lower her down. My Fives gloves rub along the rope. My hands ache from all the gripping. But determination feeds me. Cook follows, heavier yet. Fortunately Ro-emnu is exceedingly strong, packed with muscle. Afterward Coriander dashes back into the oracle's chamber and returns with treasure stolen from the chest. I don't care as long as we can get out.

Horns blare a cheerful tune, getting closer.

Ro-emnu and I lower Coriander down. Lamplight blurs the darkness below as she vanishes into an unseen passageway connected with the bottom of the shaft. Kalliarkos appears out of the passage, lit from the back, face in shadow as he looks up. He stands perhaps six body lengths below, the height of the tallest climbing post in Trees.

I think he smiles although shadows make it hard to see. A flash of sunlight could not have heartened me more. I grin even though I am sure he cannot make out my expression. All my tiredness spills away as if the sea has washed clean my flesh and spirit both.

"Jes." The walls of the shaft magnify his whisper. "You come down next."

But I'm still thinking, plotting, planning. "What about the oracle? Wouldn't it be better for the last of us to close up the bier and go out the air shaft at night? So if anyone ever opens the tomb they won't discover how we escaped?"

The sound of men singing temple hymns drifts through the slits in the walls. The High Priest approaches. I suddenly remember that the rope by which I descended the shaft is still wrapped around the exterior of the shaft up on the roof, in plain sight. All my joy and relief plunge into throat-curdling fear.

I turn to see Ro-emnu examining the oracle. The gag cuts cruelly into her mouth because Coriander tied it too tight. Her eyes have a glassy sheen, as if she were drugged with shadow-smoke. Did she give up struggling against her fate long ago, or has she always welcomed the tomb? Were she a young man I think Ro-emnu would kick her, but even a contemptuous person like him will not hit a frail crone.

He has a strong Efean face and a gaze that slices, like he is seeing beyond the mask every person must wear to disguise her secrets. "You and I have a decision to make, sullen schemer. Do you wish to force the oracle to eat the poisoned food so as to make it look as if it killed her? Or should we smother her?"

"She's just a pathetic old woman."

He lifts an eyebrow. "How Patron-bred you are. There is no such thing as a pathetic old woman, not among people who respect experience and wisdom. Only among your father's people are such women discarded like trash. It's shameful but no business of mine. All I see here is yet another Patron lady who would spit on me and have me beaten were I to get in her way on the street. We can't leave her alive."

"I guess killing is nothing to you. Your sister admitted you were arrested for murder."

His grin mocks me and makes him look dangerous. "Is that what she said?"

Retreat always looks like weakness so I take a step forward. "Are you saying it isn't true?"

Scorn curls his lips. "I did what they accuse me of, yes."

I try not to notice how the oracle stares at us, mouth slack as we talk so casually about her death. The way she clutched my brother has torn my heart open. "This can't be the only life she has known," I say, winding a path through this maze because I must find a way to convince him. "Oracles are young. Look how old she is. I think she once had a baby who died. Don't you wonder why she was locked away?"

He unties the gag and shakes her. "What is your story? What secrets do you know?"

"You cannot treat me so roughly! You are a lowly servant, no better than mud." She jerks out of his grasp, staring at something behind me.

I turn as Kalliarkos pulls himself out of the shaft.

"What is going on, Jes? Can't you hear the High Priest's procession? You must have secured the rope to the air shaft to come down. Is it untied so they won't see it?"

The oracle struggles to her knees, crawling toward him. "Kallos! My love! I thought they banished you! But you have come back. I knew you would not abandon me, my heart!"

Astonished by this outburst Kalliarkos steps full into the

lamplight. He is as handsome as an actor in a tragic play pretending rapt wonderment at an extraordinary coincidence.

Her expression crumples, her weeping an incongruous dissonance across the priests' harmonious singing. "You are not my beloved Kallos! Where is my baby that they stole from us?"

Kalliarkos kneels, gently taking her chin in his hand. "Doma, quiet your tears. Be at peace. I will let no harm come to you."

Her sobs quiet. "You look something like him, he who was my rose bower love." Her wistful tone peels away the years until the old woman becomes a young maiden caught up in the first sweet tremblings of desire. Yet her words turn sour. "But he fled away over the sea and they sealed me into the temple and told me that if I ever spoke of him again, the gods would smite him with a lance of thunder and a knife of lightning."

Ro-emnu looks like a merchant calculating an unanticipated bargain. "Who are you, Doma?"

The priests have begun to sing the morning descant in praise of the Sun of Justice. As they climb the path I can pick out words: "...righteous light...pure judgment..."

"Put the gag back on, you fool," I whisper. "They're almost here."

Startlingly loud and right up against the oracle's alcove, a stentorian voice intones a prayer. "Oracle, awake! I who am

High Priest in His Most Glorious Raiment and with the Holy Presence of the Gods' Sweet Breath and Joyous Favor attend your sanctuary."

Ro-emnu claps a hand over the oracle's mouth. I am afraid to move and almost too scared to breathe. How did the High Priest arrive so quietly?

"I, the humble living, beg you, the separated who is dead, to speak into this world through your hidden mouth. Speak the words whispered to you by the gods from their high thrones of Seeing. Speak the words which you are gloried and sanctified and required to utter."

The fragrance of the priests' holy incense wafts through the slit in the wall. The harsh scent tickles right up my nose. Ro-emnu sneezes and his hand slips off the oracle's mouth. She wails, an ululation of grief, before he slaps his hand back. Too late. Now they know someone is alive inside.

29

The oracle must always speak if she is summoned by the proper ritual words. If she does not, there is a longer ritual to coax her voice awake. I need them to go away quickly so no one notices the rope looped around the air shaft on the roof.

I run into the oracle's chamber and sit on the stool before the "mouth," the slit through which worshippers can hear her whispered prophecies. No priest would look directly through the slit so all I see are the robes they wear, dyed in colors that represent the god each priest serves: blue for Lady Hayiyin of the Sea, yellow for Lord Seon the Sun of Justice, and red for Lord Judge Inkos who rules the afterlife. The High Priest wears purple to mark his descent from royal ancestors, since only palace-born men can serve as High Priest. Whether or not he is in on Lord Gargaron's plot, I have to convince him to leave.

My pulse pounds in my ears so loudly I am dizzy with it. If the words she spoke leave my mouth, do I become the oracle?

"The tale begins with a death." I pitch my voice low to disguise it. "Where will it end? There could be a victory, a birth, a kiss, or another death. There might fall fire upon the City of the Dead, upon the tombs of the oracles. A smile might slay an unsuspecting adversary. Poison might kill the flower that bloomed brightest. A living heart might be buried. Death might be a mercy."

Silence pools like fate as a scribe writes my words down. It takes all my willpower not to bolt for the bier's shaft, but at length, singing a hymn, the priests walk away to complete a circuit of the tombs. The instant it is safe to move, Kalliarkos grabs the rope at the bottom of the air shaft.

"What are you doing?" I whisper.

"I have to climb up and cut the rope free. It'll be tricky coming down but it's nothing more than a very tight blind shaft."

"What if they see you?"

He shrugs. "If they arrest me, I won't have to go into the army, will I?"

I kiss his cheek for luck.

He rests his fingers briefly against my cheek in answer, then climbs the rope hand over hand, the muscles tight in his arms.

"Time to go, Doma, if you can pull your eyes away from the handsome prince who's showing off for you," says Ro-emnu, watching me from the arch.

I see no need to answer such an impertinent comment. Pushing past him, I stop short. Lord Ottonor's corpse has been put back into the coffin, and the oracle is gone. Only my brother remains. Ro picks up the tiny bundle and offers it to me.

"You did not tell me there were two babies, Doma. Twins are sacred."

"Twin boys are considered a sign of good fortune, and twin girls of ill fortune, but they're not sacred."

"You're speaking like a Patron. Twins are sacred to the five."

"To the Fives? The game? What are you talking about?"

"You don't know anything about being Efean, do you?" His dark gaze mocks me. "What I can't believe is that you just discarded him on the floor."

"She gave birth to him in darkness. Don't think you can judge what you were not here to experience." I am not about to confess the desperate thing I did in my panic. Instead I kiss the baby's cold forehead as a blessing. Watching me, Ro-emnu's sneer softens.

A bed-curtain sliced up makes a sling to tie the baby against my body. Unlike my new sister he feels empty: no spark heats him, and his self has long since fled. Father never had any luck with his sons.

"Where is the oracle?" I ask.

"Why do you care?" His sympathetic expression fades into his usual derision.

A thump interrupts us. Kalliarkos trots in with two lamps, the rope and harness, and a sealed reservoir of oil. He grins with a cocky confidence that looks good on him.

"They've gone on around the hill. We did it, Jes! Everyone is out!"

I can't allow myself to relax. Disaster lurks around every corner.

We tidy up the tomb, then wrestle the heavy stone lid almost all the way back over the bier.

"Tomb robbers built this so they could sneak in," I say after we set the coffin on top.

Ro-emnu scoffs. "Men from the Efean masons' guild built it, Doma. Your father's people are the tomb robbers, not mine."

Kalliarkos sets a hand casually on Ro-emnu's shoulder. "Ro, we have got to go, not argue about history."

Instead of scorching him with a retort, Ro-emnu shoves him away companionably. "You're right, Kal. We can argue later."

I'm impressed by how Kalliarkos has so quickly forged a comradeship with a Commoner criminal.

"Jes, you go first," Kalliarkos says. "You won't need the rope. It's an easy climb. Ro and I will close the bier and follow."

Even with the baby bundled against me it is indeed an easy

climb. Hand- and footholds have been carved into the rock, as if this really is a route for tomb robbers. A lantern burning at the base of the shaft guides me down. The stonework is fine masonry in a crisscrossing pattern, obviously laid by a master craftsman. At the base I look around curiously. A jagged cleft makes a passageway out of the shaft but I wait, a hand curved atop my brother's cap of hair. Above, the stone lid grinds as they shift it, then clunks into place. Ro-emnu descends. The way his feet thump as he probes for footholds betrays him as an inexperienced climber. A stream of words pours out of him, sounding like the silkiest poetry even though he is cursing about donkeys, manure, and breaking legs in holes filled with scorpions. Just above me he slips and plummets the last body length.

I press back against the wall to avoid his feet but steady him so he doesn't smash. He slams into my side, grabbing hold of me for purchase. He's very strong.

Above us, Kal laughs. "I heard that slip! Best stagger out of the way as I'm coming down."

Ro-emnu's murmur teases my ear. "Hard to imagine a petted and cosseted princeling running the Fives when he could be sitting in the stands making bets on the outcome and eating grapes offered to him by a prettily masked slave like you, Doma."

The insinuation is a slap in the face. I twist out of his arms and shove him into the cleft. "Efeans are the ones who enslaved their own people. Kliatemnos the First and his queen, Serenissima, put a stop to that evil custom. We don't keep slaves."

"No, you just call them something else and treat them worse. How your father's people love the lies they tell!"

"I'm down!" says Kalliarkos cheerfully. The lantern bobs as he picks it up and follows us into the narrow passage.

"That was fast for a pampered lord," says Ro-emnu in a tone so affably joking that I feel my neck has been wrenched by his abrupt change of mood.

"Climbing is my best skill, as both you and Jes should know by now," replies Kal in a laughing way that confounds me. His voice is as bright as the lamp, glittering with triumph. "We have only to follow the chalk marks back out to the pool we came by, and we're free."

"Good thing you brought the chalk," says Ro-emnu.

"Now you see the value of running the Fives, don't you?"

"It's a foul game that Patrons love. No offense."

"None taken. We'll contest the matter later over a drink."

Lord Gargaron is wrong to think that Kalliarkos's instinct to treat others as equals is a flaw. Even I thought so at first, believing him too nice, but his ability to respect others and set them at ease makes him strong, not weak.

The cleft opens into a perfectly square chamber. Lamplight's golden aura washes the shadows into the corners. Mother sits in the center of the room with Cook on one side and Maraya on the other. The baby suckles at her breast.

Amaya rocks back and forth, arms crossed over her belly as she groans in pain. Coriander stands guard over the oracle, who hides her face behind her hands.

"There's no door," says Coriander. "How do we leave?"

Ro-emnu snatches the lamp from Kalliarkos and swings it so its light falls full on one corner. "We climbed up this shaft."

There is no shaft, just a square depression with a grate lying beside it and grooves in the stonework where the grate would fit over a hole, if there were one.

"Where did the shaft go?" Kalliarkos prods the stone. "It must have closed after we came up."

The two men thump at the blocked depression as I walk a tour of the chamber, shining lamplight into every corner. For the life of me I cannot see another opening. It was too easy after all. Or the masons betrayed us. I sink down next to Mother. What do we do now?

"We're going to die down here," Amaya whimpers.

"Just shut up, Amiable. Let me think." There has to be a way.

"Jessamy, let me look on him," Mother whispers.

I push the linen folds away from his little face. The light gilds his perfect features. He has his father's eyes and his mother's coloring.

"He will not be cursed to lie alone in a tomb until he is dust." Tears slide down her cheeks. "Poor child. His father would not have loved that face."

"How could anyone not love such a beautiful face?" I retort, for I do not like to think that Father did not love me when he first saw me.

"Shhh. Let go of your anger, Jessamy. It will weaken you if you allow it to rule your heart."

My lips press closed over the things I would like to say but will not trouble her with. I love Father but I know Maraya is right: he could have turned his back on ambition, and he didn't.

Maraya walks over to the two men. "Could someone have shut the opening behind you to trap you here?"

Ro-emnu scratches at his shaved head and looks surprised when his fingers find no hair. "I don't think so. The masons who know about this place never enter it. It is forbidden to disturb what lies beneath. They say angry spirits eat intruders but I think fear makes a man see spirits where there are none. People are just afraid of the past."

"Maybe angry spirits shoved the stone into place to trap us so they can eat us like a fine meal," murmurs Amaya, "leaving the delicacies for last. Which means you will be eaten first, Jes."

"Then I'll be spared your whines and shrieks, which will sour your flavor!"

She laughs, as I guessed she would, but I cannot join her. The exhaustion of all our hopes weighs too heavily. What if our only choice is to climb back into the tomb?

Merry probes around the rim for a latch. She hasn't given

up. "There is no need to fear malignant spirits when a better explanation would be that springs or ropes made a stone move to close the opening."

Kalliarkos turns a slow circle, studying the blank walls. "Certainly the chambers we worked our way through to get here had pitfalls and barriers."

"The way you climbed that one shaft blind with no assistance was cursed amazing," says Ro-emnu.

He nods. "There was a lot of climbing to get here, wasn't there? Many collapsed rooms too. We had to retrace our path several times. That's why the chalk was so valuable. But if there are spirits lurking we never saw them. That this place was buried long ago is enough to make it unsafe."

Cook clears her throat, and we all look at her stoic face. "My lord, can we get out?"

"I don't know."

Maraya stands. "Ro-emnu, do you think the masons might have tricked you?"

Coriander laughs bitterly. "They would never have. Don't you know who he is?"

"No, I don't. Is he a magician to spell us free?"

Ro-emnu shakes his head with a patience he has never shown me. "The masons do not lie, Doma. My uncle is one. This is a dangerous place and we walk here at our own risk."

Maraya nods. "How did you identify Lord Ottonor's tomb from underneath?"

"When the tombs were erected in the reign of Kliatem-nos the First, they were built over old air shafts from the buried complex. The biers hide the shafts. The priests don't even know about them because the Efean workers never told them. I've heard stories about how women were rescued from the tombs but I don't know if they're true. Each tomb has a mark that gives its location to the north, south, west, and east. Here, do you see it?" He goes to the cleft and shows us simple lines depicting Clan Tonor's three-horned bull, the same mark carved into the tomb's lintel.

"Do that again!" says Amaya.

"Do what?" he asks, surprised by her command.

"Honored Lord, walk from the cleft to the grate, more slowly this time."

Ro-emnu lifts an eyebrow, not sure whether she is mock-ing him or showing respect by using the Efean honorific. Yet instead of throwing a nasty retort into her face he paces out the gap.

When he is halfway across she yelps. "Stop! The pattern of the bricks is broken *there*. You can see it when the light and shadow fall just right."

The even pattern of the bricks is broken to make a faint outline in the shape of a door. I press a hand along the out-line but nothing moves. A pattern at the center resembles the nested pyramid, a small one inverted inside a large one; this symbol marks the entrance to Traps on any Fives court.

Resting my palm flat on the center brick, I lean into it. The wall gives way.

A door opens as by magic or by the secret workings of ancient wires and pulleys.

Startled exclamations ring out. I raise a hand to stop the others from crowding forward.

"There is a trick here. Let me go through first."

Lantern in hand, I ease through the opening. No light penetrates the space beyond, except the glow of the lantern. When I lift it I cannot see ceiling or floor, for I stand on a ledge on the brink of a cliff. Water slops below like waves shushing among rocks. The air smells salty. Does the ocean reach under the City of the Dead? Or is this all an illusion?

Two bridges attach to the ledge. It is far too dark for me to see where they lead. They simply vanish as into nothingness. The stone bridge seems to be anchored with arches and pillars beneath; it looks sturdy but has no railing, so it would be easy to step off. The wider bridge is built of wood and has railings, but when I test its first plank the wood feels spongy. If this chamber has lain here for five generations, this bridge is surely rotting.

I call back. "Everyone come through at once in case there's a trap to close you in there."

They arrive in hasty procession: Maraya has the baby. Cook assists Amaya. Ro-emnu carries Mother like a sack of rice, while Coriander has slung the oracle over her shoulders.

Kalliarkos brings up the rear with the other three lanterns and our gear. We crowd the ledge, clinging together in the aura of lantern-light. Who knows what might be lurking in the dark beyond?

"I'm going first," I say, tightening the cloth that binds my dead brother against my chest. "You all follow when I give the order."

"Yes, Captain," says Ro-emnu in his sardonic voice.

With a rumbling scrape the open door suddenly slides shut.

"It looks like we have no choice but to go forward," Maraya remarks.

"Follow me single file," I say.

The bridge rises in a slow arch. We all tread cautiously on the span, step by step. I can no longer see the ledge where we started, just Kalliarkos's lamp at the end of our group. My light shines only a few paces ahead of me. Horribly, the roadway starts to narrow. From being as wide as the width of my outstretched arms it shrinks until the bridge is no wider than the distance from the tip of my fingers to my elbow. It's not so hard to walk, unless you look down into the stygian depths. Watery sighs breathe out of the abyss like a monster sleeping. There might be a sea-swallowing serpent waiting to rise and snap us up one by one as the rest plunge screaming off the bridge to their deaths.

I can't allow fear to master me.

"How much farther?" Maraya asks, her breath coming in short bursts. She has crouched to brace herself on hands and knees. Behind her Cook and Amaya are crawling. Kalliarkos has given the lit lamp to Coriander so he can coax the oracle forward. Like me, Ro-emnu remains standing. How he balances with Mother on his back I cannot fathom but it's impressive that he does.

I creep forward, holding out the lamp to see what comes next. The span narrows until it is no wider than my hand, a single course of bricks.

Maraya begins to wheeze. Amaya sobs once and is silent.

"How are we to cross without falling, Doma?" asks Cook in her phlegmatic voice.

Ro-emnu says, "I confess I do not think I could balance that even if I weren't carrying the honored lady. We will have to turn back."

"We can't turn back. The door closed behind us, just as the shaft did. It's as if we're being driven in one direction. But who would build a bridge to get narrower? There's something I'm missing." I snap a finger. "Wait. Don't anyone move."

Kneeling, I feel my way forward, pushing the lantern ahead of me. My fingers brush along the edge but it feels wrong. Air should move up into my face from the depths but it doesn't. Carefully I straddle the span so as to test its sides. A calf-length below, my legs hit stone. The span remains the same width as at the beginning. It's just this little ridge bricked atop and cunningly painted to make it look like the bridge is narrowing.

"It's a trap! An illusion. Our eyes deceive us, and our fear makes us quail."

I press forward and they creep after. In a mere twenty strides, the false painting ends and we reach the far shore and enter a vaulted chamber with four ramps leading into further passageways.

"Why would anyone want to frighten and confuse people like this?" Amaya whimpers as she huddles on the floor, clutching Cook's leg for comfort.

Maraya turns to look back the way we came. A wall of wide arches gives us a view onto the lightless gulf we just traversed, a maw of darkness.

"That is a very good question, Amiable," she says in a brisk voice. "Who built this place originally? When it was buried, why was it not totally filled in with rubble? Think how strong the roof must be to have not collapsed under the weight of a hill."

"What are those lights?" asks Mother, twisting out of Ro-emnu's supporting arm. She shades her eyes as against the sun. "What haunts us?"

Out on the gulf of night, sparks of blazing light dance like a swarm of fireflies. They spin through hypnotic circles and spirals and all in a silence that wraps us like swaddling clothes. Their uncanny glamour paralyzes when we should be running away.

As with an inhaled breath the lights collect into a pulsing mass. They spill toward us in a flood. Too stunned to move or speak, we stare helplessly. Like fiery locusts the sparks pour through the arches in such numbers that their brilliance blinds us. Sparks tumble hotly through my flesh like a thousand million falling stars. Their radiance dissolves me; my being becomes mist. Unmoored, my heart comes unanchored and slides toward the ocean of eternity.

My shadow frays and tears where it attaches to my heels. I forget my name. My breath ceases.

In the shadow-ridden flesh of my dead brother, a fierce spark lodges with a hiss of steam.

In an eyeblink the lights vanish. Silence crashes down over us like the fist of voiceless thunder, a force that jolts the whole world. My knees buckle, and I pitch forward, barely catching myself on a hand. The sling flops sideways, cloth flapping open to uncover his face. My little finger brushes the bow of his tiny lips. His mouth parts under its pressure, and an answering force clamps down.

I suck in a harsh breath, heart thudding madly, as I realize what I am feeling.

My dead brother is suckling on my finger. *He is alive.*

30

My fingertip offers no milk. A mewl of infant indignation frets him. When I look down, the baby's eyes are open. An expression no innocent baby could ever have mars the unblemished features: he is aware and he is afraid. When I met my baby sister's gaze, the threads of our hearts tangled. This stranger stares at me as if he is trying to figure out who I am and if I mean to hurt him. His eyes squish up, his chin trembles, and he wails.

A hand presses on my shoulder as the awful sound swirls around us.

"Give him to me," Mother says in the strongest voice I have heard from her since I first entered the tomb. "He's hungry."

I can't bear to touch him. I just want to fling him away. So I am relieved when she takes him.

My body aches like it has been torn apart and stitched back together. Limping to the arches I lean against the smooth stone and rub my forehead as I stare out at the stone bridge. All the lit sparks have come to rest like butterflies on the supporting arches beneath the roadway. Their light illuminates a sandy floor, not a fathomless sea. The vast cavern we crossed is nothing more than a large chamber with vaulted ceilings, not nearly as big as I imagined it. In the murky shadows concealing the far end of the span I see the mouth of a passageway but not the door we came through. There is no wooden bridge. Everything I thought I saw has vanished.

"Jes? Are you all right? I saw you stumble." Kalliarkos hurries up, and I open my arms so he can walk right into them.

"Will we ever find Bettany?" I whisper as I put my head on his shoulder.

"We'll find her," he promises. "We'll do it together, Jes."

I rest there, feeling his heart beat against mine.

After a short silence he speaks again. "I've never seen oil flare so brightly as when the reservoir shattered. The flames blinded me. Unfortunately most of our reserve oil burned up so we have to move on soon."

"The flames?" I look over at the others clustered together around the lit lamp. The ceramic jug with its reservoir of oil is indeed broken, and leaked oil has spread across the floor. "It was the sparks that blinded us."

"Sparks? What sparks?"

"Don't you see them?" The sparks gleaming along the bridge start to fall. One by one they plummet onto the sandy floor and wink out of existence to become just another grain of sand.

He eases me back. We are face-to-face with nothing between us. "Listen to me, Jes. You're exhausted. But it's all right. We can do this."

He can't see the sparks. As they fall, flash, and vanish, the bridge fades until I can no longer see the chamber, only breathe in its ancient salt-dust odor. Did I hallucinate it all? Yet when I touch my chest the sling hangs limp because they took the baby. My brother is alive.

The pressure of Kalliarkos's hand on the small of my back makes me so aware of how close he stands. His breathing quickens.

"Jes," he whispers as softly as a promise I never knew was made. I have been yearning for such a promise all my life.

"I don't have to hide behind a mask when I'm with you," I say.

"Jes! Where are you?" Maraya's frantic tone cuts between us, and I pull back from him.

She stands at the edge of the lamplight. The boy nurses industriously in Mother's arms as Cook supports her. Amaya clutches our sister as if she means to shield her from malevolent spirits. Ro-emnu has an arm thrown protectively around Coriander but it is he who looks stricken and she who seems to be whispering reassurances as they look nervously around the chamber. The oracle lies facedown on the floor.

"I'm here," I say as Kalliarkos and I walk over.

Amaya grabs my arm, shaking it like she means to yank it off. "What were those sparks, Jes?"

"You saw them?"

"Of course I saw them! They passed right through my flesh. I thought I was turning to smoke. What were they?"

"What sparks?" asks Cook, looking up.

When Ro-emnu and Coriander nod at each other I know they saw them too.

"Do you have some boring Archivist's explanation, Merry?" Amaya demands.

Maraya shakes her head slowly. "No. I can't explain that with ropes and pulleys and wires. It was like the hearts of a thousand stars pierced my body and flew right through me."

Mother whispers, "The land is the Mother of All. She gave birth to the five souls that bind us. The souls arise from the land. If we forget Her then She will forget Her children."

To hear such a superstitious utterance pour out of my mother's lips shocks me. By the sweating shine of her face I see that she is feverish.

"Why is it so cold?" she adds.

We three girls look at one another, for while it is cool here beneath the earth, it is not so cold as to make a person shiver as she is doing.

Ro-emnu kneels, offering her a flask. "Honored Lady, will you drink in honor of the five?"

"I'm so cold," she says. "I'm not thirsty."

"Amaya, get Mother to drink." I stand. "Kal, help me look for a way out."

He frowns as Cook and my sisters fuss over Mother and the babies. "We can only use one lamp at a time. We risk running out of oil now that we've lost the reservoir."

So he and I and Ro-emnu leave them in the dark and with a single lamp we discover five passages leading out of this chamber: two lead down, one up, one is level, and the fifth is the bridge. I enter the closest ramp, one of the two leading down. A few steps into the featureless passageway, I take in a deep breath of the musty air to see if I can smell sky or sea, but it is all dust and silence.

Light throws wavering shadows on the wall. They stretch with monstrous limbs reaching out for me, and I jump back.

"Careful," says Kalliarkos, coming up behind me with the lamp. I know he has my back.

Now that he's brought up light we can see that both ceiling and floor drop away in a jumble of collapsed masonry: the passage is blocked. As we retreat the light glimmers over four lines like pointed caps gouged halfway up the passageway's opening.

"Doesn't that look like the mark for Rivers?" I say.

"Kal, let's try the one that leads up," says Ro-emnu. I follow them, and as they enter I can't help but glance at that same spot halfway up the right-hand wall where, at the entrance to each Fives obstacle, its identifying mark is carved. There it is! As they go in I pause to trace five interlocked circles incised into the stone: Rings.

Inside the passage, their voices crow in triumph. "Stairs!"

Light chases shadows as they hurry back, congratulating each other, but when they reach me I grab the lamp out of Kalliarkos's hand.

"Come with me!" The other passageway leading down is marked with four parallel lines of uneven length: Trees. The arches overlooking the cavern are marked with the doubled inverted pyramid of Traps. The last passageway, the one that is level, spans a ditch and then cuts straight into what seems to be solid rock, not part of a building at all.

"Look! This is the mark for Pillars." I point to overlapped right angles incised to the right of this passage. "Like start gates on a Fives court."

"This is not a Fives court, Jes," says Kalliarkos, hands extended as if calming a crazed person. "We are buried underneath the City of the Dead. But Ro and I have found stairs—"

"Don't you see?" Like my mother I'm feverish, but it's an idea that consumes me, not illness. I begin to sing the song that announces each new Fives run: *Shadows fall where pillars stand. Traps spill sparks like grains of sand.*

To my surprise Ro-emnu joins me, slipping into harmony: *Seen atop the trees, you're known. Rivers flow to seas and home.*

Kalliarkos whistles sharply to interrupt us. "You both need to drink something and sit down. You're dizzy."

"No, she's right about the marks." Ro-emnu's agreement comes so unexpectedly that I actually smile at him. "And there *were* sparks that turned to sand."

"I didn't see any sparks," says Kalliarkos.

"You're not Efean," says Ro-emnu. "Go on, Doma."

The pattern has seized me. It's like watching Rings unfold on the court. "You said you climbed a lot to get to us. So you entered the underground complex in Trees, right?"

They glance at each other. "We entered next to a pool and crossed some streams," says Kal.

"Ah! Then you entered in Rivers. Even better! But the passage here that's marked with Rivers is blocked, so we can't return that way. What if you climbed through Trees to get to the tomb, and then we all crossed Traps together? The way the bridge was constructed is kind of a trap, right? If the stairs you found lead to Rings, then they won't take us to the surface but into the heart of the complex. We'll be stuck underneath the kings' tombs. So we have to go through Pillars to circle back to Rivers. Doesn't that make sense?"

Ro-emnu shakes his head. "This can't be a Fives court because Fives isn't an Efean game. The Saroese brought it here with their other festivals."

"How do you know the Saroese brought it? You weren't alive then. Your grandparents weren't even alive yet." Hands on hips, chin up, I challenge him. "Look around! Obviously this is not a Fives court because it isn't the game we play. But I will wager you anything you wish that if we enter the passage marked like Pillars we will end up in a maze."

"It's our lives we're wagering with," Ro-emnu retorts.

"With chalk to mark the dead ends and false turns we can get through it and back to Rivers and thus to the place you came in! Do you have a better idea?"

Of course they don't have a better idea!

In the silence, a sound flutters like wings above us. When I glance up, shadows twist along the ceiling even though the lamp isn't moving. If sparks spill in Traps, then shadows haunt Pillars. Fear runs cold through me. But I know better than to hesitate.

"Get everyone up. We have to go now."

We have four lamps. I lead the way with one, but we leave the other three unlit so that Kalliarkos must guard the rear with dark shrouding him. As we pick a route along the tunnel, the smoothness of a stone walkway gives way to a rumpled floor of awkward ropy ridges and bumpy protuberances. The ceiling is too high to touch; the walls are rough.

Maraya says, "These tunnels don't seem like they were chiseled out of rock. In the Archives it's said rough tunnels like this were made long ago by fire burning a path."

Ro-emnu breaks in. "These passages are the veins of the land through which ran the blood of the Mother of All. Hers is the blood that wells out of the earth's heart. In ancient days before people lived here, the Queen's Hill and the King's Hill were lakes of molten fire."

"Like the Fire Islands," she replies. "Yes, that's what the Archivists teach."

"It is the dames who kept this knowing knitted into the hearts of the people. Not your Archivists." His look challenges her. "Everything you Saroese have you have stolen from us."

"We have no time for this," I say. Mother sags like a sack of grain over Ro-emnu's back. Her eyes are closed, and there is blood on her legs. She will die if we don't get her to a safe place and a healer. "Keep moving."

Ahead, the path branches, and I find that my heart feels the same. All that I am has come unmoored. The mask I have worn my whole life is cracking, and what shines up from beneath will scald our eyes.

Did Lord Ottonor's shadow try to crawl into my body? Was my brother merely caught in a deep sleep that we mistook for death or did a spark give life to his dead flesh?

What lies buried beneath the City of the Dead? Is this the corpse of old Efea, the secret at the heart of the land?

You know the lies they tell you but you don't know the truth, so Coriander said to me.

I rest my right hand on the right-hand wall of the right-hand passageway. I am the tomb spider, anchored to the stone, spinning a way out of this maze. "Kal, you have the chalk."

"I'll mark the junctions, Jes," he calls forward. We both know how to unravel a maze.

I pace with slow sweeps, checking for pitfalls and traps. The ragged rock scrapes at my fingers but my gloves protect my palms. Our light reveals the mark of tools scoring the walls, places where long-dead workmen smoothed a sharp edge or erased the mark another maze traveler carved in the rock to show their path. Suddenly an unseen creature crawls over my hand and I shriek.

"Nothing," I say, although my heart pounds twice as fast as before. "It was just a bug."

"I'd have smacked it with my slipper," says Amaya. Her words give me the courage to go on.

Twice we pass a cleft that leads to an air shaft. In the first the shaft is partially collapsed. In the second we smell a fetid aroma, and the mark on the shaft indicates it is the tomb of a lord who passed, Maraya says, eighteen years earlier. Perhaps his oracle and her attendants have died.

We reach a circular space like a distended gourd. There are three possible exits. Ro-emnu sets Mother down with meticulous gentleness. She is unconscious and does not wake even when the babies fuss hungrily. Cook and Maraya let them suck broth off their little fingers. Coriander rests against a wall. The oracle stares so blankly I wonder what she sees.

Amaya sinks to the ground with head on knees, next to the opening that is the first to the right. According to my own plan we have to keep going to the right, yet the opening isn't even tall enough to walk upright. Its sloped confines hook away into the rock. What if the tunnel closes and we are stuck and can't turn around? How can Mother crawl if she can't even wake up?

I sit with her hand in mine. Her pulse is a fragile thread.

Kalliarkos crouches beside me and clasps my other hand. "The leftmost opening is another air shaft," he says. "It's clear of debris, and it doesn't stink. I'll climb it. There's a chance we can get out more quickly that way. Everyone needs a rest anyway."

He vanishes up the shaft, taking no light, climbing blind. Doubt digs its teeth into my heart. If I am mistaken in thinking this complex to have anything in common with a Fives court, then I may have doomed us to dying of thirst, lost in a maze.

Coming up beside me, Ro-emnu smiles the way a tomcat prowls. "What is your next command, Captain Jessamy? How is your campaign strategy proceeding?"

"I would like to see you do better! Since you seem to believe you know so much!"

Coriander's eyes pop open. "Ro knows more than any Archives!" she says stoutly.

"Kori, hold your tongue." His is the tone of an exasperated older sibling, one I recognize.

"I won't! Ro is trained as a poet in the Efean way, to speak only the truth. That's why the king's agents arrested him."

"For murder!" The instant the words leave my mouth I'm sorry I said them in front of everyone else.

Naturally he laughs. Cook shifts away from him. Maraya measures him anxiously. He seems so big and threatening here in this closed space where we can't run.

Coriander makes a rude gesture with her hand, right at me. "He was arrested for the play he wrote. The one the king's agents closed the night it opened."

"*The Poet's Curse?* The one that murdered the king's reputation? What is it about?"

With a chuckle he rubs the stubble of his hair. He has a laborer's callused hands, nothing like the soft skin I associate with a daydreaming poet sitting at a window gazing over a reed-choked lakeshore where egrets hunt in the misty distance. "The story may shock you, Doma."

"I'm not afraid of the truth, if that is what you mean," I retort.

"You don't have the sense to be afraid."

"Either tell me or stop boasting, I beg you."

By the way he stares at me I can tell he is about to refuse, just to spite me.

But it is Maraya who speaks. "I would like to know if the Archives are wrong. Isn't it better to chase the truth and catch it if you can?"

He glances at the oracle slumped on the ground. A glint like avarice gilds his expression, as if he sees her—the oracle—as a pot of honey that he means to slurp up before anyone can stop him. "People hide all kinds of stories," he says. "Let me tell you one of them, Doma Maraya, for I believe you truly do wish to know the truth, unlike your sister. Maybe someday you can write your own Archives."

A mask settles on his face, one that makes him look both new and ancient. As he begins the story, shadows gather like ravenous beasts around our wavering lamp.

"In the days of heaven and earth and sea and wind, the heart of All was planted in the fertile fields of Efea. So the land prospered beneath the rule of balance, a king to oversee soldiers and fieldwork and laborers and a queen to oversee diplomacy and the marketplace and artisans. But sweet food sours if left out in the sun too long. There came a bitter war for succession between two factions within the royal clans. Into this battle sailed a foreign prince, Kliatemnos, a refugee from the broken empire of Saro."

Shadow and flame weave in and out of his words. I sense something terrible crawling out of the dark as if his tale gives it life. What if death steals Mother? But her hand in mine is warm, and her heart is beating. I will anchor her in the world of the living.

"The young Efean queen took Prince Kliatemnos as her husband. With his troops to aid her, her faction won the battle and defeated her rival. In this way he became king to rule beside her."

Cook mutters, "Impiety! That is not how it happened!"

His story marches on. "After this, she gave birth to four daughters. The Saroese invaders became restless. They wondered if the gods had turned against them because there was no male heir according to the way these men measured rulership. Yet despite his council's demands, the king refused to put his Efean queen aside to marry a Saroese woman and try for a son. He could not, for she was the source of his power. So it came about that when the king sickened and died, his cunning and jealous sister invoked the law of the oracle, that a woman must be killed so her last prophecy would accompany the dead emperor into the afterlife. She drugged the queen and the queen's daughters and walled them alive into the king's tomb, claiming they had begged to attend him into death. Afterward she took the queen's name for her own, calling herself Serenissima the First and ordering that the chronicles erase the existence of the Efean queen. She placed a Saroese prince on the throne as King Kliatemnos the Second, saying this youth was the heir, the son of her brother by the last living daughter of the dead Saroese emperor, a woman who never existed."

When he pauses to look at me, the poet's heavenly mask falls away to reveal a gloating smile. "That is how your dynasty was founded. On murder and treachery."

"It's not true!" exclaims Cook. "Kliatemnos married the last living daughter of the dead emperor of Saro."

A knife-line of doubt creases Maraya's pale forehead. "The Archives say Kliatemnos the Second was the last living grandson of the empire. There is no mention of a queen of Efean descent."

His look is a jab. "What do you think, Captain?"

I want to refute him, but I no longer know what to think.

A thump startles us. Kalliarkos scrapes into view, shaking dust from his short hair. It is obvious he hasn't heard a single word of Ro-emnu's scandalous story.

His dour expression reveals his expedition's failure. "It's a sealed tomb. I heard women talking. We can't get your mother out through an air shaft if it's like the one in Lord Ottonor's tomb."

"Can't we free them?" Maraya asks. "Bring them with us?"

For the sake of the living a captain must leave the dead behind. It's what Father would do. "Their oracle may refuse and tell the priests. We can't take the chance."

"Jes! It's sickening to leave them trapped there, not even give them a choice." Maraya looks around at the others for support. Her eyes widen, and she leans forward. "Where is Amaya?"

"She was sitting right here by me!" I say with alarm.

A ghastly scream echoes out of the low tunnel, filling the space until we cower as it winds around us. With a kiss of drafty air and a curl of moving shadow, the lamp flame gutters out.

"Amaya!" I shout frantically.

A strangled cry twists out of the tunnel. "Jes! It's swallowing me!"

I can't even see my hand in front of my face. Fumbling, I find the flint and the last taper tucked into my Fives jacket. Flame licks up the little torch. The light barely illuminates but in contrast to the darkness everyone's face looks startlingly clear. Kalliarkos at once hands me another lantern. I light it and then hand him the taper as I crouch-walk into the low tunnel.

"Amaya! Don't move! I'm coming!"

My head bumps against the ropy ceiling, and the scarf tied over my hair catches and pulls down on my eye so I have to yank it back up. Parallel ridges along the floor make the footing tricky. I hold the lamp out with one hand and balance with the other.

My shadow distends along the walls, and as if alive, it separates into two shadows and then into four. What should be my head and my limbs become horns and claws. A jaw gapes as if to devour me but I drop to hands and knees to change the angle of light. Rippling, the shadows retreat. Goose bumps come out all over my skin.

The meow of a cat whispers up the tunnel. My chest tightens with hope: if a cat has made its way down here, then we can find our way out. As I scramble forward my bare wrist scrapes the rock, a hot burn along the skin.

The tunnel curves sharply and drops into a round space like a bubble of air popped amid the rock. At first I think there is no exit but then I see a gap so low I will have to wiggle forward on my belly. I raise the lantern.

"Amaya?"

She's not here, but the ceiling heaves as if liquid impossibly flows along it. Shadows elongate off the ceiling, stretching until they drip onto the floor. A shadow exactly like a crocodile hinges open vast jaws that curve along the walls as if to consume me. Hastily I turn the lantern, and it transmogrifies into a jackal's shadow gathering itself to pounce. Raising up the lantern breaks the shadow's leap into shards that skitter away like bugs. The feathery crawl of tiny legs brushes along my neck. With a shriek I flick a bug off me and jerk forward onto my knees, dropping the lantern and slapping my head to make sure nothing else is crawling there.

My moving light cuts new pathways across the chamber's smooth floor. I see another way out: a downward shaft as black as a well filled to the brim with pitch. But the moment I take one hesitant step toward it, the surface of the well slurps darkness over its rim. The shadow of a huge articulated spider's leg emerges, then a second leg and a third: a tomb spider as big as I am pulls its head and body up until it fills half the space. Its six eyes are voids, sucking away my courage.

I begin to whimper in aching, mindless fear. Its forelegs probe, their long shadow descending toward my face. With a gasp I desperately knock the lantern forward. It tips, over-balances, and my reflexes kick in: I catch it before it crashes over.

When I look up the spider's shadow is gone and I face the giant shadow of a hissing cat, ears flat, back arched. But now I know what to do. Grabbing the lantern, I leap to my feet and sweep its light all the way around to shatter any more that are forming.

And there Amaya is, where she wasn't a moment before. She has curled up on herself, lips pulled back to show her teeth, head hunched, arms drawn up as if she is ready to claw at me. The hazy golden light makes a mask of her face, reminding me of the cat mask she briefly wore in the carriage on the day we went to the Ribbon Market. For an instant her pupils look slitted.

"Amaya!"

She blinks with her ordinary eyes. "Jes?"

"What happened to you? Why did you go off?"

She snivels the way she always does when she is being accused of something. "I didn't! I was resting by the opening. A shadow ate me, Jes! It was a big cat and it just ate me in one gulp! When you shone the light on me it vanished."

I can't explain what I saw. The song people sing before each trial winds through my memory again: *Shadows fall where pillars stand.*

The only thing I really want is to get out of this awful place. Now that I can breathe again because Amaya is safe, I realize I smell water. I shine the lamp down into the shaft, mostly to make sure no spiders linger there. Light catches on a glimmer of water flowing sluggishly below. After so long in these dusty passages, its moisture tickles my nostrils. Escape surely smells like this.

Movement scratches behind us. I whirl, but it is Kalliarkos, not a tomb spider, who crawls out of the tunnel. He has pursued us without a lantern, braving the darkness. He gives me a meaningful look that I can't answer in front of my sister. "Thanks to the gods you are both safe."

My nod is my answer. "There's water at the base of that shaft, not more than a body's-length drop. If the pattern holds, then we've reached Rivers."

The lamp gutters, flame wavering. When I tip the lantern sideways the flame brightens again.

"That one is almost out of oil," says Kalliarkos. "It's going to take time to get to the entrance we came through. We've got to move."

"What about my mother?"

"She is awake. We will not leave her, Jes. I promise you." He vanishes back up the tunnel.

Amaya is rubbing her lips with the back of her hand just as a cat does. "The handsome prince is sweet on you, Jes," she purrs. Her meanest smirk peeps out. "How did that happen?"

"Shut up!" I crouch by the shaft, trying to decide how far the drop really is.

"I'll go down first," she says unexpectedly. "You need to stay here to lower down the others because you're stronger than I am."

"Are you sure?" This isn't the fussy Amaya I know.

As if my thoughts are words she shows her teeth, and a faint hiss escapes her. Then she smiles. "I'm not afraid, Jes."

And she isn't afraid. Without a complaint or a whine or a demand for attention she swings her legs over the opening. When I've hooked my elbows under her armpits I lower her as far as I can, then let go. Her splash resounds in an echoing space. She laughs.

When I lower the lamp toward her I can dimly see her staring up at me from where she sits with water eddying around her waist. Twice she slaps the water just to make it jump.

"It's shallow. Wait!" She flounders out of view.

"Amaya!"

Her voice drifts out of the darkness. "The water is just a narrow channel. I'm already up on a stone floor. It's easy, Jes! We just need more light!"

Voices murmur down the passage behind me, and Ro-emnu backs into the space. He cradles Mother's head, while Coriander moves her legs. Mother's eyes are open, tracking vaguely, and her mouth forms my name when she sees me. I kiss her.

"You go down first," I say to Ro-emnu, "and we'll lower her."

Amaya is right: it is easy. Coriander and I lower Mother into his arms. One by one we transfer the others: the listless, mute oracle; Maraya with our baby sister; Cook; Coriander with the boy and the other lanterns. Last, Kalliarkos rests a hand on my shoulder. Flame sputters as the lamp that has brought us this far flickers, catches a last flare of oil, and drives back the shadows.

Exhaling, I lean against him and shut my eyes. Just one breath to gather my strength and my courage for the last push. His lips brush mine. They're cool and a little dry and their touch makes me so warm that I can't help but remember Father ordering me never to speak to him again.

"Jes!" Maraya shouts as if she disapproves of our embrace, not that she can see us. "Hurry! Bring the light!"

Just as I open my mouth to reply, the lamp at our feet spits one last spurt of flame and dies. A soldier's curse snaps out of me. A faint flame wavers below.

"Go, and I'll follow," he says.

I feel my way over the edge, hang, and let go. Water sprays up around me as I absorb a landing in knee-deep water and then jump back blind. He hits right after me, water flung into my face. Flailing to orient myself I slap first a wall and then his arm.

I shout too loud and my voice cracks back from a cavernous space. "Merry? Where are you?"

"Over here!"

When we wade in the direction of her voice we push out of the channel up onto a stone floor covered with rubble and layered with dust. There huddle Maraya, Amaya, Mother, Cook, the babies, and a lamp that flickers and goes out, emptied of oil.

Ro-emnu and Coriander and the oracle are gone, and they have taken the last lantern with them.

31

Kalliarkos and I stand side by side. I am too bewildered to speak.

He elbows me. "There! Do you see the light?"

A golden glow sways in the distance, rising and falling like a boat drifting in the well of eternity. Then it vanishes.

Cook sobs once and then stifles her fear. At least the babies aren't crying.

"I can't believe Ro just did that to us," cries Kalliarkos. "I used my rank and my name to get him released from prison into my custody! He said he would do anything to help his sister, that an Efean man is not an honorable man if he abandons his family."

"We aren't his family." The words roll tartly off my tongue. The Rings spin in my head as I recollect his words in the tomb. "He came to help his sister. But now he wants the oracle. After the way she seemed to recognize you, he must believe she has something to do with the royal family. He must hope that she knows secrets he can use to write his scandalous plays. So much for being a noble poet! Oh gods. We've come so far and yet we are still trapped!"

Despair crashes into me so fast I can't stop my souls from sinking into wretched misery. Collapsing to my knees, I begin to weep.

He kneels beside me, crushes me against his chest. "Jes! It's all right. We're almost there."

"It's too late," I cry. "We'll never get out of here now."

His voice has all the passion and determination that I have lost. "It isn't too late. We'll walk upstream in the direction we saw the light. Ro and I entered the complex at a pool that had four streams flowing out of it. This has to be one of those streams. We'll tie ourselves together with the rope and I'll lead. You and Cook carry your mother. Your sisters will each take a baby."

His plan makes sense, and his firm tone steadies me. I sniffle, sucking up my tears as a pinch of hope lightens my heavy heart.

He whispers in my ear as intimately as if we were alone. "Instead of telling ourselves what we can't do, we have to believe in what we can do. Let's go."

He unwinds the rope and loops us together into a shuffling

centipede with ten legs, everything done by feel. To my amazement Amaya volunteers to go last.

"I'll scratch and bite anything that tries to eat us from behind," she hisses, poking me in the side with a finger. We all laugh nervously.

Kalliarkos takes the lead, followed by Maraya holding our baby sister. Cook and I make a basket with our arms to carry Mother. We stick close to the water and creep forward with slow sweeps. Small stones and uneven bits of material crunch and slide under our feet. Mother weighs like an unwieldy sack of lead. Amaya sticks so close behind that she notices when Cook or I shift at all and is there to steady us.

Kalliarkos and Maraya give warnings over their shoulders: "There's a dip in the ground." "Careful, to your right, something hard and round that rolls."

Suddenly Kalliarkos grunts in pain.

"Hold on, I just kicked a big rock." The scrape of a heavy object on stone shudders through the darkness, then he mutters a curse. "There's rubble we have to climb over."

We untie Maraya and give her both babies. She waits alone in the dark so we can shift Mother by feel up a rugged ridge of what feels like collapsed stone columns and down the other side. It's exhausting, and if we didn't have all four of us working together we couldn't manage it. But we do, and when we get down on the other side Cook and I sit with Mother's limp body braced between us as Kalliarkos goes back over the rubble to fetch Maraya.

"Do you want me to take a turn carrying Mother?" Amaya asks, squeezing my hand. "I know I'm not as strong but I can manage for a little distance."

"No, it's all right, Amiable, I'd rather you take rear guard since you're not afraid of the monsters and I am." The truth is I don't want to hold our brother, but I can't tell her that.

"That's because I'm too sweet, and they'll just spit me out. I'm not really afraid of the dark, you know. The only times I ever said I was, it was just to get my way."

Maraya's voice floats down from above. "We already knew that, Amiable. Father was the only one you ever fooled."

"I don't want to talk about him!" she snaps.

"We should go on, if you can," says Kalliarkos.

I feel him press in beside me. His hand taps my arm in a secret signal, and I tug on his sleeve in answer. I swear to the gods that I can hear him smile. His cheek brushes mine. I press a kiss randomly that touches the corner of his mouth. Then we set back to work tying us all into a line again so we can go on.

Each slow step along a cracked and uneven floor we never see is a victory as long as Mother still breathes. Her weight on my arms, the way my shoulders feel like they are pulling out of their sockets, all is a triumph as long as she still breathes.

By degrees a pallid glow begins to rise like mist off the ground. A hazy silver light clouds the air ahead of us, and we climb stiffly over a second mountain of rubble to see an oval pool gleaming below. The water shimmers like silk. Down we stagger. When we reach the rim of the pool Cook and I have to rest, so we set Mother down as Kalliarkos explores farther along the shoreline.

Her eyes are open, and with what seems her last strength she reaches until her hand meets the liquid. Lustrous mist twines up her arm until it paints her face with an eerie luminosity.

I hold my breath, not sure what will happen next.

With unlooked-for strength she sits up, seeking her children.

"Maraya. Jessamy. Amaya." She beckons us closer and we each touch a hand to our heart in the Efean way as we kneel so she can touch our foreheads one after the next. "Where is Bettany?"

"We'll find her and bring her back, Mother," I say.

She nods regally, accepting my promise, and lays her left hand on the boy's head and her right on the girl's. "This fine boy will be Wenru. This fine girl will be Safarenwe. Let it be as I say, for it is my responsibility to name them. I birthed their flesh into this world to be a vessel for the five souls the land who is Mother of All gives to them."

"But Mother," says Amaya, "those are Efean names."

"So must they be Efean, now that their father has turned his back on them." She holds her head with the pride and dignity that has been hers all along. "He made his choice. It is time to go on without him."

In the water's sheen I see my face so clearly that I wonder who I truly am and who we all are, we who walk above ground not knowing what lies beneath that we have been taught to forget.

The game called Fives has five obstacles. A person has five souls.

This cannot be a coincidence.

The City of the Dead is the mask that conceals what was here before the Saroese came. The invaders buried the magic of Efea beneath their tombs.

"This way!" calls Kalliarkos triumphantly from halfway around the pool.

We gather ourselves and trudge after him. Mother walks, leaning on Cook. I examine the cavern and its mysteries one last time, but hurriedly follow as the others vanish into an opening in the wall. Chalk marks a narrow passageway where a lit lantern hangs as a beacon. I wonder if Ro-emnu left it. When I enter, I find what appears to be a tomb robber's tunnel punched through the main wall. A crude set of steps boxed in by timbers leads me on a long and crooked path past more buried rooms and dark passages. The steps are lit at intervals with lanterns so I walk from one dim aura to the next.

I emerge into the back of a storage room carved out of rock and filled with barrels. The wall stinks so foully of urine that I cover my nose as I squeeze past. A low archway leads into another storage room stacked with crates. A curtained opening admits me to an underground warehouse filled with ceramic vessels used to transport olive oil. Tripods hold lamps burning so brightly that I shade my eyes.

Six Efean men stand guard, each wearing the trowel of the masons' guild inked into his left shoulder. Five wear the knee-length wrapped linen skirts typically worn by Commoner men, and like most laborers they go bare-chested. The sixth is an elderly man dressed in a long formal keldi and linen tunic. He is talking quietly to Kalliarkos and Mother. Maraya and Cook hold the babies. Amaya has curled up on the floor and has actually fallen asleep.

"We did not see him pass through this warehouse, my lord," the elderly man is saying. "Once you reach the steps, there are other routes by which a person may make his way to the city streets."

"So be it," says Kalliarkos with a gracious nod. "I will not ask you to speak against one of your own. Perhaps he feels he has discharged his obligation. What do I owe you, Honored Sir?"

The old man bows respectfully. "Nothing but your trust, my lord. As we agreed beforehand, we must bind your eyes to lead you out so as not to reveal the location of our gathering place."

"I gave my word and I will honor it."

Two of the men make a chair of their linked arms to carry Mother. They treat her like a great lady, although she is too weary to realize it. I like them for the respect they show her. When they pull an eyeless cloth mask over my face, I do not protest.

By the time our guides remove our masks I have lost all sense of location and time. They propel us along a walled corridor into an oval dining hall with round tables and benches in the Commoner style. It has canvas for walls, a roof raised on brick pillars, and lamplight in plenty because it is nighttime. Thynos and Inarsis stand comfortably together looking over a shadow-washed garden. In the distance the fifth night-trumpet blows, the last one before dawn's fanfare. The two men turn and see us.

"There you are, Kal." Thynos's tone is light but the way he pounds Kalliarkos on the back reveals a much deeper affection. "Nar and I were beginning to despair of you."

Inarsis examines the silent masons and our ragged party. "I admit I underestimated you, my lord."

Kalliarkos's grin dazzles. "You are pardoned, General Inarsis. This time. But don't do it again." He looks at me, and I wink at him, and he laughs.

Having deposited Mother on a bench, the masons retreat. Kalliarkos follows them into the corridor. I hear his low voice, their laughter and genial replies. His knack for making allies has served him well.

"Food!" Amaya descends locustlike upon a platter of olives, flatbread, and baked fish.

"Are those *twins?*" says Thynos with a side-eyed grimace, but we girls ignore him in favor of digging into the food while Cook offers a sampling to Mother.

"Maraya?" she says, pushing away the food. "Jessamy? Amaya?"

We hasten to her. She touches us on the lips, and then each baby in turn. She is our mother, who guards our breath.

Her hands feel so dry and hot when I grasp them. "Mother, we are taking you to a refuge. Polodos and Maraya intend to marry. They will take care of you and the babies. We'll find Bettany. Do you understand what I'm saying?"

Her half-unfocused gaze rests on me for a drawn-out while. "I dreamed we had been buried for so long," she answers in a tone so weightless I fear it will float away and take her life with it.

"You need to rest and heal, Mother," I say sternly.

When Kalliarkos reappears, Inarsis studies him with the sort of frown Father would use when he examined ranks of soldiers who hadn't prepared their kit correctly. "What of the poet?"

Kal sweeps an arm heavenward with the same gesture an actor would use to flamboyantly indicate the Path of Honor. "He has fulfilled his part. Let us be on our way."

Inarsis transfers his gaze to Mother. Her face has none of

the luster that normally makes people stare at her, nor does her kind smile light the room like an offering of peace to soothe the world's ills. Does he see beneath the grief and exhaustion to the beauty he expects from a woman whose Patron lover kept faith with her for twenty years? Or is he looking for something else? After a moment he approaches her with a dip of the knee, cupping his left hand so his little finger touches his breastbone.

"Honored Lady, with your permission I will convey you to the inn. I have arranged for a healer to examine you and the newborns."

"We need a doctor," says Cook, who has not the slightest compunction about contradicting an Efean man she cannot imagine might be a general.

Inarsis glances at the floor with a pinch of his lips, then up again. "I have already sent for a dame much experienced in midwifing."

He does not rebuke her as a Patron man would a woman speaking out of turn, but he does not back down as Efean men normally must in the presence of Patrons. Cook looks to me, and I nod to show it is all right.

Mother relaxes into the sure embrace of his command. "Thank you, Honored Sir. I accept."

I step back to allow the general to carry out his arrangements. With a frown Cook follows him into the garden. Amaya is still eating but Maraya is looking from Kal to me and back.

Lord Thynos slaps Kalliarkos's shoulder. "Well done, my nephew. There should be another attendant, though. And what of the oracle?"

"The poet took his sister, as we agreed beforehand." Kal's glance warns me to keep my mouth shut. "The oracle is dead."

"I have never approved of this barbaric practice of burying living people in tombs," Thynos mutters.

"Is it more merciful to kill oracles as they used to do in old Saro?" I retort.

When Thynos is agitated, his old-country accent gets stronger. "Only emperors ever had oracles. The custom was given up when the empire fell. Here it has become a disease, nothing more than a fashion. Every clan must bury their head of household with an oracle so as to be seen as important and honored as the next clan. It is a foul pollution."

The outburst silences me. But Kalliarkos nods as if he has heard this tirade a hundred times and takes it no more seriously than an offer of a trip to the legendary oasis of the winged snakes and gossiping trees. "It's done now, Uncle. One tomb is empty."

"Yet you will tell me nothing of how you got them out?"

"I gave my word of honor that I would respect Efean secrets."

Most Patrons would scorn the idea of their honor being subject to any oath given to a Commoner, but Thynos makes a gesture of acceptance.

Out in the courtyard Inarsis courteously assists Mother into a curtained carriage.

"Jes, aren't you coming with us?" Maraya asks. Amaya pauses with a hank of flatbread almost in her mouth, and she looks questioningly at me too.

I hurry over to the carriage for fear they will blurt out words that embarrass me. "No. I have to go back to Garon Stable."

Maraya frowns as she whispers, "Don't think I haven't noticed the way Lord Kalliarkos has been touching you and looking at you. If he's hounding you, we can come up with a way to be rid of his attentions."

"It's not like that." Possibly the lamplight is bright enough for her to see the way my cheeks grow hot, but she has already guessed by the cool edge in my tone.

"Jes, don't be a fool. He's a prince."

Amaya lowers the bread. "I think it's the funniest thing I've seen in forever, just like in a play. Be a fool, Jes. Why not? It'll be the first time you ever lost your head over a person instead of your beloved Fives."

I push between them, keeping my voice low. "I have to go back to the stable because if I run away Lord Gargaron will send his stewards to hunt me down and then he'll find out you've escaped. As soon as Mother can travel we must get her out of the city. Merry, ask Polodos if he can find out what happened to the servants who were left behind so we can trace Bettany. Amaya, I have to tell you..." My hesitation betrays me.

She clutches my hand as her lower lip trembles. "Is it about Denya?"

The words are hard to say because they will hurt her so much. "Lord Gargaron took Denya to be his concubine. I'm sorry."

She puts a hand over her face, then lowers it to shake me. "I have to see her. You have to find a way to sneak a message in to her! So she knows I'm alive, and that I haven't forgotten her!"

"Yes, I'll find a way."

"You want to train at the stable, don't you?" says Maraya. "It's what you've always wanted."

I nod, because there is nothing else to say, and then I kiss them and the babies. Sweet Safarenwe is asleep but Wenru is awake, staring around with an expression so calculating that I am ashamed of how uncomfortable I feel around him. I thank Cook. Last of all I kiss Mother yet again before the carriage rolls away through open gates onto a dark street.

Kalliarkos steps up beside me, hands clasped behind his back at parade rest. The courtyard in which we stand is wreathed with trellises of night-blooming jasmine, its scent as heady as desire. We are the only ones here, utterly alone. I lean against him, so comfortable that I know this is also a place I belong: standing beside him no matter what people might say.

He smiles without looking at me. We don't even need to speak, just share our triumph in an easy silence.

Then he hooks a finger around one of mine, and I turn to raise my mouth to his.

"Kal! Time to go!"

The speed with which I leap around must make me seem ashamed, but Kalliarkos merely releases my hand and ambles over to his uncle. Thynos has driven up in the carriage we used to go to the villa. He climbs down, giving me a once-over as if trying to determine how far I have seduced his royal nephew despite my few charms.

"This is all very like an exciting and adventurous play to the two of you, I am sure," he says. "You're young, and it's perfectly natural, but it's not real."

"It's real!" objects Kalliarkos.

"Don't interrupt! I'm impressed by what you accomplished, Nephew, but this budding little blossom of love has to wither now. Let me explain the realities of your situation to Spider, since you obviously have not."

"He's told me about his family, Lord Thynos," I say, but when Kalliarkos presses a hand to his forehead as if plagued with a headache, I'm struck by doubt.

"There are many things I don't believe you understand about our Kalliarkos, Spider. To start with, Princess Berenise is Kal's grandmother."

"I know that!"

"Did I ask you to speak? Then don't. She is the aunt of the current king and queen. Her first marriage was to King Sokorios of Saro-Urok. At that time she left Efea to live in Saro-Urok as his queen. He died in battle less than a year after their marriage. Because she wasn't pregnant, his successor sent her to an ill-wishers' temple there but she escaped before they cut out her tongue. She found safety in the camp of an Efean army that had been campaigning in Saro-Urok in support of Sokorios. That army was under the command of Menos Garon, the uncle of Lord Gargaron."

"Sent to be an ill-wisher! That's a terrible story, but what does it have to do with us now?"

"I am trying to explain to you how the endless wars between Efea, Saro-Urok, East Saro, and West Saro are complicated by the shared kinship of their royal families. You see, King Sokorios was fighting against his cousin, a man named Elkorios. And indeed Elkorios became king of Saro-Urok after Sokorios died. Elkorios did not want Princess Berenise to return to Efea lest she marry some other Saroese prince who with Efea's backing would then challenge him for Saro-Urok's throne. But she escaped Elkorios's plot by marrying Menos Garon and returning to Efea with his army."

Kalliarkos breaks in. "That's not the only reason she married Menos. My grandmother harbored her own ambitions. She's like you, Jes. Always running the next game in her head."

Thynos examines me to see how I will take this disconcerting compliment, but I wisely say nothing.

"Twenty years later she set in motion an elaborate scheme of revenge against King Elkorios for killing Sokorios," Thynos goes on. "She began by contracting a marriage between her only son and my sister—Kal's mother. For you see, my sister is the niece of Sokorios and the daughter of Elkorios."

I shake my head. "This is so complicated that only Maraya could love it. Does this mean you are the nephew of one king and the son of another, Lord Thynos?"

"I am Sokorios's nephew, yes. His sister was my mother. But I am not Elkorios's son. Several years after my mother gave birth to my sister, Elkorios divorced our mother so he could marry the king of East Saro's daughter. After the divorce our mother married again. Her second husband was my father, and he raised my sister as if she were his own. He was a good man. He died in the wars."

"I am sorry for your grief, Lord Thynos. But what is your point?"

"My point, Spider, is that you don't understand these Rings you're running through. On his father's side, through Princess Berenise, Kalliarkos is the great-grandson of Kliatemnos the Third and Queen Serenissima the Third of blessed memory. On his mother's side he is the grandson of King Elkorios of Saro-Urok and great-nephew of Sokorios the Short-Lived. Such a prince is as rare as rubies and more precious than gold."

Kalliarkos snorts quite indelicately.

"These matters are far out of my reach," I protest.

Lord Thynos's eyelashes flutter as he chuckles, but it's obviously no joke to him. "You don't see it yet, do you? You haven't spun it through your web."

"See what?"

"Our Kal can inherit two thrones."

"I just want to run the Fives," says Kalliarkos, his voice ragged with emotion.

"You and your quiet little dreams, Kal."

"Let Menoë have the glory," he says bitterly. "She wants it."

"Yes, but your precious sister made a mess of her first marriage. A bloody murdering mess. Now she rusticates with humble and lowborn General Esladas in the hope that as his star rises no one will notice how far hers fell. She's just fortunate Gar didn't have her bricked into a tomb."

Kalliarkos mutters, "Even I wouldn't wish that on her."

"Never let down your guard, my young nephew," says Thynos harshly. "Gar will callously discard you the moment he thinks you're not worth anything to him. He'll find a way to punish your defiance if you don't obey him."

"Do you think I don't understand?" His anger scorches. "I know Jessamy believes we are fighting a noble war against our implacable Saroese enemies who want to rain fire down upon our cities. But we are really just fighting over the corpse of the old empire. Brother kills brother over the right to rule a strategically located city. A son inherits, and is overthrown by his uncle. A woman marries her brother to consolidate their holdings but afterward divorces him to marry a cousin with better territory and more riches. A wife is murdered so her husband can marry a king's daughter. Or maybe she gets wind of it and murders her husband first. I refuse to be thrown into that game. I would rather walk through a pit of vipers than go to war!"

The words hit me like a slap in the face.

"I'm not mad at you, Jes," he says hastily. "Your father is an honorable man."

Thinking of my mother, I don't know how to answer him, so I say nothing.

"We're all tired," remarks Thynos, glancing around the empty night courtyard. The light has begun to sift from black to gray, heralding dawn. "I'll have one of Nar's men escort her back to the stable. You and I can drive together to the palace."

"Jes and I must arrive at the stable together so that Uncle Gar doesn't suspect why she was really gone," says Kalliarkos. "Half the people there already believe we have something between us. Everyone in the palace wonders why I don't keep a concubine. When Uncle Gar hears of it, he and I can have an argument over why it is beneath me to have a Commoner lover."

Never in all my life would I have believed a highborn lord like Kalliarkos could speak of someone like me being his lover and not bat an eye nor look ashamed. But when he catches my eye, I know we have passed the point of feeling ashamed because there is nothing to be ashamed of.

"It's a bad idea, Kal."

"You don't have a better one. Uncle Gar can't be allowed to guess what we've done."

Thynos offers Kal the reins. "Very well. If you wish to become a man, then I suppose I must treat you as a man and let you make your own decisions and deal with the consequences."

Kalliarkos grasps his hands. "Thank you, Uncle. Blessings on you. But Jes and I are going to walk, as if we've come from the Lantern District."

Thynos extricates his hands. "I have to send a pair of Nar's men to shadow you. Don't be surprised to see them behind you. Adversaries are required to be back by Firstday dawn, so hurry."

On deserted back streets lit by cheap lanterns we pass a pair of old women sweeping up horse dung into a wheelbarrow. Now that our adventure is over, an awkward silence pools between us. When we reach the West Gate of the Lantern District with its brass wheels we pause in the square to share a mug of barley beer from a yawning street-side vendor. An air of spent revelry and sad loss permeates the gloom. The soldiers and foreigners who would normally pack the district's "pleasure wharves" have all gone to make ready for war. The brass water clock ticks down the night, the last trumpet filling up for the dawn fanfare.

Thirst quenched, we walk side by side, not touching. A pair of drunks stagger behind us, propping each other up. I wonder if they are Inarsis's men, always someone within sight of Lord Kalliarkos. In his own way he has been as protected and restricted as my sisters and I were.

As we head uphill into the palace district I find my voice at last. "Will you get into trouble for taking Ro-emnu out of prison?"

"I'm a prince, remember? If the king and queen complain to my grandmother, she will tell them to go soak their heads in a vat of urine." I'm so shocked to hear such an impiety casually flung into the air that I can't speak. He takes my hand, squeezing it as he chuckles with excitement. "Can you believe what we saw? I had no idea the City of the Dead was built on top of a vast complex where people must once have lived."

I think of sparks like fireflies and my brother waking up from death. I think of Amaya eaten by a shadow, and the watery mist that brought my mother back to herself.

"Either my tutors never told me the truth or they don't know it themselves," he adds. "They're all Archives-trained. I thought they knew everything. What now, Jes? What about us?"

In the empty street, knowing my family is free, I feel bolder than ever. "Why don't you keep a concubine? Most lords do from an early age."

He stops dead and tugs me to a halt. Right there in the

middle of the street he kisses me. His lips are cool, and at first their pressure is light. It is his hands I feel more, solid along the small of my back. I savor the way our bodies fit neatly together. As the kiss deepens, the spark of my being heats, and it twines the cord of its life into the spark of his, setting off a flare of brilliant light within our hearts.

We break off. My eyes flash open, and I'm a little dizzy.

His gaze is wide and questioning. "Because she wouldn't be you, Jes. You're here with me because you want to be. Any concubine I had in the palace would be spying on me for my uncle."

I think of poor Denya. "Is it really nothing but a pit of vipers?"

"Yes."

Footfalls crunch up the street behind us, and we step apart. Inarsis's two men still shadow us, no longer pretending to be drunk. To the east the sky lightens.

"Come on," he says.

As we walk I think of the victory procession held for my father, the way the crowd went quiet when the royal carriage passed. With each step a new pattern begins to unfold in my mind's eye. "Kliatemnos the Fifth and his sister Serenissima the Fifth are not popular rulers, are they?"

"Not at all," he says blithely. To speak critical words about them is nothing to him! "My cousin Kliatemnos sits in his palace and carouses all day with his honey cakes. He sends his brother Nikonos into the field to fight his battles. Everyone knows Serenissima despises her husband and prefers their younger brother Nikonos in every possible way."

"Poets are arrested for murder for making such scurrilous accusations."

He laughs. "I'm not a poet, but I'll tell you the truth anyway. Kliatemnos and Serenissima have a sickly twelve-year-old son but everyone suspects Nikonos is the real father. Can you possibly wonder why I want nothing to do with all of that?"

Anise's warning. Thynos's explanation. Kalliarkos's angry flood of words. The path through the Rings is starting to open.

Words fumble out of me. "If I were a man like Lord Gargaron and I wanted more power in the world, I would marry my disgraced niece to the best general in the kingdom. I would force my unambitious nephew to march with the army and take credit for that general's victories. That would give the nephew a princely burnish and prestige."

His fingers clutch my elbow as if to warn me to be silent. But I go on, because Rings never stop turning until one person reaches the victory tower.

"In a time of war, an unloved and weak king and his sickly underage son may be deposed for the good of the kingdom, especially in favor of a bold military prince like Nikonos. But even Prince Nikonos may meet with an unfortunate accident on the battlefield if he has enemies on his own side. And a queen who bet on the wrong horse will find herself put out to pasture. Which leaves you and your sister next in line to become king and queen."

His voice is so soft I barely catch the words and yet his tone rings harder than I have ever heard it. "Do you know what it means to be king in Efea?"

"The king must defend the country from its enemies and honor the gods in the proper way so their peace will shelter the land."

"The king sits atop a mountain of treasure. All bow before him because his will is law. His army defends not the country but his power. That's why I don't wish to be a part of it. But I also don't despise the army and its soldiers, Jes. I'm no coward, or at least I pray I will never act the coward's part."

Driven by secrets, he quickens his pace, and I hasten to keep up.

"Uncle Gar thinks I'm soft, that I don't see the nature of his plans. He pretends to want what is best for me but I won't be his pawn. I want to be an adversary who runs my own game."

We turn at last onto Garon Street. I reach for his hand, and he clasps mine with more strength than I expected.

"I shouldn't have involved you, Jes."

"You know I'm not afraid."

He has the strong hands of a climber, and when his grip tightens on my fingers, it crushes. "You should be afraid. They are monsters waiting to eat us."

Above, the high heavens shade to a vibrant purple while the eastern horizon glows with pink and a band of light rims the world. Behind, the two men shadowing us have vanished. The guards at the stable gate see us. Kalliarkos tries to shake his hand out of mine but I hold on until their gazes drop down to our linked hands. They squelch smiles as they straighten to parade attention, offering a salute to the only male of princely descent who lives in Garon Palace. Farther up the street lie the upper gates: the monumental gate to the main palace compound, which is ablaze with so many lamps that the lights smear together, and beyond it the servants' gate where Garon Street ends in a wall. The guards there have seen us too.

I release his hand as if we only now remember we ought to do so. He offers a pleasant smile and an agreeable nod to the startled guards at the stable gate. As they open the pedestrian door they mumble greetings—"My lord prince, a good wakening to you"—in the voices of men who have been allowed to greet him before and are still grateful that he acknowledges their existence. But oh how they struggle not to stare at me, for they are Patron-born men who serve Patron lords, and I am what I am in their eyes.

As I consider how to make the most dramatic farewell, he pulls me into the stable courtyard. At this early hour the kitchen girls have already begun stoking the clay oven, soaking millet and barley for porridge, and sweeping around the tables to make sure no brown scorpions or striped asps linger on the tile. The cook appears with her baskets and two assistants, ready to head down to the market to buy her perishables. Tana and Darios sit sipping at tea whose flavor is so strong I can smell the aniseed from here. Several other early risers are emerging from the barracks, yawning and rubbing their eyes.

"Make it convincing," whispers Kalliarkos into my ear, the words as startling as the thunder of a hailstorm that drowns all hearing, all sense of the world outside the shell you live in.

I could kiss him just by inhaling but suddenly I can't remember how to smile as a doting lover would. As my mother and father would smile at each other. As they never will again.

"I can't believe you're hesitating," he whispers. His eyes crinkle. His mouth parts as he waits for me to act because he thinks it's funny that I'm the one who is hesitating.

So I cup his face in my hands and I match him, look for look. "This isn't hesitation. This is my challenge."

I press my lips to his, and after all it is easy to forget everything else and just kiss him, because we are learning who we are, as if he and I will turn by turn unfold each other until we know everything that matters about our hearts.

A bark of command slaps down over us. We break apart, but it is not anyone speaking to us. The dawn changeover of guards has arrived. The gate stands wide open and, with the sun rising, all the guards have seen.

With a parting smile he walks out the gate, leaving me standing in full sight of every awake person in the stable. My pulse eases down from a hammering gallop into a mere trot. Without meaning to, I touch fingers to my lips.

The cook chuckles as she trundles past, her assistants trailing like cowed goslings.

Mis, Gira, and Shorty are standing at the entrance to the baths, mouths agape. Talon waits apart from them. Even she has eyebrows raised in that princely style she affects without its seeming an act. Abruptly I wonder if she is related to him.

"A good wakening to you, Spider," calls Tana from the shelter, with a false cheer that warns me she isn't pleased, "although it looks as if you've not had much sleep over your Sevensday rest. Best take a few cups of tea with your morning porridge. I believe we shall have to run you hard today to remind you that you train here. Keep the rest of your business to yourself."

32

As we adversaries eat our morning porridge, not one person asks me what I did during my absence, but it is obvious by the way they whisper behind their hands that the news is spreading. When Kalliarkos shows up for training, flanked by Thynos and Inarsis, all talk ceases. People's mouths might as well have been sewn up. Inarsis catches my eye and gives a subtle nod, but I know what it means: my family is installed at the inn as a temporary refuge.

Now I can breathe. Now I can truly enjoy our victory.

Once we are through menageries, Tana and Darios ride me all morning until I am so exhausted I can barely shift one foot in front of the next. On Trees I climb until my arms give out and my vision swims. Rivers defeats me as I splash a hundred times into the shallows and once scrape my knee so bloody it stings. I am so clumsy on Traps that everyone starts calling me "Dusty," and in the maze of Pillars I keep mistaking my right hand for my left.

They whip me along, trying to make me cry. But why would I cry? My mother and sisters are free, my father did what he could for us, I am training to run the Fives, and a prince kissed me.

When the bell rings at last, I shuffle to the dining shelter. Not even Thynos and Inarsis can keep Kalliarkos from me. As exhausted as he looks, with shadows under his eyes and a fresh bruise on his chin from a fall on the court, he has a strut as he brings his platter over and sits beside me. His defiance brings a smile to my face although I am so tired it feels like the effort of grinning is the same as that of trying to hoist a massive stone.

He frowns. "Are you all right, Jes?"

"I'm about to fall asleep face-first into my soup."

He nods gravely, leaning closer. "I'll wipe off your face if you do. Promise."

I stifle a giggle behind a hand but everyone hears it. Everyone sees. Everyone disapproves. I can practically smell it, as if flesh can exude castigation.

But Kalliarkos doesn't care, and so neither do I.

I press the side of my foot against his under the table, where no one can see.

In a low voice he says, "Grandmother was very irritated with me for being out two nights running. But for once my mother spoke up. She said it meant I was behaving as a man should, not tied to their skirts. That was amusing, let me tell you."

His light voice has such charm. The way he shares the little arrangements of the life he lives in the elaborate confines of Garon Palace makes me want to know everything.

The bell rings to mark the afternoon rest.

"Kal!" Thynos calls. A prince must rest in the safety of the palace.

With his sweetest grin as a promise he departs with his uncle.

Mis walks with me to the barracks, shaking her head. "You shouldn't have done it. But he is very good-looking. There isn't a single person in this whole stable he has taken a harsh word to, like he could, being a prince who could order any of us whipped or sent to the mines if the whim took him."

"He'd never do that!"

"Oh, Jes, you sound like you're in love. Tell me about it later!"

I collapse onto my cot and sleep like the dead. Or how I used to imagine the dead slept.

A hand shakes me awake. Talon stands over me. In the dim room her expression is unreadable. She taps her chest twice. I sit up in my underclothes, blearily trying to rub the leaden weight out of my eyes and limbs. The long slant of shadows through the shutter slats in my window and the silence suggest the others have already left for the afternoon session.

"Thank you," I say, wondering why Mis did not wake me or if Gira and Shorty are mad or if Tana gave them orders to let me sleep. "Do you have another name than Talon that I can call you? Not if you don't want to, but you can call me Jes. It's short for Jessamy."

She taps her chest again, points toward the outside, and leaves me sitting on my cot.

The first warning bell rings, calling adversaries to the training ground for the late afternoon session. With more haste than care I dress, gulp down water, and arrive on the court with drops still dribbling down my chin. I do not see Mis, Gira, or Shorty anywhere, nor any of the experienced adversaries. Even Talon has vanished. Elsewhere on the court, out of my sight, Tana calls out commands as she loops the adversaries through a drill. Only the beginners remain here. Darios works us through our menagerie with the look of a man who has given up on finding a single good thing in his dreary life, of which we are the last failing hope.

How bad a sign is it that I have been cast back in with the beginners?

Darios whacks my butt with his baton. "Don't let your mind wander. Don't get above yourself."

It is a warning. But I can't explain to him that I am not a fool in a way that he'll believe. Instead I shove everything else from my mind and let myself live within the menageries: cat, ibis, elephant, snake, dog, falcon, bull, wasp, jackal, butterfly, gazelle, crocodile, horse, gull, monkey, scorpion, horned lion, crane, sea dragon, firebird, tomb spider.

When I work that deeply I never notice anything going on around me. It is one of the reasons I am good. Only after we finish with the deathly menace of tomb spider and I have the leisure to wipe the sweat from my face do I see the people who have come to sit on the viewing terrace.

Three women sit in a row: one elderly, one of middle age, and one young like me. The elderly woman looks as brittle as a misfired iron blade; her back is as straight as if a rod holds her up. No ribbons adorn her silver hair; she wears it in a single braid. Her gold gown has the flare of fire sewn out of rippling silk. The woman in the middle is no longer young and not yet old. She has a plump round moon face and a placid expression and a way of sitting that makes it seem she has been there forever and will be there forever, perhaps having forgotten where she came from or meant to go.

The young woman is shifting in her seat and impatiently tapping her fingers together. Her hair is a tower of ribbons and arches spun out of thin braids woven with yet more golden ribbons, and it shakes and shimmers with each of her impatient movements. If not for the presence of the other two women, I think she would have run out of here already. She has a look of bored disgust on her beautiful face, or else ants are crawling all over her body beneath her clothes.

This is my father's wife.

I cannot help but smirk. I have gotten the better bargain.

Above the women, with a more commanding view of the proceedings, Lord Gargaron sits beside men I do not know but who resemble him enough to be kinsmen: brothers, nephews, cousins. The youngest crows out a laugh and points to a sight elsewhere on the court that I cannot see from the ground. He has a voice like a bullfrog's, oddly deep in so small a frame.

"There he is! Ha ha! Look at Kal swing along that horizontal ladder like a monkey! I thought you said he was no good, Uncle Gar."

All the beginners turn to stare at the speaker. Upon realizing with horror that they aren't to stare at the lords, they glance accusingly at me as if my torrid love affair with the princely son will get them whipped for their part in the conspiracy, and finally fix their gazes on their feet. It happens in such unison that I would laugh if I weren't quivering because I hate Gargaron so much.

Yet it is hard to fight down the smile that wants to burst out of me. Gloating will give me away so I wear my obedient face, knowing I have saved them, beaten him, and won his nephew's trust and heart besides.

Darios whistles. We hurriedly assemble in our ranks. Lord Thynos stands in the place of honor, befitting his Illustrious status. I am sent to stand with the Novices between Gira and Dusty. Kalliarkos takes a place on the other side of Gira now that he has decided to become a real adversary who devotes his life to the Fives and not a prince playing at being one.

Lord Gargaron and his kinsmen descend to stroll up and down our columns.

He stops in front of Kalliarkos. "Well, Nephew, the Exalted Princess your grandmother and I have agreed you will be allowed one last trial at Novice rank. I have enrolled you in the victory games at the Royal Fives Court tomorrow. Lose, and you go into the army at my bidding and under my aegis."

"What if I win?" asks Kalliarkos, annoyance flickering in the corner of his mouth.

"What if you win?" echoes Lord Gargaron, the tone shaded so close to mockery that I tense. The frog-voiced boy honks a laugh. "That would be food for discussion, would it not?"

Only now do I notice that Talon is nowhere to be seen. Are they hiding her?

My distraction catches me up short. Lord Gargaron paces past me, halts, pauses, and turns back. When he glances at Kal and back to me, I know he has heard the rumor. He measures me with an insulting ugly frown. But I say nothing. I show nothing.

"They call you Spider now, so I hear." His smile is thin and his voice is thin but he is a man whose power is as weighty as the City of the Dead crushing the past into rubble. "Tomorrow you will run the first trial, Spider. Appropriate for the daughter to run in the victory games held in her father's honor, do you not think?"

He pauses.

I nod obediently although my mind spins a giddy whirl at the thought of running a trial at the Royal Fives Court. In front of my father! If I could crow aloud, I would. But I mustn't forget that I am merely an adversary on the court and he is the one in the undercourt spinning the Rings.

"Remember, Spider. I will be watching to see if you pass muster."

33

Once when Father and I were returning home after I had accompanied him on a visit to his military camp, he stared for the longest time at the terraces of ripening grain cut through by irrigation channels. Shades of brilliant green stretching away to the horizon mark the richness of the soil of Efea, the land that nourishes us.

To my astonishment he said, "Even after all this time I can never quite get over how different the fields look here."

"Father," I asked daringly, "why did you leave your home and come to Efea?"

He almost smiled. "Funny you should ask in quite that way, Jessamy. For when I told my family, kin, friends, and acquaintances that I had decided to take my chances and sail to the fabled land of Efea, that was the only question they asked me. 'Why are you leaving?'"

"What did you tell them?"

He leaned out from under the carriage awning to watch a falcon fly past. When it was gone, he sat back and addressed me.

"I told them that the choice was made for me when I was born the youngest son in a poor household. My older brothers would inherit the bakery. My father could not afford me the bride-price for a wife, so I had no expectation that I would ever marry. In Saro-Urok, men of our caste could be nothing but foot soldiers with no rank in the army, because only men of wealth and connection can become officers. But we had all heard the poets and sailors and merchants and tale-tellers. They said that in Efea a man from Saro can be anything he wants."

He took my hand in his, an affectionate gesture he so rarely made that I was stricken and tongue-tied. His grave face made me think he was about to impart his most precious secret.

"There will come a moment in your life where you find yourself confronted with two choices, and both are bad ones. For me it was to stay in a place where I was choked and had nothing to look forward to and no way to prove my talents, or to leave everyone I knew and loved behind forever for a chance that might not work out. That is how the gods test us, by laying before us what seems to be a choice and yet is no choice at all. When we come to that fork in our path down which no road is clean, all we can control is with what dignity and honor we take our inevitable step."

34

The representatives of the Garon Stable enter the Royal Fives Court in procession, Tana in the lead, Kalliarkos behind her and after him Lord Thynos, then me, with Darios bringing up the rear. To walk into a building I have only ever glimpsed from the outside numbs me. The Royal Court is built of marble and hung with painted silk tapestries depicting famous adversaries of the past. The stairs down to the undercourt are swarmed by women and men who toss flowers at the feet of those of us who are entering. Many call out Lord Thynos's Fives name of Southwind.

My feet tread on rose petals as I descend. The scent floods me with the memory of my father bringing flowers from the market as offerings for my mother.

Blinking back tears, I enter the attiring hall. Everything is polished to a shine. The benches have cushions. Mats woven of soft reeds cover raised beds where trainers work stiffness out of the muscles of waiting adversaries. Ropes mark out private curtained chambers where the Illustrious await their trials in a privacy the rest of us have not earned. I glimpse the faces of men and women I have seen win on the Fives court. I am walking into my most cherished dream.

That my father will sit in a place of honor on the royal balcony just makes me even more nervous and excited.

I have to concentrate.

Tana takes me aside. "Do not get distracted," she says.

She leaves to go up top to the trainers' balcony, from which she will watch the trials. Thynos retreats to the roped-off area to wait in privacy for the Illustrious rounds, which will come much later in the day. Darios leads Kalliarkos and me through a warm-up of menageries.

I haven't spoken to Kalliarkos since Lord Gargaron told us we would both run trials in the victory games. They have kept us apart, and I can't help but watch him moving through the patterns beside me. He's graceful and precise as he moves, although his angles are a little off. It's impossible not to marvel at his perfect profile with its strong chin, straight nose, dark eyes, and short hair. He flashes a glance at me that is almost as good as a kiss, and I purse my lips and blow a kiss back. Darios whaps me on the butt with his baton.

When Darios tells us to pause so he can adjust my gloves

and check my mask, he says, "You have a chance, Spider. Don't get distracted."

"I don't understand why I'm entered," I say, because I've been running this maze in my head. I'm sure Lord Gargaron must have an ugly motive. Perhaps he hopes I'll lose in front of my father or maybe even means to run me against Kalliarkos. "I've never competed at anything like this level."

"Tana and I recommended you be entered in the first trial today, the one for the most promising Novices."

"You did?"

He nods, his gaze steady on my face to make sure I understand how serious he is. "Think of this as a test to see how good you really are and how badly you really want this. Any Novice who wins at the Royal Fives Court automatically moves up to Challenger. We think you're ready for it. You have the potential to become an Illustrious, Jessamy."

The unexpected praise sweeps warmth into my cheeks. "What about Lord Kalliarkos?"

He yanks hard on the lacing of my gloves. "Keep your eyes on the obstacle in front of you and your heart in the court. As for his lordship, he'll be placed in the normal manner, according to his victories and a random draw."

The first warning bell rings.

The Fives have a structure so complicated it is run by accountants. Trials begin with fledglings or the lowest-ranked Novices and work up to Illustrious. That's why I'll go in the first trial whereas Kalliarkos, with five Novice wins under his belt, will go a little later.

A fanfare of blaring horns announces the arrival of the king and queen and their entourage, so loud we can hear it even down here.

I want to prove myself. I want my father to be proud. I want to run the prize circuit and pour money into Mother's hands so she never need want for anything. I want to pay the fee for Maraya to take the Archivists' exam if Kalliarkos will agree to secretly sponsor her in another city. I can accompany Amaya to the theater and buy her all the masks and ribbons she wants. *I will find Bett.* As I wait for the second warning bell I stare at the wall and envision in my mind's eye the obstacles I may encounter and how I will defeat each one.

"Jes." Kalliarkos steps in beside me and takes my hands in his with such familiarity that my pulse surges like I'm already running. "May Fortune kiss you, as I intend to do right now in front of everyone."

My cheeks flame.

"I knew I could make you blush again," he says, his bright face all the laughter he needs. He is the sun, triumphant, and tonight, one way or another, he is going to be mine.

"Leave her be, my lord," says Darios, coming up to us. "She is already on the court in her mind and so should you be. Do you forget what this trial means to you?"

Kalliarkos stiffens, releasing me as his expression closes

up like the last brick set into the door of his tomb. "No, of course not."

I grab his hand despite Darios's frowning presence. "May Fortune kiss you as I do."

Right out where everyone can see and wonder and speculate, I kiss him. It is only a brief touch, but it is my promise to him.

"It already has." He presses fingers to my cheek, the warmth of his skin and the intensity of his gaze its own kind of blossoming magic.

Darios's grimace pours vinegar over me. "If you will, my lord, let me guide you through another menageries." He ushers Kalliarkos away to a warm-up circle, deliberately leaving me behind.

But he can't take our promises away. I find my own space, as I always have, and with a sure heart pace through cat, jackal, and crane.

The second warning bell rings.

"First trial!" calls a gate-custodian. "Spider, Garon Stable!"

I tug my mask on, adjust it so the corners of the eyes fit perfectly, and enter the ready cage. My custodian hands me a brown belt that blends with my plain brown clothes. I start on Pillars. Good fortune for me.

"First trial! Firecat, Kusom Stable."

A short, stocky, but exceedingly fit young woman in a silky jacket saunters in and accepts the blue belt. Her lack of height may hurt her on Trees but she'll have balance and agility like I do and less height to fight against. She looks me up and down, unimpressed by my ordinary brown mask and my ordinary Fives gear, and she flicks a little finger against her chin, a kiss-off before the trial even begins. I'm so excited that she's honored me with a taunt that I grin. This is what it truly means to be an adversary.

"First trial! Sandstorm, Royal Stable!"

A muscular young man struts in wearing a fancy jacket with the sea-phoenix badge. He's got to be good to train at the Royal Stable, and by his cocky posture he is pretty sure he's the best in this ready cage. A custodian gives him the red belt.

I exhale a calming breath into my cupped hands. My thoughts drift to my mother and father, to the butterfly mask and the firebird rug and chair.

The butterfly is a soul given substance. For all its seeming fragility its serenity is too powerful to be quenched.

The firebird can fly vast distances, subsisting only on air and courage. It can mate with any flying creature, for its substance is not flesh but ambition.

They were right for each other but Lord Gargaron tore them apart.

He made an illegal and blasphemous arrangement with the priests in order to do so.

"First trial! Beacon, Garon Stable!"

Looking startled and angry, Kalliarkos bounces into the

ready cage as if he is about to jump out of his skin. He fixes the green belt for Trees over his gold silk tunic. His fancy gold mask blazes like lightning. The spray of sunlight from the grille above makes him all gold except for his black hair and dark eyes. There is a lift to his chin and a squareness to his shoulders that he didn't have before we rescued my family. Confidence limns him. He might be a legend walked out of the past, noble and handsome and upright in all manner of conduct as men of old Saro are said to have been, adhering to the code given to them by the gods in the most ancient times. He is a beacon, in truth.

Then it hits: I am running against Kalliarkos.

Has Princess Berenise paid off someone so her grandson can run in an easier trial?

I meet his gaze. I nod, adversary to adversary, and he nods back as with a message in his eyes but I am too stunned to know what to say or do.

We hear the cheering of the crowd as the first trial is announced. We hear our names spoken but no one chants them as they will chant Thynos's Fives name when he is announced. You can take a name with you onto the court, but the crowd has to approve and anoint you. Most hopeful adversaries run trials without ever getting the crowd to sing out their names.

"Come with me," says my custodian, startling me.

With a glance toward Kalliarkos's retreating back as he

goes his way, I follow my custodian up a ladder and down a tunnel to the small chamber where a gate-custodian awaits. I dust my hands with chalk and take my place at the foot of the ladder.

The ugly truth sinks in: This isn't Princess Berenise's doing. This is what Lord Gargaron meant when he said I had to pass muster. He didn't mean the first day at the stable. He wasn't watching then because it didn't make any difference how well the girl who let his nephew win performed in practice.

This is the only trial that matters.

Horns blare. The crowd quiets to a low rumble.

Deep in the undercourt the start bell rings.

The hatch opens.

35

As **I reach** the top of the ladder I scan the stands because I may never again see the Royal Court from the inside. The tiers of seating are splendidly caparisoned with so many ribbons flowing in the wind that they are a restless ocean of constant change. From this angle I can't get a good look at the royal balcony, but the Garon Palace balcony with its horned and winged fire dog banner lies off to my right. Lord Gargaron is watching me.

Pillars begins with a gate flanked by two large stone pillars. Here on the Royal Court each one is carved with a face, on the left the stern gaze of Kliatemnos the First and on the right the benevolent smile of Serenissima the First.

Serenissima the Murderer.

I ring the obstacle bell to mark that I'm going in. A set of rope stairs leads up into a maze whose path must be traced not by walking along the solid ground but by balancing above the ground on a series of narrow beams. A seed of suspicion blooms: What if a man who is head of a powerful princely household has bribed the officials to set up the court in a configuration that favors my strengths of balance and agility?

No point in wondering. Although I hit two dead ends, I reorient myself and recover quickly. When I climb out of Pillars onto my first rest platform, the girl wearing the blue belt is already clambering down from Rivers and heading for Trees. I hear a bell ring as one adversary starts on his second obstacle. I am pretty sure the sound comes from Rivers, which means Kalliarkos has gotten through Trees and chosen to move north around the court.

Do I want to run into him? I do not.

A bell rings from Trees as Firecat gets going, although I cannot see her, since only the tallest poles jut up above the walls that separate the obstacles.

I am not going to let Firecat or Sandstorm beat me. Dropping down, I head south.

The moment I enter Traps I see in its multilayered architecture all my favorite elements: bars to swing from, slack ropes, stairstep beams, bridges with traps triggered if you put your weight on the wrong place. Right smack in the center Sandstorm is splayed awkwardly like an outstretched frog. He has slipped while crossing a rope bridge whose skewed balance keeps tipping him sideways.

Traps always has two possible routes, one long and laborious and low to the ground, and one short and glorious with a lot of flying and balancing at dangerous heights. Kalliarkos and Firecat are already in their second obstacles, so I leap up to grasp a horizontal bar, use the momentum of my swing to catch the next higher bar with my knees, and swing up backward to yet a higher bar that skips me over a beam and up to the highest and most dangerous and thus shortest path.

The noisy spectators, the wide blue sky, the dusty heat penetrating my throat: they spur me on as I balance and swing through rope and beam and bar and trap.

More quickly than I expected I find myself poised on a narrow beam looking down on the tipping bridge, which I have to cross next. Sandstorm still clings there, upside down with his back almost touching the ground and his jacket stained with sweat. From his furious look I realize he hoped the tipping bridge would be the bottleneck and that he could stop all of us from crossing by hanging there.

Except there is another way across the gap for an adversary bold enough to make a leap from the narrow beam to a slightly less narrow platform, high enough up and far enough away that if you miss you will hurt and maybe kill yourself.

I calculate how much speed and arc I will need to get across the gap, and then I catch his eye, him all helpless caught up in the wobbling rope ladder. His glare wishes me crashed on the ground all bloody and broken. His fingers are turning white as he clings to the rope bridge.

"Kiss off, Adversary," I call down. The blood flows high in me. "I'll show you how a real adversary does it."

The height of my starting point gives me momentum and opportunity. I throw a somersault into my leap, knees tucked and unfolding as I hit a perfect landing, the kind that doesn't even jar.

The crowd roars.

The rest of Traps flies past as if I truly have spun a web through it. The approbation of the crowd lifts my feet. I show off, which is always a danger because you're more likely to miss, but I no longer care. I can't fall.

When I reach the resting platform I see no sign of Firecat, but I catch a glimpse of Kalliarkos clambering down from Rivers and therefore headed for Pillars. I drop to the dirt and run for Trees, hearing the chime of a gate bell. He's still ahead of me.

My plain brown mask has slipped a little, and as I pause to adjust it I risk a quick look at the royal balcony. It's too high and far away for me to see faces clearly, but the king and queen lounge on a grand sofa under umbrellas held by servants. On a lower level of the balcony, at their feet, sits the man who won the victory at Maldine. I would know my father anywhere by the way he holds his back and head confidently upright. The honor shown him today takes my breath away. If only Mother were here to celebrate it with him.

On Garon Palace's balcony they stand silent, watching.

I chalk my sweating hands again and enter Trees.

Immediately I run into Firecat. To enter this configuration of Trees you have to jump up, catch hold of a bar, and swing up into a nest of climbing poles on a second level. Firecat is so short she's having trouble reaching the bar.

The crowd cheers and whistles as an exciting maneuver happens in Pillars or Traps.

"Salutations, Adversary," I say politely.

She snarls at me. "Usually they offer a lower climbing entrance that eats up time. There's no way I can jump that high. It's like they want someone taller than me to win."

Because of betting scandals in which one adversary threw a trial to another in exchange for a share of the winnings, King Kliatemnos the Third proclaimed that any act of cooperation or interference among the adversaries will be punishable by expulsion. So I say nothing.

The bar is so high it takes me four tries to catch it for long enough to draw up my knees to my belly and hook them over the bar. After that it is no trouble to get onto the second level and its tangle of climbing. Before I head in, I look down.

"Kiss off, Adversary," I say with a sympathetic shake of my head.

For all her anger, she gives me a grudging smile and that flick of the finger to the chin.

This configuration of Trees uses a great deal of technically difficult climbing up perpendicular faces with handholds, or hold-less climbing between posts like in the air shaft. Scraping my back against polished wood, feet braced in tension against a post set opposite, I work up several sets of blind shafts. After escaping the tomb it just doesn't seem that hard.

As I'm climbing up to the resting platform, shaking a cramp out of my left hand, a bell rings from the direction of Traps. Kalliarkos is still ahead of me. But he has to get past Sandstorm, who for all I know is still blocking the bottleneck of the tilting bridge.

Will Kalliarkos dare to leap?

Rivers runs dry. Stepping stones are scattered across a sandy pit instead of a watery channel. The trick is that there are false stones scattered through the true ones that look stable but won't take weight. Anise taught us to look at all the clues: The way the sand is scuffed around certain stones tells me where others have slipped off. The sand around the stable stones lies unmarked. By taking time to examine the ground before I start, I make it across in one go. And because I want Father to see how good I really am, I add a flip at the very end, from the last stone to the "shore."

The crowd loves it, the terraces of spectators seething with excitement, cheering, chanting, and singing.

Just as I climb up onto the platform that overlooks Rings, Kalliarkos climbs up on the opposite side. He is working on his breathing to steady himself. His gaze strikes mine, a blow hard enough to rock me back on my heels where I crouch. He is running the best Fives of his life, showing he has what it takes to be a real adversary.

"You made good time through Traps," I say in a low voice as I catch my breath. Even as I speak I study the layout of Rings: the pattern, the varying heights, the speed of the turning wooden rings, and the way they open and close paths that lead toward the victory tower.

"I had to risk the high leap," he says in answer. "You know what will happen if I lose."

I do know.

Up in the seats, half the crowd is on its feet. Even my father is standing, shading his eyes for a better look. On the balcony of Garon Palace, Lord Gargaron is waiting to see if I pass muster.

No step you take can be retraced. Yesterday cannot be revisited. That is what my father taught me.

Lord Gargaron saw a girl cheat to let his nephew win. I see how he has trapped me.

If I win, Kalliarkos becomes the puppet adversary his uncle means to play on the Fives court of palace intrigue, a poisonous scheme brewing in the heart of the kingdom. If I win, he will be thrust into a war between the nastiest and most ruthless people imaginable. They will rip him apart.

If I lose, Gargaron will know I cheated because I am better than Kalliarkos on Rings. My father will suffer because of my rebellion. Whatever hope I have to help my mother and siblings and to find Bettany will be lost because I will be sold to the mines to die. And Gargaron will force Kalliarkos to march out with the army anyway because he'll convince everyone that I lost to let the prince they all believe is my lover win. Because I did it once before.

This is the choice my father had to make that terrible morning when Lord Gargaron came to our house, the choice that is no choice at all. Whatever promises Kalliarkos has made to me, he cannot keep them, no matter what he thinks.

Lord Thynos tried to tell me: *Our Kal can inherit two thrones.*

The world will never leave him alone. He is naïve to believe otherwise.

The Rings spin, and he hesitates, trying to unravel a pattern that is complex and dizzying because you have to shift heights and speeds. The fastest way through is already completely clear to me. Just as Lord Gargaron knew it would be.

So I make the break clean, as Father did, even though my heart is breaking.

"Kiss off, Adversary."

As he recoils, surprised and dismayed, I leap into the spinning pattern. I throw in a few extra twists and tucks for flair.

The crowd is dancing and singing to cheer me on, everyone on their feet. Deep in the crowd I hear a word rising as more voices take hold of it and lift it toward the heavens.

"Spider! Spider!"

My arms and legs burn with exhaustion as I climb the tower and grab the victor's ribbon.

Only then do I look down. Kalliarkos stands at the foot of the ladder, mask off, face stricken.

"Jes," he says in all bewilderment, although I cannot actually hear him. Everything he thought he had has been torn from him, and I had a hand in it.

On the Garon balcony, people are waving banners to celebrate my victory. I have won a trial at the Royal Fives Court, in the victory games celebrating my father's success at Maldine. I have leaped from Novice to Challenger in one trial. I worked so hard for this and dreamed of it for so long but I cannot take any pleasure in my triumph.

I turn to face the royal balcony where the king and queen are applauding politely, yet it isn't their notice I seek. My father stands at attention, looking right at me. I tap my chest twice, for I have fulfilled my orders. Across the distance, he taps his chest in answer.

Only then do I pull off my mask.

Let them see me for who I am, daughter of a Patron captain and a Commoner woman who loved and stayed loyal to each other until one man tore them apart for his own convenience. I need not choose loyalty to one parent over the other. I love them both and no one can take that from me.

Let them see me, a child of Saro and a daughter of Efea. Let them remember my face because I am going to win again. I have walked beneath the City of the Dead and discovered a buried heart that is still beating and still powerful. My enemies have weapons and magic and riches and ships and all the might of kingdoms at their disposal. But they don't have me.

Below, Kalliarkos goes as blank of expression as a man who has woken up to find himself in a vipers' pit and knows he cannot make a single twitch without being stung. Without looking at me he climbs down to the undercourt and into the pitiless maw of his uncle's ambition.

The crowd is still cheering and chanting my name.

Jessamy Tonor is dead and buried in the tomb of Lord Ottonor with all the rest of his household and their hopes and dreams, turned to dust.

Now I am Spider.

And Lord Gargaron is going to be sorry that he left me free to spin my web of revenge.